HEIDI

HEIDI

A Story for Children
and Those Who Love Children

By JOHANNA SPYRI

Translated by
PHILIP SCHUYLER ALLEN
The University of Chicago

Illustrations by MAGINEL WRIGHT ENRIGHT

RAND McNALLY & COMPANY

New York   Chicago   San Francisco

First paperback printing, 1972
Second paperback printing, 1975

THE CONTENTS

HEIDI'S YEARS OF LEARNING AND TRAVEL

The Preface

HEIDI MAKES USE OF WHAT SHE HAS LEARNED

HEIDI

THE PREFACE

More than fifty years ago, amid the tumult and clamor of the Franco-Prussian War, little Adelheid was born into the world of literature in which she has lived as a favorite figure of childhood ever since. There is something about her at once so innocent and sweet, so loyal and truthful, that she has endeared herself unfailingly to those who read her life, and she has come to occupy a secure place in the affections of young people of many different lands and languages.

The pure mountain air of Switzerland breathes in the pages of Heidi's book, as does a sincere love for nature in her simpler and grander moods. The cramped dweller in cities and towns longs for the freedom of the open spaces and the highlands quite as earnestly as do our small heroine and Meadow Nuncle. Goat Peter is the very image of unfettered country boyhood. Crippled Clara and the despondent doctor grow strong in the rude vigor that prevails on the sloping roof of the Swiss world.

Perhaps a first reason for the sure hold that Heidi has won on the hearts of her own and a later generation lies in the beautiful and unusual setting given to her story. But no one reads far into the quiet tale before its characters begin to live more really than most people he has actually met and known. Not for anything in the world would one have missed an acquaintance with Brigitte and the blind grandmother of Goat Peter's tumbledown cottage, with the village pastor and Meadow Nuncle, and with Peter, the feather-minded general of the army of goats. Prim Miss Rottenmeier is drawn from life with broad strokes of the pen, as are kind-hearted Sebastian, and the blundering tutor, and pert Tinette. Clara, the patient invalid, is a sweetheart—nothing less—and

THE PREFACE

how we do agonize over her possible betterment and recovery!
And one comes away from meeting Mr. Sesemann and his
serene mother encouraged to a renewed faith in men and
affairs.   Verily, it is difficult to say who loves best to read
and read again of Heidi and her friends: whether children or
the older folks.   The authoress, Johanna Spyri, made no
mistake when she wrote beneath the title of her unforgetable
book, "A Story for Children and for Such as Love Children."

The present translation has been a labor of love.   A con-
sistent attempt has been made throughout to modernize both
dialogue and description wherever this has been possible without harming the old-world flavor of the original.

PHILIP SCHUYLER ALLEN

The University of Chicago
Thanksgiving Day, 1920

HEIDI'S YEARS OF LEARNING AND TRAVEL

HEIDI

CHAPTER I

UP TO MEADOW NUNCLE'S

A path leads from the cheerful old market town of Mayenfeld through green and wooded fields to the very foot of the mountains whose tall slopes gaze sternly down upon the valley. The first part of this narrow trail has no great interest for the traveler, but the moment it begins to climb, the whole moor sends forth the sweet smells of its plants and grasses until the air is heavy with them. And suddenly the path strikes sharply up and goes straight to the Alps.

On one bright and sunny June morning a tall and stoutly built girl of this highland country was toiling up the road, leading a child by the hand. The cheeks of this small lassie were in such a glow that it flamed even through the deep tan of her skin. Nor was this after all so strange a thing, for, although the June sun burned hotly, the poor child was all bundled up, as if for protection from a bitter frost.

You would hardly think the little mite was more than five years old, but just what she really did look like you could never guess, because she was covered by two different dresses that anyone could plainly see. They were put on in layers, one above the other. And, to make matters worse, a big scarf of red cotton was so wound about her tiny form that she did not seem to have any shape at all as she trudged wearily along in her rough and heavy tramping shoes.

These two people had climbed some three or four miles up from the valley when they came to the group of houses which lies halfway on the long Alpine slope and which is called The Hamlet. And here they were shouted at from almost every house, now from an open window, now from a doorway or the roadside. For the highland girl had at last reached her home village. She made no stop, however, but on her way by kept calling back answers to all the questions that were asked of her. And so they came to the far end of The Hamlet and to the last of its scattering cottages. A voice hailed her—

"O Dete, wait a minute! If you're going farther up, I'll walk along with you."

The highland girl halted. The child who was with her quickly drew away her hand and sank down upon the ground.

"Are you so very tired, Heidi?" her companion asked.

"No-o-o, but I'm hot," the child said.

"You just wait, we'll be up there before long now. Only, you must try harder and take great big steps, and then we'll be at the top in an hour," her guide said, to encourage her.

At this moment a fat, good-natured woman stepped out of the house and joined them. The child got to her feet again and walked along behind the two older people. And these, who were old friends, began to talk at a great rate

about the different people of The Hamlet and of the many
other dwellings in its neighborhood.

"Say, Dete, where are you taking the youngster?" the
fat woman asked. "That's the child of your dead sister,
isn't it?"

"She's the one," answered Dete. "I'm going up to
Nuncle's with her. And she'll have to stay with him, too."

"What's that? The child's going to live with Meadow
Nuncle? You can't be in your right mind, Dete! How
can you even think of such a thing? The old man will
just pack you and your fine plan off home again, you'll see!"

"Oh, no, he can't do that. For, after all, he's her
grandfather, and it's his business to look after her. I have
been supporting the child so far. And I'll tell you one
thing, Barbel—I am not going to lose such a place as I
have now found for the sake of any youngster. It's time
Nuncle steps in and does his share."

"Of course it is," broad Barbel agreed eagerly. "Or
at least it would be if he were like other people. But you
know his sort. What on earth will he do with the child,
and with such a tiny one, too? She won't last it out in
his house. But where is it you are planning to work?"

"In Frankfort," said Dete, "and an extra good job it
is. My new employers were at the baths last summer,
their rooms were on my floor, and I looked after them.
They were determined to carry me off with them then, but
I couldn't get away. And now they want to hire me again,
and I'm going, no matter what anyone says."

"I shouldn't like to be that child," declared Barbel,
with a shudder. "For nobody knows what's wrong with

the old man up there. He never speaks to a living soul. From one end of the year to the other he never sets foot in the church. And when, once a season, he and his thick staff do come down to us, everybody runs away from him and is afraid. Those bushy gray eyebrows of his, and that awful beard! He looks so much like an old heathen and Indian that I can tell you you're glad not to run across him when you're alone."

"Suppose he does look queer," said Dete defiantly, "he's her grandfather just the same and has to take care of the child. He probably won't do her any harm. And if he does, *he* will have to answer for it, not I."

"And still," the prying Barbel said, "I'd awfully like to know what sin is on the old man's conscience. Why does he frown so? Why does he live up there on the mountain meadow, shut off .from all the world? Why does he almost never show himself among people? They tell all sorts of stories about him, but I suppose you've heard them all from your sister, haven't you, Dete?"

"Indeed I have, but that is my business. If he found that I had been gossiping, I'd get myself into trouble."

Barbel had for ever so long been curious to know what was the matter with Meadow Nuncle. Why did he glare at people as if he hated them? Why did he live on the mountain like a hermit? Why did folks always speak of him curtly, as if they did not want to be against him and still were afraid to speak a good word for him? Barbel also thought it queer that all the people in The Hamlet should call the old man Meadow Nuncle, for of course he could not be the real uncle of every one of them.

But, because they called him that, she followed their lead and never spoke of him except as Nuncle, which was the local way of saying Uncle.

Just a little while before our story opens, Barbel had married and come to The Hamlet from her girlhood's home in Prättigau, and this is why she did not yet know all the strange things that had happened in the small village and all about its odd characters and surroundings. Her friend Dete, however, had been born in The Hamlet and had lived there with her mother until the old lady had died the year before. Then Dete had gone to work in the summer resort Ragaz as chambermaid in the great hotel there. And this morning she had come back with the child from Ragaz. They had ridden as far as Mayenfeld on a hay cart which a friend of hers was driving home, and he had been glad to give her and her little charge a lift.

Barbel was not the one to let so good a chance to learn about things slip. So she took tight hold of Dete's arm and said slyly—

"You see, dearie, one can get the truth from you about what people are saying, because of course you know the whole story. Do tell me what's wrong with the old fellow. Was he always so feared? Did he always hate everybody so?"

"How do I know how he used to be? I'm only twenty-six years old, and he is seventy at least. You can't expect me to have seen him when he was young. Still, if I knew it wouldn't be gossiped all over Prättigau afterward, I could tell you a few things, believe me! Mother was from Domleschg, you know, and so was he."

"Bah, Dete, what are you afraid of?" asked Barbel, a little offended. "Don't be so hard on the poor gossips down in Prättigau. And I guess I can keep a secret if I have to. Go on and tell me, that's a good girl! You won't be sorry for it."

"All right then, I will. But see that you keep your promise!" Dete warned her. First she turned around to make sure the child was not close enough to hear what she was going to say, but the youngster was nowhere to be seen. She must have stopped some time before this, only the two companions had been too interested in their chattering to notice the fact. Although the footpath made several windings, still one could see most of it all the way down to The Hamlet, and there was no one in sight.

"Oh, now I see her!" cried Barbel. "Look over yonder!" and she pointed far to one side of the mountain trail. "She is climbing the slope with the young goatherd Peter and his goats. I wonder why he's bringing his beasts so late today. But it's all right. He can look after the child, and you can tell me all the better about things."

"Peter won't have any trouble with her," said Dete. "She's anything but stupid for a five-year-old. She has her eyes open and sees what is going on in the world, I tell you! She'll do the old man good, for he has nothing left but his two goats and the thatch on the mountain meadow."

"He used to have more, didn't he?" asked Barbel.

"I should say he did!" answered Dete eagerly. "He owned one of the finest farms in Domleschg. He was the elder son and had only one brother, who was a quiet and steady fellow. Now, Nuncle wanted to do nothing except play the gentleman, travel around the country, and be friends with bad people whom nobody else wanted to know. He gambled and drank until the farm was all gone. And then the news came that his father and mother had died one right after the other because of their grief. And the brother, who had been made a beggar, got angry and ran away, nobody knew where. And Nuncle himself disappeared, leaving nothing but a bad name behind him."

"Where had he fled to?"

"They weren't sure. Some said he went off with the army to Naples. Anyway, nothing more was heard from him for almost fifteen years. And then suddenly he appeared, one day, with a half-grown boy, whom he tried to leave with his relatives."

"And they took the lad in, did they, Dete?" Barbel asked excitedly.

"Not they! Every door was closed against Nuncle. No one wanted to have any dealings with him. This made him very bitter. He swore he would never set foot in Domleschg again, and he came up here to The Hamlet to live with his boy. The mother must have been some Swiss girl that he had met down below and soon lost again."

"But, Dete, the old man had no money!"

"There must have still been some money left, for he had the boy Tobias learn how to be a carpenter. Tobias was a nice lad and well liked by all the people in The Hamlet, but nobody placed any trust in the father. They said he had run away from the army in Naples and that he would have been put in jail if he had not fled, because he had killed a man — not in war, of course, but in a fight.

Still, we had to speak to him, since my mother's grand-mother and his had been sisters. So we called him Nuncle. And, because through our father we are related to almost all the folks in The Hamlet, they called him the same. That is why, ever since he moved up to the mountain pasture, he has been known as Meadow Nuncle."

"But whatever became of Tobias?" Barbel asked curiously.

"Have a little patience and you'll hear," said Dete. "I can't tell you everything all at once. Well, Tobias was an apprentice off in Mels. And when his term was over he came home to The Hamlet and married my sister Adel-heid, for they had always been fond of each other. And they got along finely after their marriage, but it did not last very long. Not more than two years later, when Tobias was helping to build a house, a beam fell on him and killed him. When they brought her husband home so badly hurt, Adelheid's grief threw her into a violent fever from which she never quite recovered. She was never very strong after that. She was so weak that often you could scarcely tell whether she was awake or sleeping. A few weeks after the death of Tobias they buried Adelheid, too."

"People must have pitied Nuncle then," said Barbel.

"Oh, no, they didn't. Far and near everyone was talking of the sad fate of the young couple. And they said as well as hinted that this was the punishment which Nuncle got because of his godless life. They told him to his face, too — the pastor had a straight talk with him about begging God for forgiveness. But Nuncle just grew more sullen and no longer had a good word for anybody. They took good care to avoid him, anyway."

"And is that why he left The Hamlet, Dete?"

"I suppose. Suddenly it was reported that Nuncle had gone up to the mountain meadow and sworn never to come down again. And since that time there he has stuck and lived at odds with God and men. Mother and I took Adelheid's child in with us; it was a year old. And when Mother died last summer, I wanted to earn my living down at the baths. So I took the child along and put her out to board at old Ursula's up in Pfäfferserdorf. It turned out that I could stay at the baths during the winter, for there was a lot of work to do, because I knew how to sew and mend."

"And you met your new employers there?"

"Yes. They came from Frankfort again, early last spring. They were the ones I had waited on the previous year and who want to take me back with them. Day after tomorrow we go. And the place is a good one, I'll tell you that."

"And you're leaving the child with the old man up there? O Dete, I wonder what you can be thinking of!" Barbel said in a tone of deep reproach.

"And why not?" Dete demanded. "I guess I've done my duty by the child. And what else is there left for me to do now? I surely can't take a youngster five years old to Frankfort. But — where are you going, Barbel? We're hardly halfway up to the meadow."

"I — why, I'm right where I started for," Barbel answered. "I must have a talk with Goat Peter's mother.

She is to spin for me this winter. So good-by, Dete, and good luck!"

Dete gave her hand to Barbel and then stood watching her as she walked toward the small, dark brown hut which stood a few steps to one side of the trail in a hollow that protected it somewhat from the mountain winds. The hut was situated halfway up to the summit pasture, if one measured the distance from The Hamlet. And it was a good thing that it stood in a sheltered nook of the mountain side. For it did look so shaky and tumble-down that it must have been dangerous to live in it when the storm wind blew so madly across the Alps that doors and windows rattled. At such a time all the decaying timbers of the cottage trembled and creaked. If the little house had stood out on the level pasture, it would have surely been swept down into the valley far below.

In this hut dwelt Goat Peter.

This was the eleven-year-old boy who each morning went down to The Hamlet to fetch the villagers' goats. He drove them to the highland pastures, where they could graze on the short meadow grass of the slopes until evening came. Then Peter would run down the slopes again with his nimble flock, would pause at the edge of The Hamlet to whistle shrilly through his fingers, and each owner would come to the village green to get his own goat.

It was usually the small boys and girls who would be sent on this errand, for there was nothing to fear from the gentle little animals. And these short moments at sun set were the only time during the whole summer when

Peter associated with his playmates. The rest of the days he spent with his goats.

To be sure, his mother and his blind grandmother lived with him at home. But as he was forced to leave the hut very early in the morning and never returned to it until late in the evening, spending, as he did, every minute possible in play with the Hamlet children, he saw but little of his home. In fact, there was just time enough to swallow his bowl of bread and milk at dawn and at dusk, and then off to his cot for sleep. His father, like himself, had been called Goat Peter, because in his childhood years he had also tended the flocks, but some years before this he had been killed by a falling tree which he was chopping down. The real name of young Peter's mother was Brigitte, but because of family associations everybody called her Goat Peter's wife, and the blind grandmother was known to old and young as just Grandmother.

Now Dete had been waiting some ten minutes or more to see if she could find the children. She had climbed a little higher to a spot where she had a better view of the downward sweep of the meadow lands, and from this new place she peered about her in every direction. She was becoming very impatient, for the youngsters were coming slowly the long way around. Peter knew many a hidden spot where there were shrubs and bushes good for his goats to nibble at, so he and his herd were taking their own time and not hurrying.

At first Heidi had tramped painfully along after Peter, for the heat made her gasp, and her heavy clothes were so uncomfortable that it took all her strength to keep up with the boy.   She said nothing, but she kept eyeing the young goatherd, who with bare feet and in thin trousers was jumping about here and there without the least effort. And then she looked at the goats, whose slender legs were climbing so lightly over the thin bushes and the rocks of the steep cliffs.   Suddenly Heidi sat down on the ground, peeled off her shoes and stockings quickly, pulled the thick red scarf away from her throat, and unbuttoned her little dress to wriggle hurriedly out of it.

But this, alas, was not all she had to do.   There was another dress for her to unhook, because Aunty Dete, in order to make short work of dressing Heidi and to avoid an extra bundle, had drawn the child's Sunday clothes on over her everyday ones.   Quick as light the old gown was off, too, and now Heidi stood dressed only in her thin underskirt and blouse and was stretching her bare arms happily forth from her short sleeves.   Then she rolled her things up in a neat bundle and leaped and climbed after the goats at Peter's side, as light of foot as any in all the company.

Peter had paid no heed to what the child was doing when she had fallen behind.   But later, when he saw her running along after him in her new costume, his whole face twisted into a merry grin as he turned around to look. And when he caught sight of the small heap of clothes lying down below, his grin became if possible even wider still and his mouth seemed to reach clear from one ear to the other, but he said nothing.

Now that Heidi felt so much more easy and comfortable, the two children started to talk with each other.

Peter had many a question to answer, for Heidi wished to know how many goats he had, and where he was going with them, and what he was going to do when he got there. And so it was that they and the goats at last arrived at the hut and came to the sight of Aunt Dete.

The moment Dete saw this straggling company, she cried, "Heidi, whatever are you doing? My, how you do look! Where is your Sunday dress, and the other dress, and your scarf? And the brand new shoes I bought you and the new stockings I knit for you? They are gone, every one of them! What have you done with them all?"

The little girl pointed calmly down the mountain side and said, "There they are."

The aunt looked where she was pointing. Sure enough! Something was lying there, and on top of it was a red spot that must be the scarf.

"You naughty little imp!" the aunt cried in great vexation. "What got into your head, Heidi? Why did you take your things off? What do you mean by such actions?"

"I don't need them," the child said. Nor did she seem to be sorry in the least for her deed.

"You wretched, silly Heidi, where is your common sense?" her aunty went on to scold her. "Who's to go down and get them, more than a mile away? Quick, Peter, run and fetch the things for me, and don't stand there goggling as if you were stuck fast to the ground."

"I am already too late with my goats," said Peter slowly. And he stood right where he was without budging, his hands thrust into his pockets, listening with a grin to Dete's scolding.

"Just standing and staring won't get you very far in life," Aunty Dete called to him. "Come here. I've got something nice to show you."

She held out to him a penny so new that it flashed in his eyes.

Without a word Peter ran off and tore in a straight line down the hillside. He took such big jumps that he reached the pile of clothing in a short time. He seized it and appeared with it again so quickly that Dete could not help praising him and giving him the promised penny. Like a flash Peter stuck it deep in his trousers' pocket, and his face shone and was wreathed in smiles. For such a treasure did not come his way often.

"Now carry the pack to Nuncle's for me, because you're going up there anyway," Aunty Dete said.

And they made ready to climb the steep trail that rose straight upward behind the cottage of Goat Peter.

The boy did willingly as he was asked and followed his guide as she strode swiftly on ahead of him. In his left hand he clutched the bundle of clothes, in his right he swung his goat whip. Heidi and the little animals leaped gaily on by his side.

In this way, almost an hour later, the small procession arrived at the mountain meadow. Here the cabin of old Nuncle stood on a great overhanging rock, open to all the winds that blew, but also where every ray of sunshine would strike it, and with a fine view far down into the valley. Behind the hut three old fir trees towered aloft with their long, thick branches. And still farther on, in the rear of the meadow, the trail again wound its way up the mountain side until it reached the old gray cliffs. First the road crossed heights that were rich with grass and plants, then a great patch of tangled shrubs strewn everywhere with stones, until at last the trail was lost in the bald crags that stood sharply out against the sky.

Fast to the cottage on its valley side Nuncle had nailed a bench. Here he was sitting, with a pipe in his mouth and his hands on his knees, looking calmly on as the children, the goats, and Aunt Dete climbed up the path. Heidi led. She walked right up to the old gentleman, stretched out her hand, and said, "Good evening, Grandfather!"

"Well, well, and what does this mean?" Nuncle asked. He grasped the child's hand and gazed at her from under his bushy eyebrows with a long and rather fierce look. Heidi looked steadily back at him without once winking, for Grandfather, with his thick gray eyebrows that grew together in the middle, seemed somehow so strange to her that Heidi had to stare at him quite closely. In the meantime Dete arrived with Peter, who stood still for a while and waited to see what would happen.

"I wish you good day, Nuncle," said Dete, coming forward. "Here I am bringing you the child of Tobias and Adelheid. Of course you don't recognize her, because you haven't seen her since she was a year old."

"And what is the child to do in my house?" the old man asked. "As for you yonder," he called to Peter, "run along with your goats. You're none too early. Take my goats with you."

Peter disappeared at once, for Nuncle had given him a look that was all he wanted.

"Heidi's going to stay with you, Nuncle," Dete said. "I guess I've done my share for her these last four years. It's now your turn to see what you can do."

"O-ho!" said the old man, and flashed a look at Dete. "And when the child begins to whimper, as silly young-sters will, what am I going to do then?"

"That is your business," Dete said. "There was no one to tell me how to handle the child when she came to me barely a year old. And I already had my hands full looking after Mother and myself. I have my own work to go to now, and you are the child's nearest relative. If you can't keep her with you, then you must do whatever you want with her. But it's your fault if anything bad happens to her. And I guess you've got enough to answer for already in that respect."

Dete's mind was far from easy in this matter of getting rid of Heidi. That is why she grew so excited and said more than she meant to. At her last words, Nuncle rose up quickly and looked at her so that she fell back a step or two. He stretched out his arm and said fiercely —

"Go back to where you came from. And don't you show up here again!"

Dete did not wait to be told twice.

"Well, good-by then, Nuncle, and you too, Heidi," she said quickly.

And she ran all the way downhill to The Hamlet at a fast trot, for her excitement kept driving her on like a steam engine. As she passed through the village this time, she was hailed more often than before, because everyone was wondering what she had done with the child. They were all acquainted with Dete, knew who the child was, and remembered everything that had happened in the past.

But when from every door and window the questions flew, "Where is the child, Dete?" and "Where did you leave the young one?" she kept answering back ever more and more crossly—

"Up at Meadow Nuncle's. Ye-e-es! At Meadow Nuncle's, I said. You're not deaf, are you?"

The reason she was so rude was that the women on every hand were calling to her—

"Oh, how could you do such a thing!" and—

"The poor little kitten!" and—

"Leaving that helpless little midget up there!" and—

"The poor little angel!" over and over again.

Dete ran on and on as fast as ever she could, and was glad enough when she finally got out of hearing of their words. For she was not quite easy about the whole business, since her mother on her death bed had given Heidi to her to care for. But she comforted herself with the thought that she could help the child all the more now that she was earning good wages. And so she was glad to escape from anybody who argued against her act, and at last be on her way to take a good position.

CHAPTER II

AT GRANDFATHER'S

After Dete had gone, Nuncle had sat down again on the bench, and now he was blowing great clouds of smoke from his pipe, and all the time he was staring at the ground and saying never a word. Meanwhile Heidi looked about her happily. She discovered the goat shed that was built beside the cottage and peered into it. There was nothing inside.

The child continued her search and came to the old fir trees behind the hut. There the wind was blowing so hard through the branches that it whistled and roared up in the tree tops. Heidi stood still and listened. When it grew a little quieter, the child walked around the other side of the cottage and came back to her grandfather in front. As she found him still in the same position as when she had left him, she placed herself before him, put her hands behind her back, and gazed at him. The grandfather looked up.

"What do you want to do now?" he asked as the child kept standing before him without moving.

"I'm going to see what you have in the cottage," said Heidi.

"Come on, then!" And the grandfather got up and walked ahead of her into the hut. "Bring your bundle of clothes along with you," he called to her as she entered.

"I don't need them any more," Heidi explained.

The old man turned around and looked sharply at the child, whose black eyes were shining as she thought of what would be inside.

"She can't be lacking in common sense," he said half to himself. "Why don't you need your clothes any longer?" he added aloud.

"I'd soonest go like the goats. They have swift little legs."

"And you can, too, but get your things," Grandfather told her. "We'll put them in the chest."

Heidi did as she was told. The old man now opened the door, and Heidi followed him into a fairly large room which took up all the space of the cottage. There was a table, and a chair beside it. In one corner was the bed where Grandfather slept. In another corner a great kettle hung above the fireplace. On the other side of the room there was a big door in the wall. Grandfather opened it. It led into the cupboard.

In there his clothes were hanging. On one shelf lay his shirts, his stockings, and his linen, and on another one were several plates, cups, and glasses, and on the topmost shelf a round loaf of bread, with smoked meat and cheese. Everything the Meadow Nuncle had in the world and needed for his housekeeping was in this closet. As soon as he had opened the cupboard, Heidi ran quickly up with her things and thrust them inside as far back of Grandfather's clothes as she could, so they would not be easy to find again.

Then she looked carefully around the room and said, "Where must I sleep, Grandfather?"

"Where you want to," he answered.

That just suited Heidi. She hunted in every nook and corner to see which was the best place for her to sleep. Over in the corner beyond Grandfather's couch a little ladder was standing. Heidi climbed this and came to the hayloft. There lay a fresh, sweet-smelling heap of hay, and through a round window one could look far down into the valley beneath.

"I want to sleep here," Heidi called down, "it's fine! Just come and see how nice it is here, Grandfather."

"I know well enough," came the voice from below.

"I'm making the bed now," the child called again, as she moved busily to and fro, "but you must come up and bring me a linen sheet, for there's a sheet on every bed, and that's what you lie on."

"So that's the way it is," the grandfather said below, and after a while he went to the cupboard and rummaged around a bit in it. Then he drew out from under his shirts a long coarse cloth that looked as if it might be something like a sheet. He came up the ladder with it. A very neat little bed had been made up there in the loft. At the top of it, where the head would come, the hay had been piled up high, so that one could look right through the open round window.

"That is done just right," the grandfather said. "Now comes the sheet, but wait a second"—and he snatched up a good armful of hay from the stack and made the couch twice as thick, so that the hard floor could not be felt through it—"there, now come here with the sheet."

Heidi had quickly grasped the linen sheet, but it was so heavy that she almost could not carry it. But that was a good thing, too, for then the sharp hay-straws could not stick through the firm material. Then the two of them spread the sheet over the hay, and where it was too wide or too long Heidi hastily stuffed the ends under the bed. At last it looked very trim and neat, and Heidi stood before it and looked at it thoughtfully.

"There's one thing we've forgotten, Grandfather," she said.

"What can that be?" he asked.

"A coverlet. For when you go to bed, you creep in between the sheet and the coverlet."

"Oh, you do? But what if I haven't got one?" the old man said.

"That's all right then, Grandfather," Heidi said gently. "We can take some more hay for our coverlet," and she started to go to the haymow again, but Grandfather put up his hand.

"Wait a minute," he said, climbed down the ladder, and walked over to his couch. Then he came back with a large, heavy linen sack and laid it on the floor.

"Isn't that better than hay?" he asked. Heidi tugged at the bag as hard as ever she could to unfold it, but her little hands could not master the heavy material. Grandfather helped, and when at last it was spread out on the bed everything looked quite neat.

Heidi stood admiring her new couch and said, "That is a splendid coverlet, and the whole bed is beautiful! And now I only wish it was night, so I could lie down on it."

"I think we'd better have something to eat first," said
Grandfather. "Is that your idea?"

Heidi had been so excited about making the bed that
she had forgotten everything else. But now that she
came to think about food she at once grew very hungry,
for she had had nothing except a piece of bread and a
small cup of thin coffee early that morning, and since that
time she had made a long journey.

So she said very heartily, "Yes, that's my idea, too."

"Go down then, since we're both agreed," said the old
man, and he followed right on her heels.

Then he went to the kettle, pushed the big one aside,
and drew forward the small one that hung on the chain,
sat down before it on the three-legged wooden stool with
the round seat, and blew the fire into flames. The water in
the kettle began to boil, and below it the old man held a
large piece of cheese on the end of a long iron fork over
the fire, turning it this way and that until it was as yellow
as gold on every side. All this Heidi had watched eagerly.

Suddenly a new thought had come into her mind,
for she ran off to the cupboard and kept going back
and forth. Then Grandfather brought the teapot and
the toasted cheese to the table, and it was already neatly
set with the round loaf of bread on it, and two plates
and two knives, for Heidi had quickly found where everything was in the closet and knew that it would all be
needed right away for the meal.

"That's nice that you think things out for yourself,"
said the grandfather as he laid the cheese down on the
bread, "but there's something still lacking from the table."

Heidi saw how invitingly the steam was coming out of the teapot and ran quickly back to the cupboard. But there was only a single small bowl to be seen. Heidi was not at a loss for long, as two glasses were standing right behind it. The child came back at once and set the bowl and a glass on the table.

"That's the way, you know how to help yourself. But where are you going to sit?"

Grandfather was himself sitting on the only chair. Heidi ran straight as an arrow to the fireplace, brought back the little three-legged stool, and sat down on it.

"Well, there's a seat for you at any rate," the grandfather said, "only it's down a good way. But my chair would be too short for you to reach the table, too. And now you must have something to eat, so come ahead!"

Thereupon he got up, filled the small bowl with milk, set it on the chair, and drew this quite close to the stool, so that Heidi now had a table before her. Grandfather laid a big slice of bread and a piece of the golden cheese on the chair and said, "Eat away!"

He sat down on a corner of the table and began his own noonday meal. Heidi seized her bowl and drank and drank without stopping, for all the thirst from her long journey had returned to her. Then she drew a long breath — for she had been drinking so hard she couldn't breathe for a long time — and set down her bowl.

"Do you like the milk?" Grandfather asked.

"I never drank such good milk in all my life," Heidi answered.

"Then you must take some more."

And Grandfather filled the bowl to the very top again and placed it before the child, who was eating happily away at her bread after this had been spread with the soft cheese. For the cheese had been toasted until it was as soft as butter, and it tasted very good indeed. She took frequent sips of milk and seemed quite gay.

When the meal was ended, Grandfather went out to the goat shed and was busy putting it in order, and Heidi watched carefully as he first swept it out with a broom and then scattered fresh straw for the animals to sleep on. She followed him later into the shop next door, where he cut round sticks and shaped up a board. He bored holes in it, put in the round sticks, and set it up, and there was suddenly a chair like grandfather's, only much higher. Heidi stared at the thing, speechless with wonder.

"What is that, Heidi?" her grandfather asked.

"That's my chair, because it's so high—you did it like lightning," said the child, not yet able to get over her surprise.

"She knows what things are. Her eyes are in the right place," her grandfather muttered to himself as he walked around the cottage and drove a nail here and there. Then he fixed something about the door and wandered from one place to another with hammer and nails and pieces of wood, patching or knocking things off, just as seemed best. Heidi followed his every step, watching him closely, and everything he did seemed to amuse her.

Thus the evening drew near. There was a louder rustling in the old fir trees, and a mighty wind came along and whistled and roared in the thick tree tops. It sounded so beautiful in Heidi's ears that it made her very happy. She hopped and danced about outside under the firs as if some strange joy had come to her. Grandfather stood in the doorway of the shop and watched her play.

And then a shrill whistle was heard. Heidi put a stop to her jumping. Grandfather stepped outside. Down from above, goat after goat came leaping, like a pack of hunters, and Peter in their midst. With a cry of joy, Heidi rushed into the midst of the flock and, one after another, greeted her friends of the morning.

"When the flock reached the hut, they all came to a halt, and two fine, slender goats, one white and one brown, came up to Grandfather and licked his hands, for he had some salt in them to welcome them with, as he did every evening. Peter disappeared with his troop. Heidi stroked gently first one goat and then the other, running around to pat them on the other side. She was quite mad about the small creatures.

"Are they ours, Grandfather? Are they both ours? Do they go into the shed? Are they to stay with us always?"

Heidi asked one question after another in her excitement, so that Grandfather could hardly get a word in edgewise. "Yes, yes, yes," he said. And when the goats had licked up all their salt, he added, "Go and bring out your bowl and the bread."

Heidi did as she was told and came right back. Then Grandfather milked the white goat and filled the little bowl with its milk, and cut off a slice of bread.

"Now eat your supper," he said, "and then run off to bed. Your Aunty Dete left a bundle for you—there are some nightgowns and other things in it. You'll find it downstairs in the chest when you need it. I must go and see to the goats now, so sleep well!"

"Good night, Grandfather. Good night — oh, what are their names, Grandfather? What do you call them?" the child cried as she ran after the old man and the goats, who were disappearing into the shed.

"The white one's name is Little Swan, the brown one is called Little Bear," Grandfather answered.

"Good night, Schwänli, good night, Bärli!" Heidi called with all her might, because they were just vanishing into the stable. Then she settled down on the bench and ate her bread and drank her milk, although the wind was so strong that it almost blew her from her seat. So she finished as fast as she could, and went in to climb up to bed. And she went right off to sleep and slept as soundly as if she were lying on the most beautiful bed of some princess.

Not long afterward, before it was yet wholly dark, Grandfather, too, lay down upon his couch, for he was always up with the sun mornings, and it peered over the mountain top very early in the summer time. During the night the wind blew with such force that it made the whole cottage tremble, and all the beams were creaking. It howled and groaned in the chimney like the voice of one in pain. And outside in the fir trees it raged so terribly that here and there a branch was broken off.

In the middle of the night Grandfather got out of bed and said to himself softly, "She is probably scared."

So he climbed up the ladder and went to Heidi's side. Out of doors the moon was shining brightly just then, but a moment later it hid again behind the driving clouds and all was dark. Then the moonlight shone a second time clearly through the round opening and fell right on Heidi's bed. Her cheeks were as red as fire from sleeping under the heavy coverlet. She lay quite peaceful and still on one round little arm and was dreaming of something pleasant, for a look of happiness was on her small face. Grandfather stood a long time to gaze at the gently sleeping child, until the moon again went behind a cloud and it was dark.

Then he returned to his own couch.

CHAPTER III

IN THE PASTURE

Heidi was awakened bright and early by a loud whistle. And when she opened her eyes, a golden light came pouring in through the round hole upon her bed and upon the hay beside it, so that everything around her was gleaming like gold. At first she looked about her in surprise and had no idea where she was.

But then she heard the deep voice of her grandfather outside the hut, and she remembered everything—where she had come from, and that she was now up on the mountain meadow with her grandfather and no longer at old Ursula's. Ursula was almost deaf and generally half frozen, so that she was always sitting by the kitchen fire or by the stove in the living room. And so it was that Heidi had to stay there, too, so the old lady could tell where she was, because she was too deaf to hear her. Heidi had felt very shut-in many times and would much sooner have played out of doors.

Therefore she was very glad to wake up in her new home and to think of all the new things she had seen yesterday and all there were to see again today—above all, Schwänli and Bärli!

Heidi sprang hastily from her bed and in a few minutes had put on everything she had worn the day before —which was little enough. Then she climbed down the ladder and ran out in front of the cottage. There, sure enough, stood Goat Peter with his flock, and Grandfather was that moment fetching Little Swan and Little Bear out of the shed to join the company. Heidi ran to meet him, to tell him and the goats good day.

"Do you want to go along to the pasture?" Grandfather asked.

That just suited Heidi, and she hopped round for joy.

"First go and wash yourself clean or the sun will laugh at you when it is shining so finely up above there and sees that you are dirty. Look, everything is ready for you over yonder."

Grandfather pointed to a big tub full of water which stood by the doorway in the sunshine. Heidi ran to it and splashed and rubbed until her face shone.

Meanwhile Grandfather went inside the cottage and called to Peter, "Come here, Goat General, and bring your knapsack with you."

Peter was surprised, but he obeyed and stretched out the small sack in which he carried his poor dinner.

"Open it," the old man ordered. And he put in it a big slice of bread and an equally large piece of cheese.

Peter opened his round eyes as wide as they would go, for both pieces were half as large again as the two that he had brought for his own noonday meal.

"There! And now the little bowl goes in, too," continued Nuncle, "for the child cannot drink as you do right from the goat — she doesn't know how. Milk two bowlsful for her at noon. The child is going with you and is to stay until you come down again. See that she doesn't fall over the cliff—do you hear me?"

Then Heidi came running up.

"Can the sun laugh at me now, Grandfather?" she asked earnestly.   In her fear about the sun she had rubbed her face, neck, and arms so astonishingly with the coarse cloth her Grandfather had hung up beside the water tub that she stood before the old man as red as a lobster.   He laughed a little.

"No, the sun has nothing to grin at now," he said. "But let me tell you one thing.   Tonight, when you come home, all of you is going into the tub, just like a fish.   For when you go out as the goats do, you get your feet dirty. And now you can set out."

Off they went happily up the mountain meadow.   During the night the wind had blown away the last bit of cloud.   From every side the sky looked down on them, deep blue, and in the midst of it stood the shining sun lighting up the green pasture.   And all the blue and yellow flowers on the meadow opened their eyes and looked at them joyfully.   Heidi ran hither and thither and cried aloud for happiness, for here were whole companies of dainty red primroses, and over there it was all blue with pretty gentians, and everywhere soft-leaved yellow rock-roses were laughing and nodding in the sunshine.

Heidi, because of her delight at all the gleaming, beckoning flowers, quite forgot the goats, and Peter into the bargain.   She made long trips ahead and off to one side, for here the flowers sparkled red and there yellow, luring her in every direction.   And everywhere Heidi picked great heaps of flowers.   She stuffed them in her apron, for she wanted to take them all home with her and put them in the hay in her bedroom so that it might seem like out of doors.

So today Peter was forced to look in all directions, and his round eyes, which did not move very quickly from one thing to another, had more to do than they could well attend to, for the goats acted as badly as Heidi. They flashed here and there, and he was kept busy whistling and calling and swinging his whip to drive all the runaways together again.

"And where have you gone to this time?" he was now crying in almost an angry tone of voice.

"Here," came the answer from somewhere behind him. Peter could see nobody, for Heidi was sitting on the ground behind a knoll that was thickly sown with sweet-smelling prunellas. The whole air around was so filled with their fragrance that Heidi had never smelled anything so lovely. She sat down among the flowers and took deep breaths of the perfume.

"Come on!" Peter called again. "You mustn't fall over the cliffs. Nuncle forbade you to."

"Where are the cliffs?" Heidi called back to ask. But she did not budge from the spot, for the sweet perfume was borne on each new breeze more delightfully than ever to the child.

"Up there, away up! We have a long way before us still, so come right along. And at the very top the old bird of prey sits and croaks."

That sounded interesting. Heidi jumped up at once and flew to Peter, her apron filled with flowers.

"You have enough now," he said, as together they

began climbing again. "If you don't stop, you'll never get away from here, and if you pick them all now, there won't be any left for tomorrow."

This last reason seemed good to Heidi, and, besides, she had already filled her apron so full that there was no room for any more. And there must be some left to pick tomorrow. So she tramped along with Peter, and the goats became more quiet, too, for they smelled from afar the good herbs of the high pasture grounds, and so hurried on without delay.

The pasture where Peter usually halted his goats and set up his quarters for the day lay at the foot of tall cliffs. These rocks lower down were covered with bushes and fir trees, but higher up they rose toward the sky quite bald and steep. There were great chasms in the cliffs on one side of the mountain, and the grandfather had been right in warning the children about them.

When Peter had reached this point of the heights, he took off his sack and laid it carefully in a small hollow in the ground. For the wind often swept in strong gusts at this spot, and Peter knew it and did not wish to see his precious possessions rolling down the mountain side. Then Peter stretched himself out on the ground of the sunny pasture, for he had to rest after the hard work of his climb.

In the meantime Heidi had laid aside her apron and had rolled it up neatly with the flowers inside it and had placed it beside the lunch bag in the hollow, and now she was sitting close to the outstretched Peter and gazing around her.

The valley lay far beneath them in the full morning

sunshine. Before her Heidi saw a large white field of
snow which rose high up into the dark blue sky. To the
left of this stood an enormous mass of cliffs, and on each
side of it a high rock tower stretched bare and jagged up
into the blue and seemed to stare very solemnly down upon
Heidi.

The child sat as still as a mouse and looked about her.
Everywhere there was a great deep stillness, except that
the wind moved quite softly and gently across the dainty
bluebells and the gay yellow rockroses which bloomed
about her on every side and nodded happily to and fro on
their slender stems. Peter had fallen asleep after his hard
work, and the goats were climbing up above among the
bushes.

In her whole life Heidi had never been so happy as
now. She drank in the golden sunlight, the sweet smell of
the flowers, the fresh air, and wanted nothing so much
as to stay there for always. A good while passed in
this way. Heidi had stared so often and so long at the
tall mountain blocks that it seemed as if they, too, all
had human faces and were looking down at her like old
friends.

All at once Heidi heard above her head a loud, sharp
screaming and croaking, and as she looked up there
circled over her the biggest bird she had ever seen in all
her life. It wheeled through the air with far outstretched
wings and kept coming back again in great circles of
flight, to scream loud and shrill above Heidi's head.

"Peter! Peter, wake up!" Heidi cried aloud. "Look,
there is the bird of prey—look, look!"

Peter rose at her call and together they stared after the bird, which kept flying higher and higher up into the blue sky, until it finally vanished above the gray cliffs.

"Where has he gone now?" asked Heidi, who had been following the bird with eager eyes.

"Home to his nest," was Peter's answer.

"Has he a home 'way up over there? Oh, how fine to be so high up! Why does he screech so?" Heidi went on to ask.

"That's the way he's made," Peter explained.

"Let's just climb up and see where his nest is," Heidi said.

"Ho, ho, ho!" Peter broke out. "When the goats themselves can't get up there, and Nuncle said you musn't fall over the cliffs!"

And suddenly Peter began to whistle and call so sharply that Heidi did not know what was going on. But the goats seemed to understand his noise, for one after the other they came leaping down until the whole herd was gathered on the green slope. Some kept nibbling at the spicy stalks, some ran this way and that, others were butting one another playfully with their horns.

Heidi had jumped up and was darting around among the goats, for it was lots of fun for her to see the little animals huddling together and making merry. She ran from one to another and struck up a real friendship with each, for every goat seemed somehow different and had his own peculiar ways.

While she was doing this, Peter fetched the lunch bag and placed the pieces of bread and cheese on the ground in a neat square, the large ones on Heidi's side and the small ones on his own, for he knew exactly whose they were. After that he took the little bowl, milked fine fresh milk from Schwänli into it, and placed the bowl in the center of the square.

Then he called Heidi to him. But he had to call longer than he did to get the goats, because the child was so happily excited at the amusing play of her new comrades that she had eyes and ears for nothing else. But Peter knew how to make himself heard. He screamed until the sound echoed up in the cliffs. Then Heidi appeared, and the table he had spread looked so inviting that she hopped about for joy.

"Stop your dancing. It's time to eat," Peter said. "Sit down and get started."

Heidi took her seat.

"Is the milk mine?" she asked, again casting a satisfied look at the neat square and the chief object in the middle of it.

"Yes," Peter replied, "and the large things to eat are yours too. And when you've drunk it up, you get another bowlful from Schwänli. And then it's my turn."

"And where do you get your milk from?" Heidi wanted to know.

"From my goat, from Dapple. You go ahead and eat," Peter again advised her.

Heidi started with her milk, and as soon as she set down her empty bowl, Peter got up and fetched a second one. At that, Heidi broke off a piece of her bread, and the remaining portion, which was larger than Peter's own

share had been, she handed him, together with its big
slice of cheese.

"You can have it," she said. "I've had enough."

Peter gazed at Heidi, so astonished that he could not
say a word, for never in his life had he been able to make
such an offer and to give something away. He held back
a little at first, for he could not quite believe that Heidi
was in earnest. But she kept holding the pieces out to
him, and when Peter failed to take them she laid them on
the boy's knees. Then he saw that she was not joking.
He seized the gift, nodded his head in thanks and willing-
ness to accept the present, and had the most abundant lunch
he had enjoyed since he had been a goatherd. While he
was eating, Heidi looked at the goats.

"What are all their names, Peter?" she asked.

He knew that right enough, and could keep their names
in his head all the more easily because he did not have much
else to store up in it. So he began without hesitation to
name one after the other, pointing out each goat as he
went along. Heidi listened eagerly to his teaching, and it
was not long before she could tell them apart and call
each one by its name. For they all had special marks by
which one could keep them in mind, if one but paid close
attention, the way Heidi did.

That was Big Turk with the thick horns. He always
wanted to butt all the others, and they mostly ran away
when he came, for they wanted nothing to do with the
rough fellow. Only bold Goldfinch, a lean and lively young
goat, was not afraid of him and often tore after him three
or four times in succession so quickly and sturdily that Big

Turk would halt astonished and try no further attack. For Goldfinch seemed eager for a fight and had sharp little horns.

Then came little white Snowhopper, who was always bleating so sadly and pitifully that Heidi several times had run to her and taken her head in her arms, to comfort her. And now the child ran to her again, for the pitiful young voice had once again cried out in appeal. Heidi placed her arm around the neck of the young kid and asked with much sympathy—

"What's the matter, Schneehöppli? Why do you cry so for help?"

The kid snuggled closely to Heidi and was then quite still. Peter called over from where he was sitting, pausing a few times to chew and to swallow—

"She acts that way because the old lady no longer comes along. They sold her at Mayenfeld day before yesterday, so she comes no more up to the mountain meadow."

"Who is the old lady?" Heidi asked.

"Bah, the mother, of course!" was the answer.

"Where's the grandmother, then?" Heidi called again.

"Hasn't any."

"And the grandfather?"

"Hasn't one."

"You poor little Snowhopper," said Heidi, and pressed the small creature tenderly against her. "But please don't whimper so any more. Just look, I'm coming with you every day, and then you won't feel so lonely any longer. And if anything's wrong with you, you can come straight to me."

Schneehöppli rubbed her head delightedly against Heidi's shoulder and stopped her mournful bleating. Meanwhile Peter had finished his noonday meal and had now returned to his herd and to Heidi, who was beginning to ask about all sorts of new things.

By far the two prettiest and cleanest goats of the whole herd were Schwänli and Bärli, who carried themselves with a certain grand manner, generally minded their own business, and treated the silly Turk in the way that he deserved.—

The little animals had now begun to climb again toward the bushes, and each one had his own way of doing this. Some jumped along carelessly over everything, others sniffed out the good herbs as they went more slowly, and Turk of course sought someone to attack.

Little Swan and Little Bear clambered prettily and lightly upward and, finding at once the nicest bushes, they stopped and nibbled daintily at them. Heidi stood with her hands behind her back and looked at all the goats very closely.

"Peter," she said to the lad, who was again stretched out on the ground, "Schwänli and Bärli are the prettiest of them all."

"Don't I know that?" was the answer. "Meadow Nuncle scrubs and washes them, he gives them salt and has the best stable."

But suddenly Peter sprang up and tore at top speed toward the goats, with Heidi right on his heels. Something must have happened, and she did not want to be left behind. Peter ran through the midst of the flock of

goats to the side of the mountain meadow, where the cliffs
descended steep and bare far below, and where a careless
goat, if it went too near, might easily plunge down and
break all its bones.

He had seen how the reckless Goldfinch was hopping
over in that direction. And he got there just in the nick
of time, for the silly little animal was leaping in that
moment toward the edge of the rocks. Peter was on the
point of seizing it when he stumbled and fell to the ground,
and in his fall was only able to grasp one of the animal's
legs and hold fast to it. Distelfink bleated aloud his anger
and amazement, to have his leg gripped so and to be kept
from continuing his gay stroll. He struggled to go ahead.

Peter shrieked for Heidi to help him, for he could not
get up and was almost tearing Goldfinch's leg off. Heidi
was there in a flash and saw at once the danger of both
of them. She quickly plucked from the ground some
sweet-smelling herbs and held them under Distelfink's
nose and said—

"Come, Goldfinch, come, don't be such a goose! Why,
look, you might fall down and break a leg, and that would
hurt you awfully."

The goat had turned around quickly and begun to eat
the herbs from Heidi's hand with much content. In the
meantime Peter had got to his feet and had seized the
rope by which the bell was hung on Distelfink's neck.
Heidi grasped the cord by the other side, and thus the two
led the runaway back to the peacefully grazing herd.

When Peter had brought the goat back to a safe place,
he raised his rod and was going to give him a sound

thrashing as a punishment. Goldfinch drew back in fright,
for he saw what was going to happen. But Heidi
screamed—

"No, no, Peter, you mustn't beat him! See how scared
he is."

"He deserves to be," growled Peter and started to
strike. But Heidi grasped his arm and cried angrily—

"You shan't do a thing to him, it will hurt him. Let
him go!"

Peter gazed in great surprise at Heidi. Her black
eyes gleamed at him so that he lowered his rod.

"Well, let him go, then, if you'll give me some more
of your cheese tomorrow," Peter said in surrender. He
wanted to have some reward for his fright.

"You can have all of it, every bit, tomorrow and every
other day," Heidi promised him. "I don't want it. And
I'll give you a lot of bread, too, just like today. But then
you must never pound Distelfink, nor Schneehöppli, nor
any other goat—never."

"That suits me all right," Peter remarked. And with
him that was as good as a promise. So he let the rascal
go, and happy Goldfinch leaped high into the air and then
flashed back to the herd.—

So the day had passed unnoticed, and the sun was
already on the point of setting behind the mountains.
Heidi sat down again and gazed very quietly at the bluebells and the rockroses. They were sparkling in the golden
evening light, and all the grass seemed as if touched with
gold, and the cliffs above her began to glisten and glimmer.
And suddenly Heidi jumped up and cried—

"Peter, Peter, it's burning—it's burning! All the mountains are on fire, and the big snow over there is on fire, too, and the sky. Oh, just look! The great rock mountain is all golden red! Oh, the pretty flaming snow! Peter, get up! The fire is at the bird of prey's home. Look at the cliffs! Look at the firs! Everything is burning up."

"It's always been like that," Peter now said good-naturedly, as he kept on peeling his rod, "but that isn't fire."

"What is it, then?" cried Heidi as she ran back and forth so she could look everywhere. It was so pretty in all directions that she just could not get enough of it.

"What is it, Peter? What can it be?" she asked again.

"It comes that way, all by itself," Peter explained.

"But, just see," Heidi cried very much excited, "all of a sudden it's growing rosy red! Look at the mountain with the snow, and the other one with the high pointed rocks! What are they called, Peter?"

"Mountains don't have names," he replied.

"Oh, how pretty! See the rosy red snow! Oh, and on the rocks up there are heaps and heaps of roses! Ah, now they're getting gray! Oh, my! now it's all over, Peter."

And Heidi plumped down on the ground and looked as troubled as if everything had really come to an end.

"It will be like that tomorrow again," Peter declared. "Get up, we'll have to be going home now."

The goats were whistled for and gathered together. The home journey was begun.

"Is it that way all days — every day when we are at the pasture?" asked Heidi, eagerly listening for his answer as she climbed down the mountain meadow at Peter's side.

" 'Most always," he replied.

"But tomorrow again, sure?" she insisted on knowing.

"Tomorrow, without any doubt," said Peter.

That made Heidi happy again. And yet she had seen so many new things, so many thoughts were whirling around in her mind, that she never said a word until she came to the meadow hut and saw Grandfather sitting beneath the fir trees. He had built himself a bench there and was always waiting there in the evening for his goats, which came down in this direction.

Heidi ran straight up to him, with Little Swan and Little Bear close behind her, for the goats knew their master and their shed. Peter called after Heidi—

"Come again tomorrow, won't you? Good night!"

For he was quite set on having Heidi go with him a second time.

Then Heidi flew back to him, gave Peter her hand, and promised him that she would come along next day. Afterward she jumped into the midst of the departing herd, put her arms a last time around Snowhopper's neck, and said—

"Sleep well, Schneehöppli. Don't forget I'm coming again tomorrow and remember you must never again bleat so pitifully."

Snowhopper gave her a friendly look and seemed grateful. And she ran happily off after the flock.

Heidi walked back under the fir trees.

"O Grandfather," she called out before she had reached him, "it was so beautiful—the fire, and the roses on the cliffs, and the blue and yellow flowers—just see what I've brought you!"

And thereupon Heidi poured her whole store of flowers from her folded apron at her grandfather's feet. But how the poor flowers did look! Heidi could no longer recognize them. They were all like hay, and not a single one of their cups was open.

"O Grandfather, what's wrong with them?" Heidi cried, quite frightened. "They weren't like that at all— why do they look that way now?"

"They want to stay out of doors in the sun and not rolled up in your apron," Grandfather said.

"Then I shan't ever pick any more of them. But, Grandfather, why did the bird of prey squawk so?" Heidi now asked earnestly.

"Into the water with you, while I go to the stable and get some milk. Then we'll go into the cottage together and eat supper. And then I'll tell you all about it."

Heidi did as she was asked to. And later, when she sat on her high chair with her little bowl of milk before her and Grandfather next to her, she returned again to her question—

"Why did the bird of prey croak and scream down at us so, Grandfather?"

"He is laughing at the people down below him who crowd into their villages and tease one another. He mocks at them and screams, 'If you'd leave one another and climb the heights, each his own way, as I do, then you'd be happier!'"

Grandfather spoke these words almost wildly, so that

Heidi remembered the screaming of the bird of prey even more clearly than before, if such a thing was possible.

"Why don't the mountains have names, Grandfather?" Heidi asked then.

"But they have," he answered. "And if you can describe one so that I can recognize it, I'll tell you what its name is."

Then Heidi described the rocky mountain and its two high towers exactly as she had seen it. And Grandfather, well pleased, said—

"Just right! I know that one. It's called Falcon's Nest. Did you see another one?"

Heidi went on to describe the mountain with the great field of snow, the one on which all the snow had been afire, and then grown rosy red, and finally without warning had got very pale and dead.

"I recognize that one also," said Grandfather, "that is the Cäsaplana. You liked it, then, on the pasture, did you?"

Now Heidi told him everything about the whole day— how lovely it had all been, and especially the fire toward evening. And now Grandfather must tell her, too, where that had come from, because Peter had known nothing about it.

"That's done by the sun, you know," explained Grandfather. "When he says good night to the world, he sends his very finest beams to the mountains, so they won't forget him before his return in the morning."

That pleased Heidi. She felt she could hardly wait until another day had come, so that she could go up to the pasture and again see how the sun said good night to the mountains.

But first she had to go to bed. And she slept soundly the whole night through on her couch of hay. And she dreamed of nothing but gleaming mountains with red roses on them, and in the midst of these little Snowhopper was running about with merry leaps.

CHAPTER IV

AT THE GRANDMOTHER'S

The bright sun came again on the following morning. And then Peter appeared with his goats. And they all went together back up to the pasture. And so it happened day after day.

Heidi got very tanned from this life on the meadow, and so strong and healthy that nothing was ever wrong with her. And she lived happily from one day to the next as only gay little birds can live in all the trees of the green woods.

When it began to be autumn and the wind roared more loudly across the mountains, then Grandfather would say perhaps—

"Stay at home today, Heidi. With one puff the wind can blow a little thing like you over the cliffs into the valley."

When Peter would hear such words in the morning, he looked quite miserable, for he could see nothing but unhappiness before him. For one thing, he did not know what to do when Heidi was not with him. And then he missed his generous dinner. Besides, the goats were so stubborn on these days that he had twice his usual trouble with them. For they were so used to Heidi's company that they would not go ahead without her, but would run away in all directions.

Heidi was never dull, because she always found something to do that was fun. She would have liked best to go with the goatherd and his flock off to the meadow, to the flowers and the bird of prey. There were so many things to learn about all the goats and their different ways.

But then, her Grandfather's hammering and sawing and carpentry work were very interesting to Heidi. Sometimes it happened that he was making the pretty round goat-cheeses on just the day when she was at home. Then it was quite specially enjoyable to see the remarkable work her Grandfather did with both arms bare as he stirred what was in the great kettle.

More to be desired by Heidi than all else, on such days of high wind, was the surging and roaring in the three old fir trees behind the hut. Whatever she might be doing, or wherever she might be, she had to run to them from time to time, for nothing in the world was so lovely and wonderful as this deep roaring up there in the tree tops. Heidi would stand beneath them and listen hard. And she never could get her fill of seeing and hearing what was waving and heaving and rushing with such power among the trees.

The sun no longer shone as hot as in summer, and Heidi hunted out her shoes and stockings and also her little dress. For now it kept growing colder. And when Heidi stood under the fir trees the wind blew through her as if she were a thin leaf. Still she could not bear to stay indoors, but kept running out every time she heard the sighing of the wind.

Then it grew cold in earnest, and Peter would blow on his hands when he came climbing up early in the morning. But not for long. For all of a sudden one night a deep snow fell. And next morning the whole mountain meadow was snow white, and there wasn't a green leaf to be seen anywhere, no matter where you looked.

After this, Peter came no more with his herd, and Heidi gazed much astonished out of the small window, for now it began to snow again. And the thick flakes fell and fell until the snow was so deep that it reached up to the window. And then it grew higher yet, so they could not open the window at all and they were completely packed away in the cottage.

That seemed very jolly to Heidi, and she kept running from one window to another just to see how things were getting on and whether the snow was going to cover the entire hut so that one would have to light a candle in broad day. But it did not come to that, after all. And next day Grandfather went out—for it had stopped snowing—and shoveled around the whole house. He piled big, big heaps of snow on top of one another, so that about the hut it looked like a mountain every little way.

But now the windows and door were free again, and it was a good thing they were! For that afternoon as Heidi and her Grandfather were sitting on their three-legged chairs by the fire—Grandfather had long since made a chair for the child — something suddenly staggered up, stamped on the wooden threshold, and finally opened the door.

It was Peter the goatherd.

He had not made such a great noise at the door because he was rude, but to stamp the snow from his shoes, which were all covered with it. In fact, all of Peter was covered with snow, for he had had to push his way so violently through the deep drifts that great clumps of snow had stuck to him and, because of the sharp cold, had frozen fast. But he had not given up his trip, for he wanted to go up that day to visit Heidi, whom he had not seen for a whole long week.

"Good afternoon," he said when he came in. Then he placed himself at once as near as possible to the fire and had not another word to say—but his whole face lighted up with joy to think he was there. Heidi looked at him quite puzzled, for now that he was so close to the fire the snow began to thaw on him, and Peter looked quite like a gentle waterfall.

"Well, General, how are you getting along?" Grandfather said then. "Now you are without an army and have to nibble at a slate pencil."

"Why does he have to bite at a slate pencil, Grandfather?" Heidi asked at once, curiously.

"In winter he has to go to school," the grandfather explained. "There you learn to read and write, and that's often so hard that it helps a little if you chew the end of your slate pencil. Am I right, General?"

"Indeed you are," said Peter.

Heidi's interest in the matter was now awakened, and she had a great many questions to ask of Peter about the school and everything that happened there—about what he saw and heard. And as much time was always spent in any talk that Peter took part in, he had a good chance to get quite dry from top to toe. It was always hard for him to put his ideas into words that would express what he meant. And this time it was harder even than usual, for scarcely had he answered one thing, than Heidi would ask him two or three more questions which required a whole sentence to answer.

During all this talk the grandfather had kept very quiet indeed, but the corners of his mouth had twitched several times humorously, which was a sign that he was listening.

"Well, General, now you've been under fire and need something to strengthen you. Come, join in with us!"

Thereupon the grandfather rose from his chair and fetched the supper from the cupboard, while Heidi drew the chairs up to the table. There was another seat which Grandfather had made and nailed fast to the wall. Now that he was no longer alone, he had prepared in one place and another all sorts of seats for two, because Heidi had a way of keeping close to him everywhere, no matter what he was doing.

So all three of them had places to sit, and Peter opened his round eyes very wide when he saw what a mighty piece of fine dried meat Meadow Nuncle laid on his thick slices of bread. Peter had not seen anything so good for a long time. When the merry meal was over, it began to get dark, and Peter started on his homeward way. When he had said good night and "God reward you" and was already at the door, he turned around and said—

"I'm coming again Sunday, a week from today. And you must come over to Grandmother's some time. She told me to say so."

That was quite a new thought for Heidi, that she should

go to somebody's house. But the idea became fixed in her mind, and on the very next day her first words were—

"Grandfather, now I must really go down to see Grandmother. She expects me."

"There is too much snow," Grandfather replied, shaking his head. But the idea was fast in Heidi's mind, for, you see, Grandmother had sent word to her, and that settled it. So not a day passed but that the child said five or six times—

"Grandfather, I've really got to go now. Grandmother is waiting for me."

On the fourth day it was so cold that out of doors every footstep crunched and creaked and the great crust of snow all round about was frozen stiff. But the bright sun was peeking in at the window right at the high chair in which Heidi was sitting at the dinner table, so she began again her little speech—

"Today I've just really got to go to Grandmother's, or I'll be putting it off too long."

Then Grandfather got up from the dinner table, climbed up to the hayloft, brought down the thick sack that was the coverlet of Heidi's bed, and said—

"Come on, then!"

The child skipped joyfully after him out into the shining world of snow. It was now very still in the old fir trees. The white snow lay on all the boughs, and the trees glistened and sparkled everywhere in the sunshine with such glory that Heidi jumped about for joy and called out one time after another—

"Come outside, Grandfather, come on! There is pure silver and gold in the fir trees."

Grandfather had gone into the workshop and now came out with a broad hand-sled. It had a rod fastened to the side, and from its flat seat you could thrust your feet out in front against the snowy ground and with one or the other of them steer in the direction you wanted to go.

First Grandfather had to examine the fir trees with Heidi, and then he sat down on the sled, took the child in his lap, bundled her up in the sack so that she would be warm as toast, and pressed her tightly to him with his left arm, as this was very necessary for the trip they were to take. Then with his right hand he seized the rod firmly and gave a push with both feet. At that the sled shot away down the mountain meadow with such speed that Heidi thought it was flying through the air like a bird, and she cried out aloud.

Before you knew it, the sled came to a stop right before the hut of Goat Peter. Grandfather set the child on the ground, unwrapped her coverings, and said—

"There you are! Now go in, and when it begins to grow dark, come away and start on your way home."

Then he turned his sled around and drew it after him up the mountain.

Heidi opened the door and came into a small room which looked quite black. There was an open hearth in it and some plates on a stand. This was the little kitchen. Then, right near, there was another door which Heidi opened, too, and which led into a tiny living room. For this was not an Alpine hut like Grandfather's, in which there was a single large room with a hayloft above. It was rather a very old cottage in which everything was small, poor, and shabby.

When Heidi entered the small living room, she stood right before a table at which a woman was sitting, mending Peter's jacket. Heidi recognized it at once. In the corner an old bent grandmother was sitting and spinning. Heidi had no trouble in telling who this was. She went straight to the spinning wheel and said—

"Good day, Grandmother. I've come to see you at last. Did you think I was never coming?"

The old lady raised her head and reached for the hand that was stretched out to her. When she had taken this, she first stroked it thoughtfully a little while with her own, and then she asked—

"Are you the child who lives with Meadow Nuncle? Is your name Heidi?"

"Yes, indeed," the child assured her. "I've just come down the mountain on a sled with my Grandfather."

"You don't say so! But how warm your hand is! Tell me, Brigitte, did the Meadow Nuncle himself come down with the girl?"

Peter's mother, Brigitte, who had been sewing at the table, rose and looked at the girl curiously from head to foot. Then she said—

"I don't know, Mother, whether the Nuncle came down with her or not. It isn't very probable; perhaps the child is mistaken."

But Heidi looked at the woman quite decidedly and not at all as if she did not know.

"I know well enough," she said, "who wrapped me up in the bed covering and slid down with me. It was my grandfather."

"Then there must be something in what Peter was telling us all last summer about Meadow Nuncle, even if we did not believe him," the grandmother said. "Who would have thought that such a thing was possible? I didn't imagine the child would live up there three weeks. How does she look, Brigitte?"

In the meantime Brigitte had been looking at her from every side, so she could tell pretty well what she looked like.

"She is daintily formed, as Adelheid was," she replied. "But she has black eyes and curly hair like Tobias and the old man up there. I think she resembles both of them."

Meanwhile Heidi had not been idle. She had peered about her and examined closely everything that was to be seen. Now she said—

"Look, Grandmother, there's a window blind that keeps swinging out and back. Grandfather ought to drive a nail in it right away to fasten it. If he doesn't, it will break the pane. Just see how it's acting!"

"You nice child, you!" the grandmother said. "I can't see the blind, but I can hear it fast enough, and many other things, too. It isn't only the shutter, but everything creaks and pounds when the wind blows, and it gets in every place. Nothing is tight any more. And often at night, when the other two are asleep, I get so terribly afraid that the whole house is coming down on our heads and will kill the three of us. Alas, there is no one who can mend things in the cottage, for Peter doesn't know how."

"But why can't you see what the blind is doing, Grandmother? Look, there it goes again, right over there!" Heidi pointed her finger straight at the spot.

"Ah, child, I can't see the least little thing, the blind or anything else," the Grandmother said sadly.

"But suppose I run out and open the blind wide, so that it is very light, then you can see, can't you?"

"No, no, not even then. No one can ever make it light for me again."

"But if you go out where the snow is all white, then it surely will be bright enough. You just come with me, Grandmother, and I'll prove it."

Heidi took the old lady's hand and tried to lead her away, for she was beginning to worry because it did not seem light anywhere to her friend.

"Just let me sit quietly, you dear child. Things are dark to me all the same, even in the snow and the light. They do not reach my eyes any more."

"But it's different in the summer time, Grandmother," said Heidi, still trying to find some way out of the trouble. "You know, when the sun shines down hot as anything and starts to say good night and the mountains glow as red as fire, and all the yellow flowers are gleaming, why, then it will be light again for you, won't it?"

"My child, I shall never see them again, the fiery mountains and the golden flowers up there. Never again will the earth be bright for me—never again."

At these words Heidi burst into tears. Full of sorrow, she kept sobbing aloud—

"Who can make things bright for you again, then? Can't somebody do it? Can't anyone?"

And then the old lady tried to comfort the child, but that was not so easy to do. Heidi almost never cried, but when she once started, then it was almost impossible to make her forget here trouble. The grandmother had soon tried every means of quieting the child because she could not bear to hear her sob so pitifully. She said—

"Come here, dear Heidi, come to me. I've got something to tell you. You know, when a person can't see things, it's such good fun to hear kind words. And I dearly love to hear you talk. Sit down close to me and tell me what you do up at your house, and what Grandfather does. I used to know him well long ago, but I've heard nothing about him for many years except what Peter tells me, and he doesn't say much."

That is when the new idea came to Heidi. She wiped her tears away and quickly said, comfortingly—

"You just wait, Grandmother. I'm going to tell Grandfather everything. He'll soon make it light for you again and he'll mend the cottage so it won't fall down. He can put things in fine shape."

The old lady said nothing. And then Heidi began to tell her excitedly of her life with Grandfather, of the days in the pasture, and all about her present winter life. She told her what Grandfather could make out of wood— benches and chairs, and fine mangers from which Schwänli and Bärli could eat their hay, and a big new water trough to bathe in summers, and a new milk bowl and spoon. Heidi grew more and more eager in describing the pretty things which could be made in a jiffy out of a piece of wood. She said she always stood right by Grandfather and watched him closely. For sometime she was going to do all those things herself. The Grandmother listened with great interest, and from time to time would interrupt to ask—

"Do you hear all this, Brigitte? Do you hear what she's saying about Nuncle?"

Suddenly the tale was broken off by a great clatter at the door, and Peter came stamping in. But he stopped at once and opened his round eyes wide in surprise when he saw Heidi. And he made the happiest face you can imagine as she cried out quickly, "Good afternoon, Peter!"

"My, is it possible he's out of school so soon!" the grandmother called in great astonishment. "No afternoon has gone so quickly for many a year. Good afternoon, dear Peter! How goes the reading?"

"Just like always," Peter answered.

"Oh, oh," said the grandmother, with a gentle sigh, "I had hoped there'd be a change by the time you were almost twelve years old. And your birthday's in February."

"Why must there be a change, Grandmother?" Heidi asked with sudden interest.

"I just hoped that he might be able to learn more in his reading," said Grandmother. "I have an old prayer book up there on the shelf, and there are such pretty hymns in it. I haven't heard them for such a long time and I cannot remember them any more. I had hoped Peter would learn so that he could read a hymn to me sometimes. But he can't learn. It is too hard for him."

"I believe I must make a light, it's already growing quite dark," now said Peter's mother, who all this time had been busily patching his jacket. "The afternoon has slipped away for me, too, before I noticed it."

Then Heidi sprang up from her little chair, put out her hand hastily, and said—

"Good night, Grandmother. I must go home right away, now that it's growing dark."

She offered her hand in turn to Peter and his mother and walked to the door.

"Wait, wait, Heidi! You can't go alone that way. Peter will have to go with you, do you hear? And be careful, Peter dear, that the child doesn't stumble. And don't stand still so she'll freeze, remember! And has she got a good thick muffler around her neck?"

"I haven't any old muffler," Heidi called back, "but I shan't freeze." Thereupon she flashed out of the door and scurried away so fast that Peter could scarcely catch up with her.

But the grandmother cried out urgently—

"Run right after her, Brigitte, run quickly! The child is sure to freeze out in the night that way—hurry, won't you?"

Brigitte did as she was told. But the children had gone only a few steps up the mountain when they saw Grandfather coming down to meet them. He reached them in a few long strides.

"That's nice, Heidi. You've kept your promise," he said. He bundled up the child again tightly in her covering, raised her in his arms, and set off up the mountain. Brigitte had been just in time to see the old man wrap the child up well, lift her into his arms, and set out on his homeward journey. She went back into the cottage with Peter and told the grandmother with amazement what she had seen. The old lady was also very much surprised and kept repeating—

"God be praised and thanked that he feels that way toward the child! Praise God, indeed! If he will only let her come to me again! The child did me so much good. What a kind heart she has!"

And until she went to bed that night she kept saying—

"If she will only come again! For now when I least expected it there is still something left in the world to give me joy."

And each time Brigitte would agree with her, while Peter would nod his head and grin widely with pleasure and say—

"I told you so."

In the meantime Heidi inside of her sack kept up a constant chatter. But as her voice could not be heard through the eight folds of her covering, and Grandfather therefore did not understand a word she said, he called to her—

"Wait a little while until we are home. Then you can tell me."

As soon, then, as he had reached the hut up on top and had peeled off Heidi's wraps, she began—

"Grandfather, tomorrow we'll have to take the hammer and some big nails along with us and fasten the shutter in Grandmother's house. We'll have to drive a lot more nails, too, for everything creaks and rattles at her place."

"Have to, eh? We must do that, must we? Who said so?" Grandfather asked.

"Nobody said so. I just know it, that's all," Heidi replied, "because everything is loose. And it makes Grandmother terribly anxious when things rattle so she can't sleep. And she thinks, 'Now everything is going to tumble down on our heads.' And you can't make things light for Grandmother any more. At least, she doesn't see how anyone can, but you can do it, Grandfather, I'm sure. Just think how sad it is for her to be always in the dark. And she gets so scared. And no one but you can help her. Tomorrow we'll go and help her, won't we, Grandfather?"

Heidi had clung fast to her grandfather and was looking up at him in perfect trust. The old man gazed down at the child awhile and then said—

"Yes, Heidi, we'll fix things so that nothing more rattles in Grandmother's house. And we'll do it tomorrow."

The child started to jump for joy all around the big room and to cry out one time after another—

"We're going to do it tomorrow, tomorrow!"

And her grandfather kept his promise. The next afternoon they took the same ride on the sled. Just as on the previous day, the old man set the child down before Goat Peter's door and said, "Now go in, and when it gets to be night, come back." Then he laid the sack on the sled and went around the house.

Heidi had scarcely opened the door and jumped into the room when from the corner Grandmother called out happily—

"There comes the child! There's the blessed child!"

In her great joy she dropped the thread and stopped the wheel and stretched out both hands to the girl. Heidi ran to her, dragged at once the low stool quite near to her, sat down on it, and again had a whole lot of things to tell Grandmother about and to ask of her.

But just then there started such an awful pounding on the house that Grandmother was terribly frightened. She almost knocked over the spinning wheel, she trembled so. She cried out—

"Oh, deary me! It's come at last. It's all falling to pieces."

But Heidi took her firmly by the arm and said comfortingly—

"No, no, Grandmother. Don't be afraid, it's only Grandfather with his hammer. He's mending things so you won't worry any longer."

"Oh, you don't mean it! Is it possible? Then the dear God has not quite forgotten us," Grandmother exclaimed. "Did you hear what that is, Brigitte, did you hear? It's a hammer, as sure as you live! Go and see, Brigitte, and if it's the Meadow Nuncle, tell him he must come in a minute and let me thank him."

Brigitte went out. Meadow Nuncle was that moment driving new logs into the wall with great force. Brigitte went up to him and said—

"A good afternoon to you, Nuncle, from Mother and me. We are grateful to you for your work. And Mother is eager to thank you for herself indoors. No one else would be so kind to us, and we want to thank you, for surely—"

"Cut it short," the old gentleman interrupted her. "I know exactly what you think of the Meadow Nuncle. You just go back again. I can find what needs doing without help."

Brigitte obeyed at once, for Nuncle had a way with him that was not easy to resist. He pounded and hammered all around the cottage. Then he mounted the narrow ladder that led to the roof and kept up his hammering until he had used up the last nail he had brought with him.

In the meantime it had begun to be dark again. But he had scarcely climbed down and drawn his sled out from behind the goat shed, when Heidi came out of the door. He wrapped her up, as he had done the day before, and took her in his arms, drawing the empty sled behind him. For if she had sat on it all alone, her coverings might have fallen off, and Heidi would have nearly frozen, perhaps quite so. Grandfather well knew that and kept the child warm in his arms.

Thus the winter passed away. Joy had come after the long years into the dreary life of the old blind lady. And her days were no more long and dark, each one like the day before it, for she had now always something to look forward to. The very first thing in the morning she was listening for the tripping footstep. And when the door finally did open and the child came really dancing in, then she never failed to cry out joyfully—

"Heaven be praised! There she comes again."

Then Heidi would sit down close to her and chatter away so happily about everything that she knew, that Grandmother was always pleased. The hours flew by so fast she did not notice them. And not one single time did she ask, as she used to—

"Brigitte, isn't the day over yet?"

But each time that Heidi had closed the door after her, Grandmother would say—

"Why, how short the afternoon has been, Brigitte!"

And the daughter would answer—

"It has, hasn't it? Seems as if we had hardly put away the dinner plates."

And then Grandmother would say after that—

"If the Lord God will only keep the child safe for me and will keep Meadow Nuncle in a good humor. Does she look healthy, Brigitte?"

Each time the daughter would answer—

"She looks like a strawberry apple."

And Heidi, for her part, had a great affection for the old grandmother. Whenever she remembered that no one, not even her grandfather, could make things bright for her again, a great sadness always swept over her. But Grandmother would always tell Heidi that she suffered least when the child was with her, and so Heidi went down on her sled to see her every fine winter day.

Grandfather continued to take her without saying a word against it. Each time he took his hammer and all sorts of other things along. And many a long afternoon he pounded away at the cottage of Goat Peter. This work had one good effect, too—there was no more creaking and rattling through the night. Grandmother said that she had not been able to sleep for many a long winter, and she would never forget to be grateful to Nuncle for his help.

CHAPTER V

ONE VISIT, AND THEN ANOTHER

The winter had passed quickly, and even more rapidly the happy summer that followed it. And now another winter was already drawing to its close.

Heidi was as happy and cheerful as the birds of the air, and each day she was looking forward more eagerly to the coming days of spring, when the warm south wind would rustle in the fir trees and sweep away the snow. Then the bright sun would call forth the blue and yellow flowers, and the days of the pasture would return. These were the days that brought Heidi the best gift the earth could give.

Heidi was now in her eighth year. She had learned from her grandfather how to do all sorts of useful things. She knew how to get along with the goats as no one else could. And Little Swan and Little Bear followed her around like faithful dogs, bleating aloud their joy whenever they heard her voice.

It was in this winter that Peter had twice brought word from the village school teacher of The Hamlet that Meadow Nuncle should send the child who lived with him to school. For Heidi was already more than old enough and by rights ought to have been in school the previous winter. Both times Nuncle had sent back the message that if the school teacher wanted anything of him he knew where he lived; meanwhile he certainly would not send the child. This message Peter had duly delivered.

When the March sun had melted the snow on the slopes, and the white snowdrops were peeking forth everywhere in the valley, when on the mountain meadow the fir trees had shaken off their burden of snow and the boughs were again waving merrily, then Heidi in her delight kept running back and forth from the house to the goat shed. And then she would run from the shed to the fir trees, and later to her grandfather inside the cottage to tell him how much larger the piece of green ground under the trees had grown. Afterward she would fly right back to look again, for she could not wait until everything should become green and the fair summer with all its flowers again come to the mountain meadow.

While Heidi on one sunny March morning was running to and fro in this way and was jumping across the threshold for perhaps the tenth time, she was so frightened that she almost fell backward into the hut. For suddenly she was standing before an old gentleman in black, who blinked at her very solemnly. But when he saw her fright, he said in a kindly voice—

"You must not be afraid of me. I am fond of children. Give me your hand. You are Heidi, I suppose. Where is your grandfather?"

"He is sitting at the table carving round spoons out of wood," Heidi replied as she again opened the door.

It was the old pastor from The Hamlet, who had known Nuncle well years before when he lived down below and was his neighbor. He stepped into the hut, walked up to the old man, who was bent over his wood carving, and said—

"Good morning, neighbor!"

Nuncle looked up in astonishment. And then he got to his feet and replied—

"Good morning to the pastor!" Thereupon he set his chair before the old gentleman and continued, "If the pastor is not afraid of a wooden seat, here is one."

The pastor sat down. "I have not seen you for a long time, neighbor," he went on to say.

"Nor have I seen you, Pastor," was the answer.

"I have come today to talk with you about something," the pastor began again. "I suppose you know what the business is which I want to discuss with you. And I'd like to hear what you have in mind."

The pastor was silent and looked at the child, who was standing in the doorway closely watching this strange new figure.

"Go to the goats, Heidi," Grandfather said. "You can take a little salt with you and wait until I come."

Heidi vanished at once.

"That child should have attended school a year ago, and she most certainly should have gone this winter," the pastor said after a moment. "The teacher sent you a warning about it, but you made no reply. What do you intend to do with the child, neighbor?"

"I intend not to send her to school," was the answer.

The pastor gazed in astonishment at the old man, who was sitting with folded arms on the bench and did not look as if he were going to yield.

"What are you going to make out of the child?" the pastor then asked.

"Not a thing. She grows and thrives as the goats and

the birds do. She is safe with them and learns not a bit of harm."

"But the child is not a goat and not a bird, she is a human being. If she learns nothing bad from these playmates of hers, neither does she learn anything else. But she ought to be learning something, and the time for that is here. I have come to tell you in good season, neighbor, so that you can think it over and make your plans during the summer. This is to be the last winter that the child spends without teaching of any sort. Next winter she's going to school every single day."

"I won't do it, Pastor," said the old man, stubbornly.

"Do you actually think, then, that there is no way of bringing you to reason, if you stubbornly stick to your silly actions?" the pastor asked with some heat. "You have traveled around in the world a good deal and had your chance to see and learn much. I should have thought you had better sense, neighbor."

"Oh, indeed!" the old gentleman said. His voice showed that he was no longer quite so calm in his mind. "And so the pastor believes that next winter I am really going to send a tender child on freezing mornings down the mountain, six miles' journey through storm and snow. That I'm going to have her come back again at night, when it is often blowing and raging so that we ourselves would lose our lives in the wind and snow. And, above all, a child like her! Perhaps the pastor can still remember her mother Adelheid, who walked in her sleep and was subject to fits. Is this child to be made to suffer such things because of overwork? Just let somebody come and try to drive me to it! I'll take her into any court of law there is, and then we'll see who is going to make me!"

"And you would be quite right, neighbor," said the pastor in a kindly voice. "It would not be possible to send the child to school from here. But I can see the child is dear to you. Do for her sake what you should have done long ago—come down again to The Hamlet and once more live among men. What sort of life is this you lead up here, lonely and bitter against God and your kind? Who would help you if anything should happen to you off up here? Nor can I understand why you're not half frozen in your hut all through the winter, and how the tender child can stand it."

"The child has young blood and a good roof above her, I can promise you that, Pastor. And one thing more, I know where there is wood and when is a good time to fetch it, too. The pastor can take a look in my shed. He will see there is enough so that the fire in my hut never goes out all winter long. What the pastor says about going down to The Hamlet is not for me. The people down there despise me and I despise them, so it suits both sides to stay apart."

"No, no, it is not good for you to do that. I know what's the trouble with you," the pastor said in a hearty voice. "The people down below don't despise you half so much as you think. Believe me, neighbor. Seek to make your peace with God. Pray for his forgiveness if you feel you need it. Then come and see how differently the people look at you, and how happy you can still be with them."

The pastor had stood up. He held his hand out to the old gentleman and said again with much heartiness—

"I count upon having you with us again next winter, neighbor. We are old and tried friends. It would make me very sorry to have to use force with you. Shake hands on it! Come down and live among us again, at peace with God and men."

Meadow Nuncle offered his hand to the pastor, but he said firmly and clearly—

"The pastor means well with me, but I shall not do as he wishes. I can tell him that once and for all. I shall not send the child, and I can't come down myself."

"Then God help you!" said the pastor, and went sadly out of the door and down the mountain.

Meadow Nuncle had the blues. When Heidi said, that afternoon, "Let's go to Grandmother's now," he answered shortly, "Not today."

He said nothing more the whole day, and next morning, as Heidi asked, "Are we going to Grandmother's today?" his words were as sharp as his tone of voice when he said, "We'll see."

But long before the dishes had been put away after dinner, another caller appeared in the doorway. It was Aunt Dete. She was wearing a pretty hat with a feather on it, and a dress that swept up everything on the floor, and in the Alpine hut all sorts of things lay around which would not help the looks of a dress.

Nuncle looked at her from top to toe, but said nothing. And yet Aunt Dete was intending to have a very friendly talk, for she began at once to say nice things. She said

Heidi was looking so well that she scarcely knew her any longer, and anyone could see that she had been treated finely at Grandfather's.

She said she had always intended to take the child off his hands again, for she knew very well that the little one must be in his way. But at the moment she could find no place to put her. Since that time, however, she had been figuring night and day where she could find a lodging for the child. And she had come just today because she had heard of a piece of luck for Heidi so good that she could hardly believe it. She had gone without delay to arrange the matter. It was all as good as settled now that Heidi was to be as fortunate as only one in a hundred thousand could be.

Some very rich relatives of her employers, who live in almost the finest house in all Frankfort, have an only daughter. The poor child has to sit always in a wheel chair, for she is lame on one side and otherwise not healthy. So she is almost always alone and has to study by herself with a teacher. That is quite dreary for her, and, besides, she would like to have a playmate in the house.

There had been a lot of talk about this at the house of Dete's employers, and it would be fine if they could only find such a child as the lady who kept house for the relatives described. For Dete's mistress was very sympathetic and wanted to find a good playmate for the sick daughter.

Now the housekeeper had said they wanted a really unspoiled child, an unusual child who wasn't like every one you saw on a day's march. Right then Dete had thought of Heidi, and she had run straight to the lady and

told her all about Heidi and her character, and like a flash
the lady had agreed. Now nobody could tell just what
luck and happiness might be preparing for Heidi, because
after she was once there and the people liked her, and
something might possibly happen to their own daughter—
you just couldn't tell, she was so weakly—and if the
people did not want to remain without a child, then perhaps the most unheard-of luck might—

"Are you almost through?" Nuncle interrupted her.
He had not got a single word in edgewise.

"Bah!" Dete threw back at him, tossing her head.
"You act just as if I'd been telling you the most ordinary
news. Why, there isn't high and low in all Prättigau a
single person who would not thank his lucky stars if I'd
brought him such news as I have you."

"Tell it wherever you want to, I don't care to hear it,"
Nuncle said dryly.

Then Dete flew into a rage and said—

"All right, if that's what you think, Nuncle, then I'll
just tell you how I think about things. The child is now
eight years old, and she can't do a thing, and she knows
nothing, and you won't let her learn anything. They tell
me down in The Hamlet that you won't send her to school
or to church, and yet she is my only sister's child.

"I have to see that she is well brought up. And when a
child can have the good luck that Heidi can, then there's
only one person to stand in the way, and that's a man who
likes nobody and wishes nobody well.

"But I tell you I won't give in. The people are all on
my side. There isn't a single one down in The Hamlet

who won't help me and who isn't against you. And if you want the thing to come before the court, perhaps, then you just look out, Nuncle! There are some matters which could be warmed up there that you wouldn't like to hear. For when you once have to do with the law, then lots of things come out that everybody has forgotten."

"Silence!" thundered Nuncle, and his eyes flashed like fire. "Take her and spoil her. Never come with her into my sight again. I never want to see her with such feathers on her head and such words in her mouth as you have today."

Nuncle left the house with great strides.

"You've made Grandfather angry," Heidi said. Her black eyes gleamed at her aunt in no friendly way.

"He'll be all right again soon. Come on now," the aunt said, urgently, "where are your clothes?"

"I'm not coming," said Heidi.

"What's that you say?" the aunt said angrily. But then she changed her tone a little and went on half kindly, half vexedly—

"Hurry and come, you just don't know any better. You can't think what a fine time you're going to have."

Then she went to the cupboard, took out Heidi's things, and wrapped them together.

"Come on now, pick up your little hat there. It doesn't look pretty, but it's got to do this time. Put it on and hurry along."

"I'm not coming," Heidi repeated.

"Don't be stupid and silly like a goat. You must have caught it from them. Just get things straight, can't you?

Grandfather is angry now. Didn't you hear him say we should never cross his sight again? Now he wants you to go with me and you musn't make him even angrier. You can't guess how fine it is in Frankfort and all the things you'll see there. And if you don't like it you can come back home again. By that time Grandfather won't be cross any longer."

"Can I turn straight back and come home tonight?" Heidi asked.

"Oh, pshaw, come on! Haven't I said you can go home whenever you want to? Today we'll go down as far as Mayenfeld, and early tomorrow we'll be on the train. In that you can be home again afterward in a hurry. The train just flies along."

Aunt Dete had put the bundle of clothes under her arm. She took Heidi by the hand. And so they went down the mountain.

It was not time for pasturing yet, and so Peter went down to school in The Hamlet, or at least he was supposed to go. But he took a day off now and then, because he thought there was no use in going to school. You didn't need to read things, but you did need to go around hunting for big rods, since you could make use of them. Thus he was just coming up near his hut from off one side, bearing with him the result of his day's work in the immense bundle of long, thick hazel-rods that he carried on his shoulder. He stood still and stared at the two who were coming to meet him until they overtook him.

"Where are you going?" he said.

"I have to go in a great hurry to Frankfort with my

aunt," Heidi answered. "But first I'll go to see Grandmother. She is waiting for me."

"No, no, by no means, it is too late this minute," the aunt said hastily, as she held the struggling Heidi fast by the hand. "You can go to see her when you come home again. Hurry up now!"

Thereupon the aunt dragged Heidi firmly along with her and did not lose hold of her for a moment, because she feared that if the child went into the house she might again decide not to go away, and the old lady might stand by her. Peter ran into the cottage and pounded with his whole bundle of rods on the table so terribly that everything started to shake. The grandmother jumped up frightened from her spinning wheel and wailed out loud. Peter had to find some expression for his feelings.

"Why, what's the matter! What's the matter?" the old lady cried excitedly.

The mother, who had been sitting at the table and had almost jumped out of her chair at the awful noise, said with her customary patience—

"What ails you, Peter dear? Why do you act so wildly?"

"Because she has taken Heidi away," Peter declared.

"Who has, Peterli? And where has she gone?" asked the grandmother, again all a-tremble. But she seemed to guess quickly what was going on. Her daughter had told her not long before that she had seen Dete on her way up to Meadow Nuncle's. Trembling in her haste, the old lady opened the window and cried out pitifully—

"Dete, Dete, don't take the child away from us! Don't take Heidi away!"

The two travelers heard her voice. Dete doubtless suspected what she was calling, for she seized the child more firmly than ever and walked as fast as she could. Heidi struggled and said—

"Grandmother called me. I want to go to her."

But that was exactly what the aunt did not want. She calmed the child and said they must hurry right along now or they would be too late, but that the next morning they would go on traveling and Heidi could then see if she did not like it so well in Frankfort that she never wished to leave it again. And if it turned out that she was homesick in spite of everything, then she could come back at once and find something to bring Grandmother that would make her happy. This last thought pleased Heidi. She began to go on without a struggle.

"What can I bring back to Grandmother?" she asked after a while.

"Something nice," the aunt said. "She would like some lovely, soft white rolls. You see, she can hardly eat hard black bread any longer."

"Oh, yes," Heidi agreed. "She always hands it back to Peter and says, 'It's too hard for me.' I've seen her do it. We'll have to hurry, won't we, Aunt Dete? And then perhaps we'll get to Frankfort today and I'll be home with the rolls all the sooner."

Heidi now began to run along so fast that her aunt, with the bundle under her arm, could scarcely keep up with her. But Dete was very glad they walked so fast, for they were now approaching the first house of Dörfli. And there would again probably be all sorts of questions and talk which would set Heidi to thinking. Therefore she hastened straight through The Hamlet, with the child tugging so hard at her hand that everyone could see Dete was hurrying because the child wanted her to. So she only had to answer all the questions called out to her from window and doorway—

"Don't you see, I can't stop a minute? The child's in such a hurry and we have a long way to go."

"Are you taking her back with you? Is she running away from Meadow Nuncle? It's a wonder he didn't kill her. And yet, what red cheeks she has!"

That is what they heard from every side. Ah, Dete was glad to get through The Hamlet without stopping and having to explain things—glad, too, that Heidi said not a word but kept pushing straight on with all her might.—

From that day on whenever he came down and passed through the village, Meadow Nuncle's face was darker than ever before. He spoke to nobody. With his cheese basket on his back, his mighty staff in his hand, and his thick eyebrows drawn close together, he looked so forbidding that mothers would call to their little children—

"Look out! Get out of Meadow Nuncle's way or he may harm you."

The old man had no business with anyone in The Hamlet. He only passed through it on his way far down into the valley, where he got rid of his cheeses and bought his stock of bread and meat. Whenever he had in such fashion passed through The Hamlet, people would gather in groups and stare after him. And you may be sure that each one had seen something strange in Meadow Nuncle.

They all agreed that he looked more savage, that he took no notice of anyone, that Heidi had been very lucky to escape from him, and that it was no wonder she had fled away from him as if she were afraid the old man was pursuing her to bring her back.

Only the blind grandmother still kept her belief in Meadow Nuncle. She never failed to tell each person who came up to her house to bring spinning, or to take away what she had spun, how good he had been to the child and how careful of her. She would tell what he had done for herself and her daughter, how many afternoons he had patched at their cottage, which without his help would surely have fallen down by now. In this way the news came down to the village. But most of those who heard it said that the old lady was probably too old to know what she was talking about. Perhaps she couldn't hear well any more, just as she couldn't see.

The Meadow Nuncle no longer appeared at the house of Goat Peter. It was a good thing he had mended the hut so well, because it was not touched again for a long time.

Nowadays the blind grandmother began each new day with sighs, and not one went by that she did not complain—

"Oh, when the child went, everything happy and good was taken away from us, and these days are so empty! I wish I might hear Heidi's voice once again before I die."

CHAPTER VI

BRAND NEW EXPERIENCES

In the house of Mr. Sesemann in Frankfort, Clara, the little invalid, was lying in her comfortable wheel chair. In this she spent the whole day and was pushed from one room to another.

At this moment she was in the library, as they called it, which was next to the big dining room. All the articles that furnished the room were made for comfort rather than for show, which proved that it was used as a living room. You could see how it had been named from the great beautiful bookcase with glass doors, and knew this must be the spot where the little lame girl had her lessons every day.

Clara had a pale, narrow face from which two mild blue eyes looked out. At this moment they were turned toward the large wall clock, which seemed to be going very slowly today. That is why Clara, who was almost never impatient, was saying with some uneasiness in her voice—

"Isn't it time even yet, Miss Rottenmeier?"

Miss Rottenmeier was sitting very straight beside a small sewing table and doing embroidery. She had around her a queer sort of wrap, a kind of large cape or half cloak which gave her a solemn look, and this effect was increased by something like a high cupola that she wore on her head. Since the death of Clara's mother several years before this, Miss Rottenmeier had been housekeeper

in the Sesemann home and had had entire charge of the
servants. Mr. Sesemann was traveling most of the time
and therefore left the whole house in Miss Rottenmeier's
care. But he had made one condition, and this was that
his young daughter should have a say in all things, and
that nothing should be done against her wishes.

Clara had just asked Miss Rottenmeier a second time if
it was not high time for their guests to arrive. At that
very moment Dete, with Heidi's hand in hers, was standing downstairs at the front door and asking John, the
coachman, who had got down from his seat, if he thought
she might disturb Miss Rottenmeier at so late an hour.

"That is not my affair," growled the coachman. "Ring
for Sebastian to come down, inside in the hall."

Dete did as she was told. And the butler came down
the stairs. He had big round buttons on his livery coat
and big round eyes almost as large in his head.

"I wanted to ask if I might disturb Miss Rottenmeier
at this late hour," Dete inquired again.

"That is no affair of mine," the butler replied. "Ring
for Tinette, the maid, at the other bell." And without
another word Sebastian disappeared.

Dete rang a second time. And then there appeared
at the head of the stairs Mamsell Tinette, with a dazzling
white linen cap perched on top of her head, and with a
proud look on her face.

"What do you want?" she called, without coming down.
Dete repeated her question. Mamsell Tinette went away,
but soon came back and called down the stairs—

"You are expected."

Dete and Heidi then climbed the steps and followed Tinette into the library. Here Dete remained politely standing in the doorway, holding Heidi tightly by the hand, for she was not at all sure what the child might decide to do in this place that was so strange to her.

Miss Rottenmeier rose slowly from her chair and went over to study the newly arrived playmate of the daughter of the house. The result of her stares did not seem to please her. Heidi was wearing her simple cotton dress and her old crushed straw hat. The child peered at her innocently from under the hat and looked with open amazement at the high tower of hair on the lady's head.

"What's your name?" Miss Rottenmeier asked after she had examined for several minutes the child, who never turned her eyes away from her.

"Heidi," came the clear answer in a ringing voice.

"What? What? Why, that's not a Christian name at all. Then you can't have been baptized. What name did they give you when you were baptized?" Miss Rottenmeier asked again.

"I can't remember any longer," Heidi replied.

"What sort of answer is that?" remarked the lady, shaking her head. "Mamsell Dete, is the child silly or pert?"

"Begging your pardon, and if the lady will permit me, I will do the talking for the child, for she is very shy," said Dete, but not until she had secretly poked Heidi for her foolish answer. "But you must not think her silly or pert either, for she doesn't know how to be. She means exactly what she says. Only, today's the first time she's been in a great house and she doesn't know good manners. She is willing and not stupid, if the lady will be kind and patient with her. She was baptized Adelheid, like her mother before her, my dead sister."

"Oh, very well! There's a name at last that can be pronounced," said Miss Rottenmeier. "But, Mamsell Dete, I must really tell you the child looks odd to me for her age. I informed you, you know, that Miss Clara's companion should be of her own age, so she could follow the same studies and share all her occupations. Miss Clara is already past twelve. How old is your child?"

"Begging the lady's pardon," Dete began again glibly, "I just couldn't quite figure out how old she was. She is really a little younger, but not enough to count. I can't say exactly, but she is about ten, or perhaps a little more."

"I am eight years old now. Grandfather said so," Heidi declared. Her aunt nudged her again, but Heidi had no idea why she did so, and was not in the least embarrassed.

"What is that? Only eight years old!" cried Miss Rottenmeier quite indignantly. "Four years too few, why, what can that mean! And what have you learned, pray? What books did you use in your classes?"

"No books," said Heidi.

"Eh, what?" asked the lady again. "Then how did you learn to read?"

"I didn't learn to, and Peter didn't, either," Heidi stated.

"Heavenly powers! You can't read, you really can't?" cried Miss Rottenmeier in the greatest horror. "You don't mean to say you don't read! What did you learn, then?"

"Nothing," said Heidi, which was the truth.

"Mamsell Dete," said Miss Rottenmeier after a few minutes spent in trying to calm herself, "this is not at all as agreed upon. How could you bring this creature to me?"

But Dete was not so easily frightened. She answered eagerly—

"Begging the lady's pardon, this child is just what I thought she wanted. The lady told me just what she must be, quite out of the usual run and not like other children. That's why I had to take this little one. For, you see, the bigger ones at home are nothing uncommon, and I thought this child fitted your needs perfectly. But I must be going now, for my mistress is expecting me. If she permits me to, I'll come again soon and see how the child turns out."

With a curtsy Dete was out of the door and down the stairs as fast as she could go. Miss Rottenmeier hesitated a moment and then ran after Dete. For she remembered there was a lot of things she wanted to talk over with the aunt, if the child was really going to stay there. And there the child was at any rate. And it was plain the aunt had determined to leave her.

Heidi had not moved from the place by the door where she had been standing from the beginning. Up to now Clara had been watching everything silently from her chair. She waived to Heidi and said—

"Come here."

Heidi walked over to the wheel chair.

"Would you rather be called Heidi or Adelheid?" Clara asked.

"My name's Heidi and nothing more," was the child's answer.

"Then I'll always call you that," said Clara. "It's a nice name for you, but I never heard it before. And I never saw a child that looks like you, either. Have you always had such short curly hair?"

"Yes, I think so," Heidi answered.

"Did you like to come to Frankfort?" Clara went on to ask.

"No. But tomorrow I'm going back home again to carry Grandmother some white rolls," Heidi explained.

"You're a funny child," Clara burst out. "They brought you to Frankfort on purpose to be with me and study with me. And, don't you see? it's going to be lots of fun, because you can't read at all and our study hours will be quite different. They have often been so terribly tiresome, and the morning just never would end.

"For, you see, at ten o'clock every morning the Herr Kandidat comes. And then the lessons begin and last until two o'clock, and that is so long. Even Mr. Candidate often raises the book up to his face, just as if he had suddenly become shortsighted, but he is only yawning terribly behind it. And Miss Rottenmeier, too, takes out her big handkerchief from time to time and covers her whole face with it, as if she were much affected by something we were reading. But I know well enough that she is only yawning terribly behind it. And then I have to yawn also, awfully, but have to keep swallowing it, for if I come out with only one single yawn Miss Rottenmeier runs at once and gets the cod-liver oil, pretending that I am growing faint. Taking cod-liver oil is the most horrible thing in the world, so of course I prefer to swallow my yawns. But now it will be lots more fun, since I can listen while you are learning to read."

Heidi shook her head very doubtfully at this talk of her learning to read.

"But, look here, Heidi, of course you have to learn to read. Everybody does. And the Herr Kandidat is very kind, he's never cross, and, besides, he explains everything to you. Only, remember that when you don't understand what he's explaining, you must wait and say nothing. If you don't, he'll explain a lot more, and then you understand less than ever. But afterward, when you've learned something and know it, then you'll understand all right what he has been meaning."

Just at this point Miss Rottenmeier returned to the room. She had not been able to call Dete back and was very much excited by this fact. For she had had no chance to go into details as to what the child was lacking. And as she did not know how to undo what she had done, she was all the more excited, as she had proposed the entire affair of securing the companion.

So now she trotted from the library to the dining room, and then right back again, and here she met Sebastian, whose round eyes at this moment were glancing around the table which he had set to see if there was anything wrong with his work.

"Save your deep thoughts up for tomorrow. Just see that we get to dinner some time today."

With these words Miss Rottenmeier passed by Sebastian and called to Tinette in so unpleasant a voice that the maid came mincing in with even shorter steps than usual. She planted herself before the housekeeper with so mocking a look on her face that even Miss Rottenmeier did not dare to chide her. But she grew all the angrier inside.

"The guest room must be put in order, Tinette," the lady said, struggling hard to appear calm. "Everything is ready. Just dust the furniture off."

"That is worth doing," Tinette mocked, and departed.

Meanwhile Sebastian had opened the double doors of the library with quite a crash. He was very angry, but he did not dare express his feelings by answering back to Miss Rottenmeier. Then he walked quietly into the library to push out the wheel chair. While he was straightening the handle behind the chair, which had got displaced, he noticed that Heidi had placed herself in front of him and was staring at him without blinking. Suddenly he burst out—

"Well, what is there so strange about that?"

He growled at Heidi in a way that he would not have done if he had seen Miss Rottenmeier. She was standing on the threshold and just about to enter the room, when Heidi replied—

"Thou lookest like Goat Peter."

Horrified, the lady clasped her hands. "Well, I never!" she groaned half aloud. "Actually, she is saying *thou* to the servants! The creature lacks the least idea of good manners."

The chair came rolling along. Clara was lifted out and set on her chair by the table.

Miss Rottenmeier took her place next to Clara and motioned to Heidi to take the place opposite. No one else came to dinner, and there was enough room for the three to sit far apart and for Sebastian to offer his service tray. A fine white roll lay beside Heidi's plate and the child cast a happy glance at it. Sebastian looked so much like Goat Peter that he seemed to have won her entire confidence in him, for she sat as still as a mouse and did not move a muscle until he had come to her with his large tray and offered her the baked fish. Then she pointed to the roll and said—

"Can I have that?"

Sebastian nodded and looked sidewise at Miss Rottenmeier, for he was wondering what sort of effect the question would make upon her. Without delay Heidi seized her roll and put it in her pocket. Sebastian made an awful face in order to keep from laughing, but he knew well enough that that was not allowed. Mute and without moving, he kept his position by Heidi, for he could not speak. On the other hand, he could not go away until she had served herself some of the fish. Heidi looked at him awhile in surprise, and then she asked—

"Am I to eat some of that, too?"

Sebastian nodded a second time.

"Then give it to me," she said, and gazed calmly at her plate.

The strange look on Sebastian's face was becoming very serious. The tray that he had in his hands began to shake.

"You may set your tray on the table and come back again afterward," Miss Rottenmeier said in a severe manner.

Sebastian vanished at once.

"I see, Adelheid, that I must teach you a few things about behavior," Miss Rottenmeier continued, with a sigh. "First of all I shall show you how to serve yourself at dinner."

Thereupon the lady showed Heidi plainly and in detail everything that she had to do.

"And then," she went on, "I must say that you are not to talk to Sebastian at the table unless you wish to give him an order or have some question that you must ask him. In that case, address him with 'you' or 'he' and never with the hateful 'thou.' Let me never again hear you call him that! Tinette you will also call 'you' or Mamsell Tinette. Clara herself will decide how she wishes to have you address her."

"Why, Clara, of course," said the daughter of the house.

And then there followed a number of teachings as to how Heidi should get up in the morning and go to bed at night, how she should go out and come in, should keep things in order, should close doors behind her. And during all this talk Heidi's eyes were closing, for she had risen at five that morning and had made a long journey. She leaned against the back of her chair and fell asleep. When,

after a long time, Miss Rottenmeier had finally reached
the end of her teachings, she said —

"Now think about what I have told you, Adelheid.
Have you got the straight of everything?"

"Heidi's been asleep ever so long," said Clara in high
glee. The supper time had not passed away so happily
since she could remember.

"Well, I never heard of anything like this child!"
Miss Rottenmeier cried in great excitement. And then
she rang the bell so violently that Tinette and Sebastian
came running in together. But in spite of all this noise
Heidi did not wake up. And they had the greatest trouble
to arouse her enough so she could be got to her bedroom,
first through the library, then through Clara's bedroom,
then through Miss Rottenmeier's apartment to the corner
room which had been made ready for Heidi.

CHAPTER VII

MISS ROTTENMEIER HAS A TIRING DAY

When Heidi opened her eyes on that first morning in Frankfort, she could not make up her mind at all what she was looking at. She rubbed her eyes as hard as she could, then peered out again and saw the same things as before.

She found that she was sitting up in a high white bed. And before her was a big wide room, and where the light came in there hung very long white curtains. Near by stood two chairs with large flowers on them, then came a sofa with the same flowers by the wall and a round table before it, and in the corner stood a wash table with things on it the like of which Heidi had never seen in her life.

But then, all at once, she remembered she was in Frankfort. The previous day came back to her mind, and finally even the clear teachings the lady had given her, at least so far as she had heard them.

Heidi sprang from her bed and dressed herself. First she went to one window and then to the other, for she had to look at the sky and the earth outside—the great curtains made her feel as if she were shut up in a cage. She could not push these to one side, so she crept in behind them to reach a window. But this was so high that Heidi was just able to reach up far enough to see through, and she did not find what she was looking for. She ran from one window to the other and then back to the first again.

but always the same view was before her eyes—walls and windows, and still other walls and windows.

Heidi became quite afraid. It was still early in the morning, for she was used to rising early up on the mountain meadow and going at once out of doors to see what the weather was, whether the sky was blue and the sun already shining, whether the fir trees were rustling and the eyes of the little flowers open. Heidi kept running from one window to the other, as a small bird which is put for the first time in a beautiful shining cage darts hither and thither, and tests all the bars, to see if it cannot somehow slip between them and regain its freedom. She tried to open a window, for it must be that one could then see something else than walls and windows. Down below there must surely be the ground, with green grass and the last melting snow appearing on the slopes, and Heidi fairly ached to see those things.

But the windows remained firmly closed, no matter how much the child lifted and pulled, try as she would to get her small fingers under the sash in order to gain strength to raise them. Everything stuck together as hard as iron. After a long while, when Heidi saw that all her efforts were in vain, she gave up her plan and began to think how nice it would be to go outside and around the house to where the lawn was. For she remembered that last evening in front of the house they had walked on nothing but stones. At that moment there was a knock on her door, and right after it Tinette thrust her head in and said shortly—

"Breakfast is ready."

Heidi did not know that these words were really an invitation. The scornful look on Tinette's face seemed to warn her to keep away, rather than to invite her to do anything. Heidi read the maid's look and acted as it seemed to wish her to. She drew the small footstool out from under the table, put it in a corner, sat down upon it, and then waited still as a mouse to see what would happen next. After a little while something came bustling along; it was Miss Rottenmeier. And again she seemed very excited and called out to Heidi from the doorway—

"What's the matter with you, Adelheid? Can't you get it into your head what breakfast is? Come along!"

Heidi could understand such talk as that. She followed right after the housekeeper.

Clara had been sitting at her place in the dining room for some time, and she looked up at Heidi with a pleasant greeting. She seemed to be happier than usual today, for she was expecting all sorts of strange things to happen that morning. The breakfast passed without any trouble, for Heidi ate her bread and butter just as she should, and when the meal was ended Clara was wheeled back into the library. Heidi was told by Miss Rottenmeier to follow Clara and stay with her until the Herr Kandidat arrived to begin the lessons. When the two children were alone, Heidi said at once—

"How do you see out here and away down to the ground?"

"You open a window and put your head out," Clara said, amused.

"You can't open the windows," Heidi answered, sadly.

"Silly, of course they open. You can't do it, I suppose, and I can't help you, either. But when you see Sebastian, he'll open one for you fast enough."

Heidi felt much better to know that the windows would open and let her peer out, for the room still seemed to her like a prison. And now Clara began to ask Heidi questions about her home. And Heidi, of course, was glad to tell of the mountain meadow and the goats, of the hut in the pasture, and of everything she was so fond of.

In the meantime the university student arrived. Only, Miss Rottenmeier did not lead him into the library as she usually did, because she wanted to talk with him first. So she asked him into the dining room, where she sat down before him and told him in great excitement of the awful situation she was in and how it had all come about.

She said she had written some time before this to Mr. Sesemann, who was making quite a stay in Paris, telling him how for a long while his daughter had wanted to have a playmate in the house with her—how she herself had felt such a companion would be a spur to Clara in her studies and keep her from being lonely the rest of the time. To tell the truth, the scheme was a very good one for Miss Rottenmeier, since she was very glad to have someone there to help her take care of the sick Clara, a task that was often too much for her alone.

Mr. Sesemann had answered her letter, saying that he would be glad to do as his daughter wished if the playmate was treated in every way as well as Clara herself. He wrote that he did not wish any drudgery put upon a child in the house. "And I think that was a most

unnecessary thing for Mr. Sesemann to say," Miss Rottenmeier added, "for who wants to make a drudge of a child?"

With that, the lady went on to say how terribly she
had been disappointed in the child. She told all the foolish
things Heidi had done so far, to prove not only that the
Herr Kandidat would have to begin his lessons by teaching her the ABC's, but that from every possible point her
training must start at the very beginning.

Miss Rottenmeier said that she saw only one way out
of this difficulty, and that was for the university student
to explain it was impossible to teach two such different
children together without doing real harm to the more
advanced pupil. This, she thought, might be reason
enough for Mr. Sesemann to put an end to the business.
And he would then agree to have the child sent back to
where she had come from. But Miss Rottenmeier of
course did not feel she could do this without the consent
of her employer, since he knew of the child's arrival.

Now the university student was a timid person and
not quick to decide any matter.

So he said comforting things to the housekeeper and
thought perhaps they would find that if the young child
was not so well advanced in some ways she might still
know more in others. He felt they might even things up
by being very careful about her teaching. Now, when
Miss Rottenmeier saw that the Herr Kandidat was not
going to stand by her, but was going to try to teach the
ABC's, she opened the library door for him, closed it
quickly behind him, and remained on the other side. For
she disliked the ABC's very much.

Then she walked with great strides up and down the room, for she had to decide how the servants were to address Adelheid. Mr. Sesemann had certainly written that Heidi was to be treated as his own daughter, and this command of his had especial reference to the servants, the housekeeper thought. But she did not have long to think things over in peace because all at once there came from the library a terrible crash of falling objects, and then a cry to Sebastian for help.

She rushed into the other room.

There on the floor everything lay in a heap, all the things they studied with—books, copy books, the inkwell—and on top of them the table cover, from under whose edge a small stream of ink was flowing the whole length of the room. Heidi had disappeared.

"Now she's done it!" cried Miss Rottenmeier, wringing her hands. "Carpet, books, waste basket swimming in ink! Such a thing never happened before. She's the child of misfortune, that's all there is about it!"

The scared university student stood and stared at the work of ruin. Although he was not at all quick in deciding things, this was certainly very shocking. But the delighted Clara was looking at these strange events and their results with high glee. She explained how it had all happened.

"Oh, Heidi did it, fast enough. But she didn't mean to. She just was in an awful hurry to get away and she pulled the table cover off, so everything fell on the floor. A string of carriages was going past, that's why she flew out. I guess she had never seen a cab before."

"Isn't that just what I was telling you, Herr Kandi-dat? The creature hasn't the first idea about things. She hasn't the least idea of what a lesson is, and that she ought to sit still and listen. But where is the imp of mischief? If she has run away, what on earth will Mr. Sesemann—"

Miss Rottenmeier ran from the room and down the stairs. Here, down below the opened entrance door, Heidi was standing and peering in confusion up and down the street.

"What's the matter with you? What are you think-ing of? How can you run off in such a manner?" the housekeeper shouted at the child.

"I heard the fir trees rustling, but I can't find where they are and I don't hear them any more," Heidi answered. She was looking with disappointment in the direction where the sound of the rolling carriages had died away. This noise had sounded to Heidi's ears like the roaring of the south wind among the firs, and she had followed its calling in the greatest glee.

"Fir trees! Do you think we're in the woods? What silly notions! Come up and see what you've done!"

Miss Rottenmeier climbed the staircase again. Heidi followed meekly after and was very much surprised to see the great havoc she had created in the library. For, so wild had been her haste to find the fir trees, she had not noticed what she was dragging after her.

"You can do a thing like that once, but no more," Miss Rottenmeier said, pointing to the floor. "During your lessons see that you sit still and pay attention. If you can't do that by yourself, I shall have to tie you in your chair. Do you hear me?"

"Yes," Heidi answered, "and I'll sit very quiet now." For at last she understood it was the rule not to move about when a lesson was being given.

Now Sebastian and Tinette had to come in to put things in order. The university student departed, because any further teaching was impossible. There had been no excuse for Clara to sit and yawn that morning.

In the afternoon Clara always had to rest for awhile, and Heidi could then busy herself in any way she wanted to. Miss Rottenmeier had explained all that in the morning.

So, when Clara had lain down in her chair to rest after dinner, the housekeeper went to her room, and Heidi saw the time had come for her to do whatever she pleased. This suited her finely, because there was something in her mind that she wished to try, but she could not do it without help. So she placed herself in the middle of the hall by the dining room in order that the person she wanted to see might not escape her. And, sure enough, after a short wait, Sebastian came upstairs with the great tea tray on his arm, for he was carrying the silver up from the kitchen to put it away in the china closet of the dining room. When he reached the last step of the staircase, Heidi went up to him and said very distinctly—

"You, or He!"

Sebastian opened his eyes just as wide as they would go and said very crossly, "What's that you're saying, Mamsell?"

"I'd like to ask you something, only really it's nothing naughty, like this morning," Heidi added gently, because she noticed Sebastian still seemed a little vexed, as if he were thinking of the ink she had spilled on the floor.

"All right. But first I should like to know about that 'You or He,'" Sebastian answered, still crossly.

"Oh, that's what I always have to call you," Heidi declared. "Miss Rottenmeier told me to."

At that Sebastian laughed so loud that Heidi looked at him in surprise, for she had not seen anything funny.

"And my name is not Mamsell either," the child said, in her turn a little angry. "My name is Heidi."

"So it is. But the same lady has ordered me to say, 'Mamsell,'" Sebastian declared.

"Oh, she did? Then that must be my name," Heidi said, obediently. For she had come to see that everything must go just as Miss Rottenmeier said.

"So, now I have three names," she said with a sigh.

"But what was it that the little Mamsell wanted to ask?" Sebastian said, going into the dining room and putting the silver away in the china closet.

"Show me how to open a window, Sebastian."

"Here is the way to do it," he said, and he opened the great double window for her.

Heidi went up to it, but she was too small to see out. She reached only up to the sill.

"There you are! Now the little Mamsell can peer out and see what's down below," said Sebastian. And he brought a high wooden footstool and put it in place. Heidi clambered up on this happily and she could at last have the look she had so longed for. But, with a gesture of great disappointment, she drew in her head again at once.

"You can't see anything but the stone street," Heidi said pitifully. "But if you go 'way around the house, Sebastian, what is there to see on the other side?"

"Just the same thing," he answered.

"But where do you have to go to see far, far across the whole valley?"

"For that, you have to climb up on some high tower like a church steeple. See the one over there with the gilt dome on it? From up there you can see ever so far."

Now Heidi jumped down quickly from her stool, ran out of doors, and flew down the steps out into the street. But the affair did not turn out as she had thought it would. As she had seen the tower from the window, it had seemed as if she would only have to cross the street to find it right in front of her. But poor Heidi walked down the whole length of the street without coming to the tower. And she could not find the tower anywhere else.

Down one street after another she walked, on and on, but still there was no steeple. A great many people passed her, but they all seemed to be in so much of a hurry that Heidi was sure they would have no time to direct her. Just then she saw a lad standing on the next street corner, who carried on his back a little hand organ and on his arm the strangest sort of an animal. Heidi ran to him.

"Where's the tower with the golden ball on top of it?" she asked.

"Don't know," said the boy.

"But who'll tell me where it is?"

"Don't know."

"Do you know any other church with a high tower?"

"Surely."

"Come on then and show it to me."

"First you show me what you'll give me."

The lad thrust out his hand. Heidi felt around in her pocket. Then she drew out a small picture in which a pretty wreath of red roses was painted. First she looked at it a little while, for she hated to lose it. Clara had given it to her just that morning. But, oh, to look down into the valley across the green slopes!

"There you are," Heidi said, holding out the picture. "Would you like that?"

The boy drew back his hand and shook his head.

"What do you want then?" Heidi asked, and put the little picture gladly back in her pocket.

"Money."

"I haven't any, but Clara has some that she'll give me. How much do you want?"

"Five pennies."

"Come on, then!"

So the two wandered down a long street, and on the way Heidi asked her companion what he was carrying on his back. He told her that under the cloth there was a fine organ that made wonderful music when he turned a crank. Suddenly they were standing before an old church with a high tower.

The lad halted and said, "There you are."

"But how can I get in?" Heidi asked when she saw the tightly closed doors.

"Don't know," was the answer.

"Do you think you could ring here, the way you do for Sebastian?"

"Don't know."

Heidi found a small bell in the wall and pulled at it with all her might.

"You must wait down here for me while I'm up in the tower. I don't know the way back any more, and you'll have to show it to me."

"What will you give me if I do?"

"How much do I have to?"

"Five pennies more."

Just then the old lock was turned from the inside, and the door creaked slowly open. An old man stepped out and looked at the children first in surprise, and then in some anger. He shouted at them—

"How dare you ring for me to come down? Can't you read what stands above the bell, 'For those who wish to climb the tower'?"

The lad pointed silently at Heidi.

"Climb the tower is just what I want to do," Heidi said.

"What business have you up there?" asked the sexton. "Did somebody send you?"

"No," the child said, "I only'd like to go up so I could see down."

"You hurry and go home! And don't try that trick on me again, or you won't get off so easily next time!"

With these words, the sexton turned around and was going to shut the door. But Heidi held fast to his coat tail and said in a pleading tone—

"Oh, please! Just this once!"

He looked behind him and saw Heidi's eyes fixed on his so pitifully that suddenly all his anger was gone. He took her hand in his and said gently—

"Why, if you want to go up so badly as all that, come on!"

The boy sat down on the stone before the door to show that he did not wish to go along with them.

Heidi took the sexton's hand and climbed long rows of steps. They kept getting narrower and narrower, until finally there was a flight but little wider than a ladder. At last the two people were at the top. The sexton lifted Heidi up and held her in the open window.

"Now you can see down below," he said.

Heidi looked down upon a sea of roofs, towers, and chimneys. She drew her head quickly back again and said, much disappointed—

"It's not anything like what I thought."

"Just what I expected!" said the sexton. "What can a little thing like that know about views? Well, come down now, and see you never ring a tower bell again."

He set Heidi down on the floor and led the way to the narrow steps. Where these grew broader, there was a door on the left that opened into the sexton's room, and close by it the flooring stretched out under the steep roof. In behind there stood a great basket, before which a fat gray cat was sitting and growling.

For her family lived in the hamper, and she wished the passers-by to know they must not mix themselves up with her household affairs.

Heidi stood stock still and looked surprisedly into the corner, for in all her born days she had never seen so huge a cat. Whole troops of mice lived in the old tower, and the old cat had no trouble in fetching home a half dozen selected ones every day. The sexton saw Heidi's surprise and he said—

"Come on, she won't hurt you while I'm here. Look at her kittens if you want to."

Heidi walked over to the basket and fairly squealed with happy excitement.

"Oh, the cute little things! The cunning kittens!" she cried again and again. She danced here and there about the basket so as to be sure not to miss a single one of all the funny movements and leaps the seven or eight young kittens were making. They crawled, jumped, and fell over one another without stopping.

"Would you like one for your very own?" asked the sexton, who smiled to see Heidi hopping around so happily.

"All mine, for keeps?" Heidi said. She was so excited she could scarcely believe her good fortune.

"Yes, of course. You can have more, too. You can have them all if you find a place for them," the man answered. He was glad of a chance to get rid of the kittens without doing them harm.

Heidi was very happy. Why, there was such lots of room for the little things in the big house. And wouldn't

Clara be amazed and delighted when the cunning creatures arrived!

"But how am I going to carry them?" Heidi asked. She started to catch some of them in her hands right away, but the fat cat jumped on her arm and snarled at her so fiercely that she started back in great fear.

"I'll take them home for you if you'll tell me where to go," the sexton said. He stroked the old cat to quiet her again, for she was his friend and had lived many years with him up in the tower.

"To Mr. Sesemann in the great house. The front door has a gold dog's head with a thick ring in its mouth," Heidi explained.

She did not have to tell the sexton that. For the sexton had been sitting in his tower for many years and he knew every house in the whole district. Besides, Sebastian was an old friend of his.

"Oh, I know," he said, "but whom shall I give the little fellows to? Shall I ask for you? You don't belong to Mr. Sesemann, do you?"

"No. But Clara will be so happy when the kittens come."

The sexton was going to start downstairs again, but Heidi just could not tear herself away from the interesting scene before her.

"If I could only take one or two with me! One for me and one for Clara. Don't you think I could?"

"Just wait a second, then," said the sexton. He carried the old cat cautiously into his room and placed her in the cupboard, closed the door on her, and returned.

"There! Now you can take two," he said.

Heidi's eyes shone with happiness. She chose a white kitten and one with white and yellow stripes, putting them in the pockets of her skirt. And then they started on their way down.

The lad was still sitting on the steps outside. When the sexton had shut the door behind Heidi, she said—

"Which is the way to Mr. Sesemann's?"

"Don't know," was the answer.

Then Heidi began to describe for him as well as she could the front door, the windows, and the steps, but the lad shook his head at all her talking. He knew nothing about it.

"You see," Heidi went on describing, "from its windows you can see a great big gray house, and here's the way its roof goes—"

With one finger she drew sharp points in the air.

At that the lad jumped to his feet. He only needed signs like that to find his way. He kept running straight ahead, and Heidi right after him, and in a short while, sure enough, they stood before the front door that had a dog's head in brass as its knocker.

Heidi rang the bell. Sebastian soon appeared, but the moment he saw Heidi he called out impatiently—

"Hurry up, hurry up!"

Heidi ran in as fast as she could, and Sebastian closed the door. He had not noticed the lad who was standing outside.

"Quick, little Mamsell!" Sebastian kept begging her. "Right in the dining room! They are already at dinner.

Miss Rottenmeier looks like a loaded cannon.   Whatever made little Mamsell run away like that?"

Heidi had walked into the dining room.   Miss Rottenmeier did not look up from the plate.   Clara said nothing, either, and there was an unpleasant silence.   Sebastian placed Heidi in her chair.   The moment that she was in her seat, the housekeeper began to speak.   Her face was very stern and her voice most solemn.

"Adelheid," she said, "I shall talk with you afterward, but at present I shall only say that you have been very naughty and really ought to be punished for leaving the house without telling anyone or asking permission, and wandering around until late in the evening.   I never heard of such a thing."

"Meow!" said a voice, as if in answer.

At that the lady grew angry indeed.

"What, Adelheid," she cried, and her voice kept rising higher, "you dare make such a naughty joke, after all your bad behavior?   You had better look out, I warn you!"

"I didn't say—" Heidi began.

"M-e-o-w!   M-e-o-w!"

Sebastian almost threw his tray on the table and fled away.

"That will do!" Miss Rottenmeier tried to say, but she had lost her voice in her excitement.

"Get up and leave this room!" she cried after a moment.

Very much scared, Heidi got up from her chair and once more tried to explain.

"I didn't say—"

"M-e-o-w! M-e-o-w! M-e-o-w!"

"But, Heidi," Clara went on to say, "really, when you see how cross you're making Miss Rottenmeier, why do you keep meowing?"

"But, I'm not," Heidi at last was able to say loudly enough to be heard. "It's the kittens."

"What's that? What are you saying? Cats? Kittens?" shrieked Miss Rottenmeier. "Sebastian! Tinette! Find the terrible beasts and get rid of them!"

And the lady rushed headlong into the library and bolted the door behind her to be safer from cats, which were to her the most awful things in all creation. Sebastian was standing outside the door and had to have his laugh out before he could come back in. While he was waiting on Heidi at table, he had seen the little head of a kitten peering out of her pocket and had been expecting the scene that was to come. When it arrived, he could scarcely hold in long enough to set the tray down on the table.

At last, however, he was able to go back into the room in good order, but not until the lady's terrified cries for help had long ceased. Everything in the room. was by that time peaceful and happy. Clara was holding the kittens in her lap, Heidi was kneeling down beside her, and both were joyfully playing with the tiny, graceful creatures.

"You must help us," Clara said to Sebastian as he entered. "You'll have to find a nest for the kittens where Miss Rottenmeier won't see it. For she's afraid of them and wants to get rid of them. But we want to keep the cunning little things and fetch them out whenever we're alone. Where can you hide them?"

"I'll tend to that all right, Miss Clara," Sebastian said good-naturedly. "I'll make a fine bed for them in a basket and put them in a place that the timid lady will never discover. Trust that to me."

Sebastian kept giggling a little every now and then as he went on with his work, for he thought, "There's going to be trouble, sure as you're born!" Which did not displease Sebastian, for he liked to see Miss Rottenmeier get excited.

After some while, when it was almost bedtime, Miss Rottenmeier opened the door the least bit and called through the crack—

"Have the terrible beasts been taken away?"

"Oh, yes, long ago," Sebastian said. He had been finding work to do in the dining room, waiting for this question. Quickly and softly he took the kittens from Clara's lap and disappeared with them.

The special scolding Miss Rottenmeier intended for Heidi was put off until next day. That evening the lady felt too worn out by the changing moods of anger, rage, and fright which Heidi, without meaning to, had caused her. She retired in silence, and Clara and Heidi followed her contentedly, because they knew their kittens were in a good bed.

CHAPTER VIII

EXCITEMENT IN THE SESEMANN HOUSE

Next morning Sebastian had hardly opened the front door for the Herr Kandidat and let him into the library when somebody else rang the doorbell, but with such a noise that the servant almost tumbled downstairs in his hurry.

"No one rings like that but Mr. Sesemann himself," Sebastian thought. "He must have returned ahead of time."

He tore the door open. A ragged boy with a hand organ on his back stood before him.

"What do you mean?" Sebastian yelled at him. "I'll teach you not to tear down doorbells. What do you want here?"

"I want to see Clara," was the answer.

"You dirty little tramp, you! Don't you know enough to say 'Miss Clara,' as your betters do? What's your business with Miss Clara, anyway?" demanded Sebastian roughly.

"She owes me ten pennies," the lad explained.

"You must be crazy. What makes you think a Miss Clara lives here?"

"I showed her the way yesterday for five pennies. And then I showed her the way back—that makes ten."

"Just to show what an awful lie you're telling, Miss Clara never goes out of the house. She can't walk a step.

Come, run off to where you belong, or I'll give you a push!"

But the lad was not in the least frightened. He did not move from the spot, and he said calmly—

"Just the same I saw her on the street. I'll tell what she looks like. She has short curly hair that's black, and her eyes are black, and her dress is brown, and she can't talk the way we do."

"O-ho!" thought Sebastian, and chuckled to himself. "That's little Mamsell who's been up to more mischief."

Then he pulled the lad inside and said—

"Right you are. Follow me, but wait outside the door until I come back again. If I let you go in, you must play something. Miss Clara likes to hear it."

When he was upstairs, he knocked at the library door and was told to come in.

"There's a lad here who has a message to give Miss Clara herself," Sebastian said, gravely.

Clara was much pleased to have such an unusual thing happen.

"Tell him to come right in," she said. "You don't mind, Herr Kandidat, if he wants to give me the message himself?"

The lad had already entered and, just as he had been told to, he began at once to play his organ. In order not to have to listen to the ABC's, Miss Rottenmeier had been busying herself at different tasks in the dining room. Suddenly she pricked up her ears.

Did those sounds come in from the street? But they seemed to be so close to her! How could the tunes of a hand organ possibly be coming from the library? And still—they really seemed—

She flew across the dining room and tore open the door.

There—would you believe it?—there in the middle of the library was a ragged organ grinder, and he was playing his instrument with all his might! The university student was evidently trying to say something, but you couldn't hear a sound he made. Clara and Heidi were listening with shining faces to the organ music.

"Stop it! Stop it right away!" Miss Rottenmeier called into the room. Her voice was drowned by the music.

So she ran straight for the lad—

But suddenly she felt something between her feet. She looked down at the floor. A frightful black beast was crawling under her skirts—a turtle. The housekeeper jumped high in the air, as she had not done for years, and screamed at the top of her lungs—

"Sebastian! Se-bas-tian!"

All at once the organ grinder stopped playing, for this time her voice drowned the music. Sebastian was standing outside by the half-opened door, and he was bent double with laughter, for he had seen Miss Rottenmeier's mighty leap. At last he came in. The housekeeper had sunk down limply on a chair.

"Away with them all, man and beast! Get rid of them on the spot, Sebastian," she called to him.

Sebastian obeyed willingly. He drew the lad away with him and the turtle, too, that was now tightly held in the boy's arms. When he had the lad outside, he pressed some money into his hand and said—

"There's the ten for Miss Clara and ten more for playing. You play fine."

Then he closed the front door behind the strange guest.

Everything was quiet again in the library, once more the lessons had been begun, and this time Miss Rottenmeier remained in the room to make sure that nothing further of a terrible sort should happen. She planned to look into the matter of the organ grinder after the study hours were over, and to punish the guilty person in a way that he would not soon forget.

Before long there was another knock on the door, and Sebastian again appeared with the news that a large basket had been left at the door, to be given without delay to Miss Clara herself.

"To me?" said Clara in surprise and very eager to know what it might be. "Please let me see at once what it looks like."

Sebastian brought in a covered basket and went away again hurriedly.

"I think you'd better finish your lessons first and then unpack the basket," said Miss Rottenmeier.

Clara cast longing eyes at the basket. For the life of her she could not guess what it contained.

At last she stopped right in the middle of a word she was declining. "O Herr Kandidat," she sighed, "if I might take just one quick look, so I could know what was in it, then I'd go right on with my work."

"In one way, you might as well take a look," the university student said, "in another way, you ought to wait. The reason for taking just one peep is that your whole mind is set on the thing anyway—"

The speech was never finished.

The cover of the basket was not fastened tightly, and at this moment one, two, three little kittens jumped out into the room, and then two more, and then even more. And they began to scamper around so like lightening that it seemed as if the whole room were full of the small animals.

They leaped over the Herr Kandidat's boots, nibbled at his trousers, climbed up Miss Rottenmeier's dress, scratched at her feet, jumped up on Clara's chair. They scraped and sprawled and meowed. The confusion was awful.

Clara was in raptures and kept crying, "Oh, what cunning pussies! What jolly jumps they make! See here, Heidi, look there! Oh, do see that one!"

As to Heidi, she chased them joyously into all the corners. The university student stood nervously by the table, lifting first one foot and then the other to avoid the sprawling things. For a few moments Miss Rottenmeier sat speechless with horror, and then she began to howl at the top of her voice—

"Tinette! Ti-net-te! Sebastian! Se-bas-tian!"

She could not even pluck up courage to rise from her chair, because she feared all the horrid little beasts might jump on her at once.

Her repeated calls for help finally brought Sebastian and Tinette. The butler packed the kittens one after the other back into the basket and carried them off to the bed in the basement which he had made for the two kittens the day before.

This day again there had been no cause for yawning during the study hours. Later in the evening, when Miss Rottenmeier found herself somewhat rested from her excitement of the morning, she called Sebastian and Tinette upstairs to the library in order to talk over thoroughly the disgraceful things that had happened. And so it was discovered that the trip Heidi had made on the day before was the cause of all the trouble. The housekeeper sat there white with anger and at first was unable to think of any words that would express her feelings. She waved Sebastian and Tinette out of the room, and then she turned to Heidi, who was standing by Clara's chair and could not see what she had done that was wrong.

"Adelheid," she began, in a stern voice, "I know of only one punishment which would be severe enough for you, because you are a wild girl. But let us see if down in the dark cellar with lizards and rats you will not become so tame that you will never try such tricks again."

Heidi listened quietly and in surprise to this judgment, for she had never been in a fearful cellar. The room next to the hut on the mountain meadow which Grandfather had called the cellar was rather a nice and pleasant place. The ripe cheeses and the fresh milk were kept in it, and she had never seen any rats or lizards there.

But Clara began to cry and wail.

"No, no, Miss Rottenmeier, we must wait until Papa comes back. He wrote he was coming soon. And then

I'll tell him everything and he'll decide what must be done to Heidi."

Miss Rottenmeier really could not object to Mr. Sesemann as chief judge in Heidi's case, and all the more because he was going to be home very soon. She got up and said somewhat sternly—

"Very well, Clara, I am willing. But I, too, shall have a word to say to your father."

And with that she left the room.

There followed now two or three days of peace and quiet, but the housekeeper could not seem to get over her excitement. Every hour she kept thinking of how deceived she had been in Heidi. She felt as if things had been going wrong ever since the child first appeared in the Sesemann house, and as if they would never get any better.

Clara was very happy. She never felt dull any longer, for Heidi made the study hours most amusing affairs. She really could not learn her letters and always got them mixed. And just as the Herr Kandidat would be in the act of explaining the form of some letter and, to make this clearer, would be comparing it to a small horn or to the beak of a bird, Heidi would suddenly cry out joyfully—

"It's a goat!" or, "It's a bird of prey!"

The descriptions of the university student awakened all sorts of pictures in Heidi's small brain, but no idea of the letters.

In the later hours of the afternoon Heidi would sit again beside Clara and tell her so much about the mountain meadow and the life on it that she would become terribly homesick and would end by declaring—-

"I'll really have to go right back home. I certainly must go back tomorrow."

But when Heidi had such attacks, Clara would quiet her by saying that she surely must wait for Papa to come home. Then they could see what was to be done about the matter.

One happy thought that Heidi carried secretly in her mind made her quite willing to give up her own ways and to be contented. This was the thought that every added day she stayed in Frankfort there would be two more rolls for Grandmother. For each noon and evening there was a fine white roll beside her place. And these rolls she always put right in her pocket, because she could not eat them when she remembered Grandmother had none at all and, with her poor old teeth, was hardly able any longer to eat the tough black bread.

Every day after dinner Heidi would sit all by herself for two hours up in her room, since in the city they did not permit her to run out of doors as she had used to on the mountain meadow. She understood this rule now and never broke it. Nor did she dare to have a talk with Sebastian across the hall in the dining room, for Miss Rottenmeier had forbidden that also. And she did not even dream of having a chat with Tinette. She always avoided the maid if she could, because Tinette spoke to her in a mocking tone and was forever making fun of her. And Heidi saw clearly what she was up to and knew that Tinette was laughing at her.

So Heidi would sit every day in her room, spending her time thinking of how green the mountain meadow must be growing by now, and of how all the yellow flowers must be gleaming in the sunlight. She would picture the snow and the mountains and the whole wide valley. And then Heidi would often feel as if she could not bear to be away from it a moment longer. Had her aunt not told her that she could go home whenever she wanted to?

Thus it came about that one fine day Heidi gave in to her homesickness. She hurriedly packed up her rolls in the big red neckerchief, put on her straw hat, and set forth.

But she had got no farther than the front door when her plans for escape were wrecked. She came upon Miss Rottenmeier, who was just back from a walk. This lady stopped and gazed at Heidi from top to toe. Her look seemed to dwell on the full red scarf at Heidi's neck. And then she gasped—

"What sort of dressing is that? And what does this mean, anyway? Haven't I strictly forbidden you ever to go tramping about again? Yet here you are trying to steal away another time, and looking like a perfect little ragamuffin!"

"I wasn't going to tramp about, I was only going home," Heidi answered, frightened.

"Eh? What? Going home? Going home, if you please!" Miss Rottenmeier clasped her hands in her excitement. "Running away? Oh, if Mr. Sesemann should hear of it! Running right away from his house! You'd better see he doesn't learn about it! And what is there, pray, that you don't like in his home? Aren't you treated better than you have a right to expect? Is there anything you lack? Did you ever in your life have as nice a home, or such good things to eat, or such good treatment as here? Tell me that!"

"No," Heidi answered.

"And don't I know it!" the housekeeper went on, excitedly. "There is nothing you do not have. And yet I cannot imagine such an ungrateful creature. You're so well off, you don't know your own good luck."

But poor Heidi could no longer hold back her great loneliness. She burst out—

"I just wånt to go h-o-m-e. And if I keep staying away any more, Schneehöppli will gò on grieving for me. And Grandmother is expecting me. And Distelfink will get a whipping if Peter doesn't get any cheese. And here you never see the sun say good night to the mountains. And if the bird of prey should fly over Frankfort, he would scream ever so much louder, because so many folks sit together and get cross with each other and never climb up on the rocks where it's good for them to be."

"Mercy me! The child has gone crazy," Miss Rottenmeier cried out. She flew in terror up the steps and ran straight into Sebastian, who was just starting down.

"Carry the unfortunate thing right up," she called to him, while she rubbed her head with her hand. For she had received a good hard bump.

"Yes, yes, all right! Thank you, ma'am!" Sebastian answered, rubbing his head, likewise. For his bump had been even worse.

With flaming eyes, Heidi never budged from where she stood. Her whole body was shaking with nervous excitement.

"Well, what have you been doing this time?" Sebastian asked, with a cheerful grin. But when he looked more closely at Heidi, who was standing very still, he patted her gently on the shoulder and said—

"Oh, bah! The little Mamsell mustn't take things so much to heart. Just be jolly, that's the way to do! Didn't she just this minute almost ram a hole in my head, but why be downhearted about it? Well! Still on the same spot, I see. We've got to go back in, she said so."

At that, Heidi walked up the steps, but slowly and wearily, and not at all as she generally did. It made Sebastian unhappy to watch her. He followed along behind and spoke encouraging words—

"You mustn't mind so much. Just don't be so unhappy about it! Be brave, whatever happens. Our little Mamsell is a regular soldier, has never shed a tear since she's been with us, while everybody knows that other girls of her age weep twelve times a day! The kittens are having a fine time upstairs, I'll bet. They're jumping all over the place and acting crazy. After a bit we'll just go up and take a look at them when the lady in there isn't around to see."

Heidi nodded her head a little, but so sadly that it went straight to Sebastian's heart. He looked at her with much sympathy as she slunk off to her room.

At supper that evening Miss Rottenmeier did not say a word. But she kept casting strangely keen glances at Heidi as if she thought she might at any moment do something quite unexpected. For her part, however, Heidi sat at her place still as a mouse and never made a move. She ate and drank nothing, but she slipped her roll quickly into her pocket.

Next morning, when the Herr Kandidat was coming up the stairs, Miss Rottenmeier beckoned to him secretly to go into the dining room. And there she told him how greatly she feared that the change of scene and the new manner of living had driven the child out of her head. She told him of Heidi's trying to run away, and she repeated all of the strange words of Heidi's that she could remember.

But the university student soothed and comforted Miss Rottenmeier. He said that he was well aware, on the one hand, that Adelheid was a little odd, and yet on the other hand she was certainly in her right mind. He felt sure that little by little, with the right kind of treatment, he could restore her to a proper frame of mind, and this was what he had had in view all along. He thought her case was worse just now because he simply had been unable to teach her the ABC's, since she could not learn her letters.

After this talk Miss Rottenmeier felt calmer and excused the Herr Kandidat to go to his lessons. Later in the afternoon she suddenly remembered the queer clothes Heidi had had on when she was trying to run away, and she made up her mind to put the child's clothes in suitable shape by giving her some of Clara's things to wear, before Mr. Sesemann should return.

She talked this over with Clara, and when she found the invalid agreed with her and wanted to give Heidi a lot of clothes and linen and hats, the housekeeper went up to the child's room, in order to look through her closet and see which of her dresses should be kept and which should be got rid of. But she was back again in a few minutes, looking very much disgusted.

"Can you guess what I have found, Adelheid?" she cried aloud. "Such a thing as I never expected to see! In your closet, in your clothes closet, in the bottom of this closet, Adelheid, tell me what I discovered. A heap of little rolls! Yes, Clara, bread in her closet. A big heap of them stowed away."

With that, Miss Rottenmeier called to the maid, who was in the dining room—

"Tinette, take away the stale bread in Adelheid's closet, will you? And also the crushed straw hat that's on the table."

"No, no!" Heidi screamed. "I must keep the hat, and the rolls are for Grandmother."

Heidi tried to rush after Tinette, but the housekeeper held her in a firm grip.

"You stay here! The rubbish will be put where it belongs," she said, as she hung on to Heidi.

Then the child threw herself down on Clara's couch and began to weep. Her wailing grew louder and more bitter, and she kept saying over and over in her grief—

"Now Grandmother won't have any more rolls. They were for Grandmother, and now they're all gone and she won't have any." And Heidi sobbed as if her heart would break. Miss Rottenmeier ran out of the room. Clara was scared.

"Don't cry so, please, Heidi," she begged, "but listen to me. Look here, I promise to give you just as many rolls for Grandmother when you go home, or even more of them. And they'll be fresh and soft ones too, while yours would have got all hard. They were stale already. Just don't cry so, Heidi!"

It was some time before Heidi could hold back her sobs. But all the while she understood that Clara was comforting her, and it helped her greatly, or she never would have been able to stop crying. And Heidi had to be told several times about the new rolls and asked Clara again and again, while her speech was still interrupted by sobbing—

"Sure you'll give me just as many as I had for Grandmother?"

Each time Clara answered, "Honest true, I will, and more, too, if only you won't be sad any longer."

Heidi's eyes were still red from weeping when she came down to supper. And when she saw the roll by her place, she had to start sobbing anew. But this time she held on to herself, for she knew that one must be quiet when at table.

Now this evening, whenever Sebastian got close to Heidi, he would act in the strangest way. He would point first at his own head and then at Heidi's. Then again he would nod and wink, as if he wanted to say—

"Don't you care. I saw what was up and looked out for everything."

Later, when Heidi went to her room and was going to creep into bed, why, there lay her crushed straw hat tucked under the spread! She pulled out the old hat delightedly, crumpled it even more in a fit of joy, wrapped it up in a handkerchief, and thrust it out of sight far back in her closet.

It was Sebastian who had hidden the little hat under the coverlet. He had been in the dining room with Tinette when she was called by Miss Rottenmeier, and he had heard Heidi's cries of grief. So he had followed Tinette, and when she came from the child's room with her load of bread and the hat on top of it, he had snatched the hat and said to her—

"I'll attend to that for you."

So, after all, he had saved it for Heidi, to her great delight. And that is what he was trying to tell her during supper to cheer her up.

CHAPTER IX

THE MASTER HEARS STRANGE THINGS

Some days after these happenings there was great excitement in the Sesemann household. People were running upstairs and down, for the master of the house had just returned from his journey. Sebastian and Tinette were carrying in one bundle after another from the well-filled carriage, for Mr. Sesemann always brought a host of pretty things home with him.

First of all he went to his daughter's room to greet her. Heidi was sitting with Clara, for this was the late afternoon hour when they were always together. Clara, welcomed her father with great happiness, for she loved him dearly, and the good papa greeted his little daughter no less fondly. Then he offered his hand to Heidi, who had quietly retired to a corner, and said—

"And here is our little Swiss girl. Come, give me your hand, that's the way! Now tell me one thing, are you and Clara good friends? You don't quarrel and get cross, and then cry and make up, and then begin all over again, do you?"

"No, Clara is always good to me," Heidi answered.

"And Heidi hasn't even tried once to quarrel, Papa," Clara added quickly.

"That's good. I am glad to hear it," her father said, getting up from his chair. "But now you must let me get a bite to eat, Clara dear, for I haven't had a thing all day.

I'll come back to you afterward and show you what I've brought for you."

Mr. Sesemann went into the dining room, where Miss Rottenmeier was looking over the table which was laid for his luncheon. When he had sat down and the lady, a living image of bad tidings, had taken her place across from him, the master of the house turned to her and said—

"But, my dear Miss Rottenmeier, what am I to think? You have put on a truly alarming look to welcome me with. What can be the matter? Clara seems in the best of health."

"Mr. Sesemann," the housekeeper began very seriously, "Clara is suffering, too. We have been dreadfully cheated."

"In what way?" Mr. Sesemann asked, quietly taking a sip of wine.

"Why, we had decided, as you know, to have a playmate in the house for Clara. And as I realized how set you were on having only pure and good people about your daughter, I decided on a young Swiss girl. And I fully expected to see such a creature as I have read about in books, a girl, you know, born in the fresh mountain air, one who walks through life scarcely touching the ground beneath her feet."

"Still, I suppose," Mr. Sesemann could not help saying, "even Swiss children touch the ground as they walk along, or they'd have wings instead of feet."

"Oh, you know what I mean, sir," Miss Rottenmeier continued, "one of those beings you hear so much about, who live in the pure air of the highlands and who sweep by us like a breath from another world."

"But what would Clara do with this breath from another world?"

"Please, Mr. Sesemann, it is not a thing to joke about. The matter is more serious to me than you imagine. I have been terribly, really terribly, imposed upon."

"But what is so terrible, after all? The child does not look so bad to me," Mr. Sesemann said quietly.

"There's just one thing I simply must tell you, sir. You've no idea the sort of people and animals this child has filled your house with while you were away. I'll leave that for the Herr Kandidat to tell you."

"With animals! Why, what do you mean by that?"

"It can't be explained, that's all. None of the acts of this girl can be explained unless you believe that she has spells when she is not in her right mind."

Until this moment Mr. Sesemann had not paid much attention to the housekeeper's words, but if Heidi was not in her right mind, that was another matter! That might be very serious for his daughter. He looked quite closely at Miss Rottenmeier to make sure that she herself was entirely sane. The door was opened just then and the university student appeared.

"Ah, here comes our Herr Kandidat to tell us all about it," Mr. Sesemann greeted the new arrival. "Come in, won't you, and sit down by me." And he stretched out a hand of welcome.

"The Herr Kandidat will drink a cup of black coffee with me, Miss Rottenmeier. Sit down, sir, and make yourself quite at home. And now tell me, please, what is wrong with the child who has come to be my daughter's companion and your pupil. What is all this I hear about animals being brought into the house, and what sort of mind has she?"

The university student could never give a direct answer to a simple question. First he had to tell Mr. Sesemann how glad he was to see him safe back again and to say that he had come especially to bid him welcome.

But Mr. Sesemann urged him to stick to the point, and therefore Heidi's teacher began—

"In telling you, sir, what I think of the character of this young girl, I shall have to say first of all especially that even if, on the one hand, she shows that her education is fairly weak—"

Mr. Sesemann shook his head in mild despair.

"—a lack of mental growth caused perhaps by the fact that her teaching was begun somewhat late, or perhaps it is better to say caused by the more or less quiet life which she led when dwelling up in the Alps—"

"Who is crazy now?" thought Mr. Sesemann.

"—a quiet life, sir, which can, however, not be entirely thought of as bad, but which, on the contrary, has without doubt in certain ways many good points, and if such a life is not carried on too long it may even be said—"

"But, my dear fellow," Mr. Sesemann at last interrupted him, "you are really taking too much trouble. Just tell me this. Has the child frightened you by bringing animals into the house? And do you think her society good for my small daughter?"

"Far be it from me to hurt the little girl," the university student began again, "for although, on the one hand, she shows that she does not know much about society, a lack of knowledge doubtless due to the more or less simple life that the young thing led up to the moment that she was brought to Frankfort—"

"Excuse me, Herr Kandidat—"

"—which new fact made a great change in the growth of this only half-grown and at least not yet fully developed creature, and yet, to be sure, on the other hand, one must not deny the decided talents of the child, who, if she is rightly led—"

"Excuse me, Herr Kandidat, please! But I do not wish to disturb you further—I—I must pay a short visit to my daughter at once."

The master of the house fairly ran out of the door and did not return. Across the hall, in the library, he sat down beside Clara. Heidi had got up to give him her chair, and he turned to her and said—

"Listen, little one, run and get me—wait a minute, let me see!—run and get me"—Mr. Sesemann really couldn't think of anything he wanted, and yet Heidi must be sent away, if only for a minute—"oh, yes, run and get me a glass of water, won't you?"

"Cold water?" Heidi asked.

"Oh, yes indeed. As cold as you can get it."

Heidi vanished.

"And now, dear little Clara," Papa said, drawing his chair up close to hers and taking her hand in his, "tell me straight as a string what sort of animals your little

playmate has brought into our house. And tell me, too,
why Miss Rottenmeier should think that sometimes she is
not quite right in her head."

It was easy for Clara to do this, for the frightened
housekeeper had spoken to her of Heidi's odd sayings, all
of which, however, made good sense to Clara. First she
told her father the story of the turtle and the kittens, and
then she went on to explain the odd sayings which had so
puzzled Miss Rottenmeier.

This made Mr. Sesemann laugh right heartily.

"Then you don't want me to send the youngster home?
You're not tired of her?" he asked.

"Oh my, no!" Clara begged him. "Don't do that,
Papa! Why, since Heidi's come there's something happening every day, and it's such good fun! Not at all the way
it was before, when nothing ever happened. And Heidi
tells me such lots of things."

"All right, Clara dear. And there's your little friend
back again so soon. Well, did you get me fine cold water?"
Mr. Sesemann asked as Heidi offered him a glass.

"Right fresh from the well," Heidi answered.

"Surely, you didn't go to the well yourself for it," said
Clara.

"Of course I did. And it's fresh as anything. Only
I had to go so far for it, because there were so many people
at the first well. Then I went down the street, but
there were just as many waiting their turn at the second
one. And then I went to another street, and there I got
the water. And the gentleman with the white hair wants
to be remembered to Mr. Sesemann."

"Well, that was a quick trip," laughed the master of the house. "And who may the old gentleman be?"

"He was passing the well, but he stopped and said, 'As you've a glass with you, why not give me a drink too? For whom are you getting the water?' 'For Mr. Sesemann,' I said. And then he laughed right out and sent you his greetings and said he hoped you would like the water."

"You don't say. I wonder who wanted to be remembered to me. How did the gentleman look?"

"He has a nice laugh and a thick gold chain, and a gold thing with a big red stone hangs on it, and there's a horse's head on his stick."

"That is the doctor"—"That's my old doctor," both Clara and her father said in the same breath.

Mr. Sesemann could not help laughing in secret when he thought of how surprised his friend would be at this new way of getting one's water brought in.

That same evening, when he was sitting in the dining room talking over all sorts of household matters with Miss Rottenmeier, Mr. Sesemann told her his daughter's companion was to remain in the house. He thought the child was healthy in every way, and his daughter was very fond of her society and liked it better than any other.

"And so I wish," Mr. Sesemann added, "to have this child always treated kindly. Don't think of her oddities as sins. Besides, Miss Rottenmeier, if you cannot get along with the child, there is every hope of your having good help in the near future. My mother is coming to pay us a long visit, and you remember that she can manage anyone, no matter how odd he may be, do you not?"

"Oh, yes, I know that well enough," the lady replied.

But somehow her face did not look cheerful at this promise of help.

Mr. Sesemann could take at this time only a short vacation, and after two weeks or so his business again called him to Paris. And when Clara insisted that she just couldn't let him go away so soon, he comforted her by promising that Grandmama would soon arrive and was expected a few days later.

And Mr. Sesemann had scarcely departed when a letter came to say that Mrs. Sesemann had already left Holstein, where she lived on an old estate. The letter gave the exact hour of her arrival on the next day, so that the carriage could be sent to the depot for her.

Clara was overjoyed at this news, and that evening she talked so much and so long about her grandmama that Heidi, too, began to call her "Grandmama." This action of Heidi's brought a sour look from Miss Rottenmeier, but the child paid no heed to it, for by this time she had grown used to receiving such glances and took them as a matter of course.

But, once Heidi was started on her way to bed, the housekeeper called her into her room and told her quite clearly that she must never use the name "Grandmama." When Mrs. Sesemann came, Heidi must address her as "gracious lady."

"You understand, do you?" Miss Rottenmeier asked as Heidi looked at her in a funny way. But she gave the child such a cross look that Heidi did not dare ask questions, although she did not understand what the title meant.

CHAPTER X

A GRANDMA

Next evening there were great preparations going on in the Sesemann household. In fact, there was such a to-do that it was plain the lady they were waiting for played a very important part in their thoughts. You could see that she was both loved and feared by all.

Tinette had put a brand new lace cap on her head. Sebastian had scraped together a lot of footstools and put them in all possible places, so the great lady could find one right under her feet, no matter where she might sit down to rest. Miss Rottenmeier, very stiff and straight, walked through the rooms examining everything, as if to show that her own rule was by no means at an end even if a second lady of the house was coming.

And then the carriage rolled up before the house, and Sebastian and Tinette went flying down the steps. Slowly and with dignity the housekeeper followed them, for she knew she also must be present to welcome Mrs. Sesemann.

Heidi had been ordered to stay in her room and to wait there until she was sent for, because Grandmama would first go to see Clara and of course would want to be alone with her awhile. So Heidi sat down in a corner and said over the words she was to use to the new arrival. But it was hardly any time at all before Tinette thrust the tip of her nose in at the door and said snippily, just as always—

"Off with you to the library!"

Heidi had been unable to ask Miss Rottenmeier again about the strange words she was to use with Grandmama. She thought perhaps the housekeeper had made a mistake, since always before she had heard people spoken to as Mr. or Mrs. and their real names afterward. So she settled the matter to her own satisfaction.

When she opened the library door, Grandmama called out to her in a cheery voice—

"Ah, there's the child! Come over here to me and let's have a good look at you."

Heidi did as she was told. And in her clear voice she said quite distinctly, "Good day, Mrs. Gracious!"

"Mrs. Gracious? Frau Gnädige?" laughed Grandmama. "Oh me, oh my! Is that what they say where you come from? Is that what you've heard at home in the Alps?"

"Oh, no. Nobody has such a name in my house," Heidi answered seriously.

"Well, there's no such person here, either," Grandmama said with another laugh, as she patted Heidi's cheek affectionately. "But don't you mind! In the nursery I am just Grandmama. And you can remember to call me that, can't you?"

"Surely I can," Heidi assured the nice lady. "That's what I always called you before."

"That's as it should be," Grandmama said, nodding her head and smiling.

Then she looked at Heidi very closely and from time to time would nod her head again. And Heidi kept looking steadily into her eyes, for they were so kind that they

made the child very happy. All of Grandmama, in fact,
pleased her so much that she simply had to stand and stare
at her. She had such pretty white hair, and wore a lovely
lace frill around her head, and two broad ribbons fluttered
away from her cap and kept moving here and there, as if
a gentle breeze was always blowing around Grandmama,
and Heidi thought that specially charming.

"And what's your name, dear?" Grandmama suddenly
asked.

"My real name's only Heidi. But, because I'm to be
called Adelheid, I always answer if—" and right there
Heidi suddenly stuck and felt a little guilty, for she
remembered that she did not always answer when Miss
Rottenmeier unexpectedly called her "Adelheid." You see,
she couldn't quite feel that this was her name. And here
was Miss Rottenmeier coming into the room at this very
minute.

"Mrs. Sesemann, I am sure, will justify me in choosing
a name which can at least be spoken without one's feeling
ashamed, even if just before the servants."

"My dear Rottenmeier," replied Mrs. Sesemann, "if
a human being goes and gets called 'Heidi' and answers
to that name, then that's what I call him. That's all there
is to that!"

It was very annoying to Miss Rottenmeier to have
the old lady constantly address her by name simply, without putting "Miss" before it. But there was no help for
it. Grandmama had her own way of doing things and
stuck to it, no matter how one might feel about it. What
was more, the old lady had all her five senses and knew

what was going on in a house the minute she stepped inside of it.

On the day after her arrival, when Clara as usual was lying down after dinner, Grandmama sat down beside her in an arm chair and closed her eyes for a few moments. Soon, however, she got up again, for after forty winks she was as wide awake as ever, and walked out into the dining room. It was empty.

"Clara is fast asleep," she said to herself.

So she went to the room of Lady Rottenmeier and pounded loudly on the door. After some little delay the housekeeper answered to the knocking, only to start back in much amazement at this unexpected visit.

"Where does the child keep herself at this hour, and what is she up to? I'd like to know," Mrs. Sesemann said.

"She is sitting in her room, where she might find something useful for her two hands to do if she had the least desire for such work. But Mrs. Sesemann really ought to know what silly acts the creature plans at such times, and often goes ahead and does them—things really that one can scarcely speak of in good society."

"Just what I should do myself if I had to sit bottled up the way this child does. Oh, I'm quite sure I should. And then you would see how much of my silliness could be mentioned in polite society! Go get the child and bring her into my room. I'm going to give her some pretty books I bought for her."

"But that's just what you can't do, you'll see!" cried Miss Rottenmeier, holding up her hands in horror.

"What can the child do with books, Mrs. Sesemann? In all this time she has not even learned her ABC's. You really can't get a single idea into the creature's head. You ask the Herr Kandidat if you can. If that good fellow did not have the patience of the heavenly angels themselves, he would have given up trying to teach her anything long ago."

"Indeed! That's very strange. The child does not look to me like one that cannot learn her ABC's," Mrs. Sesemann said. "Bring her to me, anyway. She can at least look at the pictures in the books."

Miss Rottenmeier had it in mind to say something more, but Mrs. Sesemann had already turned away and was hurrying to her room. She was very much surprised at what she heard about Heidi's stupidity. She thought she would look into the matter without saying anything to the university student, even though she did not like him because of his good manners. She was glad to speak to him in a very kindly way whenever they met, but she always got away from him as soon as she could and kept from having a long talk with him, because his manner of saying things was very wearying to her.

So shortly after Heidi went to her room, Fraülein Rottenmeier appeared to call her. She went into Grandmama's room and opened her eyes wide when she saw the splendidly colored pictures in the books the old lady had brought her. But all at once the child screamed loudly after Grandmama had turned over a new page. With glowing eyes she looked at the figures in the picture, and then her eyes filled with hot tears and she began to sob.

Grandmama looked closely at the picture. It showed a pretty green meadow where all sorts of animals were grazing and feeding on young shrubs. In the middle stood the shepherd, who was leaning on his long staff and gazing at the happy creatures. A golden light rested on the whole scene, for the sun was just sinking below the horizon.

The old lady took Heidi's hand in hers.

"Come, come, my dear," she said in the nicest way, "you really mustn't cry so. I suppose the picture made you think of something, but see here, there's a real pretty story about it, and I'll tell it to you this evening. And there are lots of other lovely stories in the book, too. We'll read them and tell them to each other later. And now we must have a little talk together. So wipe away your tears and stand right before me where I can see you clearly. That's good! Now we are happy again."

But it was still some time before Heidi could quite stop sobbing. Grandmama waited a few moments for her to recover, saying now and then, to encourage the child—

"There! Everything is all right, and we're just as happy as ever we were."

When at last she saw that Heidi was comforted, she said—

"Now, my dear, there's something I want to know. How are you getting along in your lessons with the Herr Kandidat? Have you learned a good deal and do you understand things?"

"Oh, no," Heidi said, with a sigh, "but I knew from the start that you couldn't learn it."

"What do you mean, Heidi, by saying that you knew the lessons couldn't be learned?"

"Children can't learn to read. It's too hard for them."

"Why, what a notion! And where did you learn this strange fact?"

"Peter told me so. And I guess he knows, for he always has to keep trying it and he can never get it, it's too hard."

"Well! Peter must be a strange lad, I must say. But, look here, Heidi, you mustn't believe everything that Peter tells you. You must just try for yourself. Surely you can't have put your whole mind on what your teacher was saying and looked carefully at his letters."

"That doesn't do any good," Heidi said in the voice of one who gives in to fate.

"Let me tell you something," said Grandmama. "You have not learned to read, Heidi, just because you believed what Peter said. Suppose you now believe what I tell you. Really and truly, you can learn to read in almost no time, just as lots of other children do who are like you and not like Peter."

"Oh, goody!"

"And then just think of what will happen when you can read. You saw the shepherd standing in the pretty green meadow? Well, the minute that you can read, this book will be your very own and then you can learn everything about him, just as if someone told you the story. You'll know all that he is doing with his sheep and his goats, and the strange things that happen to him. You would like that, wouldn't you, Heidi?"

The child had listened to Grandmama with the closest attention. And then she drew a deep breath and said, with shining eyes—

"I wish I could read this minute!"

"It will come to you, and I can see that it will not be long now, Heidi. But we must go and see what Clara's doing. Come, we will take the pretty books along."

Grandmama took Heidi's hand in hers and went with her to the study.—

There was a day, you remember, when Heidi had wanted to go home. That was the day when Miss Rottenmeier scolded her so terribly out on the front steps, and told her how naughty and bad she was to wish to run away, and what a good thing it was that Mr. Sesemann didn't know about it.

Well, from that time a change had taken place in Heidi.

She had been made to understand that she could not go home whenever she felt like it, as Aunty Dete had promised her, but that she must stay in Frankfort for ever and ever so long, perhaps for always. She had also been made to think that when Mr. Sesemann came home he would find her very naughty for wanting to leave, and Heidi supposed that Grandmama and Clara would feel the same way about it. So Heidi could tell no one that she was homesick, because Grandmama had been so good to her that she could not bear to make her cross the way she had made Miss Rottenmeier.

So it was that Heidi's heart grew heavier with each new day. She lost her appetite for food. She kept growing more wan and white. She often lay awake at night for hours, because, the moment that she was by herself and all had grown still around her, she began to see living pictures of the mountain pasture, and the sunlight on it, and the flowers. And when she did finally go to sleep, there would come to her in her dreams the ruddy sharp rocks of Falkniss or the gleaming snow fields of Cäsaplana. At such a time she would awake in the early morning prepared to dash joyfully out of the hut—only to discover that she was in her big bed in Frankfort so far away from her Swiss mountains, and she could not go home!

Then Heidi would often bury her face in the pillow and cry for a long time, but so gently that nobody heard her.

The child's grief did not escape Grandmama's sharp eyes. The old lady waited for several days to see if a change for the better would come and Heidi would lose her sadness. But as Heidi's mood continued to be the same and Grandmama often noticed early in the morning that Heidi had been weeping, she finally took the child to her room one day, looked at her very kindly, and said—

"Tell me what's the matter, dear. Have you some trouble?"

Heidi was afraid of seeming naughty to this nice grandmama and of making her less friendly, so she answered—

"There's just nothing to say."

"There isn't? Could you tell Clara about it, I wonder?" asked Grandmama.

"Oh, no, not a living soul!" Heidi said quickly. And then she looked so unhappy that the old lady's heart was filled with pity.

"Listen, dear," she said, "I'll tell you something. When we have a sorrow that we can't share with anyone, we tell it to the dear God in Heaven and we ask Him to help us, for He can take away every thought that makes us sad. You know that, Heidi, don't you? Don't you pray every night to the dear God in Heaven and thank Him for all your blessings and beg Him to keep you from harm?"

"Oh, no, I never do that," the child answered.

"Have you never said a prayer, dear? Don't you know how to pray?"

"I used to pray a little with the first grandmother, but that is so long ago I've forgotten all about it."

"See, dear, that's what makes you so sad, because you don't know anyone who can help you. Just think of how good it feels, when your heart is sad and heavy, to know you can go at any moment to dear God and tell Him your trouble, and ask Him to help you when no one else can. And He can always help us and give us things to make us happy again."

A look of joy flashed into Heidi's eyes.

"Can you tell Him everything, just everything?"

"There is nothing we cannot tell Him, Heidi."

The child drew her hand away from Grandmama and said quickly—

"Can I go now, please?"

"Of course you can," the old lady answered.

Heidi ran off to her room, sat down on a footstool, folded her little hands, and told the dear God everything that was in her heart to make it heavy. And she asked Him to help her and let her go home to her grandfather.—

A little more than a week may have passed since this day of prayer when the university student asked to see Mrs. Sesemann as he had something important to say to her. He was asked to come to her room, and the moment he entered it Mrs. Sesemann offered him her hand and said—

"I bid you welcome, my dear Herr Kandidat. Sit down by me, please, and tell me your message. It is nothing unpleasant, I hope."

She pushed a chair toward her visitor.

"Quite the opposite, dear lady!" the university student began. "Do you know the strangest thing has happened, a thing that nobody could have possibly seen in anything that went before it, for, from all that I could tell, what has just occurred appears to be absolutely impossible, and yet it has happened in the strangest way, although it is exactly opposite to anything I had a right to expect—"

"You don't mean to say the child has learned to read, Herr Kandidat?" broke in Mrs. Sesemann.

The university student stared at the old lady, greatly astonished that she had guessed his errand.

"Oh, it is very strange indeed," he said, after a while, "not only that the little girl did not learn her ABC's in spite of my clear explanations and the trouble I took with her, but also that now in no time at all, after I had decided to give up what could not be done and without explaining them at all thoroughly to present to the eyes of the young girl the naked letters themselves, so to speak—"

"She began suddenly to understand?" Grandmama asked.

"Why, yes. She learned to read overnight, you might say, and at once began to read with a correctness which I have found in few beginners. But a fact that is almost as strange to me, dear lady, is that you knew straight off the truth of my most queer message."

"Many wonderful things happen in this life of ours," Mrs. Sesemann said, with a pleased smile. "Two different things sometimes occur at the same time, such as a new interest in studying and a new way of teaching, and neither of these can do any harm, Herr Kandidat. Let's just be happy that the child has got along so well, and hope for further progress."

She walked to the door with her visitor and then went quickly to the library, in order to make sure with her own eyes that the good news was true. Sure enough! Heidi was sitting beside Clara and reading a story to her, and you could see the great surprise and the growing excitement with which she was looking into the new world that was opening up to her, now that at last people and facts stepped out from the black letters and became living and had stirring adventures.

That very same evening, as they sat down to dinner, Heidi found the big book with the pretty pictures lying on her plate. And when she looked across at Grandmama with a question in her eyes, the old lady said with a nod—

"Yes, dear, the book belongs to you now."

"For ever and ever? To take home with me?" Heidi asked, her cheeks red with happiness.

"Of course. For keeps!" Grandmama assured her. "Tomorrow you and I will begin to read it."

"But you're not going home, Heidi, not for many years to come," Clara said. "When Grandmama goes away again this time, you'll just have to stay close by me."

Heidi had to look at her book before she could ever go to sleep that night up in her room, and from that day forward it was her dearest possession. She loved nothing better than to sit over her book and read again and again the stories that went with the bright pretty pictures. When in the evening Grandmama would say, "Now Heidi's going to read for us," Heidi would be delighted, because the book had become easy for her. The stories seemed more beautiful and real to her when she read them aloud, and Grandmama made things very clear to her and told her much that was not in the book. But, best of all, the child liked to sit and gaze at her green meadow and the shepherd in the midst of his flocks, as he stood leaning so contentedly on his long staff. For he was happy to be with his father's fine herd and to walk with the happy sheep and goats who were his delight.

But right after that followed the picture where the shepherd had run away from his father's house and was living in a strange land. He had to tend the swine, and the husks, which were all he had to eat, had made him very thin. The sun no longer shone with such a golden light in this picture, and the whole scene was gray and misty.

Happily, however, there was another picture to this story. In it the father was shown coming from the house with outspread arms and running to welcome the returning prodigal son who was stealing home all ragged and hungry and sorry. This was the story that Heidi loved best. She read it over and over aloud and to herself. And she never grew tired of hearing Grandmama tell things about it.

There were a great many other beautiful tales in the book. Reading these and looking at their pictures made the days pass by very quickly, and soon the time was at hand when Grandmama had decided to end her visit.

CHAPTER XI

HEIDI IMPROVES IN SOME WAYS AND GROWS WORSE IN OTHERS

Every afternoon during the whole of her visit, when Clara lay down for her nap and Miss Rottenmeier was mysteriously absent, perhaps herself in need of rest, Grandmama settled down beside Clara for a moment. But before five minutes were gone she would be up on her feet again and would be calling Heidi into her room to chat with her, keep her busy in all sorts of ways, and entertain her.

Grandmama had pretty little dolls and showed Heidi how to make dresses and aprons for them. And almost before you knew it, the child had learned how to sew and was making the finest dresses and cloaks for the little people, for the old lady had pieces of cloth of the most gorgeous colors.

Now that Heidi could read, she was always asked to read some of her stories aloud to Grandmama. She loved to do this, because the oftener she went over her tales, the dearer they grew to her. The things which happened to the story-book people were so real to Heidi that the bond between them was very close and she was happy to spend her time in their companionship. Still, she never looked entirely happy, and her eyes no longer shone as gaily as they had formerly done.

It was the last week that Grandmama was to spend in Frankfort. She had just called for Heidi to come to her

room, for it was the hour when Clara took her nap. As
Heidi entered with her big book under her arm, Grandmama beckoned to her to come up close, laid the book
aside, and said—

"Now come, my dear, and tell me why are you not
happy? Is the same old trouble in your heart?"

"Yes," said Heidi with a nod.

"Did you take it to dear God in prayer?"

"Yes."

"And are you still praying every day that all will come
right, and that God will give you joy?"

"Oh, no, I never pray any longer."

"What's that you say, Heidi? Why, what are you
telling me? You really have stopped praying?"

"It's no use. The dear God paid no attention to me.
And I really do believe," Heidi went on, "that when so
many people in Frankfort are praying all at the same time
of night, of course the dear God can't hear what they all
say. And He certainly did not listen to me."

"Indeed! How can you be so sure of that, my dear?"

"I made the same prayer every day for many long
weeks and the dear God never answered it."

"That cannot happen, Heidi, and you must not think
it can. Don't you see, the dear God is a loving Father to
us all, and He always knows what is best for us, even
when we ourselves do not. Now if we pray to Him for
something that is not good for us, He does not grant it.
But if we keep on praying with all our heart and don't run
right away and lose our trust in Him, then He always
gives us something better than we ask for."

"Why, I never thought of that!" said Heidi.

"See? What you wanted Him to grant you was not good for you at just that moment. Be sure that the dear God heard your prayer, because he can hear and see all people at the same time. That's why he is God, and not a human being like you and me. And because He knew perfectly what was good for you, He said to Himself, "There's Heidi. Of course she must have what she asks for, but not until it is good for her, so she can get the most joy from it. For if I do what she wants right away, and if she finds out later it would have been better for me not to do it, then she will weep and say, 'Oh, I wish the dear God had not given me what I asked Him to! It isn't nearly as nice as I thought it would be.' And while the dear God was looking down from the sky to see if you really trusted Him and came every day to Him and never failed to look to Him when anything went wrong—why, you ran right away, without trusting at all, and didn't pray, and forgot the dear God entirely."

"I shouldn't have done that, should I, Grandmama?"

"No, dear. For, you see, when a person acts that way and the dear God never hears his voice raised in prayer, why, then He forgets that person, too, and lets him go wherever he will. And when he is unhappy and cries out, 'There is no one to help me!' then we have no pity for that person, but say to him, 'It was you who ran away from the dear God who could have helped you!' Do you want that to be said of you, Heidi, or do you want to go this minute to the dear God and tell Him you are sorry you turned away from Him? Will you tell Him that you will pray every day and trust Him to do what is best for you, so that your heart can be happy again?"

Heidi had listened very carefully. Each word of Grandmama's had gone straight to her heart, because she had such perfect trust in her.

"I will go this minute and ask the dear God to forgive me, and I never will forget Him again," Heidi said, truly sorry.

"That's right, my dear. And you may be sure He will always help you when the time comes," Grandmama said.

Heidi ran across to her room at once and prayed earnestly to the dear God, asking Him not to forget her but to look down on her again in pity.

The last day of Grandmama's stay had come, and it was a day of sorrow to Clara and Heidi. But up to the very moment when she rode off in her carriage Grandmama succeeded in managing things so that the children scarcely felt the sadness of the day, but looked upon it rather as a time of rejoicing. But when she had finally gone, then the house seemed as empty and quiet as if the world had come to an end. Clara and Heidi sat around all the rest of the day as if lost and had no idea what was going to happen next.

The following day, when the lessons were over and it was the usual time for the children to sit together, Heidi came to Clara with her book under her arm and said—

"After this, I'm always going to read aloud to you. Would you like to have me?"

Clara said that this suited her exactly, and so Heidi began her new duties at once. But it was not long before there came a sudden end to things, because Heidi had scarcely begun to read a story which told how a grandmother was dying, when she suddenly screamed—

"Oh, now Grandmother is dead!"

She broke down and cried, for she thought everything she read about was actually taking place, and so she firmly believed that the grandmother on the mountain meadow had died. Her cries grew louder and louder.

"Now Grandmother is dead, and I can never go to see her again, and she didn't get a single other roll from me."

Clara tried as hard as she could to show Heidi that the story was not talking about the old lady on the mountain meadow, but about another grandmother entirely. But even after Clara had finally succeeded in explaining to the excited Heidi her mistake, the child could not be quieted and kept weeping harder than ever. For the awful thought had suddenly come to her that Grandmother might die anyway while she was so far away from her, and perhaps her grandfather would die, too. And then after a long time, when she should go home again, the mountain pasture would be as still as death, and she would be there all alone, and could never again see her dear ones.

In the meantime Miss Rottenmeier had come into the room and heard Clara trying to explain to Heidi her mistake. When she saw that the child still could not stop her sobbing, she went up to the two girls with evident impatience and said crossly—

"Adelheid, that's enough of your silly screaming! I want to tell you something. If ever again while reading your stories you give way to such a fit of crying, I'll take your book and never hand it back to you."

That worked. Heidi grew pale with fear. The book was her dearest possession. She dried her tears in great hurry and choked down her sobs as hard as she could, and did not utter another peep. The housekeeper's threat had its effect. Heidi never wept again, no matter what she read. Sometimes she had to try so hard to conquer her sobs and not cry out that Clara would say to her in great surprise—

"Why, Heidi, you're making the most awful faces I ever saw!"

But Heidi's faces did not make any noise and therefore did not disturb Lady Rottenmeier. And after Heidi had got the best of her dreadful fit of grief, everything would go on as before and her grief would soon be forgotten.

With it all, however, Heidi so lost her appetite and looked so thin and pale that Sebastian could hardly bear to look on in silence and see how the child at dinner let the nicest dishes pass by untouched. So, when he passed her a dish, he would often whisper encouragingly to her—

"Take some of this, little Mamsell, it is excellent. Oh, not such a small helping! Take a large spoonful of it and then another one."

Much similar fatherly advice he gave her. But it did no good. She no longer ate much of anything, and when at night she lay on her pillow, like a flash everything at home came to her eyes. She would then be so homesick that she wept on her pillow, but quite softly, so that it would disturb no one.

In this way a long time passed by. Heidi herself
never had an idea whether it was summer or winter, for
the walls that she saw from the windows of the Sesemann
house never seemed to change. She went out of doors only
when Clara was feeling well and could be taken for a
drive in the carriage. And this was always a short drive,
because Clara was not strong enough to go very far. So
they seldom got beyond the paved streets and the walls
of the town, but usually turned around and kept driving
through the broad, beautiful city streets, where there were
to be seen plenty of houses and people, but no grass and
flowers, no fir trees, and no mountains. Heidi's longing
for the lovely natural objects she had been used to grew
greater every day. If some chance word brought up the
memory of one of these things, it was all Heidi could do
to bear the pain which came to her, and she had to struggle
with all her might not to show her unhappiness.

So autumn and winter passed by, and once again the
sun was shining so glaringly on the white walls of the
houses across from her that Heidi guessed the time was
drawing near when Peter drove the goats up to the mountain pasture. The rockroses would be again gleaming
in the sunlight, and every evening the mountains round
about would stand in flames.

Poor Heidi! She would sit down in a far corner of
her lonely room and hold both hands to her eyes so she
could not see the sunshine on the wall over across from
her. And thus she would sit without moving, silently
fighting down her burning homesickness, until Clara called
for her again.

CHAPTER XII

THE SESEMANN HOUSE IS HAUNTED

For some days Miss Rottenmeier had been wandering around the house, for the most part silently rapt in thought.

Whenever, along about twilight, she walked from one room to another or down the long hall, she would often look about her, into the corners, or steal a quick glance behind her now and then, as if she thought someone might be following her on tiptoe to pull unseen at her skirt. But when she was alone she went only into the lighted living rooms.

Now, sometimes at dusk, she had things to attend to on the upper floor where the beautifully furnished guest rooms were located. Or she would have an errand, perhaps, downstairs in the great mysterious reception hall, in which every footstep echoed back from afar, and the old councillors, with their big white ruff collars, looked down from their frames with so stern and unchanging a gaze. At such a time Miss Rottenmeier would regularly ring for Tinette and tell the maid she must come along, pretending there might be some bit of furniture to be carried up or down.

Strangely enough, Tinette did just the same thing. If she had any work to do upstairs or down she would call for Sebastian and tell him to go with her, for she might have something to shift about which she could not manage alone.

What was even more funny, Sebastian himself went through exactly the same performance. If he was sent to one of the more distant rooms, he fetched Johann and made him go along for fear he alone would not be strong enough to carry what was needed.

And each one of them was always glad to answer the other's call, although there never was anything really to be carried, and each might just as well have gone alone. But it looked as if the companion always figured that he might soon have need of the other for a similar service. And while these strange doings were going on upstairs, down in her kitchen the cook, who had been with Mr. Sesemann for many years, would stand among her pots and pans, shake her head, and sigh—

"That I should live to see this day!"

For a long time there had been something strange going on in the Sesemann house. Each morning when the servants came downstairs, they found the front door open, and yet far and near there was no one to be seen who could be blamed for the fact. The first days that this happened, all the rooms and closets of the house were eagerly searched to discover what might have been stolen. For it was thought a thief might have hidden himself in the house and escaped with his booty later in the night. But this was evidently not the state of the case, for not a single thing in the whole house was missing.

At night the door was now not only double locked, but the wooden bar was also placed across it. It made no difference. In the morning the door stood wide open. No matter how early in the morning the servants in their excitement might come trooping down, there was the door ajar. And yet there was the whole neighborhood still sunk in deep sleep, and the windows and doors of all the other houses were still tightly bolted.

At last Johann and Sebastian got up their courage and prepared to spend the night below in the room that opened off the great hall, there to await whatever might happen.

Lady Rottenmeier hunted out several of Mr. Sesemann's firearms and gave Sebastian a large bottle of brandy, so that they might feel strong enough to put up a brave fight with the robber, if it should be necessary.

The two servants took their places on the appointed evening and at once began to drink a little brandy for the sake of their strength. This made them first talkative and afterward very sleepy, whereupon they both leaned back in their chairs and dozed. When the old clock in the tower across the way struck midnight, Sebastian gathered himself together and called out to his comrade. But Johann was not easily wakened. Every time Sebastian called him he would turn his head from one side of the chair back to the other and pass off to sleep again.

Sebastian, however, now began to listen eagerly, for he was by this time as wide awake as he could be. It was as still as death about him; there was not a single sound to be heard even from the street. You may believe that Sebastian did not go to sleep again, because there was a queer feeling in the deep silence about him, and it was in low tones that he kept calling to Johann, and he shook him a little from time to time. Finally, when it struck one o'clock up above there, Johann woke up and came to realize clearly why he was sitting up in a chair and not lying safe in his bed. Suddenly he started up quite bravely and cried out—

"Well, Sebastian, we must have a look out in the corridor and see how things are. Don't be afraid. You just follow me."

The door to the hall was slightly ajar. Johann threw it wide open and left the room. At the same moment a strong gust of air from the open entrance door blew in and put out the candle that Johann was holding in his hand.

The servant started back and almost upset Sebastian, who was standing right behind him. Then he dragged his companion back into the room that they had just left, slammed the door shut, and in great haste turned the key in the lock as far as it would go. Then he got out his matches and lighted his candle again. Sebastian did not know just what had happened because, standing behind Johann's broad back, he had not felt the draught of air so plainly. But as soon as he could see Johann's face in the light, he uttered a frightened cry. Johann was as white as chalk, and trembling like a leaf.

"What's wrong? Tell me, what was that outside?" Sebastian asked anxiously.

"The door was standing wide open," Johann panted, "and on the steps there was a white figure. Look, Sebastian—right up the steps like that—swis-s-sh—and vanished into thin air!"

Cold shivers ran down the length of Sebastian's back.

Then the two servants sat down as close to each other as they could, and they didn't move a muscle until bright

daylight had come and people were again stirring about
out on the street. Then together they left the room, closed
the front door, which was still standing wide open, and
went upstairs to report to Miss Rottenmeier what had
happened.

Early as the hour was, they found this lady all ready
to receive them, because she had not slept a wink for
thinking of what might be going on downstairs. The
moment she learned what had happened, she sat down and
wrote a letter to Mr. Sesemann, one such as he had never
received before and probably never would again. She
began it by saying that she was so afraid she could
not move her fingers. She asked Mr. Sesemann to pack
his belongings without a moment's delay and come straight
home, for the most unheard-of things were happening
there. Then she told just what had occurred—the front
door was open regularly every morning, everyone in the
house was in danger of his life with the door ajar the
whole night through, and what the terrible results of this
strange situation might be, none could say.

Now, Mr. Sesemann answered by return mail that
it was impossible for him to close up his business so suddenly and come home. The ghost story surprised him
greatly, but he hoped it would be a thing of the past
before his letter was received. Meanwhile, if the ghost
refused to be laid, Miss Rottenmeier would do well to
write Mrs. Sesemann and ask her if she would not come
to Frankfort to their assistance. His mother would surely
get rid of the ghosts so fast that they would never again
dare disturb the quiet of his home.

Miss Rottenmeier was not the least bit pleased at the tone of this letter. She took the matter of the ghost too seriously to enjoy such teasing. She wrote at once to Mrs. Sesemann, but she got no better results here, either, for the old lady's reply contained some very plain words.

For example, she said she had no intention of making a special trip from Holstein to Frankfort just because Rottenmeier saw ghosts. What was more, a ghost had never been seen in the Sesemann house, and if such a thing was wandering there now, it couldn't possibly be anything more than a human being, and Rottenmeier should settle with it at once. If this were impossible, she might call in the night policeman to help her.

But Miss Rottenmeier had made up her mind to spend no more days of terror, and she knew how to help matters. Until this moment she had said nothing to the two children about the ghost, for she was afraid they would be so scared that they would not want to stay alone a single minute day or night, and that would cause her a great deal of extra trouble. Now, however, she went straight to the study, where the two were sitting together, and in a low tone of voice she told them about the unknown creature who walked around the house every night.

Clara, of course, cried out at once that she would not stay alone another second, that Papa must come home, that Miss Rottenmeier must move over into her room to sleep, and that Heidi must not be left alone either, or the ghost would get in and do harm to her. She wanted them all to stay in the same room and leave a light burning all night. And Tinette must sleep next door. And Sebastian

and Johann must come down, too, and spend the night in
the hall, so they could scream and scare away the ghost
if it got to coming down the steps.

Clara was terribly excited. It was all that Miss
Rottenmeier could do to quiet her. The housekeeper promised to write to her papa at once, to bring her own bed
into Clara's room, and never to leave her alone again.
Still, she said, they could not all sleep in a single room,
and if Adelheid was afraid, then Tinette must put up a
couch beside her. But Heidi was more afraid of Tinette
than she was of ghosts, because she had never even heard
of such creatures, and she said therefore that she wasn't
afraid of any ghost and would much sooner stay in her
place by herself.

No sooner was this decided than Lady Rottenmeier
ran to her writing desk and reported to Mr. Sesemann
that the strange things which were going on every night
in the house were having such an effect on the delicate
health of his daughter that no one could tell what awful
results there might be. She had known of cases where
terrible fits resulted from such conditions. His daughter
was exposed to any sort of misfortune if her state of
terror should last much longer.

This second letter stirred things up.

Two days later Mr. Sesemann stood before the door
of his house and pulled so hard on the bell that people came
running from all directions and stared at each other open-
mouthed. For they were sure that the evil spirit was now
beginning to play his wicked jokes without waiting for
night to come. From the second story Sebastian carefully

peered down through the crack in a window blind. But just then there was another ring at the bell, so full of impatience that no one could doubt any longer that it was a living hand behind the powerful jerk.

Sebastian recognized whose hand it was, ran pell-mell out of the room and down the stairs, and managed to land on his feet long enough to tear open the front door. Mr. Sesemann nodded quickly to him, but without a single word of greeting to him started upstairs for his daughter's room.

Clara welcomed her father with a cry of joy, and when he saw her looking as well and happy as usual the frown of worry left his brow and his face cleared. He heard from his daughter's own lips that she was perfectly well and just as glad as could be that he had come back to her. She even said that she was now fond of the ghost who was haunting the house, because it had made her papa run home to her.

"And how is the ghost behaving, Miss Rottenmeier?" Mr. Sesemann asked, while the corners of his mouth twitched with amusement.

"Ah, Mr. Sesemann," the housekeeper replied very seriously, "it is nothing to smile at. I doubt if Mr. Sesemann himself will laugh at it tomorrow. For something is going on in this house that points to an awful crime of the past which has long been kept secret."

"Well, I know nothing about that," Mr. Sesemann said, "but please don't begin to think badly of my poor ancestors. Call Sebastian into the dining room, won't you? I want to say a word to him in private."

Mr. Sesemann went across the hall and Sebastian made his appearance. His employer knew that Sebastian and the housekeeper were not on the best of terms. So he was suspicious.

"Come here, you rogue," he said, as he waved to the servant to enter, "and see you are quite honest with me. Haven't you yourself been playing the part of ghost a little, just to make things lively for Miss Rottenmeier, eh?"

"No, sir, on my honor, I haven't. Please believe me, sir. I haven't felt at all right about the matter, myself," Sebastian answered with evident honesty.

"Well, if that's the way you feel, I'll have to show you and that brave Johann tomorrow how a ghost looks in the daytime. Be ashamed of yourself, Sebastian! A strong young fellow like you running away from ghosts! Now, go straight to my old friend Doctor Classen. Give him my greetings and ask him to please come to the house at nine o'clock this evening, without fail. Tell him I've come home from Paris especially to consult him. Say I'm so badly off, he'll have to spend the night with me. He must arrange things so that he can. You understand, Sebastian?"

"Of course, sir. Rely upon it, sir."

Sebastian departed. Mr. Sesemann went back to his little daughter to quiet her fears about the ghost. He promised that he would clear the matter up that very day.

Promptly at nine o'clock, after the children had gone to bed and Miss Rottenmeier had retired for the night, the doctor arrived. In spite of his gray hairs, he had a very young looking face and two eyes with a friendly

twinkle in their depths.   At first he seemed to be quite
anxious.   But the moment his friend greeted him, he broke
out into a hearty laugh, clapped the pretended invalid on
the shoulder, and said—

"Well, I must say, old man, that for a sick person who
needs sitting up with, you look fairly healthy!"

"You just wait, my dear fellow," Mr. Sesemann
replied.   "The one you're sitting up for will look worse
than I do, when we've once caught him."

"So you have a sick man in the house?   And one who
has to be caught, into the bargain?"

"Worse than that, Doctor, far worse.   We have a
ghost in the house.   We're haunted."

The doctor laughed out loud.

"A lot of sympathy you have, Doctor!" Mr. Sesemann said.   "It's a pity my friend Lady Rottenmeier cannot be here to enjoy it.   She firmly believes that some old
Sesemann is wandering about because of some secret deed
of violence."

"How did she make the ghost's acquaintance, do you
suppose?" the doctor asked, still greatly amused.

Mr. Sesemann then proceeded to tell his friend about
the whole affair, how, according to the testimony of all
the people in the house, the front door swung wide every
night.   He said further that, just to be prepared for anything that might happen, he had had two loaded revolvers
put in the place where they were to watch.   For the whole
business might, of course, prove to be only a poor joke
which some one of the servants' friends was playing in
order to frighten the people in the house while the master

was away. In that case it might be a good idea to scare the ghost by shooting off a pistol. Or, on the other hand, thieves might be mixed up with the affair, who had been first passing themselves off as ghosts, so that later they would be safe from anyone's interfering with them. In that case a good weapon would not be out of place.

While Mr. Sesemann was thus explaining things to the doctor, they went downstairs to the same room in which Johann and Sebastian had sat to watch. On the table lay the two revolvers and in the center stood two brightly lighted candelabra, for the master of the house did not want to await the coming of the ghost in half darkness.

They closed the door all but the merest crack, because too much light must not shine out into the hall or the ghost might be frightened away. Then the gentlemen settled down comfortably in their arm chairs and fell to talking about all sorts of things, now and then taking a sip of the wine which Sebastian had brought for their refreshment. And so, before they realized how time was passing, the clock struck twelve.

"The ghost knows we are here and probably won't come tonight, after all," the doctor suggested.

"You just wait. They say it does not appear until one o'clock," his friend replied.

They went on with their talking. One o'clock struck. There was a deep silence all around them; the sounds of the street outside had died away. Suddenly the doctor made a warning gesture—

"Sh-h-h! Sesemann, don't you hear something?"

They both listened intently.

Softly, and yet quite distinctly in the silence, they heard the sound of the bar as it was pushed back. The key was turned twice in the lock. The door was being opened. Mr. Sesemann reached out for his revolver.

"You're not afraid, surely!" said the doctor, rising.

"You can't be too careful," Mr. Sesemann whispered. He seized a holder with three candles in his left hand and a revolver in his right. Then he followed the doctor out of the room into the hall.

The pale rays of the moon streamed in through the widely opened door and lighted up a white figure that was standing quite still on the threshold.

"Who's there?" bellowed the doctor so loudly that the sound rang down the long hall.

Both of the men started toward the figure, with lights and weapons waving. It turned on them and uttered a low cry. Heidi!

There stood Heidi, with bare feet, in her white nightdress, blinking at the bright flames of the candles and at the firearms, shaking and trembling from top to toe like a small leaf in the wind. The men looked at her in the greatest astonishment.

"I honestly believe, Sesemann, it's the little girl who carries water to you," the doctor said.

"My child, what does this mean?" Mr. Sesemann asked after a moment's pause. "What were you after? Why did you come down here?"

Pale with fright, Heidi stood before him and answered weakly, "I don't know."

Then the doctor took a hand in what was going on.

"Sesemann," he said, "this is a case for me to deal with. Go in the other room and sit down for a while in the easy chair. First of all, I'll take the child back where she belongs."

With these words he laid his revolver down on the floor, took the shivering child's hand in his, and went off upstairs with her.

"Just don't you be afraid of anything," he said kindly, as they climbed slowly up the steps, "but we must be quiet so as not to wake people. Don't you care, nothing bad has happened."

When they were in Heidi's room, the doctor set his candlestick on the table, lifted Heidi up, and put her in her bed. He covered her carefully and then he sat down in a chair by her side and waited until she was a little quieter and no longer shook so terribly. He put his hand on hers and said—

"There we are! Everything's all right again. Now suppose you tell me where you were trying to go."

"I wasn't trying to go anywhere, of course," Heidi assured him. "And I didn't go down there, either. I just found myself down there all of a sudden."

"Oh, I see. Do you know if you were having a dream that made you see and hear things just as plain as day?"

"Yes, I have a dream every night, and it's always the same one. Then I think I'm back at Grandfather's, for I hear the fir trees rustling out of doors. And I say to myself, 'Now the stars are gleaming so brightly up in the sky.' Then I run fast and open the door of the hut, and oh, it is so beautiful there! But when I wake up, I'm always back in Frankfort."

Heidi began to twist about and to swallow down the lump that somehow would rise in her throat.

"Uh-huh! And do you ever feel any pain anywhere? In your head or in your back?"

"Oh, no. There's just something that presses here all the time, sort of like a big stone."

"I see. Sort of as if you'd eaten something bad for you, and then wish you could get rid of it again."

"No, not like that. But it feels so heavy, as if you had to cry hard."

"Oh, that's the way it feels! And do you ever go and cry hard?"

"Oh, no, I'm afraid to cry. Miss Rottenmeier said I musn't."

"Then you just swallow it down again, like this, don't you? That's good! Do you like to live here in Frankfort very much?"

"Oh, yes," was the low answer. But it sounded more as if she really meant just the opposite.

"Hm! And where were you living with your grandfather?"

"Always up on the mountain meadow."

"I see. But it isn't such awfully good fun there, is it? Isn't it sometimes pretty dreary?"

"Oh my, no! You can't think how nice it is there."

Heidi could not go on. The thought of her dear mountain home, the excitement she had just passed through, the weeping she had been holding back so long—these things got too strong for her. The tears began to flow from her eyes in a perfect stream, and she broke out into loud and violent sobbing.

The doctor got up from his chair.. He laid Heidi's head gently down on its pillow and said—

"There! Now you can go ahead and cry a little. That won't hurt anybody. Then have a nice fine sleep. To-morrow everything will be all right."

Then the doctor stole from the room.

When he was down again in the room where they had kept watch, he settled into an arm chair across from his waiting friend and explained things to him. Mr. Sese-mann listened with eager attention.

"First of all," he said, "your little girl walks in her sleep. Without knowing it, she has opened your front door every night like a ghost and scared your servants within an inch of their lives. Next, the child is pining away with homesickness and has lost flesh until she is almost a skeleton. If you're not careful, she will really be one. Something must be done in a hurry. There is only one cure for her first trouble and for the bad state of her nerves—send the child back to the pure air of her moun-tain home. There is only one cure for her second trouble, and that is to do the very same thing. So you have my prescription—the child goes home tomorrow."

Mr. Sesemann jumped from his chair. He walked up and down the room in the greatest excitement. Finally he broke out—

"Nonsense! Walking in her sleep? Sick? Longing to be back home? Getting to be a skeleton? And all this in my house! Without anybody's noticing it or suspecting it in the least! The child came to my house happy and healthy, Doctor. Do you think I'm going to send her back to her grandfather wretched and thin as a rail? No, Doctor, that's too much to expect. I can't do it and I never shall. You take the child in hand, treat her, do anything you want, but make her healthy and sound for me again. Then I'll send her home if that's what she wants. But first I must have your help."

"Sesemann," the doctor answered earnestly, "just remember what you are doing! Her sickness is not one that can be cured with powders and pills. The child is not very strong, but if you send her back at once to the bracing mountain air she is used to, she probably will get entirely well. But even suppose she doesn't, you don't want to send her home to her grandfather too late to be cured, do you? Or perhaps never send her home at all?"

Mr. Sesemann stood still, terrified.

"Why, if that's what you think, Doctor, then there's only one thing to do. And we must get right to work."

With these words Mr. Sesemann put his arm in that of his friend and walked up and down with him while they talked the matter over further. Then the doctor started for home, because their talk had lasted a good while. The bright morning light streamed in through the front door, which this time was opened by the master of the house.

CHAPTER XIII

A JOURNEY BACK TO THE MOUNTAIN MEADOW

Mr. Sesemann climbed the stairs in much excitement and went straight toward Lady Rottenmeier's bedroom. His knock on the door of this apartment was so unusually loud that the housekeeper started out of her sleep with a cry of fear. She heard the master's voice outside saying—

"Please come to the dining room as fast as you can. We have to get things ready at once for a journey."

Miss Rottenmeier looked at her clock. It was half-past four in the morning. She had never in all her life got up so early. What on earth could have happened? She was so curious and eager that she did everything wrong and could hardly get dressed. She kept hunting around the room for clothes that she had already put on.

In the meantime Mr. Sesemann went down the hall and rang each one of the bells that was used for calling the servants. And in each room that had a bell a terrified form sprang out of bed and started to put on his clothes wrong side before, because, one and all, they immediately thought the ghost had somehow got hold of the master of the house, and this was his summons for help.

So, one by one, they came stealing down, each one, if possible, looking worse than the one before him. And they drew up in surprise before the master of the house, for Mr. Sesemann was walking up and down the room

looking fresh and cheerful, and not in the least as if he
had been scared by a ghost.

Johann was at once sent to harness the horses to the
carriage, so it might be ready when wanted. Tinette was
ordered to waken Heidi without delay and to dress her
for a journey. Sebastian was told to run to the house
where Heidi's aunt worked and to bring her back with him.

Meanwhile Miss Rottenmeier had finally finished dressing. Her clothes were all on straight enough, except for
her boudoir cap, which was on wrong side before, so that
from a distance it looked as if her face was on backward.
Mr. Sesemann realized that her odd appearance was due
to the fact that she had risen so early, and he therefore
went straight to the business before them. He explained
to the surprised lady that she was to get down a trunk at
once and pack in it all the things that belonged to the Swiss
child. He spoke of Heidi usually in this way, because her
name still seemed somewhat strange to him. He also told
the housekeeper to put in a good many of Clara's clothes,
so the child might have a proper outfit to take home with
her. But everything must be done quickly and without
waiting to decide one way or the other.

Miss Rottenmeier stood as if rooted to the spot, staring
at Mr. Sesemann in great surprise. She had thought he was
going to tell her some terrible story about the ghost he had
met the night before, and now that it was bright daylight
she would have listened gladly. Instead of which, he was
now giving her these everyday orders. She was not quick
enough to hide her disappointment. Without a word she
kept standing there, waiting for what he would say next.

But Mr. Sesemann had no intention of clearing up matters. He let the lady stand where she was and went to his daughter's room. Just as he had feared, the unusual stir had awakened Clara, and she was listening to all the sounds about her and wondering what was going on.

Her father sat down beside her bed and told her the whole history of the ghost affair. He said that the doctor thought Heidi was in very bad shape, and unless something was done about it she might start wandering in her sleep farther and farther away and even climb out on the roof, which would be a very dangerous thing. So he had made up his mind to send Heidi home on the spot, because he was afraid to run such a risk. And Clara must not feel bad at losing Heidi, for she could see that it was the only thing left for Papa to do.

Clara was much surprised at this news and at first wanted to find some way of keeping Heidi with her, but all in vain. Father remained firm in his decision, and yet he promised to go to Switzerland with Clara the following year if she would be sensible now and not start to fret.

So Clara gave in cheerfully to what could not be helped, but begged as a reward for being good that Heidi's trunk might be brought into her room and packed there so that she could put in it whatever she took a fancy to. Her papa granted her this favor very willingly, and, besides, he encouraged Clara to fit out Heidi with a fine stock of clothes.

It was then that Aunt Dete arrived and stood in the reception hall with great expectations, for it must have taken something quite out of the usual run to make her

coming at such a strange hour necessary. Mr. Sesemann
went out to see her and told her how things stood with
Heidi. He asked her if she would take the child home
with her at once that very day.

The aunt looked very much disappointed. She had
expected anything but that.

She still had a very clear memory of the parting words
that Nuncle had hurled after her, "Never come into my
sight again!" And to bring him the child he had not
wanted, then to take her away again, and then to fetch
her back—no, that did not seem to be exactly a good
stroke of business for her.

So, without thinking the matter over at any length,
she said that unfortunately it would be impossible for her
to take such a trip that day. And the day after it would
be even more out of the question because of all the things
she simply must do then. And afterward, she doubted
if she could go any better.

Mr. Sesemann saw through these excuses and sent
Aunt Dete away without bothering about her further. He
then sent for Sebastian and informed him that he must
get ready to make the trip right away. He would travel
with the child that day as far as Basel; the next day they
would reach her home. Then he could start back at once.
He would have no explanations to offer, for a letter to
Heidi's grandfather would make everything clear to him.

"But now, Sebastian," Mr. Sesemann said in conclu-
sion, "there is one thing I want you to do especially, and
you just see that you don't forget about it! I know the
hotel in Basel, the name of which I've written down on

this business card for you. When they see the card, they will show you a good room for the child. As to your own self, you know what to do. Go first thing into Heidi's room and nail every window so tightly shut that it can't be opened except by the greatest force. And after the child is once in bed, then go and lock her door on the outside, for the youngster wanders around in her sleep and might run into any sort of danger, in a strange place, if she should, for instance, leave her room and try to open the front door. Are you sure you understand?"

"A-ha! So that's what it was? That's the way of it?" Sebastian gasped, in the greatest surprise. For he had that moment seen a great light about the ghost business.

"Yes, that is exactly what was up. And you are a fraidy-cat, and you can tell Johann from me that he is another just like you. In fact, you are a silly crowd of people."

With these words Mr. Sesemann went to his room and sat down to write a letter to Meadow Nuncle.

As for Sebastian, he felt terribly put out. He stood in the middle of the room and kept repeating to to himself over and over——

"If I only hadn't let that coward Johann jerk me back into the room where we had been watching! If I had only gone after that little white form myself! And I'll bet I would have done it, too!"

The butler quite convinced himself of his own bravery. For at this moment the clear sunshine was brightly lighting up every corner of the usually dim apartment.

Meanwhile Heidi, with never a thought of what was going to happen, stood waiting in her best Sunday dress. For Tinette had merely shaken her out of her sleep, taken her clothes from the closet, and helped her to dress, without saying a word. She never talked with Heidi, whom she thought uncitified and beneath her notice.

With his letter in his hand Mr. Sesemann walked into the dining room, where breakfast was awaiting him, and called—

"Where is the child?"

Heidi was sent for. When she went up to the master of the house to wish him good morning, he looked into her face questioningly and asked—

"Well, what have you to say to all this, my dear?"

Heidi gazed up at him in astonishment.

"I suppose you don't know anything about it even now," Mr. Sesemann said with a laugh. "Well, you are going home today, and almost right away."

"Home?" Heidi repeated after him dully, and grew as white as snow. For a moment she could scarcely breathe, her heart was beating so violently at the statement.

"Would you like to hear some more about it?" Mr. Sesemann asked, smiling kindly.

"Oh, yes, indeed I should," Heidi finally managed to gasp, and her cheeks had got dark red.

"Good! Then you shall hear," her companion said encouragingly. He seated himself and motioned to Heidi to do likewise. "But first you must eat a hearty breakfast, and then into the carriage and off with you!"

Hard as she tried, Heidi could not swallow a mouthful, although she obediently tried to force herself to do it. She was so wrought up that she did not know whether she was awake or dreaming. She feared she would suddenly wake up and find herself standing in her nightgown at the entrance door.

"Sebastian must remember to take plenty of provisions," Mr. Sesemann called to the housekeeper, who was just coming into the room. "The child can't eat now, nor would one expect her to."

Then he turned to Heidi and said kindly—

"Why don't you run in to see Clara and wait there until the carriage comes?"

That was just what Heidi wished for, and she ran across the hall to Clara. In the middle of her friend's room there was an enormous trunk, the top of which still stood wide open.

"O Heidi, come here," Clara called to her, "come see what I have packed for you. Don't you like it?"

And she told off on her fingers a whole list of things— dresses and aprons, towels and sewing material. "Look here, Heidi!" Clara cried, and held a basket aloft in triumph. Heidi peered into it and then had to jump around for joy, because in the basket there was a round dozen of pretty white rolls, all for Grandmother.

So happy were the children that they both quite forgot that the moment of their parting was at hand. And when the call did suddenly come, "The carriage is waiting!" there was no time left to be sad in.

Heidi flew to her room. The pretty book Grandma

had given her must be lying there still. No one could
have packed it, for it lay under the pillow, because Heidi
could not bear to be separated from it day or night. She
found the book and laid it in the basket on top of the rolls.
Then she opened her bureau to see if there was any other
nice thing that had also not been packed. And there, sure
enough, lay the old red neckerchief. Miss Rottenmeier
had thought it too poor a thing to be worth packing. Heidi
wrapped it around some other object and put it on the
very top of the basket, so that the red package became
very noticeable. Then she set her fine new hat on her
head and left the room.

The children had to say good-by quickly, for Mr.
Sesemann was waiting to take Heidi down to the carriage.
Miss Rottenmeier stood at the head of the stairs to bid
Heidi farewell. As she caught sight of the strange little
red bundle, she snatched it from the basket and threw it to
the floor.

"No, Adelheid," she said reprovingly, "you can't leave
this house looking like that. You don't need to take any
such stuff with you, anyway. And now good-by!"

After this reproof Heidi did not dare pick her bundle
up again, but she looked at the master of the house with
an imploring glance, as if she were being robbed of her
greatest treasure.

"Oh, no, no," Mr. Sesemann said in a very decided
tone of voice. "Heidi is going to take home with her
just whatever she wants to. Even if it turns out to
be kittens or turtles, we won't bother about it, Miss
Rottenmeier."

Heidi quickly picked her bundle up from the floor, and her eyes shone with thankfulness and joy.

When she had got to the carriage, Mr. Sesemann took her hand in his and told her very nicely she must not forget him and his daughter Clara. He gave her his best wishes for a pleasant journey, and in her turn Heidi thanked him with her whole heart for the kindness he had shown her. Her final message was—

"And I leave a thousand greetings for the doctor, and many, many thanks."

For she had not forgotten that he had told her the night before, "Tomorrow everything's going to be all right." Now it had all come true, and Heidi thought he had brought it about.

Then the child was lifted into the carriage, and the basket and the bag of provisions and Sebastian followed. Mr. Sesemann again called to her, "Pleasant journey!" and the carriage rolled away.

Soon afterward Heidi was sitting in the train and holding the basket firmly in her lap. She would not let it out of her hands for a single minute, because Grandmother's precious rolls were inside it. She had to guard them carefully and take a look at them from time to time, just for fun.

For several hours Heidi sat as still as a mouse. She was just beginning to understand that she was really on her way home to Grandfather on the mountain meadow, to Grandmother, and to Goat Peter. Happy scenes from the past came to her mind, one after the other, and she dreamed of all the things she was again going to see and wondered how everything would look. New thoughts flooded in upon her, and suddenly she grew a little afraid.

"Sebastian, didn't Grandmother on the mountain meadow really die, after all?" she asked.

"Oh, no," he said, consolingly, "we'll hope she didn't. She will be alive all right."

Then Heidi again was buried in her thoughts. But every once in a while she would take a peek into the basket, for her dearest wish in life had now come to be to lay all the rolls on Grandmother's table. After some time she asked again—

"Sebastian, don't you suppose that we can be certain sure that Grandmother's still alive?"

"Why, of course we can!" her companion answered, half asleep. "She's alive, fast enough. Don't see why she shouldn't be, do you?"

After awhile Heidi's eyes closed, too. Because of the restless night and her early rising, she was so dead with sleep that she did not wake up until Sebastian gave her arm a good shaking and called out to her—

"Wake up in a hurry, Heidi! Get out right away, we've come to Basel!"

Next morning their long journey continued for many hours. In the child's lap again rested the basket; which she would on no condition let Sebastian take care of. But today she did not speak a single word, because each new hour that came made her eagerness greater. She could hardly wait. And then suddenly, just when she least expected it, the loud call was heard—

"All out for Mayenfeld!"

Heidi jumped up from her seat, and so did Sebastian, who was as surprised as she was. In a moment they found themselves out on the platform with the trunk, and the train was whistling farther on up in the valley.

Sebastian cast a longing look after the departing train, for he much preferred traveling so safely and easily to starting out on a foot tour which would end in a stiff bit of mountain climbing. Besides, he feared that the climb would be hard and dangerous in this land where everything seemed to him to be still in a half-wild condition. So he looked around for someone who would show him the safest way to The Hamlet.

Not far from the railway station a small rack wagon was standing, with a lean horse attached to it. A broadshouldered man was occupied in loading it with several large sacks of flour that had been brought up by the train. Sebastian hailed him and asked which was the safest way to Dörfli.

"All roads are safe hereabouts," was the short answer.

But Sebastian persisted in asking him the best way to take, so as not to fall over the cliffs, and how one could have a trunk sent up to this particular place called The Hamlet. The man looked at the trunk and measured its weight with his eyes. Then he said that if it was not too heavy he himself could take it on his wagon, as he was bound for Dörfli. After some little further talk the two men at last agreed that the child and the trunk should be taken along in the rack wagon, and then Heidi could be sent from Dörfli up to the mountain meadow with some one later in the evening.

"I can go by myself. I know the way from The Hamlet up to the mountain meadow," Heidi said at this point, for she had been listening eagerly while the two men bargained.

A heavy load was taken from Sebastian's heart when he saw himself freed from the necessity of clambering up the mountain. He beckoned to Heidi secretly to come to one side with him, and he handed her a thick round bundle and a letter for her grandfather. The round bundle, he explained, was a gift from Mr. Sesemann. She must hide it in the bottom of the basket away down under the bread rolls. And she must take good care to see it was not lost, or Mr. Sesemann would be awfully angry and would never get over it his whole life long. Little Mamsell would do well to remember this.

"Oh, I won't lose it," Heidi said. And she placed the thick roll and the letter in the lower part of the basket.

The trunk was then set on the wagon, and Sebastian lifted the child and her precious burden up to the high seat beside the driver. The servant shook hands with her, said good-by, and once more urged her, with all sorts of signs, to keep careful watch of the contents of her basket. For the driver was close by them, and Sebastian was by no means easy in his mind, because he knew that he himself should have gone with Heidi to the end of her journey. At last the driver swung himself up on the seat next to Heidi, and the wagon rolled off toward the mountains, while Sebastian, happy to escape the dreaded climb, sat down beside the little railway station to wait for the return train.

The man on the wagon was the baker of Dörfli, who was driving home with his sacks of flour. He had never seen Heidi before, but, like everyone else in The Hamlet, he knew about the child that had been brought to Meadow Nuncle. What is more, he had known Heidi's father and mother, and so of course he guessed at once that she was the girl people talked about so much. He could not help being surprised that the child was coming back home so soon, and while they were driving along he began to talk with Heidi—

"I suppose you must be the child who lived up at Meadow Nuncle's, at your grandfather's."

"Yes."

"Did they treat you so badly in Frankfort that you came home before you expected to? And all that distance!"

"No, I got along fine. Nobody could be treated better than I was in Frankfort."

"Why are you running right home, then?"

"Just because Mr. Sesemann said I could, or I shouldn't have gone away at all."

"Bah! Why didn't you want to stay down there anyway, even if they did let you go?"

"Because I'd a thousand times rather go home to Grandfather up on the mountain meadow than do anything else in the world."

"I guess you'll think differently when you're once up there again," the baker said with a grunt. And he said to himself, "But I wonder if she knows how bad it is."

Then he began to whistle a tune and had nothing more to say.

Heidi looked around her, and she was so excited that she fairly trembled. She recognized the trees by the roadside, and up above loomed the sharp peaks of the high Falkniss Mountain, looking down at her in greeting like good old friends. Heidi waved her hand to them joyously. Every step the horse took, Heidi's excitement grew more intense, and she almost thought she would have to jump down from the wagon and run with might and main until she reached the very top of Falkniss.

But she sat still and made no move, although her brain whirled on and on until she was dizzy. The clock struck five just as they drove into The Hamlet. In no time at all a troop of women and children crowded around the wagon, and a couple of men from neighboring houses came out to join the company. For the sight of a child and a trunk on the baker's wagon had attracted the attention of all the people, and everyone wanted to know where they had come from, where they were going, and to whom they belonged.

Hardly had the baker lifted Heidi to the ground when she said to him quickly—

"Thank you. Grandfather will be down for the trunk soon."

And she would have run away. But she was held in on every side by the crowd. There was a chorus of voices, all talking at once, and each asking a different question. Heidi forced her way through the throng with such a look of anxiety on her face that they made room for her to pass. And they said to each other—

"You see how frightened she is, don't you? Well, she has good reason to be."

Then they started to tell one another how, during the past year, Meadow Nuncle had been getting worse than ever. He would no longer exchange a word with anyone, and if you happened to get in his way, he glared at you as if he wanted to kill you. And if the child only had the sense that she was born with, she wouldn't be running up there to the old dragon's nest.

But at last the baker managed to get a word in edge-wise. He said he knew more about it than all the rest of them put together. And then, with a great air of secrecy, he told how a gentleman had brought the child as far as Mayenfeld. There he had said good-by to the girl in the friendliest sort of way. Then, without trying to beat down the price the baker asked for her fare, the gentleman had paid it, and had added a good tip, too. And besides, he knew for sure that the child had been well cared for in Frankfort and herself had wanted to come back to her grandfather.

The baker's news caused much amazement, and his story was spread like lightning through Dörfli. And that evening there was not a cottage in all The Hamlet where they did not gossip about the child who wanted to give up a life of ease and plenty to return to her grandfather.

Heidi ran up the mountain from The Hamlet as fast as ever she could, stopping a moment every now and then to catch her breath. The basket on her arm was fairly heavy for her to carry, and besides, the higher she went, the steeper grew the trail. There was room for but a single thought in Heidi's heart—

"Will Grandmother still be sitting at her place by the

spinning wheel in the corner? Did she die while I was gone so long?"

Now Heidi caught sight of the hut up in the hollow by the mountain meadow, and her heart began to pound. She ran still faster, and her heart began to beat more loudly. At last she was there! She could scarcely open the door, she was trembling so, but finally she managed to lift the latch. She sprang into the middle of the little living room and stood there, all out of breath and unable to utter a sound.

"Heavens above!" a voice cried from the corner. "That's the way our Heidi used to run in. Oh, if she could only be with me once more before I die! Who is it?"

"Here I am, Grandmother. It's really me," Heidi called.

She rushed over to the old lady in the corner and plumped down on her knees beside her. She seized Grandmother's arm and her hands, pressed tightly against her, and was speechless, she was so happy. At first Grandmother herself was so surprised that she also could find nothing to say, but then she began to stroke Heidi's curly hair and to say over and over again—

"Yes, yes, that's her hair, and that's her voice. I thank Thee, dear God, that Thou hast let me live to see this day!"

And two great tears of joy fell from the old blind eyes down on Heidi's hand.

"Is it really you, dear? Have you come back to me at last?"

"Oh, surely it's me Grandmother," Heidi said gently. "But don't you cry, for I'm back here to stay and am coming to see you every day and will never leave you again. And you won't need to eat hard bread for many a day, either. See, Grandmother, what I brought you!"

And Heidi now drew one roll after another out of her basket until she had heaped all twelve of them on Grandmother's lap.

"O my dear child, what is this blessed gift you have brought me?" the old lady cried in her astonishment, for it seemed as if the supply of rolls would never end, they followed one another so endlessly. "But the greatest blessing of all is just you, child!"

Then she ran her fingers again through Heidi's curls and stroked the hot cheeks and said—

"Say just one more word, dear. Anything, so I can hear the sound of your voice."

Then it was that Heidi told Grandmother how fearfully afraid she had been that she might die when her little child was far away. Then she could not have brought her the promised white rolls and could never have come to see her again.

Peter's mother came in while they were talking together. She stopped short and stared, as if she could not trust her eyes. Then she cried—

"As I live, it's Heidi! But how can that ever be?"

Heidi got up from her knees and shook hands with her, and Brigitte could not get over her surprise at Heidi's changed appearance. She walked around the child once or twice and said—

"Grandmother, if you could only see what a lovely dress the child has on and how fine she looks, you would hardly recognize her.   And the little hat trimmed with feathers there on the table, is that yours, too?   Do put it on, so I can see if it's becoming."

"No, I don't want to," said Heidi firmly.   "You can have it if you'll take it.   I don't need it any longer.   I have another one I like better."

Then Heidi unwrapped her small red bundle and took out her old hat, which had become still more cracked during her journey from Frankfort than it was before.   But that did not bother Heidi any.   For she had never forgotten how, when she was leaving Grandfather, he had shouted after her that he didn't ever want to see her in a hat trimmed with feathers.   And that was the reason Heidi had saved her old hat so carefully, because she was always dreaming of the time when she would be going back to him.

Brigitte told her not to be so silly.   If she did not want to wear the hat, it was such a splendid one that she could sell it perhaps to the daughter of the Dörfli school teacher. She could get a lot of money for it.

But Heidi stuck stubbornly to her decision.   When Brigitte was not looking, she put the hat quietly in the corner behind Grandmother, where it was out of sight. Then she slipped quickly out of her pretty dress, and she wound the red neckerchief over her underwaist, in which she was now standing with bare arms.   She seized Grandmother's hand and said—

"Now I must run home to Grandfather, but I'll come to see you again tomorrow.   Good night, Grandmother!"

"Yes, do come again, Heidi, by all means! Until to-morrow, then!" said the grandmother. And she squeezed the child's hand in both of hers and could hardly let her go.

"But why did you take off your pretty dress?" Brigitte asked.

"Because I'd rather go to Grandfather this way, or perhaps he would not know me. You hardly did."

Brigitte followed Heidi out of the door and said a few words secretly to her—

"You could have kept on the dress, and he would have known you fast enough. But in other ways you must be careful, for Peterli says Meadow Nuncle is always in a bad temper now and won't say a word to anyone."

Heidi said good night and climbed up the mountain slope, carrying her basket on her arm. The evening sun shone all round about on the green mountain pasture, and at this moment the vast snow field of Cäsaplana came into view and shone afar.

Every other step or so Heidi had to stand still and look over her shoulder, for the high mountains were behind her as she struggled on up the trail. Suddenly a red glow shone on the grass at her feet. She turned around, and oh! she had forgotten that the glory of the world was so great. It had not been like this even in all her dreams. The horned cliffs of Falkniss Mountain flamed up to the sky, the broad snow field was all alight, pink clouds were moving slowly across a blue heaven. The grass about her on the meadow was melted gold, the light twinkled and shone from the crags, and below her the valley swam in a sea of golden mist.

Heidi stood in the midst of this splendor, and bright tears of joy streamed down her cheeks. She folded her hands and gazed up at the sky above her and gave thanks aloud to dear God that He had brought her back home again. She thanked Him that all His works were so beautiful, much more beautiful than she had thought, and that they were once more hers to enjoy. And Heidi found herself so fortunate and so rich in this great glory that was all around her, she could hardly find the right words with which to thank her God.

Heidi could not tear herself away from the spot until the light around her began to pale. But then she ran up the mountain so fast that it was not long before she saw ahead of her the tops of the fir trees above the roof. A moment later the roof itself hove into sight, and then the cottage, and finally the figure of Grandfather as he sat on the bench by the hut and smoked his pipe. And above the whole scene the tops of the old fir trees rocked and rustled in the evening breeze.

Then Heidi ran all the faster. And before Meadow Nuncle could see what was coming, the child flew straight up to him, threw down her basket, and clasped her arms tightly about him. She was so excited at seeing him again that she kept repeating the one word over and over—

"Grandfather, Grandfather, Grandfather!"

Nor did the old gentleman have anything to say. His eyes grew wet for the first time in many years, and he had to brush his hand across them. Then he loosened Heidi's arms from his neck, set the child upon his knees, and studied her closely for a moment.

"So you've come home again, Heidi," he said, after a pause. "How does that happen? You don't look especially proud and haughty. Did they send you away?"

"Oh, no, Grandfather," Heidi assured him, eagerly, "you musn't think that. They were all so good to me—Clara, and Grandmama, and Mr. Sesemann. But you see, Grandfather, I just couldn't stand it any longer not to come back to see you. But I never said anything about it, of course, for that would have been naughty. And then one morning, all of a sudden, Mr. Sesemann sent for me very early, but I do really believe the doctor made him do it—but I suppose that is all written down in the letter—"

Heidi wriggled down from Grandfather's knees, took her letter and the rolled package from her basket, and handed him both of them.

"This belongs to you," the old gentleman said, and laid the roll of money down beside her on the bench. Then he took the letter and read it through. Without a word he thrust it into his pocket.

"Do you think you could still drink a little milk with me, Heidi?" he then asked, taking the child's hand to go into the hut with her. "But bring your money along. You can buy yourself a whole bed with that, and clothes enough to last you for several years."

"I don't need the money for anything, Grandfather," Heidi said. "I have a good bed already, and Clara packed so many clothes for me, I surely won't need any more, ever."

"Take it, just the same. And put it in your closet, for the time will come when you need it."

Heidi obeyed him and hopped along after him into the cottage. She was overjoyed to see everything again, she ran into the corners, she climbed up the ladder. But in the loft she stopped suddenly and called down to him—

"O Grandfather, I've lost my bed!"

"It will be back again soon," he called to her from below. "We didn't know you were coming home. Here's your milk now."

Heidi climbed down and sat in her old place on the high stool. She seized her bowl and drank the milk so eagerly that you would think she had never had anything so delicious in all her life. When she finally set down her bowl with a deep breath, she said—

"Nothing in the world is half so good as our milk, Grandfather!"

At that moment a shrill whistle sounded outside. Heidi shot out of the door like a flash of light.

There came the whole troop of goats, skipping, dancing, and jumping down from above, and Peter himself in the midst of them. When he saw Heidi he stood stock still, as if he had suddenly taken root in the ground, and stared at her in silence.

"Good evening, Peter," Heidi called, and fairly rushed in among the goats. "O Bärli dear, and Schwänli, do you still remember me?"

And it truly seemed as if the goats knew her voice, for they rubbed their heads against the child and began to bleat aloud for joy. Heidi called them all by name, one after the other, and they ran around in wild confusion and crowded upon her. The impatient Goldfinch sprang over the backs of two other goats to reach her without delay. And even Snowhopper, with an unexpected lowering of his head, butted aside Big Turk, who in great surprise at such treatment could only raise his bearded head high into the air to show who he was.

Heidi was almost beside herself with joy to have her old companions back. She hugged delicate little Schneehöppli again and again, stroked Distelfink, and was pushed and thrust one way and another by the affectionate goats, until she finally came up to Peter, who had not moved from where he stood.

"Come down here, Peter, and wish me good evening," Heidi now called to him.

"So you've come back again!" he exclaimed, in much surprise. And then he came forward and took Heidi's hand, which she had been holding out to him this long time, and he asked, as he always did when they were coming home in the evening—

"You're going to be with me tomorrow?"

"No, not tomorrow, but the next day, perhaps. Tomorrow I have to go to Grandmother's."

"It's fine to have you back again," Peter said, and his face got all twisted up in a grin of huge delight. Then he prepared to start on with the goats.

But never before had he had such trouble with them. First it was all he could do, coaxing and threatening, to gather the goats around him. And then, when Heidi had started off, with one arm about Schwänli's neck and the other about Bärli's, the whole herd suddenly wheeled and ran after the three. Heidi had to take her two goats into the shed and close the door, or Peter never would have managed to get his flock headed down the mountain.

When the child came back into the cottage, she found her bed already made up. It was high and sweet-smelling, for the hay had been freshly brought in and Grandfather had spread the clean linen sheets over it very carefully.

Heidi lay down on it with real pleasure and had the best night's sleep that she had had for a whole year. During the night Grandfather must have got up at least ten times to climb into the loft, and to listen carefully to Heidi's breathing, so he might be sure she was having a good rest. He examined the window where the moon used to shine in on Heidi's couch, to see if the hay was still where he had stuffed it, because from now on he intended to keep the moonlight out, so as not to allow it to waken the child with its brightness.

Heidi slept on without waking, and she no longer wandered about in her sleep. Her great longing for home had been stilled. She had again seen all the mountains and cliffs caught in the evening glow. She had once more listened to the deep roaring of the fir trees and was at home on the mountain meadow.

CHAPTER XIV

SUNDAY, WHEN THE CHURCH BELLS RING

Heidi stood beneath the swaying boughs of the fir trees and waited for her grandfather, who was going along to get the trunk up from The Hamlet while she made a call on Grandmother. The child was all eagerness to see Grandmother again and to find out how the rolls had tasted. And yet the time did not seem long to her, for she could not tire of listening to the whispering voices of the firs, of drinking in the sweet odors and the brightness of the green meadows and their golden flowers.

Grandfather came out of the hut at last, took a long look at the scene around him, and said contentedly—

"Well, I guess we can go now."

Today was Saturday, the time of all the week when it was Meadow Nuncle's custom to clean the hut and put things to rights in the shed and all around. He had taken the morning to do this, so he could make the trip with Heidi in the afternoon. That is why everything looked so neat. They parted at the door of Goat Peter's hut, and Heidi ran inside. The grandmother had already heard her coming, and she called out to her fondly—

"Are you there, dear? Have you come to us again?"

Then she grasped Heidi's hand and squeezed it a little, for she was still afraid the child might be taken away from her again. And then Grandmother had to tell how the rolls had tasted. And she said that they had strengthened

her so that she was much better that day than she
had been for a long time.   Peter's mother added, however,
that the old lady was much worried lest the rolls would
disappear too soon, and so she could be persuaded to eat
only one of them the day before and that day together.
The mother thought she would gain in strength faster if
she would agree to eat one roll a day for a whole week at
a stretch.

Heidi listened carefully to what Brigitte said and she
was thoughtful for a little while.   But then she had found
a way out of the difficulty.

"I know what we'll do, Grandmother," she said with
great eagerness.   "I'll write a letter to Clara, and she will
be sure to send me as many rolls again, or perhaps even
twice as many, for I had a great pile of such rolls hidden
in my closet.   And when they took them away from me,
Clara said she'd give me just as many more.   And she'll do
what she said she would."

"Oh, dear me," Brigitte said, "that is a fine idea! But
they will be hard before they get here, don't you think?
If we only had a spare penny now and then, we could get
the rolls from the baker down in Dörfli.   He has them for
sale, but it's all I can do to pay for the black bread we eat."

It was then that a bright ray of joy came into Heidi's
face.

"Oh, I've got a great lot of money, Grandmother," she
shouted gaily, and she couldn't stand still, she was so
happy.   "Now I know what I'll do with it.   Every single
day, you're going to have a fresh roll, and two on Sunday.
Peter can fetch them up from The Hamlet."

"Oh, no, my dear," the grandmother said, "that would never do. The money was not given you for any such purpose. You must hand it to your grandfather. He'll tell you how to spend it."

But Heidi would not have her nice plan spoiled. She crowed and danced around the room and kept calling—

"Now Grandmother's going to eat a roll every day and grow strong! And oh, Grandmother," she cried out again in her delight, "when you get healthy, things will be bright for you again, surely! I think they're dark only because you're so weak."

The grandmother kept silence, because she did not wish to spoil the child's happiness. While she was gaily dancing around, Heidi caught sight of Grandmother's old hymn book, and she was suddenly struck with a bright idea.

"Grandmother, do you know I can read nicely now? Shan't I just read you a song out of your old book?"

"Do!" said the grandmother, in pleased surprise. "So you really can do that, can you?"

Heidi had climbed up on a chair and taken down the book. It was covered with thick dust, for it had not been touched for a long time. She wiped it clean, sat down with it on the stool beside Grandmother, and asked what she should read first.

"Whatever you like best, dear," said the old lady very eagerly, pushing the spinning wheel away from her.

Heidi turned over the leaves, reading here a line and there a line. "Oh, here's something about the sun! I'll read that, Grandmother."

And Heidi began in a low voice to spell out the words
of the beautiful comforting hymn, and as she read she
grew more eager and her voice more full and warm:

> Sun golden gleaming,
> Joyously beaming,
> Brings to our regions
> Thy countless legions
> Of spirit-quickening, glorious rays!

> For long I stumbled,
> Bowed down and humbled;—
> But now arisen,
> With swift decision
> Turn I to heaven my enraptured gaze.

> I view, impassioned,
> What God has fashioned
> To tell the story
> Of His great glory—
> Infinite, endless the tale of His might!

> All pious creatures
> See there His features,
> When, happy-hearted,
> They have departed
> From earth to bask in His heavenly light.

> Worldly things sever,
> God stays forever;
> There is no changing
> Of His arranging;—
> His word and will are eternal law.

> His grace and favor
> Swerve not, nor waver:

They cure each breaking
Heart of its aching —
Filling our souls with a holy awe.

Today we languish
In grief and anguish,
But all our sorrow
Shall fade tomorrow; —
After the storm the sun shines bright.

Sweet peace and pleasure,
Boundless in measure,
We know are given
In the garden of heaven; —
Thither my thoughts turn day and night.

When she had finished, Grandmother sat quietly with folded hands, on her face a look of joy such as Heidi had never seen there before, even if the tears were streaming down the aged cheeks.

"O Heidi," she said at last, happily, "that hymn makes the world light for me, with its lines about the sun that shines in the garden of heaven. It makes my soul light indeed. Oh, how much good you have done me, dear!"

Grandmother repeated the joyful words over and over. Heidi glowed with happiness and kept her eyes fixed on the old lady's face, for she had never seen her look so before. Grandmother's face no longer had its troubled look, but glanced up at her so brightly that it seemed as if she was already seeing with the glad eyes of faith the fair garden of heaven of which the hymn sang.

Then someone knocked at the window, and Heidi saw her grandfather beckoning to her to go home with him. She went quickly, but not until she had given Grandmother

her promise to come again next day. Even if she went up
to the pasture with Peter, she said that she would be back
for the afternoon. It had become the dearest joy that
Heidi knew to make the world bright and gay for Grandmother, a joy much greater, even, than to be in the sunlit
pasture with her flowers and her goats.

Brigitte ran out of the door after Heidi, carrying the
dress and hat which had been left behind. And Heidi took
the dress to carry off with her, for she was now sure that
Grandfather would know her in the new costume. But
the hat she stubbornly refused to accept. She told Brigitte
to keep it for herself, she never wanted to put it on her
head again.

The child was so full of what had recently happened
to her that right away she had to tell Grandfather everything that was in her mind. She said they could get the
white rolls for Grandmother down in The Hamlet if they
had money enough. She said things had suddenly grown
bright and happy for Grandmother. And when Heidi
had told her whole story down to the end, she went back
to the beginning and said to him hopefully—

"Listen, Grandfather! Even if Grandmother doesn't
want me to, you'll give me all the money in the roll, won't
you, so I can hand Peter a penny every day for a roll, and
two on Sundays?"

"But how about the new bed, Heidi?" Grandfather
said. "A real bed would be a fine thing for you, and there'd
be enough money left to buy lots of rolls with."

Heidi gave her grandfather no peace, however. She
proved to him that she slept better on her couch of straw

than she had ever done in her feather bed in Frankfort.
And she kept pleading with him so earnestly and constantly
that he finally said——

"It's your money, Heidi, to do with as you please. You
can get bread for Grandmother with it for many a year."

Heidi called out happily——

"Hurrah! Now Grandmother will never have to eat
any more hard black bread, and oh, Grandfather, things
were never so splendid before in all our lives!"

She seized the old man's hand and jumped up and
down as happy and free as the birds in the sky. Then all
at once she grew serious again and said——

"Oh, suppose the dear God had done right on the spot
what I begged Him so hard to do, then things wouldn't have
turned out as they have. I should have come home with
only a few rolls for Grandmother and could not have read
aloud to her, which does her so much good. But dear
God had already planned it out so much better than I
thought. Grandmama said He would, and it has all come
true. My, but I am glad the dear God did not give in to
me when I prayed and made such a fuss! From now on
I'll pray as Grandmama told me to, and be grateful to the
dear God, even when He doesn't do what I ask. For
I can always think, 'It is just as it was in Frankfort.
Dear God is planning something much better for me.'
And now we'll pray every day, won't we Grandfather?
And we'll never forget Him, so the dear God will never
forget us."

"But suppose one did not pray, what then?" muttered
Grandfather.

"Why, then, he would not succeed, for the dear God would forget him, too, and leave him all alone. And when he got into trouble and complained, then nobody would pity him at all. They would say, 'He ran away from the dear God first, so now God who could help him doesn't pay any attention to him, either.'"

"How true that is, Heidi! But who taught you that?"

"Grandmama told me. She explained it all to me."

The old gentleman walked up and down awhile in silence. Then, following his own thought, he said to himself—

"Still, suppose that is the way of it. It's too late to go back afterward, and whom God has forgotten, He has forgotten."

"Oh, no, Grandfather, it's never too late. Grandmama told me about that, too. Besides, the beautiful story in my book says the same thing, but I never read that one to you. We'll be home in a minute now, and then you'll just see how lovely the story is."

In her mad hurry to be home Heidi hurried faster and faster during the last of their climb. And scarcely had they reached the top, when the child let go of Grandfather's hand and flew into the cottage. The old gentleman took from his shoulders the basket, into which he had put half of the things that were in Heidi's trunk, for the whole trunk was too heavy for him to carry up all at once. He sat down on the bench and gave himself up to his thoughts. Heidi came running to him with the book under her arm.

"Oh, that's fine, Grandfather, that you're sitting right there!"

With a bound Heidi was at his side and had found
her place in the book. She had read the story through so
often that the book always opened at this page. And Heidi,
with emotion, went on to read the saddest, gladdest story
in all the world, the tale of the Prodigal Son.

"Isn't that a beautiful story, though?" Heidi asked,
as she finished it and closed her book. But Grandfather
made no reply to the question. She had expected him to be
surprised and glad, instead of which he sat in silence and
seemed not to hear her.

"Yes, Heidi, the story is indeed beautiful," Grandfather said, after a long pause. But his face was so
solemn that Heidi grew very quiet and opened her book
to look at its pictures. Gently she pushed the book in front
of Grandfather and said—

"See how happy he is!"

Heidi pointed with her finger to the picture of the
Prodigal's return home, where he is standing in fresh
garments beside his father and once more belongs to him
as his son.—

A few hours later, when Heidi had long been fast
asleep, Grandfather climbed up the small ladder. He put
his lantern down beside the child's bed so that its rays
fell on her sleeping form. She lay before him with her
hands clasped, for she had not forgotten to pray. On her
little pink face there was a look of peacefulness and happy
trust which gave its own message to Grandfather. He
stood there a long time without moving, with his eyes fixed
on the sleeping child. Then he too clasped his hands
together and, with bowed head, he whispered—

"Father, I have sinned against heaven and in Thy sight and am no more worthy to be called Thy son!" And two great tears ran down the old man's cheeks.—

Not many hours after this scene, in the early hour of dawn, Meadow Nuncle was standing in front of his hut and looking around him with shining eyes. The Sabbath light glistened and beamed above mountain and valley. Single notes from the early chiming of church bells stole up from the lands far below, and high above in the pine trees the birds were singing their morning songs.

Then Grandfather stepped back into the hut.

"Come, Heidi!" he called up to the loft. "Here's the sun. Put on a pretty dress, and we'll go to church together."

It did not take Heidi long to dress. There was a new note in Grandfather's voice which made her eager to obey.

In a short time she came hurrying down with her dainty Frankfort dress on, but she stopped in front of Grandfather and gazed at him unbelievingly.

"Why, I never saw you look that way," she broke out at last. "That's the first time you've worn your coat with the silver buttons. Oh, you're so handsome in your fine Sunday clothes!"

The old gentleman looked down at the child with an amused smile and said—

"So are you, my dear. And now, let's start."

He took Heidi's hand in his, and together they wandered down the mountain path. They could now hear the clear church bells ringing on all sides of them, their tones growing deeper and sweeter the nearer they drew to them. Heidi listened blissfully and said—

"Do you hear them, Grandfather? It's like some big festival."

Down below in Dörfli all the people were already in church and were just beginning to sing a hymn as Grandfather and Heidi came in and sat down far back in the last pew. But right in the midst of the singing the person who sat next to them nudged his neighbor with his elbow and said—

"Have you noticed it? Meadow Nuncle is in church."

And the neighbor nudged the one next to him, and so on and on. In the shortest time imaginable the news was being whispered in every nook and corner—

"It's Meadow Nuncle! Do you see Meadow Nuncle?"

Almost all the women had to turn around and gaze for a moment, and most of them got behind in the tune, and the leader of the singing had the greatest difficulty in keeping time at all.

But the moment the pastor began to preach they paid strict attention, for his sermon contained such warm words of praise and thanksgiving that all his listeners were very happy. It seemed as if a new joy had come into every heart.

When the service had ended, Meadow Nuncle walked out, holding Heidi's hand in his, and went toward the parsonage. All the worshipers who came out with him and those who were already standing outside the church stared after him, and they followed behind a little way, to see if he really was going into the manse. He did so.

Then they gathered about in small groups and excitedly spoke of this unheard-of thing, that Meadow Nuncle had come to church. And they kept their gaze fixed on the entrance of the parsonage to see how he would next appear. Would he come out in anger and at strife with the world, or would he have made his peace with the pastor? None could guess which it would be, for the simple reason that nobody knew what had brought the old gentleman down the mountain or what his coming meant.

But it was easy to see that there was already a change of feeling in the hearts of many of the church-goers, for one would say to the other—

"It may well be that Meadow Nuncle is not so bad as he is painted. You can tell by the way he holds the little one's hand, he's so careful!"

And the other would answer, "That's just what I always said, you remember? And he wouldn't be going to call on the pastor if he was so terribly bad, he'd be afraid to. People always exaggerate such things."

But the baker who had driven Heidi up from Mayenfeld said—

"That's what I've been claiming from the first. Since when does a little child that has everything it wants to eat and drink, and all sorts of good things besides, run away from its fine home and go back to its grandfather, if that grandfather is wicked and wild and a man to fear!"

A very tender feeling for Meadow Nuncle was now shown by the men. And this increased when the women joined them, for they had heard from the lips of Goat

Peter's mother and grandmother many things that went to prove Meadow Nuncle was quite a different sort of man from what people usually thought him to be. And this good opinion grew until all at once it seemed as if they were all waiting there outside the manse to welcome back into the fold an old friend whose absence they had long been sorry for.

In the meantime Meadow Nuncle had gone to the pastor's study door and knocked upon it. The preacher himself opened the door and met his callers, not with the surprise that was to be expected, but as if he had awaited their coming. The pastor, of course, could not help but know that Grandfather had been to church. He seized the old gentleman's hand and shook it again and again, but Meadow Nuncle stood before him silently and could not find a single word to say. For he had not expected so friendly a greeting. At last, however, he said—

"I have come, Pastor, to ask you to forget the words I said to you, last year, up on the mountain meadow. Also, to beg you not to be angry with me for being stubborn and not listening to your sensible advice. You were right in everything you said, Pastor, and I was wrong. But I'm going to follow your advice now, if it is not too late, and take up quarters here in The Hamlet this winter. For the child is too delicate to endure the severe weather above. And even if the people down here look sidewise at me, because they do not trust me, why, I do not deserve any better treatment! But I know, Pastor, that you will not treat me so."

The fine eyes of the pastor shone with joy. He took

the old gentleman's hand, pressed it in his own, and said with feeling—

"Neighbor, you went to the right church before you came down to visit mine. Thank God for that! And you won't be sorry if you come back to live among us. You will always be a dear friend and neighbor to me, and I look forward to spending many a happy evening hour with you this winter. For I enjoy your society very much, and the little girl will find good friends, too."

The pastor laid a very friendly hand on Heidi's curly head, and then he took her hand in his to lead her outside as he walked along with her grandfather. And not until they were in front of the parsonage did he say good-by to them.

So it came about that all the people who were standing there saw the preacher shaking hands with Meadow Nuncle quite as if he were his best friend and could hardly bear to part with him. And the door of the manse had scarcely closed behind the pastor when the whole gathering crowded up to Meadow Nuncle, and each one seemed to wish to be the first to welcome him. In fact, so many hands were held out to him at the same instant that he did not know which one to take first.

One said to him, "I am so pleased, Nuncle, that you are coming back to be with us again."

Another said to him, "I have been wanting for this long time to talk with you again, Nuncle."

Such things were being said on every side, and when to their friendly words of greeting Nuncle answered that he had decided to take up his old quarters in The Hamlet, to pass the winter there with his old friends, then there was excitement! You would have thought, indeed, that Meadow Nuncle was the most popular fellow in all Dörfli, and that they had had a terrible time getting along without him.

Most of his new-found friends walked with Grandfather and the little child far up the pasture slopes, and before they left him each one wished to make Meadow Nuncle promise to pay him a call after he had moved down. When at last the people turned to go down the mountain, the old man stood and gazed after them a long time. A warm light rested on his face, as if some inner sun was shining through. Heidi looked at him steadily and said with joy—

"Grandfather, never in your life did you look so handsome as you have today."

"Do you really think so?" asked Grandfather with a smile. "Well, you see, Heidi, I am better off than I deserve to be, and am at peace with God and men. And that makes one feel so happy! The dear God was good to me the day he sent you to the mountain meadow."

When they got as far as Peter the Goatherd's hut, Grandfather straightway opened the door and went in.

"God greet you, Grandmother," he called out. "I think we must get to patching again before the autumn winds blow."

"Why, heavens above, that's Nuncle!" cried the old lady in joyful surprise. "That I should live to see this day! I can thank you now for all you've done for us, Nuncle. May God reward you!"

Trembling with happiness, the old grandmother held out her hand, and after her visitor had given it a hearty shake she still clung to his hand and went on to say—

"There's another thing in my heart to ask of you, Nuncle. If I have ever done anything to hurt you, then don't punish me by letting Heidi go away before I lie in my grave down in the churchyard. Oh, you don't know what the child is to me!" And she drew Heidi close to her and hugged her tightly.

"Don't worry, Grandmother," Nuncle said, soothingly. "I'll punish neither you nor myself in that way. We're all going to stick together now and, if God so wills, for a long time to come."

Then Brigitte drew Nuncle secretly off to a corner of the room and showed him the pretty hat trimmed with feathers, and told him how it came to be there, and said she of course would not accept such a gift from the child.

But Grandfather, well pleased, looked in Heidi's direction and said—

"The hat is hers, and if she doesn't want to wear it on her head, she doesn't need to. And if she gave it to you, take it."

Brigitte was greatly pleased at this decision, which she had not expected She said—

"It is certainly worth more than ten francs. Just look at it!" In her joy she held the hat high for his inspection. "What real blessings this Heidi has brought back from Frankfort with her! I have been thinking whether I ought not to send Peterli to Frankfort for a little while, too. What do you say, Nuncle?"

Grandfather's eyes twinkled gaily. He said in his opinion it could not do Peter any harm, but he would wait until there was a good chance for him to go.

And then the person they were talking about came in the door. But first he banged his head against it so hard that it made everything rattle. He seemed to be in a tearing hurry. Out of breath and panting, he now stood in the middle of the room and held out a letter. That was a thing that had never happened before—a letter which they had given him in the Dörfli post office to deliver.

They all sat down around the table, and Heidi opened her letter and read it aloud, without making a single mistake. The letter had been written by Clara Sesemann. She said in it that since Heidi had gone away, the house had grown so dreary that she couldn't bear it. And she had begged her father so long that he had finally agreed to make the trip to the baths at Ragaz the coming autumn. And Grandmama would come with them, too, for she wanted to visit Heidi and Grandfather up on the mountain meadow.

And, further, Clara wrote that Grandmama had asked her to tell Heidi that she had done right in wishing to take the rolls to Grandmother. And, so the old lady would not have to eat them dry, she was sending along some coffee, which had already started on its way. And when she came to the mountain meadow, Heidi must take her to pay a visit to Grandmother.

Then there was such joy and surprise at this news, and such a world of things to talk about and ask, because all of them were interested in what was going to happen, that Grandfather himself did not notice how late it had grown. They were all so happy to think of the days that were coming, and almost more contented at being together on this very day, that the Grandmother finally said—

"But the nicest thing of all is for an old friend to come and give us his hand again, just as he used to long ago. It is such a comfortable feeling to have in one's heart, to realize that we have found again everything that is dear to us. You will come again soon, won't you, Nuncle, and you, Heidi, tomorrow?"

They gave their promise to Grandmother at once. And now it was time to go. Grandfather wandered with Heidi up the mountain pasture. And just as that morning the clear bells from near and far had called them down into The Hamlet, so now the peaceful ringing of the evening chimes gave them company on their way to the sunlit meadow hut, which smiled its welcome in the Sunday evening light.

HEIDI MAKES USE OF WHAT SHE HAS LEARNED

CHAPTER I

PREPARATIONS FOR A JOURNEY

The kind doctor who had insisted that Heidi be sent back to her home was walking down Broad Street toward the Sesemanns'. It was a sunny morning in September, so clear and lovely that you would think anyone would find joy in it. But the doctor was staring so hard at the stone sidewalk beneath his feet that he never once noticed the blue sky above him. There was a sadness in his face which had not been there in former days. And since the first of the year his hair had grown much more gray.

The doctor had had an only daughter, and after his wife's death she had come to mean everything to him—to be the one great happiness of his life. But some months before this the girl, whose youth was just beginning, also had been taken from him by death. And, from that time on, the doctor had never again seemed the light-hearted man of earlier years.

He climbed the steps that led to the handsome Sesemann house and rang the bell. Hardly had the sound of its ringing stopped when Sebastian opened the door, and the moment he saw who was waiting outside he was very polite and respectful in his manner. This was not only because the doctor was the best friend of the master of the house and of his sick little daughter, but here, as everywhere else, he had by his kindness of heart won the good will of the whole household.

"Everything going along all right, Sebastian?" the doctor asked in his usual friendly tone.

He mounted the stairs that led to the second floor, followed by the butler, who was still bowing and scraping most devotedly, although the doctor of course did not know this, as his back was turned.

"It's a good thing you came, Doctor," Mr. Sesemann greeted him. "We must talk over that trip to Switzerland once more. I want to know if you still think it necessary for us to give it up, now that Clara's health has taken a turn for the better."

"My dear Sesemann, what on earth am I to think of you?" the doctor replied, taking a seat beside his friend. "I'd give a good deal if your mother were here. It's always straight sailing with her from the word 'go.' But there's no getting along with you at all! This is the third time in one day that you've sent for me so that I can have the pleasure of saying the same thing over again."

Mr. Sesemann laid his hand almost humbly on the doctor's shoulder. "Yes, I know, you are right. And the matter must make you impatient. But, dear friend, I do want you to understand how hard it is for me to deny the child what I promised her so definitely, and what has made her so happy day and night for months."

"Hard for you, I know," said the doctor. "But, after all, does that change anything?"

"Oh, perhaps not! But don't you remember how patient the poor child has been during all these recent days, always hoping that the Swiss journey was to be soon and that she could visit her little friend Heidi in the Alps?

And now, after the child has had to give up so much happiness, you ask me to destroy at a single blow the hope that she has lived on for so long. Oh, I tell you it is not possible!"

"Sesemann, you must," the doctor said, decidedly. And then, when he saw that his friend sat in silence and looking quite wretched, he went on to say, after a pause—

"Just think how the matter stands. For years Clara has not had so bad a summer as this last has been. There is no question of her taking so long a journey without the greatest danger to her health. Besides, it's now the month of September. It may still be fine weather in the Alps, but it certainly will be cold up there by now."

"At night, yes, perhaps. But during the day—"

"Ah, but the days are growing short. And as Clara can't stay overnight on the mountain, but would have to live elsewhere, she would have altogether a bare two hours to be up there. It's a trip of some hours up the mountain from Ragaz, especially as she would have to be carried up in a chair. To make a long story short, Sesemann, it can't be thought of!"

"Oh, oh, oh! What will poor Clara say?"

"Oh, we'll go in and talk with her about it. She is a sensible girl, and I'll tell her what my plan is. Next May, say, she can go to Ragaz and take the baths there for some time, until the weather is fine and warm in the Alps. Then she can be carried up every once in a while, and after she has once got back her strength somewhat she will enjoy these mountain trips twice as much as she would now. I suppose you know, Sesemann, if we want to have the slightest hope of your child's getting well again, we must use the greatest care and treat her very tenderly."

Mr. Sesemann, who had been listening quietly and with much attention to these last words, suddenly jumped to his feet.

"Doctor," he cried, "be honest with me! Have you the least hope that Clara will get well?"

The doctor shrugged his shoulders sadly.

"Not much," he said softly. "But come, my dear fellow, think of me for a moment. You have a dear child who longs for you when you are away from home and is happy when you come back. You never have to return to an empty house and sit down to a lonely dinner. Your child is well cared for at home. It is true she must go without many things that other children have, and yet in some ways she is more spoiled than they are. No, Sesemann, you and Clara are not to be so greatly pitied. You are fortunate to have each other. But think of my lonely house!"

Mr. Sesemann was striding up and down the room, as he always did when he was thinking deeply of some matter. Suddenly he came to a stop and tapped his friend on the shoulder.

"Doctor, I have an idea. I can't bear to see you like this. You're not the man you used to be. You must get away for a while from your own thoughts, and do you know how to do that? You go to Switzerland in our place and visit Heidi."

The doctor was very much surprised at this offer and would not have consented to it if Mr. Sesemann had given him time to object. But the master of the house was so delighted with his new idea that he took his friend's arm and marched him over to the room of his small daughter. The doctor was a great favorite of the sick girl, because he always treated her so nicely, and every time he came he had some funny story or other to tell her. She knew, of course, why he was no longer as lively as he used to be, and she did wish with all her heart that she could think of some way to make him happy again.

She stretched out her hand the minute he came in and sat down beside her. Her father also drew his chair up to the beside and, with her hand in his, began to talk about the Swiss journey and the joy with which he had looked forward to it. He passed quickly over the fact that the trip was now out of the question, for he was afraid of the tears that were coming. Then he went on to tell of the new plan and showed Clara how great a help it would be to their dear friend to have this short vacation.

True enough, the tears did come and swam in Clara's blue eyes, try as she would to hold them back, for she knew that Papa hated to see her cry. But, oh, it was hard to give it all up now, when her only joy and comfort during the long, lonely hours of the past summer had been looking forward to her visit to Heidi! Clara never questioned what her father did, and she knew, of course, that he was asking her to give up the trip because it would be bad for her and so she must not go. She choked down her sobs and turned to the only hope that was left her. She took her good friend's hand and stroked it, and said—

"Oh, you will go to see Heidi, won't you, Doctor? Then you can come back and tell me how things are on her mountain, and what she is doing, and her grandfather, and Peter, and the goats. They're all such friends of mine! And you can take the things I want to send Heidi and the grandmother. I've got them all thought out. Please, Doctor, do go. And while you're gone, I promise to take all the cod-liver oil you want me to, honest!"

It is hard to say whether this promise of Clara's decided the matter or not, but it seemed to do so, for the doctor smiled and said—

"Then I certainly shall have to go, little Clara, so you'll get plump and strong as Papa and I want you to be. Have you decided just when I must start?"

"First thing tomorrow morning would be best, Doctor," Clara answered.

"Clara is right, so it would," her father chimed in. "The sun is shining, the sky is blue, and there's not a moment to be lost, for it is a shame not to be enjoying every such day in the Alps."

The doctor had to laugh a little.

"In a minute you'll be telling me, Sesemann, that it's my fault I'm not already at Heidi's house. So I'd better hurry away as fast as I can," he said.

The doctor rose to go, but Clara held him fast. First, you see, there were so many things he had to tell Heidi for her. Then there were all the things he had to pay special attention to, so he could tell her about them afterward. She would send over later what she wanted him to take to Heidi, for Miss Rottenmeier would have to help her with the packing, and the housekeeper was off on one of her shopping tours in town and might not be back right away.

The doctor promised to do everything just as she told him to. He would start on his journey, if not the first thing tomorrow, at least in the course of the following day. And when he returned, he would give her an exact account of everything he had seen and done.

Servants in a house often have a wonderful way of finding out what is going on about them long before anyone thinks to tell them about it. Sebastian and Tinette must have had this gift of discovering things quickly, for hardly had the doctor, accompanied by Sebastian, reached the staircase when Tinette came into Clara's room—this, in spite of the fact that she had been rung for only a second before.

"Bring me this box full of nice fresh cakes like those we have for coffee, Tinette," said Clara, pointing to a little chest which had been standing there for just this purpose a long time. The maid seized the object by one corner and let it dangle carelessly from her hand. After she had shut the door behind her, she said snippily—

"Little things like that are no trouble at all."

When Sebastian had opened the front door with his usual politeness, he said, with a bow—

"I hope the doctor will not forget to give little Mamsell Sebastian's best wishes."

"Why, look here, Sebastian," the doctor asked pleasantly, "how did you find out about my trip so soon?"

The butler coughed slightly.

"I am—I have—I don't quite know myself—oh, yes, now I remember. I just happened to be going by the dining room a minute ago and heard the little Mamsell's name mentioned. And as one does in such a case, you know—I put this and that together—and that's the way—"

"Oh, of course," the doctor said, with a smile. "And, the more you put this and that together, the more you know. Good-by, Sebastian. I'll deliver your message."

The doctor had just passed through the opened entrance door when he met with a surprise. The high wind that was blowing had kept Miss Rottenmeier from continuing her shopping tour, so she had returned and was on the point of coming in. The wind had puffed out the big shawl in which she was wrapped until she looked like a ship under full sail. The doctor moved back at once to make room for her. But Miss Rottenmeier had always shown a marked respect and politeness for this man of medicine, and she, too, on her side, drew back for him to pass.

For a time the two stood facing each other, each waiting for the other to go through first.

Finally such a strong gust of wind came along that the housekeeper, with all sails spread, was blown straight against the doctor. He just managed to give her room to pass, and the good lady was borne by the wind quite a way beyond him, so that she had to come back in order to greet in proper form the guest of the house.

This flying on the wings of the wind had put her in a bad humor, but the doctor had a way all his own of soothing her ruffled temper and making her good-natured again. He told her about his intended trip and asked her in his most gracious manner if she would not pack for him the things that were going to Heidi, as only she knew how to pack them. With this bit of flattery, the doctor went away.

Clara fully expected to have a struggle with Miss Rottenmeier before she would consent to give away all the things which were intended for Heidi. But for once she was pleasantly disappointed, for the housekeeper was in the best of tempers. She at once took everything off the large table so she could spread out on it all the objects that Clara had gathered together and pack them where the invalid could watch.

This was no light task, since the articles that had to be wrapped up were of all different shapes.

First came the small, thick cape with the hood which Clara had chosen for Heidi so that next winter she could visit Grandmother whenever she wanted to, and not have to wait until her grandfather could come and wrap her up in the sack to keep her from freezing. Then came a thick, warm shawl for the grandmother so she could wind it around her and not have to freeze when the wind should again begin to rattle at the hut so dreadfully. Then followed the big box of cakes, also intended for Grandmother, so that she might once in a while have something else than a roll to eat with her coffee.

Next in order came an enormous sausage. Clara had first meant this gift for Peter, because he never got anything but bread and cheese, which must be tiresome. But later she changed her mind, because she was afraid that Peter would like the sausage so much he would devour it at a single meal. So his mother Brigitte was to have it and first cut off a big piece of it for herself and for the grandmother, and then she was to serve Peter his share at different times, as she thought best.

Then there was a small sack of tobacco for Grand-father, who was so fond of smoking his pipe when he sat out in front of his hut of an evening. Last of all, there was a number of mysterious sacks, packages, and boxes, which Clara had especially enjoyed collecting because Heidi was going to find in them all sorts of surprises which would make her very happy.

Finally the work was ended, and a large bundle lay on the floor ready for the journey Miss Rottenmeier looked down at it, and her mind was full of deep thoughts about the art of packing bundles well. Clara, for her part, could hardly keep her eyes from it, for her mind was dwelling on how Heidi would jump in the air and shout with joy when the enormous package should arrive.

Then Sebastian came in and, with a mighty swing of his arms, lifted the heavy bundle to his shoulder, so that he could send it at once to the doctor's house.

CHAPTER II

A GUEST ON THE MOUNTAIN MEADOW

Early dawn was glowing on the mountain tops, and a cool morning wind rustled in the pine trees, rocking the old branches to and fro.

Heidi opened her eyes, for the voice of the wind had awakened her. The deep roaring of the wind always excited Heidi, and its magic drew her outdoors under the firs. She darted from her bed and could hardly wait to get dressed properly. And yet this must be done, for Heidi by this time had learned that one should always look clean and tidy.

Then she came down the ladder, to find that Grandfather's bed was already empty. She ran outside. And there before the door stood Grandfather, gazing first up at the sky and then in all directions of the compass, as he always did, to see what sort of day it was going to be.

Pink cloudlets were floating slowly by above them, and the sky grew ever a deeper blue, and there was a stream as of pure gold on the heights and the sloping pastures, for at that very moment the sun had risen above the lofty cliffs.

"Oh, how beautiful! Good morning, Grandfather!" Heidi cried as she ran up beside him.

"Hello! So the sleep is out of your eyes, too, so early?" the old gentleman answered, offering his hand by way of greeting.

Then Heidi ran beneath the pine trees and skipped about with delight to the rushing and roaring music of the swaying boughs. And at every new puff of wind and loud surge of sound in the tree summits, she shouted for joy and jumped a little higher.

In the meantime Grandfather had gone to the goat stable and milked Little Swan and Little Bear. Then he curried and washed them, until they were all clean for their trip to the mountain, and brought them out on the lawn. The moment Heidi saw her friends, she ran to them and clasped them about the neck. She greeted them fondly, and they bleated back at her happily and with perfect trust. Each of the goats seemed anxious to show still greater affection and kept pressing its head closer and closer to her shoulders, so that she was almost crushed between them. But Heidi was not afraid, and when the lively Bärli began to shove and push so hard with its head, the child said—

"Why, Little Bear, you're butting just like Big Turk!"

And at that, Little Bear at once drew back her head and withdrew to a proper distance. Thereupon Schwänli had stretched her head high above her and bleated in a superior sort of way, so you could see clearly enough that she was thinking—

"No one can honestly claim that I'm behaving like Turk."

As a matter of fact, the snow-white Schwänli was a bit more dignified than brown Bärli.

Peter's signaling whistle was now heard from below, and soon all the lively goats came leaping up the slope, nimble Goldfinch in the van, springing higher than any.

Again Heidi was at once in the center of the flock, pushed this way and that in their rough welcome. But she shoved them all aside in order to get to timid Snowhopper, who was always bullied by the larger goats when she wanted to reach Heidi.

By this time Peter made his appearance, giving one last shrill whistle to start the goats and send them scurrying off to pasture, for he wished to have a chance to exchange a word with Heidi. The goats scattered somewhat when they heard his loud signal, and this made space for him to come to a stand in front of his friend

"You might come along with me today if you want to," was his rather surly greeting.

"No, I can't do it, Peter," Heidi answered. "They may be coming from Frankfort any moment now, and I must be at home to receive them."

"That's what you always say," Peter growled.

"But that's the way things are, and the way they'll stay until the people do come. Don't you think I ought to be home, seeing they are traveling all the way from Frankfort just to visit me? Tell me, Peter, how you feel about it."

"Well, they can visit with Nuncle, can't they?" Peter answered with a snarl.

Their talk was interrupted at this moment by the loud voice of Grandfather—

"Why isn't the army moving forward? Whose fault is it, the general's or the troops'?"

The next second Peter faced about, swung his rod through the air so that it whistled, and at this well-known sound all the goats started off on a run with Peter after them full speed toward the mountain.—

Since Heidi had been back home this time with Grandfather, every now and then something would occur to her which she had never thought of before. For example, she now made up her own bed each morning and did her level best to smooth it out until it was all even. Then she trotted about the hut, set every chair in its proper place, and hid neatly away in the closet whatever she found lying around loose. Then she got a cloth, climbed up on a chair, and rubbed the table with her linen rag until it shone. Whenever Grandfather appeared, he would look around him well pleased and say—

"Every day is like Sunday in our house now. I tell you, Heidi didn't go away for nothing."

So it was that today, too, after Peter had disappeared and she had had breakfast with Grandfather, Heidi set herself at once to work. But it seemed as if she never would get through. It was such a lovely morning out of doors, and every minute something turned up to interrupt the child's tasks.

First a sunbeam came darting gaily in through the window and actually seemed to say, "Come out to play, Heidi!" She felt she could not stay in the house another instant and ran outside. The sparkling sunshine rested on the meadow about the house, and it spread its brightness on all the mountains and far off down into the valley. The ground on the slope where she stood looked so dry that she had to sit down on it and look all around her for a little while.

Then suddenly she remembered that she had left the three-legged stool right in the middle of the hut and that she had not polished the table since breakfast. She jumped up at once and ran quickly back into the hut.

But it was not long after that when there was such a mighty rustling in the fir trees that the music of it got somehow in all Heidi's limbs. So she was forced to drop her work, run out again, and dance a little with the trees, as their branches were rocking and swaying gracefully.

While all this was going on, Grandfather had been busy at one thing and another in the shop. Every once in a while he would come to the door and look smilingly on as Heidi pranced about. He was just turning back from one of these trips when he heard the child suddenly scream at the top of her lungs—

"Grandfather, please come right away!"

He strode quickly out again, in deathly fear that something might have happened to Heidi. But he saw her streaking it off toward the cliff, shouting as she ran—

"They're coming! Oh, they're coming! And the doctor's got here first of all."

Heidi, with arms outstretched, ran up to her old friend. When she was near enough, she seized the hand he was holding out to her and cried with the greatest glee—

"Good morning, Doctor! And I thank you again millions of times."

"God greet you, Heidi!" said the doctor with a kindly smile. "But why do you thank me the moment I arrive?"

"Because you let me come back to Grandfather," the child answered.

The doctor's face lighted up as if with sunshine. He had not hoped for so hearty a welcome in the Alps. He had felt very lonely while toiling up the mountain path, and had been so wrapped in his own thoughts that he had had no eyes for the beauty of the scene about him and had not noticed how it kept ever increasing in beauty.

He had been afraid that Heidi would have almost forgotten him, for they had seen so little of each other. And, besides, as the message he had for these people was sure to be a disappointment to them, he felt they would not care to welcome him, because he had not brought the expected friends along.

Instead of this, however, Heidi's eyes were shining with pure joy, and here she was, filled with thankfulness and love, clinging to her good friend's arm as if she would never let go.

With a sudden rush of fatherly tenderness, the doctor took the child's hand in his.

"Come, dear," he said, with his kindliest smile, "take me straight to your grandfather and show me where your home is."

But at this Heidi stood still and looked wonderingly down the mountain slope.

"Where did you leave Clara and Grandmama?" she asked.

"That's just it! Now, I'll have to tell you something that will hurt you as much as it does me," the doctor answered. "You see, Heidi, I'm all alone. Clara was very sick and no longer fit to travel, and so Grandmama didn't come with me, either. But early next year, as soon as the days get warm and long again. they are coming, sure as anything!"

Heidi was completely taken back by this news. For a moment she just could not grasp the fact that what she had all along thought to be so certain had suddenly become untrue. She stood without moving when she heard this unexpected message. The doctor had nothing to say, and there was absolute quiet all about them. The only sound that broke the stillness was the roaring of the wind in the trees high above their heads. Then, all at once, it dawned on Heidi why it was that she had run down the mountain, and that the doctor had come. She looked up at him.

There was something so sad in the gaze that rested on her that she had never seen one like it before. The doctor had never looked at her that way in Frankfort. It went straight to Heidi's heart. She couldn't bear to have anyone unhappy, and least of all the nice doctor. It must surely be because Clara and Grandmama could not come with him. She sought for some way of comforting him, and hit upon it at once.

"Oh, spring will be here before long again, really, and then they're sure to come," Heidi said, to comfort him. "It never takes long where we live, and then you see they can stay all the longer with us, and Clara will like that lots better. And now let's go see Grandfather."

Hand in hand the two good friends started up for the hut. Heidi wanted so very much to make the doctor happy again that she once more assured him it never took long on the mountain meadow for the long summer days to come back—really, almost before you noticed it! And

so Heidi talked herself into a happier frame of mind, and
when they gained the top of the climb she called gaily to
Grandfather—

"They haven't come yet, but it won't be long now
before they are here, too."

The doctor was no stranger to Grandfather, for Heidi
had already spoken of him very often. The old gentleman
held out his hand to their guest and bade him a hearty
welcome. Then the men sat down on the bench beside
the hut and did not forget to save a little place for Heidi.
The doctor, with a friendly wave of the hand, motioned
to her to sit close by him.

Then he began to tell how Mr. Sesemann had urged
him to take the trip, and how he himself had imagined it
might do him good, as he hadn't felt quite strong for a
long time. He whispered to Heidi that a certain something that he had brought from Frankfort for her would
soon be coming up the mountain. And this, he felt sure,
would be more fun for her than just seeing the old doctor.
The child was all on edge with excitement to know what
the thing would turn out to be.

Grandfather urged the doctor as hard as he could to
spend the beautiful autumn days on the mountain meadow.
Or at least he must come up every day when it was good
weather, for Meadow Nuncle could not exactly ask him
to spend his nights with them, because he did not have a
bed to offer him.

He advised their guest, for this reason, not to go back
every evening 'way to Ragaz, but to take a room down
in The Hamlet. He would find the little hotel there simple

but well cared for. Then he could come up to see them on the meadow every morning. And this, Nuncle thought, would do him a world of good. Then, too, he could show the gentleman other points of view farther up the mountain which would be sure to please him. The doctor thought this a fine idea, and said it suited him exactly.

Meanwhile it had got to be noon. The wind had gone down long since, and not a leaf was stirring in the pine boughs. The air was still mild and lovely for such a height, and was fanned into a delicious coolness around the sunny bench where they were sitting.

Meadow Nuncle rose and went into the hut, to come back in a moment carrying a table, which he placed in front of the bench.

"There we are! Heidi, now go and get what we have to eat," he said. "Our guest must put up with what we have, for even if our cooking is the plainest, our dining room certainly is the best in the world."

"That's what I say, too," the doctor answered as he gazed down into the sunlit valley. "And I accept your invitation most gladly, for everything must taste good up here."

Then Heidi ran back and forth like lightning and brought them everything she could find in the cupboard, for it was the greatest fun on earth to have the doctor eat a meal with them. In the meantime Grandfather was getting the dinner ready, and he now appeared with a steaming jug of milk and toasted strips of yellow cheese. Then he carved from the pink meat of the joint, which had long been drying in the open air, slices so thin that you could see through them. And the doctor swore that for a whole year he had not eaten a single meal that tasted so good as this one.

"Oh, I tell you, our Clara must come," he said after a little. "She would gain new strength here, and after she'd been eating a while the way I have today, she'd be plump and firm as never before in her life."

Not long afterward a man came climbing up the trail with a great bundle on his back. When he reached the hut, he threw his burden on the ground, stretched out his arms, and drew in deep breaths of the cool highland air.

"A-ha! There's the luggage that came from Frankfort with me," the doctor said as he rose to his feet. He took Heidi's hand and walked over to the bundle and began to untie it. When the first heavy wrapping had been removed, he said—

"There you go, my child! Open it yourself, and see what treasures you can find in it."

This Heidi at once began to do, of course. She tilted the big round parcel on its side, and as its many contents started to roll out, her eyes grew wide with surprise. But she made no sound until the doctor reached down and lifted the top from a large box, saying, "See what the grandmother gets to eat with her coffee!"

And then Heidi did cry out with joy, "Oh, oh! Now at last Grandmother has nice cakes to eat!"

She danced gaily about the box, and was all for packing the gifts together again and running right down to Grandmother's. But Grandfather said that they would go down when the doctor left, toward evening, and carry the things with them.

Then Heidi discovered the pretty little sack of tobacco and took it to Meadow Nuncle. He was very much pleased with it. He filled his pipe at once from it, and the two men then sat on the bench and surrounded themselves with great clouds of tobacco smoke, and had a good long talk together. Heidi gave her whole attention to her beautiful treasures.

Suddenly, however, she again stood by the bench in front of her guest, waiting until there was a break in the stream of conversation. Then she said—

"I don't care what you say, my presents haven't been any more fun than seeing the old doctor again."

The two men burst out into a shout at this. And the doctor said he was mighty glad to hear it.

When the sun was on the point of setting behind the mountains, the guest got up to make his way back to The Hamlet, where he was to rent lodgings. Grandfather tucked the box of cakes, the long sausage, and the shawl under his arm, the doctor took Heidi's hand in his, and they all set off down the mountain for Goat Peter's hut. There Heidi left them, for she had promised to wait at Grandmother's until Nuncle had walked with their guest down to Dörfli and should return to call for her.

As the doctor was shaking hands with Heidi and saying good night, she asked—

"What would you say to our going up to the pasture with the goats tomorrow?"

That was the nicest thing to do that she knew of.

"That's exactly what we will do, go up there together," he answered heartily.

Then the men went on their way, and Heidi slipped into Grandmother's house, but try as she would she had to make three trips of it. First it was all she could do to drag the box of cakes in. Then she had to go out again to bring in the sausage, for her grandfather had set the things all down in front of the door. And she had to go back a last time to fetch the big shawl. She carried every thing as close up to Grandmother as she could so the old lady could feel the things and know what they were. She laid the shawl across Grandmother's knees.

"It's all from Clara and Grandmama in Frankfort," she said.

Brigitte was so astonished that she could not move hand or foot, but stood and watched Heidi drag in the heavy articles and spread them out before their eyes.

"Now, Grandmother, aren't you pleased about the cakes?" Heidi asked several times. "Just see how soft they are!"

And each time Grandmother answered her—

"Of course I am, my dear! What lovely people they must be!"

Then she would run her hand gently over the thick soft shawl and say—

"My, but that's a splendid thing for the cold winter! It's so wonderful, why, I never dreamed I'd have its like!"

Heidi could not understand why the old lady seemed to like the gray shawl better than she did the cakes. For her part, Brigitte could not get far away from the sausage which lay on the table, and she gazed at it with great astonishment. She had never even dreamed of such a giant sausage, and here it was just she that was to have it for her own and even cut into it! That seemed to her a miracle, nothing less. She shook her head and said timidly—

"We'll have to wait and ask Nuncle whose it is."

But Heidi had no doubts at all about it and said—

"It's for you to eat, and for nothing and nobody else."

Just at that moment Peter came clumping in. "Meadow Nuncle is right on my heels and wants Heidi to"—so far he got in his speech and no farther.

For his eyes had fallen on the table where the sausage was lying. And the sight of it so overcame him that words failed him. But Heidi understood what he was about to say and stretched out her hand to say good-by to Grandmother.

It is true that Meadow Nuncle no longer went by the hut nowadays without stepping in for a moment to pass the time of day with Grandmother. And she was always more than pleased to hear his step, for he was sure to have a cheering word for her. But today it was late for Heidi, who rose every day with the sun. And her grandfather said, "The child must have her sleep," and was firm about it.

So he called good night to Grandmother through the open door and took Heidi's hand as she ran out to meet him. And under the canopy of twinkling stars the two wandered toward their peaceful cottage.

CHAPTER III

A REWARD

Early next morning the doctor was climbing up the mountain from Dörfli, in company with Peter and his goats. This well-meaning gentleman tried more than once to start a talk with the goatherd, but with no success. For it was not easy to get Peter to say anything, and the best the doctor could do was to draw a few short words in reply to his questions.

So the whole company wandered silently up to the meadow hut, where they found Heidi waiting for them with her two goats, all three of them as lively as crickets and as full of gladness as the sunshine that bathed the heights.

"You coming along?" Peter said. It was the question he never failed to ask whenever he caught sight of Heidi.

"Surely. At least, I will if the doctor goes, too."

Peter looked at her guest out of the corners of his eyes.

Then the grandfather came out of the house, carrying their luncheon bag in his hand. First he saluted the doctor very respectfully, and then he walked over to Peter and hung the bag over his shoulder.

It was heavier than it usually was, for Nuncle had put quite a piece of ruddy dried meat in it. He thought their guest might like to have it by the time they had reached the upper pasture, and might enjoy eating dinner up there with the children. Peter smiled almost all the way from one ear to the other, for he guessed that there was something specially fine in the bag.

The climb up the mountain was now begun. Heidi was entirely surrounded by her goats. They kept butting one another out of the way, for each animal wished to be next to her. And so for a while she was shoved along in the midst of the flock. But at last she stood still and said—

"Now run along like nice children and don't keep coming back to push me about so! I want to walk a way with the doctor."

Then she gently patted the back of Schneehöppli, who was always right beside her, warning this animal especially to be very obedient. With that, she edged her way out of the herd and walked with the doctor, who took her hand and held it fast.

He had more success in getting Heidi to talk than he had with Peter. She started at once to chatter, and she had a thousand things to tell him about the goats and their queer ideas, about the highland flowers, and the cliffs, and the birds—so many things, in fact, that before they knew it they had got to the pasture.

But while they had been thus busy during their way up the mountain, Peter had been frequently frowning at the doctor and casting at him sidelong glances which would have scared him terribly if he had noticed them. The doctor, however, remained ignorant of this fact.

When they came to the end of their journey, Heidi led her dear friend straight to her favorite spot, to the place where she always went to sit down and gaze about her.

And here they dropped down on the ground and began to drink in the beauty of the scene.

The golden sun of autumn shone on the peaks round about them and on the green valley far below. The tinkling of goat bells came up to them from the lower mountains on every hand, gentle and sweet as if they were promising peace to all the world. Golden sunbeams flashed twinkling and gleaming lights here and there in the great glacier above them, and grim Falkniss reared its towers of rock with all its oldtime splendor high into the deep blue of heaven.

The wind of morning breathed softly and deliciously over the face of the mountain and stirred with its gentle touch the few bluebells still left from the thousands of summer. And they nodded their tiny heads sleepily in the warm sunshine. The big bird of prey flew high in the air in ever-widening circles, but he did not scream today. With wings widespread, he floated peacefully through the blue haze of light and took his ease.

Heidi's eyes missed no part of it all. It was so beautiful, every bit—the flowers nodding gaily, the blue sky, the happy sunshine, the birds contentedly hovering in mid air! The child's eyes shone with joy. She glanced at her friend to see if he was noticing all this loveliness, for until this moment the doctor had been silently looking about him, sunk in his own thoughts. But now, as he caught Heidi's glowing look, he said—

"Ah, my dear, it might be very beautiful here! But tell me, if a man brings a sad heart to this spot, how can he go about things so that he can enjoy it all?"

"O-ho!" Heidi cried happily. "Your heart is never sad here—but only when you're in Frankfort."

A smile passed over the doctor's face, but it went as quickly as it had come. Then he said again—

"Suppose a man should come up here and bring all the sadness from Frankfort with him. Do you know of anything that could help in such a case?"

"When he no longer knows how to help himself, then he must just tell all his troubles to the dear God," Heidi answered with perfect trust.

"That is a fine thought, my child," said the doctor. "But suppose that what makes you so sad and miserable comes from Him in the beginning, what can you say to the dear God then?"

Heidi had to stop and think what might be done in such a case. But one thing she was sure of, and that was you could get help from the dear God, no matter what your sorrow might be. She found the answer she wanted in her own experience.

"Why, then you just have to wait," she said firmly, after a moment's pause. "And you have to think to yourself, 'The dear God knows at this very moment of some happiness that is coming to me later on, so I must just be patient and not run away from him.' Then all at once things will turn out so that you can tell the dear God was only planning for your good all the time that you were doubting Him. But you couldn't be expected to see that at first, because you were only thinking of the awful sadness of the moment and didn't know that would change by and by."

"You have a beautiful faith, and you must never lose
it, Heidi," the doctor said.   He looked for a while without speaking at the vast rocky mountains across from
them, and then down into the sunlit valley of green.
Then he went on to say—

"You see, Heidi, a man might be sitting here with a
great shade over his eyes, so that he could not take in
any of the beauty which surrounded him.   And then his
heart might be sadder than ever, just here where it is so
lovely.   Can't you see that?"

A pain shot through Heidi's happy heart at these words.

The great shade which the doctor said lay across his
eyes made her think of Grandmother, who was never again
to see the bright sun and the beauty of the uplands.   That
was a sorrow that always woke to new life in Heidi's
heart whenever the memory came to her.   For a time she
had nothing to say because of the grief that had so spoiled
her joy.   But then she said earnestly—

"Yes, Doctor, I understand what you mean.   But
there's another thing I know, and that is, when you feel so
badly you must say one of Grandmother's hymns.   It's sure
to make you feel a little brighter, anyway, and sometimes
it helps so much that you're quite cheerful again.   Grandmother says so."

"What hymns **are you** speaking of, Heidi?" the
doctor asked.

"I only know the one about the sun and the beautiful
garden," Heidi answered, "and a few verses from the
other long hymn that Grandmother's fond of.   I always
have to read them three times to her."

"Say those verses for me, won't you? I'd like to hear them, too." And the doctor settled down to listen very carefully.

Heidi folded her hands and thought for a moment before speaking.

"Shall I begin at the place where Grandmother says faith always comes back into her heart?"

The doctor nodded his head in assent.

Then Heidi began:

> Have faith that He will lead thee,
> Thy Savior wise and true,
> That He will ever feed thee
> In wondrous pastures new.
> He shows the ways of living
> To those who heed His word,
> His love and counsel giving
> Where'er His voice is heard.
>
> At times He seems to leave thee,
> Nor sees thy searching hand;
> Though doubt and sorrow grieve thee.
> He hears not thy demand,
> As if His face were hidden
> Forever from thy sight
> And hope itself forbidden
> To pierce the gloom of night.
>
> But if thy faith uphold thee
> Through evil's loud alarms,
> He comes again to fold thee
> Within His tender arms.
> He never fails to quicken
> The spirit sore oppressed.
> All who are heavy stricken
> Find His eternal rest.

But, after she had been reciting for quite a while, she suddenly came to a stop, for she was not sure that the doctor heard what she was saying. He had put his hand over his eyes, and was sitting perfectly still.

Heidi thought perhaps he had dozed off for a moment. She decided to wait until he woke up again, and then if he wanted to hear some more verses he would tell her so. Not a sound came to break the deep silence.

The doctor did not speak, but he was not sleeping. His mind had been carried back to long-forgotten days. He was again standing, a little boy, beside the chair of his dear mother. She had put an arm around his neck and was reciting to him the hymn that Heidi had just been saying, the verses that he had not heard for many long years. Again he heard the voice of his mother and saw her dear eyes resting so fondly upon him, and after the words of the hymn had died away, the pleasant voice seemed to be speaking other words to him. The doctor must have loved to listen to them again and must have been thinking of them, for he sat there a long time, his face still buried in his hands, silent, without movement of any sort.

When he finally straightened up, he noticed that Heidi was looking at him oddly. He took the child's hand in his.

"Your hymn was lovely, Heidi," he said, and his voice was more cheerful than it had yet been. "We must come up here some other day, and then you can recite it for me again."

While this was going on, poor Peter was just as busy as he could be getting rid of his anger. It was several

days now since Heidi had come with him up to the pasture, and now that she had got there at last, this old
gentleman spent all his time with her and gave him no
chance to be with her at all. This made him hopping
angry, and he didn't think it fair.

So he sat down quite a way off and behind the gentleman's back, so that the unsuspecting doctor could not see
him when he doubled up his fist and shook it threateningly, or yet later, when he clenched both his fists and
waved them in the air. And the longer Heidi remained
sitting beside her friend, the more wildly did Peter double
up his fists, the more madly did he shake them at the back
of his enemy's head.

In the meantime the sun had got to that point in the
sky where it stands when the hour has come for dinner.
Peter never made a mistake in this important matter.
So suddenly he howled down with all his might to the
others—

"We've got to eat!"

Heidi rose to her feet and started to get the luncheon
bag so that the doctor could have his noonday meal right
where he sat. But he said he was not hungry and only
wanted a glass of milk to drink. After that he'd like to
walk around the mountain a bit and then climb higher
up. Thereupon Heidi found out that she was not hungry
either, and also wanted nothing but milk, and then she'd
like to take the doctor up to the big moss-covered stones
where Distelfink once upon a time had almost jumped
down and where all the spicy herbs grew. She ran over
to Peter and explained it all to him. She told him first

to get a bowlful of milk from Schwänli for the doctor, and then another one for her.

Peter gaped open-mouthed at Heidi for an instant, and then he asked suddenly—

"Who's to have what's in the sack?"

"You are," Heidi answered. "But first you must hurry and get us our milk."

Hurry, must he? Never in his life had Peter done anything half so quickly as he now milked Schwänli. For he saw the luncheon bag right there before him, and he didn't know what the contents looked like, and they belonged to him.

The moment his two companions had quietly drained their milk and turned away, Peter opened the bag and took a peek at its inside. When he caught sight of the wonderful piece of meat it contained, Peter was all a-tremble, and he had to have another look in the bag to make sure that the meat was real. Then he thrust in his hand to take out the welcome gift and eat it, when suddenly he drew his fingers back again as if he did not dare seize it.

For he remembered how he had stood there behind the gentleman's back and shaken his fist at him, and now that very same person was giving him a whole dinner the like of which he had never seen. And suddenly Peter was sorry for what he had done, for he felt as if his silly act now kept him from taking out the fine present and eating it. Then all at once it came to him what to do.

He jumped to his feet and ran back to the spot where he had stood a few minutes before. When he got there, he stretched his open hands high above him as a sign that clenching his fists no longer meant anything. And in that position he stood for some little time, until he felt that the whole matter was forgiven and forgotten. Then he tore back to the luncheon bag. And now that he had straightened things out with his good conscience he was able to set to work upon his unusual dinner in perfect enjoyment.

The doctor and Heidi had been wandering around together for a long while and had been enjoying themselves extremely. But then the doctor found that it was time for him to go back, and thought, too, that the child would not be sorry to spend a little while longer with her goats. Heidi, however, had no idea of doing this, for if she did, the guest would have to make the long return trip all by himself. So she insisted that she would walk with him as far as her grandfather's hut, at least, and perhaps a little way farther.

She went along with her good friend, therefore, her hand in his, and on their march there was no lack of things to show him and tell him about. He had to see all the spots where the goats liked best to graze, and where in summer the thickest masses of yellow roses and red centauries bloomed. She knew about these flowers and many others, for Grandfather had taught her their names, as far as he himself knew them.

But at last the doctor said that he really must be going. They said good-by to each other and he took the path down the mountain. But every now and then he would turn back to see Heidi still in the place where he had left her, following him with her eyes and waving her hand to him. Just so had his own dear daughter done whenever he used to go away from home.—

It was a clear, sunny autumn month. Each morning without fail the doctor would come up on the mountain, and then they would start off at once on some delightful trip or other. Often he accompanied Meadow Nuncle on an excursion high up into the rocky mountains, where old weather-beaten fir trees nodded down at them. And the great bird of prey must have had his nest somewhere about there, for he often shot past quite close to the heads of the two men with a mighty whir of feathers and loud screaming.

The doctor found great pleasure in his companion's conversation and could not but be amazed at Nuncle's store of knowledge about the many plants around them on the mountain side. He knew what they could be used for. He found something precious and valuable in all of them, as, for example, in the resinous pines and in the dark firs with their fragrant needles, in the curly moss sprouting between the roots of the old trees, as well as in the delicate, small plants and the half-invisible flowers that spring late in the year from the sturdy soil of the Alps.

And the old gentleman had just as exact a knowledge of the life and habits of all the highland animals both great and small. And he had a great stock of amusing tales for the doctor about the ways of the little folk which dwell in the rock caves and in the earth caverns, and even in the branches of the lofty firs.

Time passed as if by magic on these excursions, and often at dusk, when the doctor was shaking Nuncle's hand at parting, he would say—

"My dear friend, I never say good-by to you but that I am the wiser by having learned something new."

But on many days and generally on the very finest of all, the doctor wished to go with Heidi. At such times the two often sat together on the beautiful spur of the mountain where they had been the first day after his arrival, and here Heidi had to recite the verses of her hymn again and tell the doctor everything she was thinking about. And Peter would often be crouched behind them as they sat and talked, but by now he had grown quite tame and no longer shook his fists at them.

So the fair month of September drew to its close.

Then, one morning, the doctor came, but he did not look by any means as happy as he usually did. He said that this was his last day and that he had to go back to Frankfort. He did not like this at all, for he had grown to be as fond of the mountain as if it were his own home.

This news, as you might expect, was unwelcome to Meadow Nuncle, for he, too, had come to enjoy the doctor's conversation very much indeed. And as for Heidi, she had grown so accustomed to seeing her beloved friend every day that, for the life of her, she could not understand why their joy should have such a sudden end. She looked up at him in wonder, thinking she might have made a mistake. But it was just as the doctor said. He bade Grandfather farewell and then asked if Heidi would not walk with him a piece. She tucked her hand in his and went down the mountain with him, but still she just could not get it through her head that he was really going.

After a while the doctor stopped and said that Heidi had walked far enough now and must be turning back. He ran his hand once or twice through the child's curly hair and said—

"And now I must leave you, Heidi. How I wish I could take you back to Frankfort with me and keep you always!"

At these words the picture of Frankfort rose before Heidi's eyes. She saw the long rows of houses and the many stone streets, and Miss Rottenmeier and Tinette. So she answered her guest a little timidly—

"But I'd rather have you come back and stay with us again."

"Now you speak of it," the doctor said, pleasantly, "I believe that would be better."

He held out his hand to the child. Heidi laid hers in it and looked at her friend who was so soon to go away. The kindly eyes that were gazing down at her filled with tears. Then the doctor swung around and hurried off down the mountain.

Heidi stood stock still. The doctor's fine eyes and the tears that she had seen in them went straight to her tender heart. Suddenly the child burst out into violent weeping and ran as fast as her legs would carry her after the disappearing doctor. She called to him as loudly as she could, in the midst of her sobs—

"Doctor! Doctor!"

He turned around and waited for her.

By now the child had caught up with him. The tears ran down her cheeks as she sobbed out—

"Oh, surely I'll go with you right away to Frankfort. And I'll stay with you as long as ever you want me. But first I must run fast and tell Grandfather about it."

The doctor patted and stroked the little excited face.

"Oh, no, you mustn't, Heidi dear," he said in his kindest tones. "Not right now, anyway. You must stay on here under the fir trees so you won't scare us by getting sick again. But, see here, I want to ask you something! Suppose I get sick and have no one to nurse me, will you come then and stay with me? Can I think then that there is one who cares for me and is fond of me?"

"Oh, yes, you can. If you're sick, then I will surely come to you the very same day And, anyhow, I love you almost as much as I do Grandfather," Heidi sobbed forth.

Then once more the doctor pressed her hand and hurried away. But Heidi stood where she was and waved her hand again and again so long as there was the slightest speck of her disappearing friend to be seen in the distance. When he had turned around for the last time to look at the sunny mountain where Heidi stood and waved at him, he said softly to himself—

"It is good to live up there on the mountain where there is healing for the body and the soul, and where the joy of living is given back to one."

CHAPTER IV

WINTER IN THE HAMLET

On the mountain meadow the snow lay so deep around the hut that it looked as though the windows were standing on the level of the ground, for beneath them not a bit of the cottage walls was to be seen, and even the entrance door had entirely disappeared.

If Meadow Nuncle had been living up there, he would have had to do the same thing Peter did every day when, as usual, there had been a fresh snow the night before. Each morning the goatherd was forced to jump out the window of his room, and if it had not been cold enough during the night to form a stiff crust he sank down almost over his head in the soft snow. Often Peter had to struggle and strike out around him with his hands and his head and feet, in order to work his way out to freedom.

Then his mother would hand him the big broom out of the window, and with this Peter would push and scrape the snow in front of him until he had come to the door. Nor was that the last of his task, for, when he came to the door, all the snow had to be dug away. For, you see, the snow was either still soft and so, when the door was opened, it would fall bodily into the kitchen; or it was frozen solid, and in that case they were completely walled in. And then no one could force his way through this cliff of ice, and of the three who lived in the hut Peter was the only one small enough to slip out through the little window.

Peter rather liked the weather when things froze hard. If he was bound for Dörfli, all he had to do was open the window, crawl through it, and stand on the level surface of the firm field of snow. Then his mother would shove his small sled through the window after him, and Peter could sit on that and start off wherever he wanted to. For, however he might go, he slid downhill just the same because the whole pasture land was nothing but a great continuous path of ice.

Nuncle had been as good as his word and was not living on the mountain meadow that winter. As soon as the first fall of snow had come, he closed the hut and the stable and, together with Heidi and the goats, moved down to The Hamlet.

There, near the church and the parsonage, stood a large, roomy building. In olden days this had been a fine piece of property, as might still be seen in many places, though the mansion was now more or less in a state of ruin. A brave soldier had lived in it once upon a time. He had fought in the Spanish wars and done many courageous deeds and returned with a great deal of money. He had come back to his native village Dörfli and with his riches, and had built himself a splendid house, for here he wished to end his days.

But, after all, he did not stay long. Life in the quiet Dörfli was too slow for him, and he had lived too many years in the noisy world to endure such peace. So, off he marched again one day, and never was seen afterward.

Many years came and went before it was surely known that the soldier was dead. And then a distant relative from down in the valley moved into the mansion, but by that time it had already begun to fall to pieces, and the new owner did not care enough for his property to repair it. So poor people rented the house for next to nothing, and when a part of the building would fall off they let it lie wherever it struck the ground.

Since that time many years had again passed by. And when Nuncle brought his young son, Tobias, back to Dörfli, he took the ruined house and lived in it. But since those long-forgotten days it had stood empty most of the time, for no one could possibly live in the place unless he knew how to keep the house from further ruin, and unless he could at least to some extent stop up the holes and gaps in its walls. For winters up in The Hamlet were long and cold.

The winds blew and blustered through the rooms from all directions, so that the candles were put out, and the poor people in the house shivered with cold. But Nuncle knew how to put an end to that. The moment he had decided to spend the winter in Dörfli, he rented the old mansion again and often during the autumn had been coming down to the village to repair it whenever he had a few moments to spare. And about the middle of October he and Heidi had moved down.

If you entered the house the back way, you came at once to an open room. One of its walls had quite fallen in, and the other was half gone. Above this space a bay window was still to be seen, but its glass had long been broken and matted ivy twined around it, climbing up to the roof, which was in great part still solid. This rear apartment was beautifully arched, and there was no doubt but that it had once been a chapel.

From this an opening, the door of which was lost, led directly into a large hall. Here and there handsome tiles were still remaining in the floor, but between them thick grass was growing. In this place, too, the walls were half fallen and great pieces of the roof were missing. In fact, if two huge pillars had not still held up parts of the ceiling, one would have expected it to fall down at any moment upon the heads of those who stood beneath it.

Here Nuncle had put up a partition of boards and had covered the floor thickly with straw, for the goats were going to lodge in this old hall.

Then there were all kinds of corridors, always half open to the weather, so that from one you could look straight at the sky, from another at the meadows and the path outside. But in the front part of the house, where the heavy oak door still hung firmly on its hinges, there was a large room which was in good repair. Its four walls were still upright, its dark panels of wood unbroken, and in one corner stood a monstrous stove that reached almost to the ceiling, and on its white glazed tiles big blue pictures were painted.

There were pictures on the tiles of old castles set on heights flanked by tall trees, and down below a huntsman was walking with his dogs. Then again there were scenes of a peaceful lake under wide-spreading oak trees, with a fisherman standing on the bank and holding his rod far out over the water. All about the stove was built a bench, so that one might sit down and study the pictures close at hand.

Heidi fell in love with this spot at first sight. The very moment she entered the living room with her grandfather, she had run to the stove, sat down on the bench, and begun to gaze at the pictures.

But when she had slipped along on the bench until she was in behind the stove, something new happened to attract her whole attention. In the fairly large space between the stove and the wall four boards had been set up, as if to form a bin for apples. But there were no apples in the bin. In their place stood Heidi's bed, unmistakably put together just as it had been up on the mountain meadow—a high couch of hay, with the linen sheet and the sack to cover· it. Heidi cried aloud—

"O Grandfather, here's my bedroom! And it's beautiful! But where are you going to sleep?"

"Your room must be right by the stove so that you don't freeze," Grandfather said. "But you can find mine, too, if you'll hunt for it."

Heidi hopped across the broad room after Grandfather, who was on the other side, opening a door that led into a small cabinet where he had set up his bed. But then there was another door on beyond. Heidi pulled this quickly open and then stood still in her amazement, for she was looking into a kind of kitchen, the most enormous one she had ever dreamed of.

There had been much work for Grandfather to do in this room. In fact, there was still a good deal to be done, for everywhere in the walls there were holes and wide cracks where the wind blew in. And this in spite of the fact that he had nailed so many of them shut with boards.

It looked as though he had made a row of small cupboards all around the place. The old gentleman had also managed to fasten together the very ancient entrance door with wires and spikes so firmly that it could be tightly shut. And it was well that he could, for it looked out on the most ruined part of the house, where the rank weeds grew thickly and where whole swarms of beetles and lizards lived.

The new mansion pleased Heidi very much, and by the following day when Peter came to see how they were getting along in it she had examined all the nooks and corners so thoroughly that she felt quite at home there and could show Peter everything. And she would not let him rest until he had seen every last one of the wonderful things which the new home contained.

Heidi slept like a top in her corner by the stove. But, when morning came, she would always imagine she was walking up on the mountain and that she must open the door of the hut at once to find out why the fir trees were so quiet. She would think it might be because their boughs were weighted down by the deep, heavy snow which lay on them.

So at first she had to look around her every morning for a long time before she could remember where she was. And the moment she did remember, she would feel a choking sensation and her heart would be heavy because she was not in her home on the mountain pasture. And then she would hear her grandfather outside talking with Little Swan and Little Bear. And, perhaps, the goats would bleat loud and happily, as if they were calling, "It's fine out here, Heidi. Come right away!"

Then she would decide that she was indeed at home, after all. She would spring gaily out of bed and hurry at the first possible moment to the big goat stable. But, after she had taken scarcely a step out of the house for several days, she finally said one morning—

"I must be sure to go and call on Grandmother today. I must not leave her alone so long."

Grandfather, however, did not agree to this.

"Let's not talk about going today, or tomorrow, either, for that matter," he said. "The pasture land is buried under six feet of snow, and it's snowing this very minute. Peter himself is hardly strong enough to force his way through. Such a little creature as you, Heidi, would be snowed under the first thing and so covered up that your body would not be found before spring. You just be patient until it freezes hard, and then you can walk on top the crust as easy as anything."

To sit and wait like that made Heidi very wretched. But before long her days were so filled up with work that one day flew by after another without her realizing the fact.

Each morning and each afternoon Heidi now spent at school, and she learned very rapidly whatever was given her to do. She hardly ever saw Peter in school, for he was absent a good deal. The teacher was a mild man and had little to say about this, except—

"It seems as if Peter were not here again today. I wish he would come, for he needs to learn. But I suppose there's a lot of snow up where he is, and he can't get through."

It was surprising, though, how often Peter could force his way through the snow and call on Heidi the moment school was out, along about dark.

After a few days the sun came out again and shone down upon the white earth. It would remain only a short while and would then disappear behind the mountains very early, as if it did not care for what it saw nearly as much as in the summer time, when everything was green and in blossom. In the evening, on the other hand, the moon rose very bright and big, to shine the whole night on the broad snow fields, and the next morning the whole mountain would glisten and gleam from top to bottom, like a crystal.

On one such morning Peter jumped out of the window as he had done the day before, thinking to sink down into the deep snow. And then something happened that he did not expect.

He made his jump all right, but, instead of sinking in, he took a bad tumble on the unexpectedly hard surface, and the next minute he was skidding a long way down the mountain, like a sled with no one to guide it. In great surprise, he finally managed to get his footing and stamped as hard as he could on the crust of snow, to make sure that there was no chance about what had just happened to him. And he quickly found out the truth. No matter how much he might stamp and hack with his heels, he could scarcely break out the smallest splinter of ice. The entire mountain meadow was frozen as hard as a rock.

That suited Peter to a *T*. He knew this was the way things had to be so that Heidi could get up to his house.

He hastily went back home, gulped down the milk which his mother had just set down on the table, tucked a slice of bread into his pocket, and said—

"I've got to go to school."

"That's nice," his mother said agreeably. "Be a good boy and study hard."

Peter crawled out of the window again, for the door was wedged in tight by the solid block of ice before it, got out his little sled, sat on it, and started down the mountain like a shot.

Faster, ever faster he flew, like lightning!

When he reached Dörfli in his flight and came to the road that leads on down to Mayenfeld, Peter held to his course without stopping, since he feared he might hurt himself badly and injure his sled if he should come to a sudden halt. So he stuck to the path until he reached a long strip of level ground, and there of course the sled stopped of its own accord.

Then he climbed off and looked about him. The great force of his downward flight had carried him quite a way beyond Mayenfeld. He figured out that he was too late for school anyway, because the morning session had already begun and it would take him more than an hour to climb back up the mountain. So he did not need to hurry about the return trip. Nor did he. He came into Dörfli just as Heidi had got back home from school and was sitting down to dinner with her grandfather. Peter went in to see them. And, because he had one idea fixed in his mind so hard that he could not think of anything else, he started to speak right away.

"She's got it at last," Peter burst out the moment he had thrust his head in the door.

"Got what. What has she 'got,' General? That is a very warlike statement," said Nuncle.

"The snow," Peter replied.

"Oh, I know!" Heidi cried out gaily, for she at once understood what Peter was trying to say. "He means I can go up to Grandmother's now. But why didn't you come to school, you naughty? It was just as easy for you to slide down as it is for me to walk up."

A little frown was on Heidi's face and her voice was suddenly disapproving, for she did not think it was right to stay away from school when you could go just as well as not.

"Went too far on my sled before I could stop," Peter answered. "And then it was too late."

"In the army they call that deserting," Nuncle said. "And they punish deserters by pulling their ears, did you know that?"

In sudden terror, Peter tried to pull down his cap. For nobody in the world scared him quite as much as Meadow Nuncle.

"And besides, a commander-in-chief like yourself ought to be twice as ashamed to run away," Nuncle went on.

Peter hung his head and felt almost like crying.

"What would you think," the old gentleman asked, "if your goats should go on strike, refuse to follow you any longer, and not do what they ought to do? What would you do in that case, General?"

"Beat them," answered Peter shortly.

"And suppose a boy acted like an unruly goat and got beaten a little, himself? What would you say to that?"

"I'd say it served him right."

"Well, then, let me tell you something, Colonel of Goats! The very next time you go flying past the schoolhouse on your sled during school hours, you come right in here to me, sir, and get what is coming to you."

Then Peter knew well enough what Meadow Nuncle meant when he said a runaway boy was like an unruly goat. He was a little frightened by the old man's words, and secretly he looked around in the corners to see if he could find any trace of the thing he used on his goats at such a time.

But nowhere did there seem to be a rod, and the next words of Nuncle were very encouraging—

"Come to dinner now and join in with us. Then Heidi can go up with you. You can bring her back this evening and find supper waiting for you here."

This made Peter quite happy. His face twisted into a shy grin. He obeyed without delay and sat down beside Heidi. But the child had already had enough to eat and couldn't swallow another bite, she was so delighted at the thought of going to see Grandmother. She pushed the big potato and the toasted cheese that still stood on her plate over to Peter, whose dish had already been filled by Nuncle. So he had a regular mountain of food in front of him, and he was not backward in attacking it.

Heidi ran to the cupboard and got the little cloak that Clara had sent her. And so she was ready, all wrapped warmly up in it and with its hood over her head, to start on the journey. She took her stand by Peter's chair, and no sooner had he thrust the last mouthful of food into his mouth than she said—

"Come on, now!"

So off they started. The very first thing, Peter had to hear all the latest news about Schwänli and Bärli. When they had been put in their new stall, neither of them would eat a blessed thing. The whole day they had just hung their heads and had not uttered a sound. And when she had asked Grandfather what was the matter, he told her that the goats felt exactly the same as she did in Frankfort, because they had never been off the mountain pasture before in all their lives. And Heidi added—

"You just can't imagine what a feeling that is, Peter."

Peter did not have a thing to say until they had almost come to the end of their journey. He seemed to be so busy thinking of something or other that he hardly heard what Heidi was chattering about. But just as they reached the hut, Peter stood still and said rather sulkily—

"Well, then, I'd sooner go to school than go to Nuncle and get what he said was coming to me."

Heidi said she thought he was right and did what she could to encourage him in his good resolution.

They found Peter's mother alone in the living room bent over her sewing. She said that Grandmother had to spend the day in bed because it was so cold, and then, too, she was not feeling quite herself. That was a new idea for Heidi. She always pictured Grandmother in her place by the spinning wheel in the corner. She ran straight into the bedroom. All wrapped up in the gray shawl, the old lady was lying on her narrow bed with its thin coverings.

The moment Grandmother heard Heidi's light footsteps, she raised her head a little and said—

"God be praised and thanked!"

All through the autumn she had had a secret fear about which she had told no one, a fear that she could not get rid of, especially if Heidi did not come to visit her for a while. Peter had told her all about the strange gentleman who had come from Frankfort and was forever walking up to the pasture to talk with Heidi. And Grandmother of course could not be persuaded that the gentleman had not come to take Heidi away with him again. And even after the doctor had gone off alone, she was still afraid that somebody else would be sent from Frankfort to carry the child away. Heidi ran to the sick woman's bed and asked with much sympathy—

"Are you dreadfully sick, Grandmother?"

"Oh my, no!" the invalid said, soothingly, stroking Heidi's cheeks as she loved to do. "The cold has got into my old limbs a little, that's all."

"Will you get well just the second it's warm again?" Heidi asked her eagerly.

"I promise I will. And, if God is willing, even before warm weather, for I want to get back to my spinning. I was thinking just this morning that I'd try getting up. But I'll be all right tomorrow, anyway."

Grandmother spoke as she did because she had noticed from the tone of Heidi's voice that the child was worried. And her words did comfort the little visitor, who had

had quite a shock this first time that she had seen Grandmother sick abed. She looked at the old lady in some surprise and then said—

"In Frankfort they put on a shawl when they go out to walk. Did you think, Grandmother dear, that it was meant to go to bed in?"

"You see, Heidi," the sick woman said, "I put the shawl around me in bed so as not to freeze. And I'm so glad to have it, because the bed covers are pretty thin."

"But, Grandmother dear," Heidi went on to say, "your head lies down hill when it ought to lie the other way. That's a funny bed, I must say."

"And don't you suppose I know it is, child? But, you see, the pillow never was very thick, and I've been sleeping on it for so many years that I've made it pretty flat."

Grandmother hunted around on her pillow to find a better place to rest her head, but without success. The old thing seemed as flat and hard as a board.

"Oh," cried Heidi, "if I had only asked Clara when I was in Frankfort to let me bring my bed home with me! Why, it had three great fat pillows, one on top of the other. And I couldn't sleep, because my head was always sliding down to a flat place and then I had to put it back again so that I could sleep right. Could you sleep on so many pillows, Grandmother?"

"Surely I could. That keeps you warm, and then you can breathe more easily when your head is high."

The old lady lifted her head from the pillow with some difficulty, as if to find a higher place for it.

"But we won't talk about that any more," she said. "I

have so much to thank God for that other sick old ladies do
not have.   There are the nice rolls that come every day,
and there is this fine, warm shawl, and then, besides, there's
you to come and see me.   I wonder if you'll read something
to me again today, Heidi."

Heidi ran out of the room and soon came back with
the old hymn book.   Then she sought out one beautiful
song after another, for by this time she knew them all well
and enjoyed going through them once again.   It had been
many days since she had heard all these verses of which
she was so fond.

Grandmother lay beside her with folded hands, and
there was now a happy smile on her face which had at
first looked so troubled.   She seemed to think that some
great good fortune had happened to her.   Suddenly Heidi
stopped reading.

"Grandmother, are you all well again?" she asked.

"You have done me good, Heidi.   I've been getting
better all the time you've been reading to me.   Finish
the hymn, dear."

The child went on to the very end of the song.   And
when she was reading the last words, which speak of
the light God pours into the sad eyes of men, Grandmother recited them with her, and said them over yet
again afterward.   A look of joy came into her face.

Heidi was happy to watch the change come in Grandmother's eyes.   She suddenly remembered how the sun shone
the day she returned home, and she cried out happily—

"O Grandmother, I've already learned how one feels
when he is going back home!"

There was no answer, at least not in words, but Heidi could tell that the old lady had understood perfectly what she said, for the look that she so loved to see stayed in Grandmother's face.

After a short silence the child said again—

"Now it's growing dark and I must go down to The Hamlet. But I am glad that you are so much better."

Grandmother took Heidi's hand in hers and held it fast.

"Yes, I'm so happy again," she smiled. "Even if I must keep to my bed, I am content. You see, until one has been through it himself, nobody knows how miserable it is to have to lie for days and days abed and all alone. Never to hear a word from another's lips, never to see a single ray of light! Then it is that such gloomy thoughts pop into your head, and you often feel as if the light of day would never come again, and as if you just could not stand it another minute. But when you hear such words of promise as you have read to me, then it's as if a light shines into your heart and all the darkness is driven away."

Grandmother drew her hand away. Heidi said good night to her and ran back to the other room. She made Peter scramble out after her through the little window as fast as he could, for it was now growing late. But, although it was evening, the moon outside was up in the sky, and it shone as brightly on the white snow as if a new day were dawning.

Peter got his sled ready, sat down on the front part of it, with Heidi close behind, and they shot off down

the mountain pasture quite as if they were two birds
hurtling through the air.

Later on, that night, when Heidi was lying behind
the stove on her fine high couch of hay, she thought about
Grandmother again. She remembered how uncomfortable
her head had been on its hard pillow. She heard again all
that had been said, and saw the happy light the words of
the hymn had kindled in the old face.

And she could not help thinking that if Grandmother
heard the words every day, then she would always feel
more cheerful. But Heidi knew that a whole week, and
perhaps two, must now pass by before she could go
up for another visit. What could be done? It seemed so
sad to Heidi that she kept thinking harder and harder
how it might be so managed that Grandmother could
hear her hymns every day.

The way of help suddenly occurred to her. And she
was so happily excited about it that it seemed as if she
could not wait until daylight came so that she could carry
out her plan. All at once she sat straight up in bed, because
she had been so busy thinking she had forgotten to say
her evening prayer to the dear God, and she did not want
to let that slip by even once, no matter what happened.

When she had ended her prayer for herself, and for
Grandfather and Grandmother, she fell back on her soft
hay and slept soundly and peacefully until broad daylight.

CHAPTER V

THE WINTER CONTINUES

Next day Peter came down to school at just the right time. He brought his dinner with him in his bag, for that was what all the pupils did, except those that lived in the village.

When the Dörfli children went home at noon, then the others who lived at a distance sat down on the classroom desks, planted their feet firmly on the seats in front of them, spread out on their knees the food that they had brought, and proceeded to eat.

They had until one o'clock for play, and then school began again. When Peter had finished his school day, he went the moment it was over across to Nuncle's to pay a visit to Heidi.

This day, when after school he had gone to Nuncle's and entered the big living room, Heidi ran to meet him, for he was just the one whom she had been waiting for.

"Peter, I've got something to tell you," she called to him.

"Out with it!" he said.

"You've got to learn to read right away."

"Haven't I been doing it?" demanded Peter.

"Oh, sort of, Peter! But I don't mean that kind of reading," Heidi said, excitedly. "I mean so that you can read by yourself."

"No use!" the boy answered.

"Pshaw! Nobody believes you can't learn, and I don't either," Heidi said firmly. "Grandmama in Frankfort knew it wasn't true, and she told me so."

Peter was greatly astonished at this news.

"I'll teach you to read, if you'll let me. I know how to do it fine," Heidi went on to say. "You just have to learn first from me and then afterward you can read a hymn or two every day to Grandmother."

"Bet you I can't. There's no sense in it," growled Peter.

The way that Peter just wouldn't try to do anything that was good and right, when she wanted him to so much, made Heidi very angry. Her eyes flashed as she stood in front of the boy and said, in a threatening manner—

"All right then! I'll tell you fast enough what's going to happen to you if you get sulky and won't learn. Didn't I hear your mother herself tell you twice that you'd have to go to Frankfort and learn all sorts of things you didn't want to? And I guess I've seen the school that they go to, the bad boys!"

"Aw, how'd you ever see that?"

"Well, I did! When we were driving, Clara showed me the great big house. And they don't stop going there when they're only boys, but they keep on going, even after they've grown to be great tall men. I've seen them myself. And don't you go thinking they only have one teacher, the way we have here, and a nice teacher, too. No, sir. Whole rows of them are always walking into the house, ever so many of them together, and they're all

dressed in black, like when they go to church. And they
have black hats on their heads as tall as that—"

Heidi showed the size of the hats by holding out her
hand quite a way up from the floor.

A shiver ran up Peter's back and then down again.

"And then you have to go in there among all those
teachers," Heidi went on to say, eagerly. "And when it
comes your turn, you can't read anything at all and make
mistakes in spelling. Then you just wait and see how
those teachers will laugh at you! They say it's even
worse than when Tinette laughs at you, and you ought
to see how it feels when she gets started!"

"Oh, I'll learn then," Peter said, half whining and half
angry.

Heidi grew soft and gentle at once.

"Now you're a nice boy," she said happily. "We'll
begin this minute." She hurried Peter over to the table
and got out all the necessary tools.

In the big bundle that Clara had sent, there was a
small book that pleased Heidi immensely. When she had
been thinking things over in bed the night before, it suddenly occurred to her she might use this book to teach
Peter out of. It was an ABC book with rimes.

Then they both sat down at the table, their heads bent
over the little book, and the lesson hour began.

Peter was made to spell out the first rime again and
again, for Heidi wished him to know the sentence nicely
and without any stumbling. At last, however, she said to
him—

"You don't know it still, but I'll read it over to you

several times. After you know how it runs, then you can
spell it out better. And Heidi read—

> If in A B C you fail,
> They will send you off to jail.

"I won't either," said Peter, sulkily.

"Won't what?" Heidi asked him.

"Won't go to jail," the boy answered.

"Then you see to it that you know those three letters,
and they won't send you there," Heidi told him.

At that, Peter again set to work and repeated the three
letters steadily, until Heidi said—

"Now you know the first three."

But, because she had seen what an effect the rime
made on Peter, she decided to read ahead a little for the
lessons that were to follow.

"You wait, and I'll read you the other rimes," she
continued. "Then you'll see what's going to come next."

And then she began to read in a clear and distinct
voice—

> D E F G you now must say,
> Or you'll have bad luck all the day.

> If you forget H I J K,
> The same bad luck will come to stay.

> Now if at L and M you stick,
> You pay a fine and then feel sick.

> There's something fine that waits for you
> When you've learned N O P and Q.

> And if at R S T you halt,
> Whatever happens is your fault.

Here Heidi stopped a while, for Peter had become as still as a mouse, and she had to see what was the matter. All the threats and secret things that the rimes spoke of had taken such hold on his imagination that he could not move a muscle. He was staring at Heidi with eyes full of fear.

That touched Heidi's tender heart, and she said to soothe him—

"Don't be afraid, Peter. If you'll only come in every afternoon and learn as well as you have today, then after a while you'll know all the letters by heart and then nothing bad will happen to you. But you'll have to come every day now, and not play hookey as you do in school. Even if it snows, it won't do you any harm."

Peter promised to be good, for fear had made him quite tame and obedient. Then he started for home.

In the days that followed he did exactly what Heidi told him to, and every afternoon he studied the other letters of the alphabet so eagerly that he soon knew the rimes by heart.

Grandfather would often sit in the living room and listen to the lesson while he contentedly smoked his pipe. But, do what he would, he could not keep the corners of his mouth from twitching sometimes, he had such a great desire to laugh.

As a reward for his great struggles Peter was usually asked to stay for supper with them. And he always felt that this more than paid him for the awful efforts that he had had to make to learn the day's rime.

So the winter days passed quickly by. Peter was regular in his attendance and soon began to make real progress with his letters.   His worst moments were when he was fighting his rimes.

Finally they got as far as the letter *U*.   When Heidi read him this rime, he grew sulky and growled.

> If you mix up your U and V,
> You'll go where you don't want to be.

"I'll bet they couldn't make me!" he muttered.

But he learned his rimes thoroughly just the same. And it looked as if he really did believe someone might secretly take him by the collar and carry him off to the bad place where he did not want to go one little bit.

On the following afternoon Heidi read—

> Whate'er you do, don't stick at W,
> Or here's the stick that's sure to trouble you.

Then Peter looked around him and said in triumph— "Aw, there isn't any stick!"

"Oh, isn't there?" Heidi asked.   "Don't you know what Grandfather keeps in his big chest?   It's a stick as big around as my arm almost.   And when he takes that out, you have to say, 'There's the stick that's sure to trouble me!'"

Peter was well acquainted with the big hazel cane that Grandfather often carried when he went on a long tramp. So he immediately bent over his letter *W* and did his best to learn it.

Next day after that he read—

> If you the letter X forget,
> Your place at the table won't be set.

Peter looked questioningly in the direction of the

cupboard where the bread and cheese were kept, and he demanded crossly—

"Did I ever say that I would forget the letter *X?*"

"That's good! And now, as you're not going to forget *X*, we can learn the next letter right away," Heidi proposed. "Then tomorrow, we'll have only one letter left to learn."

Peter did not see the sense of such hurrying. But Heidi had already begun to read—

> If you can't learn the letter **Y**,
> We'll scorn and shame you till you cry.

When he heard this rime, there before Peter's eyes stood all the teachers in Frankfort, with their tall black hats on their heads, and scorn and shame for him written in their faces. So he at once tackled *Y*, and did not let go of it until he knew it so well that he could close his eyes and still tell how it looked.

The following day when he got to Heidi's house, Peter was feeling a trifle puffed up, for you see there was only one letter left for him to work at. Heidi read him the rime—

> Send the bad boy who knows not **Z**
> To Hottentot Land across the sea!

Peter said sneeringly, "I don't suppose anybody knows where that place is."

"They do, too, Peter," Heidi answered confidently. "My grandfather knows all about it. Just wait a minute and I'll ask him right away where the Hottentots are. He's only at the pastor's house."

Heidi had already jumped to her feet and was walking toward the door. Peter was badly scared.

"Wait won't you?" he howled in great alarm, for in his imagination he saw Meadow Nuncle and the pastor coming in. And he almost felt them seize him and start to bundle him straight off to the Hottentots since he couldn't remember what the name of Z was. His cry of alarm halted Heidi before she reached the door.

"Why, what's the matter?" she asked in amazement.

"Nothing's the matter," Peter stammered. "Come back and I'll learn it, honest!"

But Heidi really wanted to know for her own information where the Hottentots lived and so was going to ask her grandfather about them, anyway. But Peter screamed at her so that she gave up her plan and came back. He had to work hard, however, to pay her back for her kindness. She not only made him repeat the letter Z over and over, until it stuck fast in his mind so he could never forget it, but she took up the subject of syllables. And on that afternoon Peter learned so much that he took a great step forward.

In this manner the lessons went on day after day.

The snow had grown soft again, and lately there had not been twenty-four hours without a fresh fall of snow, so for almost three weeks Heidi had been unable to go up to Grandmother's. That made her all the more eager to get Peter to the point where he could take her place in reading the hymns. And so it came about that one evening Peter returned from Heidi's and ran into the sitting room of his mother's house, saying—

"I can do it."

"What can you do, Peterli?" his mother asked.

"Read," he answered.

"Why, is that possible! Do you hear what he is saying, Grandmother?" Brigitte called.

Yes, the old lady had heard Peter's boast and was dumb with amazement, wondering how it all happened.

"Heidi said I had to read a hymn to you," Peter went on to report.

His mother ran to take the book from its shelf, and Grandmother was pleased, because she had not heard the good words read for a long time. Peter sat down at the table and began to read, while his mother sat down beside him to listen. At the end of each verse she said in much surprise—

"Who would have thought it possible?"

And Grandmother found nothing to add to Brigitte's words, but she listened with great interest as Peter read to her one verse after another.

The day after he had shown what he could do with the hymn book, it happened that Peter's class in school had a reading lesson. When it came to Peter's turn, the teacher said—

"Peter, must I again pass you by, as I generally do, or do you wish once more to try to blunder through a line?"

The boy's only answer was to read three lines one right after the other without stopping.

The teacher laid down his book. He stared at his pupil in silent amazement as if he had never seen his like. At last he said—

"Peter, a miracle has happened to you. Although I almost worked my head off to teach you, you were never able to get even the alphabet straight. And now, the moment that I give you up as a bad job, much as I hate to do so, you come right out with a knowledge not alone of spelling, but of reading correctly and clearly. Who in these days can perform such miracles?"

"Heidi," Peter answered.

Much taken back by this simple remark of Peter's, the teacher looked at Heidi. But she was sitting in her place looking so innocent that there seemed to be nothing unusual about her. So the teacher went on to say—

"I have noticed other changes in you, Peter. You used to stay away from school a week at a time, yes, several weeks even. And now you are never absent. Who has brought about in you this great change for the better?"

"Nuncle," was the answer.

The poor schoolmaster kept getting more surprised than ever. He looked from Peter to Heidi and from Heidi back to Peter.

"Let us try it once more," he then said, in order to make sure. And again the boy had to show his knowledge by reading the next three lines. But he got through all right. He had learned to read.

The moment school was over, the teacher hastened to the pastor's house to tell him what had happened and how much good Nuncle and Heidi were doing in the village.

Peter now read a hymn at home every evening. In so far he obeyed Heidi, but not a step farther. For he never read a second hymn, and Grandmother never asked him to.

His mother, Brigitte, never ceased to wonder that Peter had learned so well, and many an evening after the reading

was over and the boy was in bed, she would say to Grandmother—

"We just can't be happy enough that Peter has learned
to read, in spite of everything.   Now there's no telling
what he may do."

Then Grandmother would answer—

"Oh, yes, it is nice of him to have learned.   But, just
the same, I shall be glad when the dear God sends His
spring weather to us again, so that Heidi can come and see
us.   I always feel different about a hymn when she is reading it.   There seems to be something left out when Peter
is reading a verse, and I am always hunting to see what it
is.   And then I lose the thought of a hymn, and it doesn't
go straight to my heart, the way it does when I am listening
to Heidi's words."

One reason for Grandmother's trouble was that Peter
fixed the hymns up a little so they would not be too hard
for him.   When he saw a word coming that looked too long
or too difficult, he simply left it out.   He thought it would
not really matter to Grandmother whether there were three
or four words more or less in a line, or not.   There were
enough words left, anyway.

So it came about that there were not many nouns left
in a hymn when Peter got to reading it.

CHAPTER VI

NEWS FROM DISTANT FRIENDS

The month of May had come.

From the highlands the waters of the brooks, swollen by the spring thawing, rushed down into the valley. The mountain was bathed in warm, bright sunshine. The last snow had melted away, and, awakened by the soft charm of the sunlight, the whole earth had grown green again. The bright eyes of the first flowers were peering forth from the new grass.

The merry breezes of spring were blowing through the fir trees and shaking off their withered dark needles so that the bright green new needles might come out and give the trees a dress of fresh splendor. The old bird of prey flapped his wings in the blue air high above the world. And all around the hut on the mountain meadow the golden sunshine lay warm upon the ground and dried up the last wet places so that one could stretch himself at ease wherever he wished to be.

Heidi was back on the mountain again.

She ran here and there and did not know which spot she found the loveliest.

At one time the wind tempted her to listen to its deep and mysterious notes as it roared down from the cliffs above. It would come nearer and grow in power. It would dart to the trees, shake them and toss them, and then the wind would seem to howl in loud delight. And Heidi, too, would cry out in her joy while she was being blown to and fro like a tender leaf.

At another time she would run back to the sunny spot in front of the hut, sit down on the ground, and hunt about in the short grass to find out how many flower cups were open or nearly so. Such swarms of gnats and young beetles were hopping and crawling and dancing madly about in the sun that Heidi must be happy, too. She breathed in the sweet air of spring that seemed to rise from the freshly opened earth, and she felt that surely the mountain had never before been so beautiful. And the thousand little creatures liked it as well as she, for they were all humming and singing into Heidi's ears the chorus—

"On the mountain, ah, on the mountain, ah!"

From the shop behind the cottage came the frequent sounds of hammering and sawing. Heidi paused to listen to these familiar noises that she knew so well, for they had greeted her ears ever since she first came to live on the mountain meadow. Every now and then she just had to jump up and run to the shop to discover what Grandfather was doing. Before the door of the shop a fine new chair was standing all ready for use, and the old gentleman was skillfully at work on a second one.

"Oh, I know what that's for," Heidi cried gaily.

"Do you really?" Grandfather asked.

"We'll need that when they come from Frankfort. This one's for Grandmama, and the one you're making is for Clara, and besides—oh, I suppose we'll have to have one more," Heidi went on to say, more slowly. "Or, do you think, Grandfather, that perhaps Miss Rottenmeier won't come, after all?"

"I can't say, of course, but the safest thing is to have one ready so we can ask her to sit down if she does come."

Heidi looked doubtfully at the small wooden chairs, which were without arms and backs, wondering quietly how they would suit Miss Rottenmeier. After a while shaking her head doubtfully, she said—

"Grandfather, I don't believe she'd sit on them."

"Then we'll ask her to sit on the sofa that has the beautiful green sod for a covering," the old gentleman answered calmly.

While Heidi was wondering where the beautiful sod covering might be, there suddenly came from above them the sound of whistling and calling. A rod swished through the air. Heidi knew at once what that meant. She darted away and was quickly surrounded by the goats that ran down to meet her.

They must have felt as good as Heidi did to be up on the mountain again, for they jumped higher and bleated more fiercely than ever before. And they crowded Heidi one way and another in their eagerness to get close to her and tell her how glad they were. But Peter shoved them aside right and left, for he himself had a message to deliver to Heidi. When he had got close enough, he handed her a letter.

"There you are," he said, leaving Heidi to find out the rest for herself. She was very much surprised.

"Why, did you find a letter for me in the pasture?" she asked in her amazement.

"No," was Peter's only answer.

"Well, where did you find it then?"

"In my dinner bag."

And he told the truth, but not all of it. The evening before, the postmaster in The Hamlet had given Peter the letter for Heidi. He had thrust it into his empty bag. That morning, when he was starting from home, he had put his cheese and bread in on top of it. To be sure, he had seen both Nuncle and Heidi when he had come for the goats. But not until he had finished eating his bread and cheese that noon, and was hunting around for the last crumbs in the bag, had he again come upon the forgotten letter.

Heidi read the address on the envelope carefully. Then she ran back to the shop and, wild with joy, held the letter out to Grandfather.

"It's from Frankfort," she cried happily, "from Clara! Shall I read it to you, right off, Grandfather?"

The old gentleman said he wanted to hear it, and so, it seemed, did Peter, for he had followed Heidi and settled himself to listen. He leaned back against the doorpost so he could have a firm support for his body and devote all his attention to following the reading of the letter.

It was a long letter, and here it is:

"Dear Heidi—

We have everything packed up and are going to start in two or three days, as soon as Papa leaves. But he is not coming with us, he has to go first to Paris.

The doctor comes every day, and the second he's in the house he calls, 'All aboard for the mountains!' He just can't wait until we get off.

You can't imagine what a nice time he had in your Alps. The whole winter he's been coming to see us almost every day. He says he has to keep coming to my house so that he can talk it all over again.

Then he sits down in my room and tells me of each day he spent with you and Grandfather on the mountain, and he talks of the cliffs and the flowers, and of the peaceful quiet up there above all the villages and streets, and of how fresh the pure air is. He often says, 'Everybody must get well up there.'

He himself is very much changed from what he used to be, and now he seems quite young and happy again. Oh, how glad I shall be to see it all myself, to be with you on the mountain, and to be friends with Peter and the goats!

First, I have to go to Ragaz for a six weeks' stay. That is what Doctor orders. Then we are to live in Dörfli, and when the weather is nice I shall be carried up the mountain in my chair to spend the day with you.

Grandmama's coming along to stay with me. She is looking forward to seeing you again. But what do you think! Miss Rottenmeier does not want to come. Almost every day Grandmama asks her, 'How about a journey to Switzerland, my worthy Rottenmeier? If you want to go along, don't be backward in saying so.' But she always thanks her politely and says that she would only be in the way.

But I know what the housekeeper is thinking about. Sebastian told her such a terrible yarn about the mountain when he came back from his trip! He said frightful cliffs frowned down on you and there was always danger of falling into ravines and pits, and the way up was so steep that you might fall off backward at any minute. He said he believed goats might climb up the trail, but no human being could do it without constant danger of his life.

Miss Rottenmeier shuddered at what Sebastian said, and hasn't been so fond of Swiss journeys since. Tinette, too, got scared and she isn't coming. So we are coming by ourselves, just Grandmama and I. Sebastian travels as far as Ragaz with us, and then turns back again.

Good-by, Heidi dear. Oh, I just can't wait until I get to you! Grandmama sends you a thousand good wishes.

Your true friend,
Clara"

When Peter had heard what the letter said, he sprang away from the doorpost and swung his rod right and left so crazily and angrily that fear seized all the goats and they fairly flew down the mountain. In fact, they took such enormous jumps as they had very rarely taken before.

Peter tore after them, waving his rod in the air as if he was trying to work off his evil rage on some enemy that could not be seen. This enemy of Peter's was his thought about the guests who were coming from Frankfort, and just thinking about them filled his heart with bitterness.

Heidi, on the other hand, was so full of joy and happiness the next day she just had to go down and pay the

grandmother a visit. She was longing to tell her everything
—who was coming from Frankfort and, especially, who
was not coming.

Grandmother, Heidi felt sure, would find her news of
the greatest importance, for she knew all the people so
well and always showed deep interest in anything that
had to do with Heidi. So, early next afternoon, Heidi
set out, for now she could again go alone to make her visits.
At this season of the year the sun shone brightly again and
remained a long time in the sky, and it was fun running
down the mountain over the dry ground. Besides, the
merry May wind roared along behind her and pushed her
on at a great rate.

Grandmother no longer lay abed. She was back again
in her corner at the spinning wheel, and yet there was a look
on her face as if her thoughts were not entirely happy ones.
That look had been there since the evening before, and all
through the night her bad thoughts had pursued her and
kept her awake. For Peter had come home white with
rage, and, so far as Grandmother could make out from his
confused statements, a big crowd of people seemed to be
coming from Frankfort to stay in the hut on the mountain
meadow. Just what the meaning of this was, he did not
know, but Grandmother could not stop thinking about it,
and that is the reason her mind got so troubled that she
could not sleep.

Then Heidi ran in and went right over to the old lady.
She sat down on the little footstool that was always there
and began to pour forth her story with such eagerness
that she got more and more excited by it. But then, all

at once, she broke off in the middle of a sentence and asked anxiously—

"Why, Grandmother dear, whatever is the matter? Don't you like to hear this even a little bit?"

"Of course I do, Heidi. I am glad because you are going to enjoy it so," she answered, and tried to seem somewhat happier.

"Then, Grandmother, why can I see that you are worried about it? Are you afraid, perhaps, that Miss Rottenmeier will change her mind and come?"

To tell the truth, Heidi herself was slightly worried on this account.

"Oh, no, it's nothing, I tell you!" Grandmother said to comfort her. "Let me hold your hand a while, dear, so that I can know you are by me still. This visit will be a good thing for you, even if I don't live to see the end of it."

"I don't want any good thing that you won't live through, dear Grandmother," Heidi said very decidedly.

In fact, she spoke so firmly, as if everything was settled, that a new fear came to rest in the old lady's mind. She began to think the people were coming from Frankfort to take Heidi away again. For now that the child was well once more, surely they would want her back with them.

This was what Grandmother feared the most. And yet she did not feel that she ought to mention the matter before Heidi. The child might be so sorry for her that she would refuse to go, and that must not be. She sought to find a way out of her difficulty, and she did not have to hunt long, for there was one thing she wanted always.

"I tell you, Heidi," she said, after a short pause, "what will make me feel better and bring back my happy thoughts. Read me the hymn that begins, 'God is warder.'"

Heidi had come to know the old hymn book so well that she found at once the place that Grandmother wanted and read in a clear voice:

> God is warder,
> He will order
> Thy life as is best for thee.
> Billows foaming
> In the gloaming
> Daunt not thy security.

When she had finished, the old lady said—

"Yes, that is just what I wanted to hear."

And it did seem as if her heart was lighter, for the look of sorrow had now disappeared from her face. Heidi glanced at her thoughtfully a moment before she asked—

"Grandmother, the word 'best' in the hymn means that everything is healed and made whole again, doesn't it?"

"Yes, that's just what it means," the old lady said, nodding her head. "And because it's the dear God who promises to make things whole, you can count on its turning out all right, no matter how dark the future looks. Read it once more to me, Heidi, so we can learn the words by heart and never forget them."

Heidi read the closing lines of the hymn once, twice, three times, for God's promise of safety pleased her very much.

When it grew dark and Heidi again was strolling up the mountain side, one star after another appeared in the sky. They gleamed and sparkled down at her, exactly as if each one of them wished to send a ray of happiness to her heart. And almost every instant Heidi had to stop and look up at them, for they seemed to be twinkling at her more brightly from every part of the sky. So she called up to them—

"I know what you want to tell me, you dear stars! It is because God knows so well what is wholesome and best for us that we can be so happy and walk so safely."

Then the eyes of every star blinked and twinkled and winked at Heidi all the way up to the hut. And there she found Grandfather standing and looking up at the sky, for he said the stars had not shone so brightly since he could remember.

And in this month of May not only the nights were brighter and clearer than they had been for many years, but the days were, too. Grandfather would often look out of the door mornings and be surprised to notice how the sun rose in a cloudless sky as gloriously as it had set on the previous evening. And he would say repeatedly—

"It's an uncommonly sunny year. It will give sap to the grass and herbs. Look out, General Peter, or your springers will have such good fodder that they'll get the best of you!"

When Peter heard that, he swung his rod swishing through the air. And the look on his face said plainly enough—

"Huh! I'd just like to see them try it."

So May sped by with its budding and greening and June came with its warmer sun and with the long light days that tempted every flower on the mountain side to put forth blossoms. They shone and glowed round about on all sides, and the air was filled with their sweet odors.

And this second month of June was drawing to its close when one morning Heidi, who had already finished her work about the house, came running out of the hut. She was intending to go quickly over to the fir trees and then to climb a little higher up, to see if the great bush of centauries was yet in bloom, for these flowers were the prettiest sight in the world when the sun shone through them. But just as soon as Heidi started to run around the hut, she suddenly screamed at the top of her lungs. Nuncle stepped out of his shop, for he knew something unusual had happened.

"O Grandfather," the child cried, beside herself with joy, "come here and look!"

The old gentleman came at her call, and his eyes followed the outstretched arm of the excited child.

A strange procession, such as the mountain meadow had never seen before, was winding up the trail. First came two men carrying an open basket chair, in which a young girl was sitting wrapped up in many shawls. Then came a horse on which a stately lady was sitting, looking about her interestedly and having a lively chat with the young guide who walked at her side.

A little way behind there followed a wheel chair pushed along by still another young man. The chair was empty, because the sick girl who really belonged in it could be carried up the mountain trail more safely in a basket seat. Last of all came a porter, who had the hamper on his back

piled so high with rugs and shawls and furs that they
reached high above his head.

"There they are!" called Heidi, jumping up and down
with happiness.

And there was no longer any doubt who it was that
Heidi stood and watched. Nearer and nearer they came,
and finally, after what seemed years of waiting, they were
there.

The porters set the basket chair on the ground. Heidi
ran to it, and the two children hugged one another joyfully. Then Grandmama came up on her horse and dis-
mounted. Heidi ran to her in turn and was greeted with
a tender kiss. And then the old lady saw Meadow Nuncle,
who had stepped forward to bid her welcome. There was
no stiffness in the way they spoke to each other, for,
because of Heidi, they felt as if they had been friends
for years.

Hardly had the words of welcome been spoken, however, when Grandmama said with much enthusiasm—

"My dear Nuncle, what a beautiful estate you have up
here! Who in the world would have imagined it? Many
a king would envy you the possession of such a place. And
see how my Heidi is blooming, like a June rosebud!"

The old lady drew the child to her and stroked the red
cheeks. And then she turned to her own little grand-
daughter.

"What a glory there is all about us! What do you
say, Clara?"

The sick child was looking around her as if enchanted.
She had never dreamed of anything like this in all her life.

"How beautiful it is here!" she cried again and again. "I never imagined it. O Grandmama, I'd like to stay here always."

In the mean time Nuncle had pushed up the wheel chair, had taken some shawls out of the hamper, and made a soft seat with them. Then he went up to the basket chair.

"If we put the little girl into her chair now, she probably will rest more easily," he said. "The seat in the other one is too hard for comfort."

He did not wait for anyone to help him, but at once lifted weak Clara up in his strong arms and set her very gently down in the soft place he had prepared. Then he spread the rugs across her knees and wrapped up her feet on the cushion as comfortably as if he had done nothing all his life but look after invalids. Grandmama looked at him as if she could not believe her eyes.

"My dear Nuncle," she exclaimed, "if I knew where you learned to care for the sick, I'd have all the nurses sent to the same place for their hospital course. Who taught you how?"

Nuncle smiled a little.

"It comes more from experience, I suppose, than from study," he answered.

But, in spite of the smile, there was a trace of sadness in his eyes. From out the long-forgotten days of his past, Nuncle's mind again turned to the suffering face of a man who used to sit wrapped up in a chair, just like Clara, and who was so badly crippled that he could scarcely move a muscle.

The dream figure from the past was Nuncle's army captain, whom he had found lying on the ground, after a fierce battle in Sicily, and had carried on his back from the field.   And from that time on the captain wanted none but Nuncle as a nurse, and never let him out of his sight until death at last put an end to his great suffering.   The face of his sick friend again appeared to Nuncle and seemed to say that it was now his duty to nurse poor Clara and to show her all the comforting care that he understood so well.

The sky stretched dark blue and cloudless away over the hut and the pines and the lofty cliffs that rose high into the air, gray and shimmering.   Clara could not tire of gazing at the view, her heart was so stirred by it.

"O Heidi, I wish I could go around with you!" she cried out longingly.   "Around the corner of the hut, and under the fir trees!   And then I could visit every place that I've heard of so much but have never seen."

Just then Heidi made a great effort.   And, sure enough, she succeeded in wheeling the chair across the dry sward until it was beneath the firs.   Here she halted.

Clara had never before seen anything like these tall old pine trees, whose long and widespread boughs grew down to the ground and became larger and thicker there.   And Grandmama, too, who had followed the children, stood and gazed at the trees in wonderment.   She hardly knew which to think more lovely, the rustling summits so full of foliage or the straight strong tree trunks like pillars.   The mighty branches told their own story of the long row of years that they had been standing up there, while down below in the valley men had come and gone and everything had changed. But the trees were as they were in the beginning.

After a while Heidi pushed the wheel chair up to the goat stable and opened wide its small door, so that Clara could see all of it. There really was not much inside, as the occupants of the stall were not at home. Clara called, with much regret—

"O Grandmama, if I could only wait for Schwänli and Bärli and all the other goats, and Peter! I can never see them at all if we have to start home as early as you said. And that would be such a shame!"

"Dear child," said her grandmama, "let's just enjoy all the lovely things that are here, and not mind so much about what isn't." She followed after the chair, which Heidi was pushing.

"Oh, see the flowers!" Clara cried a moment later. "Whole bushes of delicate red flowers, and then all the little swaying bluebells! I wish I could get out and pick some of them."

Heidi ran off at once and brought back a large bunch of them.

"Oh, but they're nothing at all, Clara," she said, as she laid the flowers in her friend's lap. "You just ought to go with us up to the pasture, and then you'd see something, I tell you. In one spot all together there are ever so many bushes of red centauries and lots more bluebells than there are here, and, besides, so many bright yellow wild roses that the whole field looks as though it was pure gold. And then there are some flowers with big leaves and a big name, too, heliopsis. That's what Grandfather calls them, and he is always right, but Peter says they are only sun's eyes. Oh, and then there are the brown ones, too—you know the ones I mean, with little round tops, which smell so good. My, but it's fine in that place! When you once sit down there, you never, never want to get up again, it's so lovely!"

As she went on to tell about all this, Heidi's eyes sparkled with longing to see it again. And Clara caught the flame of her friend's excitement, until in her own soft blue eyes one could see reflected every bit of Heidi's enthusiasm.

"O Grandmama, do you suppose I could go up there? Do you think I could be carried so high?" the sick girl asked eagerly. "O Heidi, if I could only go climbing on the mountain with you, wherever I wanted to!"

"I'll push you if you want me to," Heidi said quietly.

And, to show how easy it would be for her, she ran around with the chair so fast that it almost got away from her hands and flew down the mountain. But Grandfather was standing close enough to catch the chair at just the right moment.

While they had been chatting under the fir trees, Grandfather had not been idle. The table and several chairs were now placed by the bench before the hut, and everything was ready for them to eat their dinner out of doors. Their food was still steaming in the kettle over the fire inside the hut, or toasting on the long fork over the coals. But it was not long before Grandfather had carried everything out to the table and the whole company had sat happily down to its meal.

Grandmama was quite enthusiastic about this dining room of theirs, from which one could see far down into the valley and beyond the mountains into the blue distance. A gentle wind fanned the faces of the table companions and whispered so charmingly in the fir trees that one might have thought it music especially ordered for the feast.

"I never had such an experience before," cried Grandmama. "It is just splendid! But what do I see?" she added in a tone of the greatest surprise. "I really do believe, Clara, that you have started on a second piece of cheese."

There was a second piece of shining yellow cheese on Clara's slice of bread, sure enough!

"O Grandmama, that tastes so good! It's better than the whole hotel dinner in Ragaz," Clara cried, taking a big bite of the appetizing food.

"Eat away, all you can!" Meadow Nuncle said, well pleased. "Our mountain winds are a great help to the appetite, even if the cooking isn't very good."

So the happy meal went on.

Grandmama and Meadow Nuncle had liked each other from the very first, and they kept the talk going in a most lively manner. They seemed to have the same thoughts about men and things and the way the world was wagging. You would really have thought they had been close friends for years. A long time had passed when suddenly Grandmama looked toward the west and said—

"We must be starting along, Clara. The sun will be setting before we know it. It's time for the people to be coming back with the horse and the basket chair."

At these words a sad look stole into Clara's face, which until that moment had been so merry, and she begged eagerly—

"O Granny, just an hour or two more! Why, we haven't even seen the cottage yet and Heidi's bed and everything. I wish the day was ten hours longer."

"Well, it isn't," Grandmama said, "so I guess we'll have to get along the best we can."

But she wished to see the hut. And so they all got up from the table, and Nuncle steered the wheel chair with steady hand to the door But when they got there the chair would go no farther, for it was too broad to pass through the opening. Nuncle paused only a moment when he saw this new difficulty. He raised Clara into his strong arms and carried her into the house.

Grandmama walked all around, looking carefully at the way it was furnished, and she seemed to be very merry at sight of some of the household objects, all of which were so clean and tidy and so well arranged.

"That's your bed up there, Heidi, I suppose," she said.

And before anyone realized what she was doing, she had quickly climbed the ladder that led to the loft. She walked over to the window and peered through it.

"My, how nice it smells up here!" she cried. "It must be a very healthful place to sleep."

By this time Grandfather had climbed up, too, with Clara still in his arms. And Heidi followed right on his heels.

They stood grouped around Heidi's bed that was so neatly made up, and Grandmama, lost in pleasant thoughts, was gazing straight before her, taking deep breaths of the sweet odors of the hay. Clara couldn't think of anything finer than Heidi's bedroom.

"What a jolly room you have, Heidi!" she exclaimed. "From your bed you can look straight at the sky, and everything has such a nice smell, and just hear the fir trees rustling out there! It's the sweetest, dearest room in all the world!"

Nuncle cast a quick look at Grandmama.

"I have a fine idea," he said, "if only your grandmama will listen to it and not say no. How would it be to keep this little girl up here on the mountain for a while? It might be just the thing for her. Why, we could make an entirely separate bed, soft as down, from all the shawls and rugs that you've brought! And Grandmama need not worry about the care her little girl will get, for I'll look after her myself."

Clara and Heidi burst into a duet of happy shouts. You would have thought them two birds just free from their cage. As for Grandmama, her face lighted up with joy.

"My dear Nuncle, you are a splendid fellow!" she said. "What do you think I just had in mind? I was saying to myself, if you please, 'Wouldn't life up here be the finest thing in the world for our child! But who would look out for her? And what a nuisance her care would be for the one that nursed her!'"

"Nonsense! No trouble at all!"

"And here you are suggesting it yourself, quite as if it were an everyday matter. Oh, how grateful to you I am, dear Nuncle! I thank you from the bottom of my heart."

In her excitement the old lady shook Nuncle's hand time and time again, and he seemed more than delighted to see her so glad.

Nuncle became very busy at once.

He carried Clara back to her chair in front of the hut, and Heidi tagged along after them, feeling that she could not jump high enough to show her joy at the unexpected turn of events. Then Nuncle picked up all the shawls and rugs lined with fur and piled them in his arms. Smiling with satisfaction, he said—

"It is lucky that Lady Grandmama provided enough coverings for a winter campaign. We shall need them all."

"My dear Nuncle," replied the old lady, briskly, "I was taught that an ounce of prevention was worth a pound of cure. A traveler in your mountains is indeed lucky to escape high winds and storms and cloudbursts. And we had such luck and are grateful for it. But still my wraps are going to be of good use to you, are they not?"

While the old people were having this talk, they had been on their way back up to the hayloft. A moment later, they were spreading the shawls across the bed, one at a time. Finally there were so many of them on the couch that it looked like a small fortress.

"Now just let me see a single wisp of hay sticking through!" Grandmama said defiantly.

She pressed down again hard with her hands on all sides of the bed, but the soft mass of rugs made such a thick wall that nothing really could stick through it.

Entirely satisfied with her work, Grandmama then climbed down the ladder and went out to see her two

little wards. They were sitting close together, their faces
were shining with joy, and they were planning what they
would do from morning to night all the time that Clara
stayed on the mountain.

But how long would this visit be? That was now the
burning question that must be laid before Grandmama at
once. She answered by saying that Nuncle would know
best about that, and they must ask him. And, as he
happened to come along at just that moment, the question
was put to him. He said he thought they ought to be able
to tell in four weeks whether the mountain air was doing
good to the little patient or not. And then the children
really did scream in their delight, for they had not dared
even to hope for such a long time together.

Soon after this the porters with their basket chair and
the young guide with his horse were seen marching up the
trail. The porters were sent right back again, for there
was no longer any need of their services.

When Grandmama was on the point of mounting her
horse, Clara called up to her happily—

"O Grandmama, this is no real good-by, for you'll be
coming to visit us every so often to see what we're doing.
And that's going to be great fun, isn't it, Heidi?"

Heidi's joys that day had been heaped upon her with
so generous a hand that she no longer knew how to find
words for things. So she said yes by jumping as high
as she could in the air.

Then Grandmama mounted the trustworthy beast
of burden. Nuncle at once seized the horse's bridle rein
and started to lead it carefully down the steep path. The

old lady tried to persuade him not to bother about her safety; she said there was not the slightest need of his doing so. But Nuncle declared he wouldn't be satisfied unless he kept her company at least as far as Dörfli, because the mountain was so steep that horseback riding was not without its dangers.

Grandmama decided, now that she was to be alone, not to take lodgings in The Hamlet, for she would be too lonesome there. She preferred to go all the way back to Ragaz, and from there she could take her Alpine journey again whenever she wished to do so.

Long before Nuncle had returned, Peter came running along with his goats. When the animals saw Heidi, they all rushed in her direction, and in an instant Clara in her chair, together with Heidi, was surrounded by the herd. And one goat would keep crowding and shoving to see over the head of his fellow until he was called by name to come forward and be introduced to the invalid.

So it happened that, almost before she realized it, Clara had struck up the much-longed-for friendship with little Snowhopper, merry Goldfinch, Grandfather's clean pair of goats, and all the rest, including Big Turk. While this was taking place, however, Peter hung off to one side and cast occasional frowning looks at happy Clara.

As the children both called out to him a friendly "Good night, Peter!" he did not answer, but slashed at the air with his rod so angrily that you might think he wanted to cut it in two. Then he started to run down the trail, his followers after him.

There was one last thing to come, to be the end of all

the lovely things that Clara had seen that day on the mountain.

When at last she was lying on the broad, soft bed up in the loft, with Heidi close beside her, she looked through the open round window right into the heart of the twinkling stars and cried out, quite carried away by their beauty—

"O Heidi, look! It feels as if we were being driven straight to heaven in a high wagon."

"Doesn't it? And, Clara, do you know why the stars are so happy and keep winking at us so?"

"No. How should I know that? What do you mean?" demanded Clara.

"Why, the stars up there in the sky see how nicely the dear God arranges everything for people. No one has to worry or to feel unsafe, because he knows everything will turn out for the best. And that makes the stars so happy that they wink to us to be joyful, too. But you know, Clara, we mustn't forget to pray, and ask the dear God to think of us while he's looking after others so nicely. And then we can always feel so safe, too, and never be afraid of anything."

At that, the children popped up in bed again and said their prayers for the night. Then Heidi put her head on her little round arm and was asleep in a second. But Clara lay awake a long time, because she had never before known anything half so wonderful as this place to sleep in in the starlight.

Besides, she had hardly ever seen the stars, for she had never been outside the house at night, and inside the thick shades had been pulled down long before the stars appeared.   But now, every time she started to close her eyes, she had to open them just for once, to make sure the two big bright stars were still shining through the window and to see if they were really winking in that funny way that Heidi had spoken of. And they always were. So Clara just could not look enough at their sparkling and gleaming, until at last her eyelids closed of their own weight, and in her dreams she was still seeing them, the twin stars that were so large and brilliant.

CHAPTER VII

FURTHER HAPPENINGS ON THE MOUNTAIN

The sun was just rising up behind the cliffs and casting its golden rays across the hut and down over the valley.

Meadow Nuncle had been watching with quiet eagerness, as he did every morning, the thin mists lift from the heights and the valleys round about him and the whole countryside come forth from its twilight shadows and awake to a new day.

Clearer and brighter grew the light clouds of early morning, until the sun had quite appeared to bathe cliffs and forests in its golden glory.

Then Nuncle walked back to the cottage and climbed the frail ladder. Clara had just opened wide her eyes and was staring in the greatest amazement at the bright sunbeams that streamed in through the round window to dance and gleam on her bed. She had forgotten where she was and did not recognize the scene about her. But then she noticed Heidi sleeping beside her and heard the kindly voice of Grandfather asking—

"Sleep well? You're not tired, are you?"

Clara said that she was not tired at all—in fact, she had not once moved after she had got to sleep. This pleased the old gentleman, and he set to work at once to care for the invalid so skillfully that you might have imagined he had no other occupation in life than to attend to the needs of sick children.

By this time Heidi was also awake, and surprised to find that Grandfather had got her little friend dressed and up in his arms and all ready to carry downstairs. She did not want to be left behind. So she dressed herself as quick as lightning and flew down the ladder and out of doors, but there she halted in great surprise to find what her Grandfather had been doing.

When the children were safely tucked away in the loft the evening before, he had planned a way of bringing the broad wheel chair inside the house. The door of the hut was too narrow to admit the chair, and so he had to hit upon some other scheme. All at once an idea came to him. He took off two wide boards from the back wall of the shop and so made a large opening. The chair was wheeled in through this, and then the boards were put back in their places but not nailed fast.

Heidi appeared just as Grandfather was settling Clara in her chair. He had taken off the boards and was going to wheel the child out of the shop into the morning sunshine. When he had done this, he left the chair standing in the middle of the lawn and went back to the goat shed. Heidi ran to Clara's side.

The cool breeze blew about the faces of the children, and a spicy smell from the fir trees drifted down to them on each new breath of wind. Clara filled her lungs with it and leaned back in her chair with a feeling of such health as she had never known before.

In all her life she had never drawn in deep breaths of fresh morning air under the open sky, and at this moment the pure mountain breeze was blowing about her so cool and refreshing that every touch of it brought new enjoyment. And, above all else, there was the clear, sweet sunshine which was so lovely and warm upon her hands and upon the dry lawn at her feet. Clara had not imagined that it could be like this up on the mountain.

"O Heidi, I wish I could stay up here with you for ever and ever!" she cried. She twisted happily in her chair first one way and then another, so as not to miss a bit of the air and sunshine.

"Now you see it's just as I said it was," Heidi answered, smiling. "Grandfather's place on the mountain meadow is the nicest spot in the world."

At that moment Grandfather came from the stable toward the children, carrying in his hands two bowlfuls of frothy milk as white as snow. He handed one to Clara, the other to Heidi.

"That is good for a little girl I know," he said, nodding at Clara. "It's Schwänli's milk and makes people strong. To your good health! Drink hearty!"

Clara had never drunk goat's milk before, so she had to sniff at it first just a bit, to see what it was like. But when she saw that it tasted so good that Heidi drank her whole bowlful down without pausing for breath, she waited no longer. She started and drank and drank until there was not a single drop left. For, honestly, it was so sweet and nourishing you'd have thought there was sugar and cinnamon in it.

"Tomorrow we'll have two apiece," Grandfather said. He chuckled with pleasure to see how closely Clara had followed Heidi's lead.

Peter now appeared with his troop, and while Heidi was receiving her morning greetings from all the pushing goats Nuncle took Peter off to one side so he could hear the message that he had for him. For the animals were bleating so, each one trying to express his love and joy more loudly than the others, now that Heidi was in their midst, that you could hardly hear yourself think.

"Now you just mind what I say," Nuncle warned Peter. "From now on, let Schwänli go wherever she wants. Her instinct teaches her where the best grazing is, so if she wants to climb 'way up, you follow along. The pasture she finds will be good for the others, too. Even if she starts to go much higher than usual, don't hold her back— do you hear? She knows better than you do where to go, and it won't hurt you any to do a little work for once in your life. We want Schwänli to have the best food, so her milk is perfect. Why are you looking over yonder, as if you wanted to swallow somebody? No one's going to hurt you. Come, be off with you, and don't forget what I have said!"

Peter always did just what Nuncle told him, so he began his march without delay. But you could see that he was thinking about something, for he kept turning his head around and rolling his eyes. The goats followed his lead and shoved Heidi along a little way with them. This suited Peter all right.

"You must come with me," he called to her in the middle of the flock, threateningly. "You've got to come if I have to follow Schwänli wherever she goes."

"No, I can't," Heidi answered, "and not again for a

long time, either, for all the time Clara stays with us. But Grandfather said that perhaps some time we could go up together."

With these words, Heidi twisted her way out of the herd and ran back to Clara. And then Peter shook his fists in such hate toward the sick girl's chair that the goats sprang away from him. But he ran after them quickly and, without stopping, kept on until he was out of sight, for he was afraid that Nuncle might have seen his threatening gestures. And he was just as glad not to know what the old gentleman might say about all that shaking of fists.

Clara and Heidi had so many plans for that day that they did not know where to start. Heidi suggested that they first write a letter to Grandmama, for they had agreed to write one every day. The old lady had not been quite sure how Clara would like such a long visit up on the mountain, or whether it would be really good for her, and so she had made the children promise to write as often as they could and tell her everything that was going on. In that way she could tell whenever she might be needed on the mountain meadow, and until that time she could quietly remain where she was.

"Do we have to go inside to write?" Clara asked.

She was quite ready to send the report to Grandmama, but she did not want to go in the house, it was so lovely out of doors.

Heidi knew how that could be managed. She ran quickly into the cottage and soon came back, loaded down with her school things and the low three-legged chair.

Then she set her reading book and her writing tablet on Clara's lap, so she could rest her hand upon them, and she sat down on the stool by the bench.   And then they both began their story for Grandmama.

But Clara could not write more than a sentence without laying down her pencil and gazing about her.   It was too lovely for words!   The breeze was now not so cool as it had been.   It fanned their faces gently and murmured in the fir trees above them.   Gay little insects were humming and darting about in the pure air, and a great stillness brooded over the broad, sunlit fields.   Tall cliffs of rock looked down big and immovable, and deep peace rested on the valley below them.   Only now and then was the stillness broken by the glad cry of some shepherd lad and by the soft echoes repeated by the crags round about.

The morning passed away like a dream, and the first thing the children knew, Grandfather was bringing their steaming bowls out to them, for he said they must stay out in the air with the little girl as long as there was a ray of light left in the sky.   So their dinner was got ready in front of the cottage, just as on the previous day, and eaten with enjoyment.

After the meal Heidi wheeled Clara in her chair over under the pines, because they had decided to spend the afternoon in the fine shade there and tell each other everything that had happened since Heidi had left Frankfort. Even though there had been nothing during that time at all out of the usual run, still Clara had all kinds of little things to tell about the people who lived in the Sesemann house and whom Heidi had come to know so well.

So the children sat together under the old pine trees. And the more eagerly they talked, the louder became the twittering of the birds on the branches above them, for all the chattering down below interested the birds a great deal and they wished to take part in it. Again the time fled quickly by, and evening was there before they knew it, and the goat army was rushing down upon them, with their leader close behind, a frown on his brow and anger in his face.

"Good night, Peter," Heidi called to him, when she saw he had made up his mind not to stop.

"Good night, Peter," Clara also shouted pleasantly.

But he did not return their greeting and, with a grunt of anger, drove the goats on down ahead of him.

Now when Clara saw Grandfather lead dainty Schwänli off to the stable to be milked, she was at once seized with such a strong desire to have the spicy milk that she could scarcely wait until it was brought to her. She was as much astonished as anybody at her appetite.

"Isn't it funny, Heidi?" she asked. "As far back as I can remember, I have eaten only when I had to, and everything I put in my mouth tasted like cod-liver oil. A thousand times I have thought to myself, 'Oh, if I never had to eat another bite!' and now it's all I can do to wait until Grandfather gets here with the milk."

"Yes, I know what that feeling is," Heidi answered sympathetically, for she was remembering the days in Frankfort when everything stuck in her throat and wouldn't go down. But Clara could not understand what had happened to her. As long as she had lived, she had not spent a single day in the open air until now, and in air as pure and bracing as that of the mountain.

When Grandfather appeared with their bowls, Clara lost no time in seizing hers and thanking him for it. Then she drank the milk down in long, eager swallows and finished ahead of Heidi.

"Could I have a little more?" she asked, holding out her bowl to Grandfather.

He nodded, with a pleased smile, took Heidi's bowl, too, and went back to the hut. When he appeared later, he was bringing with each bowl a thick cover, which was, however, made of different material from the ordinary top. In fact it looked somewhat like bread.

That afternoon Grandfather had taken a stroll over to green Maiensäss, to the herdman's cottage where sweet yellow butter was churned. He had brought back from there a fine round pat of it. Then he had taken two nice slices of bread and spread the sweet butter on top of them, fine and thick. They were for the children's supper. The two girls both took such big bites into the delicious slices that Grandfather stood and watched what was going to happen, he was so pleased.

Later on, when Clara was looking up again at the twinkling stars, she could not keep awake, but imitated Heidi. Her eyes closed almost immediately, and a sound, healthful sleep overtook her, such as she had never known before.

In the same delightful way the next day passed, and then the next one, and finally there came a great surprise for the children.

Two strong porters came climbing up the mountain, each carrying on his shoulders feather mattresses already arranged in beds, both covered over exactly alike with a white spread that was spotless and brand new. The men also had a letter from Grandmama to deliver.

The letter said that the beds were for Heidi and Clara, so they could now get rid of the hay couches and from that time on sleep in a regular bed. In winter Heidi could take one of them down to Dörfli with her, but the other was always to stay up on the mountain so Clara might find it when she came back there. Then Grandmama praised the children for their nice long letters to her and begged them to keep writing her one every day so that she could have all the fun they had, just as if she were there with them.

Grandfather had gone into the house, thrown Heidi's couch of hay over on the heap of straw, and put away her coverings. Then he returned in order to help the men carry the beds up into the loft. Then he shoved them close together, so that from both pillows the view out the window might be the same, for he knew the joy the children took in the light that shone in there morning and evening.

Meanwhile Grandmama stayed down in the summer resort Ragaz and was very much pleased with the good news that came to her day by day from the mountain.

Clara's delight in her new manner of life kept daily increasing, and she could not speak highly enough of the kindness and loving care given her by Grandfather. She wrote of how funny and gay Heidi was, a lot more so than she had ever been in Frankfort, and of how each morning when Clara woke up her first thought was—

"Praise be to God, I am still on the mountain!"

Such news as this was delightful to Grandmama. She decided therefore that, as everything was going on so well, she would put off her visit to the mountain a little longer. And she was not sorry to do this, because the ride up the steep trail and down again was rather difficult for her

Grandfather must have taken quite an unusual interest in the recovery of his small ward, for not a day passed that he did not think of something new that might help her to gain strength. Every afternoon he now went climbing farther and farther up the cliffs, and from each walk he brought back a small parcel which sweetened the air for a long distance like spicy pinks and thyme. And when the goats came home in the evening, they would all begin to bleat and jump and try to crowd through the door of the shed where the bundle lay, for they recognized its smell.

But Nuncle had closed the door tightly, for he did not propose to scale the high cliffs where the rare plants grew just so the herd of goats could have a fine meal without effort. No, indeed. The herbs, one and all, were for Schwänli and were meant to make her milk richer. And it was plain to see how much good this unusual care did Little Swan, because she now tossed her head more actively than ever, and her eyes fairly flashed fire.

And so it got to be three weeks from the day that Clara first reached the mountain. For several days past, whenever Grandfather carried her down in the morning to be placed in her chair, he would be sure to ask—

"Isn't this little girl going to try just once to stand on her feet for a moment?"

Each time Clara would try to do as he wanted her to, but would cry out after a moment, "Oh, it hurts too badly!" Then she would cling to him for support, but next time Grandfather would see that she tried just a little longer.

There had not been so fine a summer on the mountain for years. Every day the shining sun moved across a cloudless sky, and all the little flowers opened their cups wide so the sun could drink in their beauty and their sweetness. And in the late afternoon it cast its purple and pink lights across the rocky horns of the mountain peaks and the glacier, and then sank into a flaming sea of gold.

Heidi told her friend Clara about this sight again and again, for it could be seen in all its glory only if you were up in the pasture. And she was never tired of telling about the place on the slope far above, where there grew large masses of gleaming golden wild roses. And she described the bluebells, of which there were so many that one would think the grass itself had turned blue. And then, near by, were the great bushes of brown mace flowers that had so sweet a smell one wanted to stay on the ground close to them and never go away again.

It was while Heidi had been seated beneath the firs, talking with Clara about the flowers up there and the evening sun and the shining crags, that she was suddenly overcome by such a longing to see the place again, she had to jump to her feet and run to Grandfather, who was in the shop at his carving bench.

"O Grandfather," she called out before she had even

reached his side, "won't you take us up to the pasture tomorrow? It is just perfectly lovely up there now."

"That suits me all right," the old gentleman said with a nod. "But then the little girl must do me a favor in return. She must try this evening to stand on her feet just as long as she can."

Shouting for joy, Heidi ran back with her news to Clara, and the invalid promised to stand on her feet just as often as Grandfather wanted her to. For she was very eager to take this trip up to the beautiful goat pasture. The moment she saw Peter coming down that evening, Heidi was so full of happiness that she called out to him—

"Listen, Peter! We're coming up with you tomorrow to spend the whole day."

Peter's only answer was a growl, like that of an angry bear. In his rage he struck at Distelfink, who, innocent of any wrongdoing, was trotting at his side. But the agile Goldfinch had seen his movement in time and jumped out of reach over Schneehöppli's back. So Peter's blow fell on the empty air.

Clara and Heidi went to bed that night filled with the greatest expectations. They were so occupied with their plans for the next day that they made up their minds to stay awake all night so they could keep talking until it was time to get up. But hardly had their heads touched the pillows when their chatter ceased. And Clara saw before her in a dream a great big field all sky-blue, it was so thickly sown with just bluebells, while Heidi heard the bird of prey scream down from the heights, "Come on! Come on!"

CHAPTER VIII

THE UNEXPECTED HAPPENS

Very early the next morning Nuncle came out of the hut and looked about him to see what the weather was going to be.

On the high mountain peaks rested a ruddy golden light. A cool wind was beginning to stir the branches of the pine trees. The sun was about to rise.

For a while the old man stood and watched with earnest attention as first the lofty summits and then the green hills caught the golden gleam. Then the dark shadows rolled softly back from the valley, and a rosy light streamed into it, until suddenly heights and depths alike were bathed in the full glory of day. The sun had risen.

Nuncle brought the wheel chair out of the shop, put it in front of the hut so that it would be ready for the journey, and then entered the house to tell the children how fine the morning was and that it was time to get up.

Just then Peter came climbing up the path. His goats did not follow him so trustingly as usual this time, nor were they so close behind, beside, or yet before him. They kept darting away from him in one direction or another, because he was striking at them without any excuse whatever, like a madman. And when he hit anywhere, it hurt badly.

Poor Peter had reached the depths of vexation and bitterness.

For weeks he had not had Heidi all alone to himself, as he once had. By the time he arrived in the morning the strange child had always been carried out in her chair and Heidi was paying attention to her. When he came down again in the evening, the wheel chair with its occupant was still standing under the fir trees, and Heidi was busied with her guest.

She had not gone up to the pasture the whole summer long, and now today she was planning to go, but with the wheel chair and the strange girl in it, and she would give up all her time to her. Peter could see how it would turn out, and this is what had brought his secret rage to the boiling point. His eye now lighted on the chair as it stood there so proudly on its rollers. And he frowned at it, as if it were an enemy that had already done him all kinds of harm and was plotting new mischief for today.

He looked quickly about him. Everything was quiet; there was not a single person in sight. Then, like a savage, he rushed at the chair, grasped it with his hands, and gave it such a violent shove toward the slope of the mountain that the chair fairly flew away from his angry clutch and immediately disappeared over the edge of the lawn.

Now he had done it!

As if borne along on wings, Peter rushed off up the mountain meadow, and never once stopped for breath until he had reached a great blackberry bush behind which he could hide. For he did not in the least wish to have Nuncle spy him.

But he did wish to see what became of the chair, and the bush on a spur of the mountain was well situated for this purpose. Peter, himself half hidden, could look down on the meadow and still be able to duck out of sight in a hurry if Nuncle should appear. He peered down from his hiding place, and what a sight met his eyes!

Far beneath him his enemy was rushing to destruction, constantly driven on by stronger forces. It turned one somersault after another. It sprang high into the air and crashed down to earth again. It rolled over and over as it hurried on to ruin.

Parts of it were already flying in all directions—its legs, its back, its padded cushions were flying through the air. Peter was unable to restrain his joy at this glorious sight, and he clicked his heels together and jumped as high as he could. He laughed aloud, he stamped his feet blissfully, he danced around in circles. But he always returned to the same spot to take a new look down the slope. And then he had to laugh afresh and dance anew for joy. Peter was fairly out of his head with delight at the destruction of his enemy, for he felt sure only good would come of it.

Now, he was certain, the strange girl would have to go away, for she would have no means of getting from one place to another. Heidi would be left alone again and would come to the pasture with him. She would be on the lookout for him morning and evening when he came along, and everything would again be just as it used to be. But Peter had not yet had time to consider what happens to one who has done a wicked deed, nor had he thought of the consequences that follow.

Heidi was the first to come out of the hut and run to the shop. Behind her came Grandfather, with Clara in his arms.

The door of the shop stood wide open, both boards had been laid aside, and it was as light as day in the farthest corner. Heidi peered all about the shop, then darted around the corner of it, and then returned with a look of great amazement in her face.   Just then Grandfather came along.

"What's up?" he asked. "Did you wheel the chair away?"

"Why, I'm looking for it everywhere, Grandfather," the child answered, still keeping up her search. "You told me it was standing beside the door of the shop."

Meanwhile the wind had increased in force. It was making the door rattle and, at just that moment, slammed it back with a crash against the wall of the shop.

"Grandfather, the wind did it!" cried Heidi, and her eyes blazed at the thought. "Oh, if the old chair's been blown down into Dörfli, it will be a long time before we can get it back, and then too late for us to go at all."

"If it has rolled down there, it will never come back," said Grandfather as he walked around the shop and looked down the mountain, "for it will be in a hundred pieces. But it's funny how it happened," he continued, looking back at the course the chair must have taken around the edge of the hut in order to get started downhill.

"Oh, what a shame!" Clara wailed. "Now we can't go at all, and perhaps we never can. Oh, I'll have to go home if I haven't any chair. It's just too bad!"

But Heidi looked up at her grandfather trustfully.

"Grandfather, you'll find some way so it won't be as bad as Clara thinks, won't you?" she asked. "And so she won't even have to go home?"

"This once we'll go up to the pasture, just as we decided
to," the old man said. "Afterward we'll see what can be
done."

The children shouted for joy. .

He went back into the hut, brought out a large share of
all the shawls, laid them beside the cottage in the sunniest
spot that he could find, and set Clara down on them.
Then he fetched the morning's milk for the children and
led Schwänli and Bärli out in front of the shed.

"I wonder why that rascal is such a long time coming
up?" Nuncle said to himself, for Peter's signaling
whistle had not yet sounded. Then he took Clara up on
one arm and the shawls on the other.

"Well, let's start!" he said. "The goats can come with
us."

That arrangement just suited Heidi.

With one arm around Little Swan's neck and the other
around Little Bear's, she strolled along beside her grandfather. And the goats were so overjoyed to be with
Heidi again that between them they almost squeezed her to
death as proof of their affection.

When they had got up to the pasture grounds, all at
once they saw the goats standing around in small groups
here and there on the slopes, peacefully grazing, while
Peter in their midst was stretched out full length upon the
ground.

"Next time you pass us by, I'll attend to you, you
booby!" Nuncle hailed him. "What did you mean by that?"

"Nobody was up yet," Peter answered. At the sound
of that well-known voice he had jumped up in a hurry.

"Did you see any sign of a chair?" Nuncle asked again.

"Of what?" Peter called back surlily.

Nuncle said nothing further. He spread his shawls on the sunny slope, set Clara down on them, and asked her if she was comfortable.

"Just as cozy as I'd be in my chair," she said gratefully. "And here I am in the nicest place in the world. O Heidi, it is so beautiful here!" she cried, as she drank in the splendor of the view unrolled before her.

Grandfather was now ready to go back. He told them to have a good time together and when it was noon then Heidi could get out their dinner, which was packed in the bag that he had left over in the shade. Peter would get their milk when they wanted it, as much as they could drink, but Heidi must remember to see that it came from Schwänli. Grandfather promised to come back at dusk. He was now going down to see what had become of the chair.

The sky was deep blue and, whichever way you looked, not a single cloud was to be seen in it anywhere.

The great glacier across from them sparkled as if with the light of countless thousands of gold and silver stars. The grim horns of the cliffs, tall and massive, stood in the place that had been theirs through the ages and gazed solemnly down into the valley. The big bird of prey swept high above them in the haze, and the breeze from the mountains came across the heights and refreshed the sunlit summits with its cool breath.

The children were as happy as they could be. From time to time a little goat would come to lie down beside them a while. Soft-hearted Schneehöppli was their most frequent visitor. She would rest her small head on Heidi's lap and stay in that position until some one of her fellows came to drive her away. Clara thus learned to know the goats so well that she could tell them apart quite easily, for she saw that each face differed from the others, and each animal had its own peculiar ways.

They soon felt that they could trust in Clara, and so they would come up close and rub their heads against her shoulder, which was an unfailing sign of friendship and affection.

Several hours sped by in this fashion. And then Heidi decided that she would like to go over to the place where all the flowers were, just to see if they were open still and as lovely as they had been the year before.

Of course, she knew that when evening came and Grandfather was back they could take Clara with them, but by that time perhaps the flowers would have closed their eyes. Heidi's longing grew until she could no longer resist it. A little timidly she asked—

"Would you mind so very much, Clara, if I should run away for just a twinkling and leave you all alone? I'm so anxious to see how the flowers are getting along. But wait—"

Heidi had had a sudden thought. She darted off a little way and pulled up a few fine bunches of green plants. The moment Schneehöppli saw this, she came running toward Heidi, and the child put her arms around the goat's neck and brought her to Clara.

"There! Now you won't be left alone, after all," she said. And she pushed Schneehöppli up a little closer to

Clara. The goat seemed to know what was wanted and lay down. Then Heidi threw the green stuff she had gathered into Clara's lap, and the invalid said very happily that Heidi could now go and have a good look at the flowers, as she was glad to be left alone with the goat. That would be quite a new experience for her.

So Heidi ran off on her errand and Clara began to hold out her plants to Schneehöppli, a leaf or two at a time, and the young goat was so trustful that she nestled close to her new friend and slowly nibbled at the leaves in her hand. It was plain to be seen how contented she was, for she gave herself up quietly and peacefully to Clara's care. When she was with the herd and no one came to her rescue, she always had to suffer from the attacks of the larger and stronger goats.

It seemed wonderfully good to Clara to be able to sit this way off on a mountain, all alone except for the little tame goat that looked up at her so helplessly. She felt a great desire to be her own master and now and then to be able to help someone else, instead of always having to rely upon the services of others.

Many thoughts which she had never had before came flooding into Clara's mind, and with them a new desire to go on living in this world full of beautiful sunshine and to do things that would make others happy, just as she was now gladdening Schneehöppli. A strange joy entered her heart, and it suddenly seemed to her as if all the things she had ever known might be more beautiful and different from what she expected. And in her newly won feeling of happiness she was so contented that

she threw her arms around the little goat's neck and
cried—

"O little Snowhopper, how lovely it is up here! If I
just never had to leave you again!"

Meanwhile Heidi had reached the spot where the
flowers bloomed. She cried out with joy. The whole
mountain side lay covered with shining gold!

There were the gleaming rockroses. Thick purplish
clusters of bluebells were swaying in the gentle breeze.
A strong, spicy smell enveloped the sunlit slope, as if
most precious cups of balsam had been poured out upon
the ground. All this sweet odor, however, came from
the small, brown mace flowers that reared their round
tops shyly from among the yellow trefoil. Heidi stood
still and gazed, drinking in deep draughts of the sweet
air. Suddenly she turned and ran back to Clara, all out
of breath with excitement.

"Oh, you've just got to come!" she called out, even
before she reached Clara's side. "They are so lovely,
and everything there is so beautiful, and perhaps it won't
be that way hours from now. Don't you think perhaps
I might carry you?"

Clara looked at her excited friend with no little surprise, but she shook her head.

"What are you thinking of, Heidi? Of course you
couldn't. Why, you're a lot smaller than I am! But I do
wish I could go."

Then Heidi looked around on every side, trying to find
some way out of their difficulty. And a new plan was
slowly forming in her determined young mind.

There above the children, where he had been stretched out at full length on the grass, sat Mr. Peter staring down at them. He had been sitting that way for hours, gazing fixedly at them as if he could not understand what he saw. Had he not destroyed the hateful old wheel chair to make an end of the strange guest and to keep her from going anywhere at all? And yet, only a short time after he had sent the chair off down the slope, she had appeared up there and was perched beside Heidi right in front of him. It couldn't have happened, and still it was true all right, for there she was whenever he cared to look at her.

And now he saw Heidi's eyes upturned to him.

"Come down a minute, Peter!" she called very firmly.

"Won't do it," he yelled back.

"You will, too; you have to," Heidi said, threateningly. "Come ahead! I can't do it alone and you've got to help. Hurry up!"

"Won't either," was the surly answer.

Then Heidi ran a little way up the mountain toward Peter and confronted him with eyes aflame. She cried—

"If you don't come here to me this minute, you Peter, I'll do something to you that you won't like at all. You just see if I don't!"

These words made Peter tremble, and he was seized with a great fear. He had done a wicked deed which must be kept secret at any cost. Until this very minute the thought of his naughty act had made him happy. But now Heidi was talking as if she knew all about it and was going to tell her grandfather on him. And Peter was more afraid of that old man than anyone else alive. Suppose he found

out what had happened to the chair! Peter's blood ran cold
to think of it. He got up and went to meet Heidi.

"I'm coming, but then you must promise not to do it,"
he said. And his fright made him so tame that Heidi
felt quite sorry for him.

"All right, then I won't do it now," she assured him.
"You come with me. There's nothing to make you afraid
in what I want of you."

When they got to Clara, Heidi showed what was to
be done. Peter was to take hold of Clara by one arm, Heidi
by the other, to lift her to her feet. And they did that
all right, but then came the hardest thing. The invalid,
of course, could not stand by herself, and how were they
going to hold her so that she could walk along? Heidi
was too short to support the sick girl on her arm.

"You must put your arm very firmly around my neck,
Clara—like that. And you must take Peter's arm and
lean on it hard, then we can move you along."

The young goat herd had never given any girl his
arm before. Clara took hold of it properly, but he let it
hang stiffly down by his side, like a long pole.

"Oh, that's not the way, Peter," Heidi said disgustedly.
"You must make a circle of your arm and then she can
put her hand through it and press as hard as she wants
to. Whatever you do, don't let go, and then we're all
ready for the march."

This plan was tried, but nothing much came of it.
Clara was fairly heavy, and the team of helpers was too
unlike in size. She had to reach up on one side and down
on the other, and that made her support very uncertain.

Clara tried to advance first one foot and then the other, but found she could not bear her weight on either and so drew them painfully back again.

"Just plant them right down hard," Heidi suggested. "And then you'll find it won't hurt so much."

"Do you think so?" Clara asked timidly.

But she did as she was told and tried to take a couple of steps along the ground. This made her cry out with pain. After a moment she raised a foot and set it down again more gently.

"Why, that didn't hurt half so badly," she said gaily.

"Try it once more," Heidi urged eagerly.

Clara obeyed. Then she tried her foot several times. And suddenly she screamed—

"O Heidi, look at me! I can do it! I can take one step right after another!"

Then Heidi started to shout much more loudly than her friend.

"Honest true? Really, can you take steps like that? Why, you can! You're walking, all by yourself, you're walking! If Grandfather could only see you!"

It seemed as if there was no end to Heidi's great joy.

To be sure, Clara was leaning hard on both of them. But, with each step she took, she gained a little more confidence, there was no question about it. Heidi was almost bursting with delight.

"Oh, now we can go to the pasture together every day!" she exclaimed. "And walk wherever we want to on the mountain. And all the rest of your life you can go around like me, and be strong, and never be shoved in a chair again. Oh, isn't that the very nicest thing that could have happened to us!"

Clara said yes to that with her whole heart. Surely she knew no greater piece of luck in all the world than to be healthy and walk about like other people, and not be condemned to spend her days miserably in an invalid's chair.

The slope where the flowers bloomed was not far away. They could already see the gold roses gleaming in the sunlight. Then they came to the tufts of blue-bells, where the sunny earth showed through so invitingly.

"Can't we sit down here?" Clara asked.

That was just what Heidi wanted to do. So the children settled down among the flowers, and Clara was more happy than you would ever guess, for this was the first time that she had ever sat on the bare ground. And she found it warm and dry.

All about her she saw the waving tops of the bluebells, the glinting gold roses, the red centauries. And everywhere was the sweet odor of the brown mace flowers and spicy prunellas. It was lovely beyond words!

Heidi, too, who was seated beside her, felt that it had never before been quite so beautiful up there, and she really could not herself have told why there was so fierce a joy in her heart that she wanted to cry it aloud to the sky. And then suddenly she remembered that Clara had been made whole again, and that was the greatest happiness that could be added to all this worldly beauty.

Clara had grown quiet. She was quite carried away with delight at the scene before her, and even more at the thought of all that the future held for her, now that she had passed through the remarkable experience of her cure. Her heart was so full that there was hardly room in it for this new happiness. And the sunshine and the sweet odor of the flowers were doing their part in giving her an overpowering sense of joy. So she was speechless.

Nor was Peter inclined to talk. In the midst of this field of flowers he lay quiet and motionless, half asleep.

The wind blew softly and gently from behind the wall of cliffs and rustled overhead in the bushes. Now and then Heidi would bestir herself and hunt for some new spot, for there always seemed to be a place more beautiful than the last one, where the flowers grew in a thicker tangle, where the air was sweeter as it was stirred about by the breeze. And everywhere she had to settle down for a moment.

So fled the hours away.

The sun was long past midday when a company of goats came walking most seriously up the flowery slope.

It was not their usual pasturage ground. They were never brought to it, because they did not care to graze on the flowers. Their troop looked more like an embassy, with Distelfink at its head. The goats had apparently come in search of their companions who had neglected them so long and, against all rules of the game, had stayed by themselves so completely. For, you see, the goats knew very well what the time of day was.

The moment Distelfink discovered the whereabouts of the three deserters, he set up a loud bleating, and the others joined at once in the chorus and trotted along making an awful hubbub. That woke Peter from his dreams. But he had to rub his eyes hard to find out where he was, for in his dream the wheel chair had again been standing before the hut, upholstered in red and uninjured. And even now, when he was wide awake, he could still see in the sunshine the gleam of the gilt nails around the cushions. But these he soon discovered to be only the glittering yellow flowers in the ground about him.

At that moment there came back to Peter the fear which he had quite forgotten when in his dream he had again seen the uninjured chair. Even though Heidi had promised not to do anything about it, still Peter was greatly afraid that he would not escape from the consequences of his sin so easily. He was entirely tamed, and willing to be a guide or anything else, and did exactly what Heidi asked him to.

When, therefore, all three had come back to the pasturage, Heidi quickly fetched her dinner bag full of provisions and set about making good her promise. For, although Mr. Peter did not know it, her threat a while before had been that if he was not nice he could not share their food with the girls. Heidi had noticed especially that morning what goodies grandfather had packed in the bag, and she had been looking forward happily to having Peter share a generous portion of them. But when the boy had been so stubborn, she had been quick to warn him he might not get any dinner, only Peter had not understood her hint because of his uneasy conscience.

Now Heidi was taking piece after piece out of the bag and stacking the food in three small heaps. And these piles gradually grew so tall that she said to herself with satisfaction—

"And, besides, he can have all the food we leave when we're no longer hungry."

Then she presented a little heap to each one and sat down beside Clara to eat her own portion. And, after all the exercise they had had, the children thoroughly enjoyed their hearty meal.

It turned out just as Heidi thought it would.

After the two girls had eaten all they wanted, so much food remained that Peter was given a second pile of it almost as tall as his first share had been. He ate it all silently and without pausing for breath even, down to the very crumbs. And yet, as he accomplished this feat, he did not feel any great contentment. There was something within him that gnawed at his stomach—or was it his conscience?—so that he fairly choked over every mouthful of food.

The children had got to their dinner so late that almost as soon as it was over Grandfather was seen coming up the mountain meadow to get them. Heidi rushed to meet him. She wanted to be the first to tell him what had happened. But she got so excited trying to tell him the wonderful news that she could hardly put her thoughts into words, and yet he seemed to understand at once what she was striving to say, and his face grew bright with joy. He hastened his steps, and when he reached Clara he said with a happy smile—

"So we got up our courage, after all! And we won out, didn't we? That's fine!"

Then he raised Clara from the ground, put his left arm around her waist, and gave her his right hand to take and lean on. And, with Grandfather's arm like a stout wall at her back, she struck out with her feet more surely and with less fear than before.

Heidi hopped along beside her and crowed with glee, and Grandfather looked as if he had met with an unexpected piece of great good fortune. But all at once he lifted Clara into his arms and said, warningly—

"We must be careful not to overdo it. And, besides, it's time to be going back."

With that, he started on his way immediately, for he knew that Clara had had exercise enough for one day and was in need of rest.

Late that evening, when Peter and his goats came into The Hamlet, a large number of people were standing together in a crowd and shoving each other aside, so as to get a better view of something that lay on the ground in their midst. Peter went up to have a look, too. He pushed and nudged his way right and left, and finally managed to slip through.

Then he saw what it was.

On the grass lay the middle part of the wheel chair, and a piece of the back was still clinging to it. The red cushions and the shining nails showed how splendid the chair had been before it came to ruin.

"I was here when they were carrying it up," the baker said at Peter's side. "I'll bet anybody it was worth at least five hundred francs. But it beats me how it ever got smashed so."

"Nuncle himself said the wind probably blew it down," remarked Barbel as she studied the red upholstery with a hungry gaze.

"It's a blessing that nobody else broke it," the baker went on to say. "He'd be in an awful hole. If the gentleman in Frankfort hears about the accident, he'll get the police to find out how it happened. You bet I'm glad I haven't been up on the mountain meadow for two years. Anybody may be suspected who was up that way about the right time."

A good many other people said what they thought, but Peter had heard all he could stand. He crept away from the crowd as quietly and meekly as he could, and a moment later he was tearing at top speed up the mountain as if the Evil One were right at his heels.

The baker's words had given him an awful scare. For now he realized that any moment a policeman might come from Frankfort to spy into the matter. And then it would come out that he was the guilty one, and they would seize him and carry him off to prison. Peter saw all this happening, as in a vision, and he grew so frightened that his hair stood on end.

He reached home in a state of despair. He would not answer when he was spoken to and refused to eat his potatoes. As soon as he could, he crawled into bed and began to groan.

"Peter's been picking sorrel upon the slope and eating it again," his mother said. "It's resting on his stomach, and that's what makes him groan so."

"You must give him a little more bread for his lunch,"

Grandmother added, "then he won't be so hungry. Give him a piece of my bread tomorrow."—

That night, as the two little girls looked up from their beds at the starlight, Heidi said—

"Haven't you been thinking all day, Clara, how fine it is that the dear God doesn't give in, when we pray to Him so terribly hard, and yet when He knows of something better?"

"Why do you say that just now?" Clara asked.

"Don't you see, dear, in Frankfort I thought the dear God had not heard my prayers, because I begged so hard to go home right away and He wouldn't let me? But, you know, if I had got my wish and gone straight home, you would never have come to the mountain to visit me and would not have got well."

Clara grew thoughtful as she heard these words.

"Why, then, Heidi," she said after a while, "we oughtn't to pray for anything at all, because the dear God always has something better in mind for us than what we ask Him for."

"O Clara, how can you talk that way!" Heidi cried, almost angrily. "We must pray to the dear God at all times and about everything, for He wishes to hear us say that we have not forgotten Him and owe Him whatever good thing we have. And your grandmama told me that if we forget the dear God, then He puts us out of His mind. But then, you see, if we do not receive what we wish for, we must not stop praying and think the dear God has not heard us. No, we must turn to Him and say, 'Now I know, dear God, that You have something better in mind for me, and I am thankful that You are so good to me.' "

"Where did you hear about all that?" Clara asked.

"Grandmama explained it to me at first, and then things turned out just as she said, and then I knew she was right. But I think, Clara," Heidi went on to say, as she sat straight up in bed, "that tonight we ought certainly to thank the dear good God, because He has given us the happiness of seeing you walk."

"You're right, Heidi, and I feel that way, too. And I'm glad you reminded me of my duty, for in my joy I had almost forgotten it."

Then the children said their prayers and, each in her own way, thanked the dear God for sending such a wonderful blessing to Clara after she had been sick such a long time.

Next morning Grandfather said he thought they ought to write Grandmama and tell her that they had a surprise in store for her when she came to the mountain. But the children had thought out another plan, for they wished to give Grandmama a great big shock. First, Clara must learn to walk better so that, with Heidi's support, she could go quite a little way, but the main thing was not to let Grandmama have the least suspicion of what was up. They would let Grandfather say how long he thought this would take. And he said he thought a week was plenty of time, so in their next letter to Grandmama she was urged to come up the mountain just a week from that date. But not a word was said about anything unusual.

The days that followed were by far the most lovely

that Clara had spent on the mountain. Each morning she awoke with a loud voice in her heart crying joyously—

"I am well, I am whole again! I don't have to sit in my wheel chair. I can walk around by myself like other people."

Then would follow her exercises in walking. And each day it went more easily and a little better, and she could walk greater distances. Her exercise gave her such a splendid appetite that Grandfather had to keep making her thick slices of bread and butter even thicker, and he was glad to see how fast they disappeared. He always brought a large pot of foaming milk along with the sandwiches and filled one bowl after another for Clara.

And so the end of the week came, and with it the day that Grandmama had set aside for her visit.

CHAPTER IX

PARTING IS SUCH SWEET SORROW

A day before her arrival on the mountain meadow Grandmama had sent a letter to say exactly when she was coming. Peter brought this letter with him early next day when he was on his way up to the pasture.

Grandfather and the children had already come out of the cottage, and Little Swan and Little Bear were both standing outside with them, shaking their heads happily in the cool morning air while the children stroked their backs and wished them a pleasant journey up the mountain side. Nuncle stood by in much contentment, studying in turn the fresh faces of the children and his clean and shining goats. Both must have given him pleasure, for he was smiling with satisfaction.

And then Peter made his appearance.

When he caught sight of the little group, he approached more slowly. He seemed fairly to crawl along as he delivered the letter to Nuncle. But the moment he had surrendered it, he jumped shyly backward, as if something had frightened him. And then he looked quickly around him as if there was another something behind to be afraid of. Then he gave a leap and ran away up the mountain.

Heidi had been watching these actions with great surprise.

"Grandfather," she said, "what makes Peter act the way Big Turk does when he feels the rod about to strike him? Don't you know, he sheers off with his head and shakes it at everything and then makes sudden leaps in the air?"

"I suppose Peter thinks there's a rod after him, too, and he knows he deserves it," Grandfather answered.

It was only the first incline that Peter ran up without stopping for breath. The moment he was out of sight of the people below him, he stood still and turned his head fearfully in every direction. Suddenly he jumped and looked behind him, as much afraid as if someone had just grasped him by the back of the neck. For behind every bush, from every hedgerow, Peter was now expecting to see a policeman from Frankfort rush out at him. The longer he had this intense fear in his heart, the worse he became. He did not have another moment's peace.

And now Heidi had to set the hut to rights, for when Grandmama came she must find everything in perfect order.

Clara always took such an interest in Heidi's furious housekeeping that it was fun for her just to sit at one side and watch while the work was going on.

So the first hours of the morning passed before the children realized it, and it was soon time for them to look forward to Grandmama's arrival at any moment.

Then the children came out of the house again, but this time all dressed for the occasion and prepared to welcome their expected guest properly. They sat down on the bench in front of the hut to await her. Grandfather came to join them. He had been off for a walk and had returned with a great big bouquet of dark blue gentians, and the flowers looked so lovely in the light of the clear morning sun that the children cried out with delight when they saw them. Every now and then Heidi would jump up from the bench to run and see if she could catch sight of Grandmama's party.

But then—there it was suddenly coming up from below, just exactly as Heidi had pictured it. First came the guide, then the white horse with Grandmama on it, and last of all the porter with the high wicker hamper, for you may be sure the old lady would never have started out for the mountain without plenty of wraps to protect her.

Nearer and nearer came the procession. At last the top was reached. Grandmama was looking from her horse down at the children.

"Why, what is that? What do I see, Clara? You're not in your chair? Why, how can that be?" she cried out in alarm, and hastily climbed down from her horse.

But even before she could get to where the children were standing, she was wringing her hands in the greatest excitement and crying—

"Clara! My little Clara girl, is it you? Why, your cheeks are as red and round as apples! Child! I simply don't know you any longer!"

And then Grandmama started to rush toward Clara.

Heidi slipped unnoticed from her place on the bench, Clara quickly found the support of her shoulders, and together the children wandered away, quite calmly starting to take a short walk. For the first few seconds Grandmama stood stock still from sheer fright. She was afraid Heidi was doing something that might have terrible results.

And then, what was it that she saw right before her!

Clara was moving along erect and sure by Heidi's side. And now they had turned around and were coming back again, both with beaming faces, both with cheeks as red as fire.

Then Grandmama literally plunged forward to meet them. Laughing and weeping in the same breath, she hugged Clara tightly to her. Then she clasped Heidi, and then again Clara. Her happy heart was too full for words.

Suddenly her gaze rested on Nuncle, who was standing by the bench and smiling happily as he watched the scene before him. Then Grandmama took Clara's arm in hers and walked with her to the bench. And all the time she was crying out with joy that the miracle had really happened and here she was walking along with her healthy child beside her. She stood aside from Clara and stretched out both hands to the waiting old gentleman.

"My dear Nuncle, what can we ever do to show how grateful we are? It is your work, every bit! Your care and nursing—"

"Added to the sunshine and the highland air of our Lord God," Nuncle interrupted her with a smile.

"Yes, and Schwänli's fine, pure milk too," Clara said in her turn. "Grandmama, you just ought to see how I can drink goat's milk and to know how good it tastes!"

"I can tell all that by your cheeks, Clara," the old lady said, laughing. "No, sir, no one would ever know my little girl now. You've grown plump and broad as I never even dreamed you could, and you are taller, Clara. My! Can it really be true? I simply can't take my eyes off you!

I must send a telegram right away to your father in Paris, begging him to come. I shan't tell him why, for it is to be the biggest joy his life will ever have. My dear Nuncle, how can we have the telegram sent at once? You let the men who brought me here depart, didn't you?"

"Yes, they have gone," he answered. "But if the Lady Grandmama is in such a hurry, why not have the goatherd take it down. He has time for anything."

Grandmama insisted on having the telegram sent off at once, for she was not willing to keep this happiness from her son a single day.

Then Nuncle went off a short distance and gave so tremendously shrill a whistle through his fingers that you could hear the high notes coming back from the rocks above, so far away had the sharp sound awakened the echoes. Before very long Peter was seen running down toward them. He knew that whistle!

The poor chap was as white as chalk, for he thought Meadow Nuncle was calling him down for his punishment. But all that was given him was a piece of paper on which Grandmama had written something! And here was Nuncle explaining to him that he had to carry it down to Dörfli right away and leave it at the post office. He was to say that Nuncle would pay for it himself later, for Peter could not be trusted to remember very many things at the same time.

And so the lad went off with the paper in his hand, for the time being very much relieved that Nuncle had not whistled for him to go away to court and that no policeman had appeared.—

At last they could sit down in sober quiet together around the table in front of the cottage, and then Grandmama had to be told from the very beginning how things had come about. First she heard how Grandfather had encouraged Clara to stand on her feet a little each day and afterward try to walk. Then she listened to the story of the chair that the wind blew away just as they were setting out for the upper pasture. Then she learned of Clara's great desire to see the flowers, of her first real walk, and of how one thing had led to another. But it was a long while before the children had brought their tale to an end, because every now and then Grandmama would break out in amazement and exclaim, full of praise and gratitude, again and again—

"Can it really be possible? Then it's not just a dream after all? Are we actually all awake and sitting here on the mountain meadow before the hut? And is this girl beside me, this creature with the round, flushed face, the same pale, weak Clara that I used to know?"

As for Clara and Heidi, there was no end to their delight, because the surprise which they had so carefully planned had turned out so well that Grandmama just could not recover from the shock of it.—

During the last few weeks, however, Mr. Sesemann had been finishing up the business that kept him in Paris, and had likewise been preparing a surprise. Without writing a single word to his mother about it, he took the train one sunny summer morning and traveled straight through to Basel. He left there as soon as he could the next day, for he was growing terribly homesick for his little daughter from whom he had been separated the whole summer long. And so it came about that he arrived in Ragaz but a few hours after his mother had left to go to the mountain.

The news of her trip to pay a visit to Clara suited his plans exactly. The moment that he could, he set off in a carriage to be driven to Mayenfeld. But when he learned that there was a carriage road to Döfli, he drove on to that point because he felt sure that the climb on foot up the mountain slope would be as much as he cared to undertake.

Nor was Mr. Sesemann mistaken in this, for the steady climb up the sloping trail seemed very long and tiresome to him. Even after he had been toiling up the steep mountain path for quite a while, there was still no hut of any sort in sight, and yet he knew that he ought to come to Goat Peter's house when he was halfway to the mountain meadow, for he had often heard that this was so.

All about him were the footprints of people who had passed that way, and often he came to footpaths that led off in all directions. But the trouble was that Mr. Sesemann was not at all sure he was on the right road, and he thought perhaps the hut was located on the other side of the mountain. He looked about him, to see if he could discover any human being from whom he could ask the way. But on every hand it was as still as death. Far and wide there was nothing in sight, there was no sound to be heard. The mountain breeze alone occasionally moved the air, small insects buzzed in the haze of sunlight, now and then a bird piped merrily from the branches of a lonely larch tree. Mr. Sesemann halted for a few moments and bared his hot forehead to the cool highland breeze.

Just then someone came running down from above. It was Peter with the telegram in his hand. He was not keeping to the worn trail, but rushing straight ahead of him, no matter how steep it was. As soon as the speeding boy came close enough, however, Mr. Sesemann waved to him to stop and come over a minute. Shy and hesitating, Peter approached, not coming directly toward his questioner, but edging along, as if he could move properly with only one of his feet and had to drag the other after him.

"Come on, boy! Don't be afraid," Mr. Sesemann said to encourage him.

But his words seemed to have a curious effect on the young mountaineer. He halted for an instant, apparently in doubt as to what course he should pursue, and then again crept slowly toward the trail, but at a snail's pace.

"I only want to know," said Mr. Sesemann, "if this is the way up to the hut where the old man lives with the child Heidi, and where the people from Frankfort are."

A hollow groan of awful terror was the sole answer to this simple question. Peter darted away with such tremendous leaps that he went plunging down the steep slope head over heels and kept rolling over and over in most unexpected somersaults. In fact, he acted much as the wheel chair had done in its descent, with the exception that Peter did not come to pieces like the chair.

The only thing that suffered was the telegram. This received such harsh treatment that it floated away on the breeze, quite torn to shreds.

"That mountaineer is remarkably bashful," Mr. Sesemann said to himself, for he thought that the appearance of a stranger was the cause of such strange actions on the part of this simple son of the Alps.

After he had spent a few moments more watching Peter's violent descent, Mr. Sesemann continued his weary climb.

In spite of all his efforts Peter was unable to find a spot level enough to let him regain his footing. He rolled on and on as if he were never going to stop, and from time to time he curved about in the air in the strangest fashion imaginable.

Such turning and tumbling, however, were by no means the worst that fate had to offer him at this moment. Far more terrible were his inward anguish and fear, now that he knew the policeman from Frankfort was really on his track. For he never doubted that this stranger who was asking about the Frankfort people up at Meadow Nuncle's was a detective in plain clothes.

At last, when he had reached the last high bluff above Dörfli, Peter managed to clutch a bush and cling to it long enough to stop his downward progress. He lay still a moment before rising, to collect his thoughts and decide what was the next thing to be done.

"Well, I'll be blessed! Here comes another one!" said a voice right above Peter. "I wonder who the next victim will be that gets a shove and starts flying downhill like a badly sewed potato sack."

It was the Dörfli baker who stood there making fun of him.

He had climbed to the top of the bluff, to get a little cool air after his hot morning's work, and had been quietly watching the goatherd as he came racing down the slope for all the world like the ill-fated chair.

Peter sprang to his feet. Here was a new fright. For it seemed that the baker had already learned the chair had been shoved off by somebody, and so, without once looking behind him, Peter turned around and started to run up the mountain again.

What he wanted to do most was to go home and creep into bed, for no one would find him there and of all the places that seemed the safest. But he had left his goats up in the pasture, and Nuncle had told him particularly to hurry back so the herd would not be alone too long without their master. And he was more afraid of Nuncle than of anybody else, and stood in such awe of him that he did not dare disobey his lightest word.

So Peter groaned aloud and went limping onward. He had to go back up the mountain. Only he could not run any longer, for his terror and the many hard knocks that he had got in his falling were beginning to have their effect. Staggering and limping badly, groaning with pain and fear, he climbed up to the mountain meadow.

Mr. Sesemann had reached the halfway hut soon after his meeting with Peter, and from that moment he knew that he was on the right path. He climbed on with renewed courage and at last, after a long, hard pull of it, he saw his goal before him. There stood the hut on the mountain meadow, and above it waved the dark branches of the old pine trees.

The traveler climbed the last part of his way with delight, for he was soon to take his child by surprise. But he had already been seen and recognized by the group of people sitting in front of the cottage, and a surprise was being prepared for the father that he little expected.

When he had taken the last step up to the height, two figures came toward him from the hut. A tall young girl with light yellow hair and rosy face was leaning for support on little Heidi, whose dark eyes were fairly sparkling with glad excitement.

Mr. Sesemann started back in amazement. He stood and gazed at the approaching children with wide, staring eyes.

What scenes did memory bring back to his fond heart! Tears suddenly flooded his eyes. Just so had Clara's mother looked as a young girl—clear blonde, and with cheeks slightly tinged with red. Mr. Sesemann could not tell whether he was awake or dreaming.

"Papa, don't you know me any longer?" Clara called out to him then, and her face beamed at him joyfully. "Am I so changed?"

The father rushed toward his little daughter and folded her tightly in his arms.

"I should say you were changed! Is it possible? Can it be?"

And, his heart almost bursting with happiness, the father stepped back a short distance, as if to see whether the vision would remain or vanish wholly from his sight.

"Is it really you after all, Clara?" he had to cry one time after another. He took the child back in his arms,

and then he had to look her all over again to make sure
that it was actually his Clara who stood erect before him.

At that moment Grandmama appeared, for she could
not wait any longer to feast her eyes on her son's happy
face.

"Well, my dear fellow, why don't you say something?"
she called in greeting. "This surprise you've given us is
very nice indeed, but what do you think of the one we're
giving you?"

And the delighted mother kissed her son with fond
affection.

"But now, dear," she said after a moment, "come over
yonder with me and be introduced to our good Nuncle,
who is the greatest benefactor in the world."

"Surely and at once! But first we must say 'how do
you do' to little Heidi," Mr. Sesemann remarked, and he
shook hands with the young Swiss girl. "How are you,
Heidi? Fresh and blooming as usual up here on your
mountain? But my! I don't need to ask, do I? No Alpine
rose could look more flourishing. And that's a great joy
to me, child, to see you so again!"

Heidi looked up with shining eyes at her nice Mr.
Sesemann. How good he had always been to her! And
it made Heidi's heart beat faster to think that he should
be finding such great happiness up here on the mountain
meadow.

Then Grandmama led her son over to Meadow Nuncle,
and the two men shook hands most heartily. Mr. Sesemann insisted on expressing his grateful thanks for the
wonderful change in Clara and said he was utterly amazed

that such a thing could ever have happened. But when her son began his speech, Grandmama stole away, for in this matter she had already said everything that there was to say and she thought she would like to have a look at the fir trees.

But here another surprise was waiting for her.

Under the pines, where the long branches had left a free space, an enormous bunch of wonderful dark blue gentians was standing. And they were as fresh, as sparkling with dew, as if they had just grown there. Grandmama clasped her hands in delight.

"Why, how perfectly wonderful! How exquisite! What a lovely sight!" she cried. "Heidi, Heidi dear come here! Did you gather these for me? I never saw anything so splendid!"

The children joined her in a flash.

"Oh, no, I really didn't," Heidi answered. "But I can guess who it was that picked them."

"That's the way they are up in the pasture, Grandmama, only more beautiful still," Clara chimed in. "But just guess who it was that fetched you these flowers, early this morning, all the way down from the highland pasture!"

And Clara smiled so mysteriously at her grandmother that for one mad moment the old lady thought from what the child had said that she had been up there herself that day. But then Grandmama realized how impossible this would have been.

A soft voice was heard to come from behind the fir trees. It was Peter who had now returned. But when he saw who was standing with Nuncle in front of the cottage, he made a big circle around the lawn and was trying to creep quite stealthily behind the pines. But Grandmama recognized his figure at once, and a new idea came to her mind. Had Peter been the one to gather the flowers for her, and was he now stealing away secretly because he was too shy and modest to want to be thanked for his pretty gift? Oh, no, they could not let such a thing happen! The nice boy must have his reward.

"Come here, my lad, and don't be the least afraid!" she called to him loudly. And she thrust her head a little way in between the trees.

Peter came to a halt, stiff with fear. After all that he had recently suffered, he no longer had strength to fight. There was only one thought in his mind—

"It's all up with me now!"

His hair stood on end, and his pale face was distorted into an expression of great anguish.

"Come right here, and no hanging back, mind!" Grandmama said, encouragingly. "Now tell me, sir, did you bring me these flowers?"

Peter never lifted his eyes to see what the old lady was pointing at. He only knew that Nuncle was standing over there by the corner of the hut and had his sharp gray eyes fixed upon him. And right beside Nuncle was the most terrible sight that Peter could imagine, the policeman from Frankfort. So, shaking in every limb, and in a trembling voice, Peter managed to utter just one sound—

"Yes."

"Well," Grandmama said, "that is surely nothing to be afraid of."

"But I'm scared—scared—because it's all broken to pieces and can't ever be mended again," Peter stammered with great difficulty. And his knees knocked together so that he could hardly stand. Grandmama walked over to the corner of the hut.

"Tell me, my dear Nuncle," she asked, sympathetically, "is there something wrong with this boy's upper story?"

"Why, no," Nuncle assured her. "Only this boy is the wind that blew away the wheel chair, and now he's come to get the punishment that he so richly deserves."

Grandmama could not bring herself to believe it. For she thought that Peter did not look at all like a naughty boy, and, besides, he could have had no reason for destroying the chair which was so necessary to them. But the boy's stammering words had only made Nuncle more sure of what he had already suspected from the start.

Grandfather had not failed to notice the sour looks that Peter had been casting at Clara since the first moment he met her. And there had been plenty of other signs of bitterness the boy felt toward these newcomers on the mountain. Grandfather had been putting one thing and another together in his mind, and so had figured out just how the whole affair had happened. He told this all very clearly to Grandmama, but at the end of his story she interrupted him in no little excitement.

"A thousand times, no! We must not punish this poor chap any further, my dear Nuncle. Let's try and be just. Strange people from Frankfort break into his life and steal Heidi away from him for weeks at a stretch. So he loses what he loves most, his one great blessing, for

Heidi is all that to him. And all the poor lad can do is to sit quietly to one side and wait for her to come. Don't you see we must not be unreasonable with him? His anger got the better of him and spurred him on to a revenge which was very silly. But, then, we're all foolish when we get angry."

Whereupon Grandmama marched back to Peter, who was still shaking in his shoes.

She sat down on the bench underneath the fir trees and said to him in the nicest way—

"Come over here to me, my lad, for I have something to say to you. Don't shiver and shake any more, but just listen to me as you should. You made the wheel chair fall down the slope because you wanted to smash it. That was a wicked thing to do, as you know very well. And you realized, too, that you deserved a good whipping for your naughty deed, and in order to dodge this punishment you tried as hard as you could to hide what you had done away from people. Isn't this all true?"

"Yes," muttered Peter, and hung his head.

"But, look here! The boy who commits sin and then thinks that no one knows about it is badly mistaken. For the dear God sees and hears everything that goes on. And the moment He sees that a little boy wants to hide his sin, the dear God wakes up the watchman that was put in the boy when he was born and sleeps in him until the boy has done something wrong. And do you know, Peter, what the small watchman has in his hand?"

"What?" asked Peter, interested in spite of himself.

"He has a pin. And with this pin the watchman keeps pricking the boy, so that he never has a quiet moment to

himself.   And with his still small voice the watchman
plagues the boy and keeps telling him, to torment him,
'You just wait! It will be found out! You're going to be
punished, you are!'   And then the boy lives in constant
fear and trembling, and he has no more fun, not one bit.
Isn't that the way you feel about it, Peter?"

Peter nodded sorrowfully, but like a person who knows
that he has just heard the truth spoken to him.

"And in another way you were mistaken," Grandmama
went on.   "See how the wrong that you did turned out
to be just the best thing that could have happened to the
girl you wanted to harm.   Because Clara had lost her chair
and yet wished so much to see the beautiful flowers, she
tried with might and main to walk.   And she learned to
use her feet and keeps on improving.   And if she stays
here, she will finally be able to walk up to the pasture every
day, much oftener than she could ever have been carried
up in her chair.   Don't you see how it is, Peter?   When a
boy wants to do something bad, the dear God can take his
act quickly into His own hands and make a blessing out of
it.   And the wicked boy has had all his trouble for nothing
and the only one he hurts is himself, isn't it?"

"Yes," said Peter, for he knew that was true.

"Are you sure you have understood me, Peter?   Yes?
Well then, you just think it over.   And every time you
want to do something naughty, remember the little watchman inside you, and the pin he carries, and his croaking
voice.   Will you?"

"Of course I will," Peter answered.   But he was still
feeling very down in the mouth, because he didn't know

how things were going to turn out with the policeman standing over there by Nuncle.

"Well, that is good, and then the matter is all settled," Grandmama concluded. "But now you must have something very nice, to make you remember the Frankfort people. Tell me, my dear boy, is there anything that you've always been wishing to have? Tell me the one thing you'd like best in all the world."

Then Peter raised his head and stared at Grandmama in astonishment. His eyes were as round as marbles. Here he had been expecting something awful to happen, and now there was talk about giving him what he wanted most! That young mind of Peter's was certainly getting all mixed up.

"Oh dear, yes, I mean it!" Grandmama said. "You're to have a nice present, to make you think of the people from Frankfort, and to show you they have forgotten all about the naughty thing you did. Don't you understand, laddie?"

It began to dawn on Peter that he no longer needed to be afraid of punishment, and that the kind lady who sat before him had saved him from the policeman. Then he suddenly felt as light and happy as if a mountain that had been resting on his chest had suddenly fallen off. And he was coming to see that it is better to tell your faults without delay. So he said—

"And I lost the paper, too."

Grandmama had to think for a while before she got the connection of ideas. But then she remembered, and she said kindly—

"I'm glad you told me about it. Always tell what is

wrong immediately, and then it can be straightened out. And now, tell me, what is it that you would most wish to have?"

Now Peter could choose anything in the wide world that he wanted to own. It made him dizzy just to think of it. The whole fair at Mayenfeld danced before his mind, and he thought of all the pretty wares in the booths at which he had looked for hours, but which he had never hoped to have. For Peter's whole wealth consisted of five pennies, and the tempting wares at the fair had always cost at least twice as much as that. He thought of the fine red whistles that would be just the thing to call his goats with. He thought of those fascinating knives with round handles that they called toad-stabbers. Oh, those would make quick work of a hedge of hazel rods!

Peter stood there deep in thought. He was trying to decide which of these two things was the most desirable, and he could not make up his mind. Then, suddenly, he had a happy thought. He had found a way by which he might have until the next fair to settle the matter.

"Ten pennies," Peter said very firmly.

Grandmama could not keep from laughing.

"At least that is not extravagant," she said. "Come to me!"

She took her purse out of her pocket and drew from it a bright new gold piece. On this she laid two ten-penny pieces.

"There!" she continued. "And now we'll do a little example in arithmetic. Let me show you. In this sum of money you have just as many different ten pennies as there are weeks in a year. So, you see, every Sunday you can take ten pennies to spend, and the money will last a year."

"Every year of my life?" Peter asked innocently.

At that Grandmama went off into such a gale of laughter that the men over by the corner of the hut stopped their talk to hear what was going on.

Before she could continue her dealings with Peter, however, the old lady indulged in another fit of laughing.

"Yes, my boy, every year of your life! I'll put it in my will, do you hear? And when I come to die, there in the will the words will be—'To Goat Peter, ten pennies a week as long as he lives.'"

Mr. Sesemann nodded, to show that he agreed with Grandmama, and smiled over at them.

Peter cast just one more look at the present in his hand, to see if it was really still there. Then he said, "Thank God!"

And off he ran, taking unbelievably long leaps, but this time he stayed on his feet instead of turning somersaults, for he was not now driven by fear, but by such joy as he had never before known in his life. All his cares and his anguish had vanished, for was he not to have ten pennies a week so long as he should live?

Later on, when the little company in front of the hut on the mountain meadow had finished their jolly dinner and were still sitting together, talking of all sorts of things, Clara took her father's hand in hers. His face still shone with the joy he felt, and each time he looked at her he seemed if anything a little more happy than before. And his daughter said to him in a lively manner not at all like that of the limp Clara of other days—

"O Papa, if you only knew all that Grandfather has done for me! He's been so good every single day that I can't even begin to tell you all about it, but I'll never forget it as long as I live. And I shall always wish that I could do something in return for his loving care, or give him something that would make him at least half as happy as he has made me."

"And that's just exactly the way I feel, my dear child," said her father. "I've been trying right along to think of some way in which we can show a small part of our gratitude to this prince of all good men."

Then Mr. Sesemann got to his feet and walked over to Nuncle, who was sitting beside Grandmama and having the finest kind of a chat with her. The old man rose politely at his guest's approach. Mr. Sesemann grasped him by the hand and said in the friendliest manner—

"My dear friend, let's have a word together. You will understand me when I say that for many long years I have had no real joy. What did I care for all my money and possessions when I looked at my poor child whom all my riches could not restore to health! Next to our God in heaven, you have made my daughter whole and have given me a new life, as well. Now tell me how best we can show our deep thankfulness. I can never hope to repay what you have done for me and mine. But whatever is in my power to do, that shall be done. Speak, my friend, what shall it be?"

Nuncle had listened quietly and had gazed at the happy

father with a smile of pleasure. When the other had finished speaking, he said in his decided way—

"Mr. Sesemann will believe me when I say that I, too, have a large share of joy in this recovery on our meadow. My trouble has already been richly rewarded. Many thanks, my dear sir, for your generous offer, but I am in need of nothing. I shall have my child with me as long as I live, and I have enough for both of us. But there is one wish which I should like to have granted, and then I should never have any further anxiety."

"Just name it, my dear friend," Mr. Sesemann urged.

"I am old," Nuncle went on to say, "and my days on this earth are numbered. When I pass away, I cannot leave the child anything. And she has no relatives, except a single one who might take advantage of her innocence. If Mr. Sesemann feels that he can give me the assurance that Heidi will never in her life be compelled to go among strangers to earn her daily bread, then he will have more than repaid me for the little I have done for him and his child."

"But, my dear friend, that goes absolutely without saying!" Mr. Sesemann burst out. "The child belongs to us. Ask my mother or my daughter if Heidi shall be given to other people than to ourselves! But now, dear chap, if it will be the slightest comfort to you, why, there's my hand on it! I promise you solemnly that this child shall never in her life earn her bread among strangers. I'll see to it, even after my life is ended, through my will."

"You are a good man," Grandfather said. And for a moment he covered his eyes with his hand.

"Nonsense, sir! I will say even more. Heidi is not made to live happily in a strange country, no matter how things turn out. We discovered that fact in Frankfort. But she has made friends. One of them I know in my own home town. He is settling up his affairs there so that after a little he can go wherever he likes and have a good rest. I speak, of course, of our friend the doctor. He is coming up here this autumn to ask your advice about where he should locate in this region. For he has enjoyed your company and Heidi's more than anyone else's. So, you see, Heidi is going from now on to have two guardians near her. And may they both be preserved to her for a long time yet to come!"

"God grant it!" said Grandmama piously.

And, as if to say Amen to her son's statement, she shook Nuncle's hand very cordially and for a long time. Then, as she saw Heidi standing close beside her, she suddenly put her arms about the child's neck, and drew her toward her.

"And you, dear Heidi, must be questioned, too, just a bit. Come and tell me, isn't there some wish that you would like to have granted?"

"Oh, of course there is," the little girl answered, and looked delightedly up at Grandmama.

"That's very nice, so out with it!" the old lady said, encouragingly. "What would you like to have, child?"

"I'd like awfully well to have my bed from Frankfort, with the three thick pillows and the heavy quilt. And then Grandmother would not have to lie with her head downhill and almost not breathe at all. And she'd be warm as toast under that quilt, and wouldn't always have to take her shawl to bed to keep from freezing."

In her eagerness to get what she was after, Heidi had said all that in a single breath.

"Why, my dear child, what are you telling me now!" Grandmama cried excitedly. "It's a good thing you reminded me. In our selfish joy it is so easy to forget the things we ought to think of first. When the dear God sends us a wondrous blessing, then we should at once think of the poor people less fortunate than we. We'll telegraph straight off to Frankfort. This very day Rottenmeier will be told to pack the bed, and in two days it will be here. If God wills, the grandmother's going to have a fine rest in it."

Heidi danced gaily in a circle around Grandmama. But all at once she paused and said hastily—

"Now I'll surely have to race right down to Grandmother's. She'll be worrying because I haven't been to see her for ever so long."

For Heidi was on pins and needles. She just could not wait another minute to carry the joyful news to the bedridden old lady. And she remembered how sad grandmother had been the last time she had been to see her.

"No, Heidi. What are you thinking of?" said her grandfather in stern reproof. "When one has guests, one certainly does not go running off like that."

But Grandmama stood firmly by Heidi.

"My dear Nuncle, excuse me, but I think the child is right," she said. "Poor Grandmother has for a long time been a loser because of us. Why shouldn't we all of us go right down to see her? I can wait for my horse at Goat Peter's just as well as here. And when it comes, we can continue on our way and send the telegram from Dörfli. Son, what do you say to this plan?"

Until this moment Mr. Sesemann had had no time to speak of what he intended to do. So he had to ask his mother to wait just a little while, if she would, so he could talk his plans over with her.

It seems that Mr. Sesemann had made up his mind to take a short trip through Switzerland with his mother. And first of all he had wished to see if Clara was in a condition to go a short distance with them. But now there was no reason why he could not take the most enjoyable sort of journey with his little daughter, and he was very anxious to make use of these lovely late summer days while they lasted. He thought it best, therefore, to spend the night in Dörfli, and next morning to come up to the mountain meadow to get Clara. Then they two would go down and meet Grandmama in Ragaz, and from there they could travel wherever they wished.

Clara was a little taken back when told to say good-by to the mountain at such short notice. But there were many other things to be happy about, and, besides, there was not any time to waste in being miserable.

Grandmama had already risen and taken Heidi's hand to lead the procession down to Goat Peter's. But then she suddenly remembered.

"Why, what in the world are we going to do with Clara?" she cried, in much concern. For it occurred to her that the walk would be much too long for the little girl.

She found that Nuncle had already taken his little foster-child up in his arms, just as he usually did, and was following with sure tread in the footsteps of Heidi and herself. She nodded back at him with great satisfaction. Mr. Sesemann closed up the rear, and so the little company started on its way.

Heidi could not keep from dancing with joy by Grandmama's side and telling her all she wanted to hear about Peter's old grandmother. She told her of the life in the halfway hut, of all they did there, and of how dreadfully cold it was in winter.

Heidi reported everything down to the smallest detail, for she knew just how they got along. And she drew a clear word picture of Grandmother in her corner, as she sat all bent over and shivering with the cold. She knew everything they had to eat, and all the things they had to go without, too.

Grandmama listened with the keenest sympathy to Heidi's chatter until they came to the hut.

Brigitte was just in the act of hanging Peter's second shirt out in the sun so that it would be ready for him to change into when his other one had been worn long enough. She saw the procession approaching and dived quickly into the living room.

"Now they are all going away, Mother," she reported. "It's quite a company of them. Nuncle is with them, too. He is carrying the sick child."

"Oh, isn't there any other way?" Grandmother sighed. "Did you notice if they're taking Heidi along? If the child would only stop in for a minute, long enough to take my hand in hers! I wish I could just hear her voice once again!"

Then the door was suddenly flung back, as if a high wind had struck it, and Heidi came jumping over to the corner where Grandmother was and clung to her almost fiercely.

"Grandmother, you can never, never guess! My bed's coming from Frankfort, and all three of the pillows, and the thick quilt too. It will be here day after tomorrow. Grandmama said so."

Heidi couldn't get her message out fast enough to suit her, because she did not want to wait a second to see the old lady's great joy. Grandmother smiled, but she said a trifle sadly—

"Oh, what a good woman she must be! I ought to be glad that she is taking you away with her, Heidi, only I may not live long enough to welcome you back."

"What's that? Who has been telling such tales to the nice old grandmother?" asked a friendly voice at this point. Clara's grandmother had come into the hut and heard what had been said, so she walked over to the blind woman and pressed her hand heartily.

"There's no talk of Heidi's going with us," she went on to say. "The child is to stay here and make you happy. We are planning to see Heidi again, of course, but we're coming here to visit her. We shall be up on the mountain meadow every year, for we have the best of reasons for coming to the spot where the great miracle was done to our child, and offering up our special thanks to the dear God."

Then Grandmother's face was lighted up with a real joy and she pressed good Mrs. Sesemann's hand again and again, for she could not voice her thanks in words. Two great tears, but not of sadness, found their way slowly down her old cheeks. Heidi had seen the glad light that flashed into Grandmother's face and felt very happy.

"Now it's turned out just as we were reading last time, hasn't it, Grandmother?" she said, snuggling close to the blind woman. "Don't you remember about the word 'wholesome' in the hymn book? And the bed's going to make you wholesome again, isn't it?"

"Oh, yes, Heidi," Grandmother said with deep feeling, "and the dear God is giving me many other things besides healing my body. How can there be such people in the world, to go and bother about a poor old thing like me, and to do so much for me? There is nothing that so strengthens one's faith in the good Father in heaven who remembers the least of His children as to find that there are people full of kindness and pity for a useless old woman like me."

"My dear Grandmother," Mrs. Sesemann here interrupted her, "in the sight of our Father in heaven we are all poor and needy, and it's equally necessary to us all that He does not forget. And now we have to say good-by, but only for a few months. And we'll want to look you up the first moment we come back to the mountain next year. We shall never forget you, be sure of that!"

Then Mrs. Sesemann took the old lady's hand in hers for the last time and gave it a hearty squeeze.

But, after all, she was not able to tear herself away

quite as soon as she expected to, because Grandmother could not stop her flow of gratitude and kept wishing her visitor all the blessings that the dear God had to bestow on herself and all her household.

Then Mr. Sesemann went down the valley with his mother, while Nuncle was carrying Clara back home again. And Heidi, without stopping once, danced madly along beside them, for she was so delighted at what the next days were to bring Grandmother that she had to hop a little almost every step she took.

Ah, but the next day there were hot tears enough, when she and Clara parted! The little guest could not bear to leave her lovely mountain meadow, where she had found the greatest happiness of her life. But Heidi comforted her and said—

"It will be next summer again before you know it, and then you'll come again, and it will be nicer than ever, lots nicer. Then you can walk right from the start of your visit, and we'll go up to the pasture with the goats every day, and we'll see the flowers and everything. And it all will be jolly from the word 'go.'"

Mr. Sesemann came, just as he said he would, to carry off his daughter. And he stood and talked a short while with Grandfather, for the two men found much to say. Clara was wiping away her tears as best she could, and finding much comfort in Heidi's words.

"Don't forget to say good-by to Peter for me," Clara said again. "And tell the goats good-by, especially Schwänli. I wish I could think of a present to give Schwänli, she helped me such a lot to get well."

"You can do that fast enough!" Heidi assured her. "Just send her a little salt. Don't you remember how she likes to lick the salt from Grandfather's hand at dusk?"

This advice Clara found most pleasing.

"Oh, then I'll surely send her a hundred pounds of salt from Frankfort," she cried, joyfully. "She must have something to remember me by."

Then Mr. Sesemann beckoned to the children, for the time had come to start. Grandmama's white horse had come for Clara to ride, and so there was no more need for the basket chair.

Heidi took up her position at the extreme edge of the slope and waved her hand to Clara until the last small speck of both horse and rider had disappeared.—

The bed came safely, and Grandmother sleeps in it so soundly that she is regaining some of her old strength.

Kind Grandmama, when she got back to her home in Holstein, did not forget about the grim winter on the mountain. She sent an enormous package of clothes to the hut of Goat Peter. There were so many warm things packed away in it that Grandmother could wrap herself up until she was almost lost beneath her coverings. And never once again did she have to sit in the corner and shiver with the cold.

A great house is being built in The Hamlet. The doctor came and for a short spell went to live in his old lodgings. But, on the advice of his friend Meadow Nuncle, the doctor bought the old building where Heidi had lived the winter before, and which had formerly been a lordly mansion, as could be easily seen from the lofty living room with the handsome stove and the fine paneling. This part of the old house the doctor is having rebuilt for his own quarters.

The other side of the spacious building is being fitted up for the winter home of Nuncle and Heidi, for the doctor realizes that Grandfather is an independent sort of man and must have his own house. Back of it all is a warm goat stable with thick walls, and here Schwänli and Bärli can spend their winter days in vast comfort.

The doctor and Meadow Nuncle grow to be better friends every day. And while they are climbing around the walls together, watching the progress of their new building, their thoughts never fail to turn to Heidi. For to both of them the chief joy in their new house is that they are to move into it with their happy child.

"My dear Nuncle," the doctor said recently, as he was standing on the wall with the old gentleman, "you must look at the matter as I do. I share all joys with the child, just as if next to you I were her nearest relative. But I also want to share all the duties that have to do with the care of the child. In that way I can hope to have a claim on Heidi, too, and can look forward to her living with me in my old age and caring for me. This is my dearest hope. Heidi shall share in my possessions as if she were my own child, and therefore we can leave her behind us without fear when the time comes for us to go, you and I."

Nuncle pressed the doctor's hand gratefully. He said nothing, for he was a silent sort of man. But his good friend could see in his eyes how deeply Nuncle had been touched and how happy these words had made him.

Meanwhile Heidi and Peter were sitting with Grandmother. And the young girl had to talk so much, and the
young lad had to listen so hard, that they almost lost their
breath in their excitement and kept almost stumbling right
over the happy old blind lady.

And then, too, there was such a lot to tell Grandmother
about what had happened during the summer, for they had
not met very often all that long time.

And each of the three looked happier than the other
two, because here they were all back together again, and
also because such amazing things had happened. But
happier than any other face was perhaps that of mother
Brigitte, for now with Heidi's help she at last got the
straight of the story about the ten penny pieces that were
to go on forever.

Finally, however, Grandmother said—

"Heidi, read me a hymn of praise and thanksgiving. I
feel as if I could never fail to give praise and glory to our
God in heaven for all the blessings that he has so richly
showered upon us."

Printed in U.S.A.